BERLIN RED

"A tremendous victory for suspense—well plotted, historically evocative, beautifully written, and addictive."
- LIBRARY JOURNAL

"Eastland's excellent seventh and final Inspector Pekkala novel, [*BERLIN RED*] convincingly explores the motivations of everyone from Pekkala to Stalin in this deeply personal story set against the broad canvas of horrific war."
- PUBLISHERS WEEKLY (STARRED REVIEW)

"Excellently plotted and paced, with a lively cast, real and fictional."
- THE TIMES OF LONDON (BOOK OF THE MONTH FEATURED REVIEW)

Praise for SAM EASTLAND/PAUL WATKINS

"As the cold nights of winter close in, Sam Eastland's *Red Icon* is one of the best thrillers a fan can pick up from the bedside table...the novel's canvas, a cyclorama of vivid scenes shot through with tension and drama, holds the reader. The author's descriptions — sharp, palpable and distinctive — are to savor."
-THE WASHINGTON POST

"The author's portrait of Stalinist Russia is vivid, his characters are compelling, and his stories downright captivating..."
- BOOKLIST (RED ICON)

"*The Beast in the Red Forest* is a complex and atmospheric thriller in a standout historical series."
- KIRKUS REVIEWS

"Highly imaginative ... History mixes with fiction in an exciting story."
- USA TODAY

"*Red Icon* will keep readers wide awake so they can see the story play out until the very end. Watkins is known as a gifted storyteller and readers will find that this novel is no exception."
- SUSPENSE MAGAZINE

"Pekkala's compelling character in this thriller series combines the literary sensibilities of Paul Watkins with the storytelling of Sam Eastland."
- ALFRED HITCHCOCK'S MYSTERY MAGAZINE

"Watkins leaves us practically breathless."
–VOGUE

"Among literati he is already a legend."
–ESQUIRE

"Paul Watkins is without question one of the most gifted storytellers of his generation."
– TOBIAS WOLFF

"[a] suspense-driven, beautifully written, heart-stopping, breathless thriller of World War II … [*The Beast in the Red Forest*] is a fascinating, labyrinthine tale of death, deceit and disappearances … It will keep you guessing throughout."
- PROVIDENCE JOURNAL

"Mr. Watkins has joined the ranks of the great war novelists: Mailer, Crane, Remarque and particularly Hemingway, whom he most resembles. But while Mr. Watkins also writes in a staccato style, his mordant wit and angle of vision are uniquely his own – along with his remarkable command of narrative."
- THE NEW YORK TIMES BOOK REVIEW

"An astonishing triumph of the imagination."
- THE NEW YORKER

"The raw elegance of the human experience itself … dazzlingly rendered …Watkins is an author whose work should be read with great respect."
- LOS ANGELES TIMES

"Superb … a brilliantly conceived and perfectly executed mystery.
- THE TORONTO GLOBE AND MAIL

"Daring and remarkably assured … provocative."
- THE NEW YORK TIMES

"Rich in detail, chokingly tense and gorgeously romantic … hoists the author to the top of his class."
–SAN FRANCISCO CHRONICLE

BERLIN RED

AN INSPECTOR PEKKALA NOVEL OF SUSPENSE

PAUL WATKINS WRITING AS

SAM EASTLAND

BERLIN RED

First published in the U.S. by OPUS

by arrangement with Faber and Faber, Ltd. London

All rights reserved.

Copyright © 2017 Sam Eastland

The right of Sam Eastland to be identified as the author of this work has been
asserted in accordance with Section 77 of the Copyright,
Designs and Patents Act 1988

ISBN: 978-1-62316-090-6

FIRST EDITION: 10 9 8 7 6 5 4 3 2

RED BERLIN is also available in OPUS e-book editions.

A Division of Subtext Inc., **A Glenn Young Company**

P.O. Box 725 • Tuxedo Park, NY 10987

Publicity: E-mail: opusbookpubpr@aol.com

Rights enquiries: E-mail GY@opusbookpublishers.com

All other enquiries: www.opusbookpublishers.com

OPUS is distributed to the trade by
The Hal Leonard Publishing Group
Toll Free Sales: 800-524-4425
www.halleonard.com

Printed in the United States of America.

For John and Johanna

BERLIN RED

9 April 1945, Moscow. His footsteps echoed in the empty street.

Above him, framed by the snub-toothed silhouettes of chimney pots, the darkness shuddered with stars.

With hands shoved deep into the pockets of his coat, Pekkala made his way towards the Café Tilsit, the only place open at this time of night.

The windows of the café, blind with condensation, glowed from the light of candles set behind them.

Pekkala put his shoulder against the heavy wooden door and a small bell, tied to the handle, clanged as he entered the room. He paused for a minute, filling his lungs with the smell of soup and cigarettes, before heading to a quiet table at the back.

Pekkala had been coming here for years.

Before the war, most of the patrons who wandered in after midnight had been workers coming off their shifts – taxi-drivers, whores, museum guards. But there were also those who had no place to live, and some who, like Pekkala, fled whisperings of madness in the quiet of their empty rooms.

Here, at the Café Tilsit, alone but without being lonely, they chased all their demons away.

Nine years at a labour camp had taught Pekkala the value of this strange, wordless communion. Schooled in the art of solitude by the lacquer-black winters of Siberia, he had come to know a silence so complete that it appeared to have a sound of its own – a hissing, rushing noise – like that of the planet hurtling through space.

Soon after he arrived at Borodok, the director of the camp had sent him into the woods, fearing that other inmates might learn his true identity.

Pekkala was given the task of marking trees to be cut by inmates of the camp, whose function was the harvesting of timber from the forest of Krasnagolyana. In that vast wilderness, Pekkala lacked not only the trappings of a civilised existence, but even a name. At Borodok, he was known only as prisoner 4745.

Moving through the forest with the help of a large stick, whose gnarled root head bristled with square-topped horseshoe nails, he daubed his hand-print in red paint on trees selected for cutting. These marks were, for most of the other convicts, the only trace of him they ever saw.

The average life of a tree-marker in the forest of Krasnagolyana was six months. Working alone, with no chance of escape and far from any human contact, these men died from exposure, starvation and loneliness. Those who became lost, or who fell and broke a leg, were usually eaten by wolves. Tree-marking was the only assignment at Borodok said to be worse than a death sentence.

Everyone assumed that Pekkala would be dead before the ice broke up in spring, but nine years later he was still at work, having lasted longer than any other marker in the entire Gulag system.

Every few months, provisions were left for him at the end of a logging road. Kerosene. Cans of meat. Nails. For the rest, he had to fend for himself. Only rarely was he seen by those logging crews who came to cut the timber. What they observed was a creature barely recognizable as a man. With the crust of red paint that covered his prison clothes and the long hair maned about his face, he resembled a beast stripped of its flesh and left to die which had somehow managed to survive. Wild rumours surrounded him – that he was an eater of human flesh, that he wore a breastplate made from the bones of those who had disappeared in the forest, that he wore scalps laced together as a cap.

They called him the man with bloody hands. No one except the commandant of Borodok knew where this prisoner had come from or who he had been before he arrived.

Those same men who feared to cross his path had no idea this was Pekkala, whose name they'd once invoked just as their ancestors had called upon the gods.

For Pekkala, after those years spent in the forest, some habits still remained. Although there was a bed in his flat, he never slept in it, preferring the hard planks of the floor and his coat rolled up as a pillow. He wore the same clothes – a hip-length double-breasted coat, heavy brown corduroys and a grey waistcoat – no matter what season or occasion. And, thanks to the Café Tilsit, he often ate his dinners in the middle of the night, just as he had done out in Siberia.

Now, in the sixth year of the war, almost all the men who dined at the café were in the military, forming a mottled brown horde that smelled of boot grease, *machorka* tobacco and the particular earthy mustiness of Soviet Army wool. The women, too, wore uniforms of one kind of another. Some were military, with black berets and dark blue skirts beneath their tunics. Others wore the khaki overalls of factory workers, their heads bundled in blue scarves, under which the hair, for those employed in munitions factories, had turned a rancid yellow.

Most of them sat at one of two long, wooden tables, elbow to elbow, eating from shallow wooden bowls.

As Pekkala passed by, a few of them glanced up from their meals, squinting through the smoky air at the tall, broad-shouldered man, whose greenish-brown eyes were marked by a strange silvery quality, which people noticed only when he was looking directly at them. Streaks of premature grey ran through his dark hair and a week's worth of beard stubbled his windburned cheeks.

Pekkala did not sit at the long tables. Instead, he made his way to his usual table at the back, facing the door.

While he waited to be served, he pulled a crumpled photograph from his coat pocket. White cracks in the emulsion of the picture criss-crossed the image and the once sharp corners were folded and torn like the ears of an old fighting dog. Intently, Pekkala studied the image, as if he were seeing it for the first time. In fact, he had looked at this picture so many times over the years that his memory of the moment it was taken remained far clearer than the photograph itself. And yet he could not stand to let it go. As the owner of the café made her way towards his table, shuffling in a worn-out pair of felt *valenki* boots, Pekkala tucked the picture back into his pocket.

The owner was a slender, narrow-shouldered woman, with thick, blonde hair combed straight back on her head and tied with a length of blue yarn. Her name was Valentina.

In front of Pekkala, she set a mug of kvass: a half-fermented drink which looked like dirty dishwater and tasted like burned toast.

'My darling Finn,' she said, and rested her hand on his forehead, as if to feel a fever on his brow. 'What dreams have brought you to me on this night?'

'For dreams, there would have to be sleep,' he replied, 'and I've had very little of that. Besides, it's past midnight now. I might as well just stay awake.'

'Then I will bring you your first meal of the day.'

He did not need to ask about the choice of food because there was none. At the Café Tilsit, they served what they made when they made it, and he'd never had cause for complaint.

As Valentina sauntered back into the kitchen, Pekkala retrieved the photograph and looked at it again, as if some detail might have risen from the frozen image.

The picture showed Pekkala, leaning up against a waist-high stone wall, his eyes narrowed as he squinted into the sun. He smiled awkwardly and his arms were crossed over his chest. His face looked thinner, and his eyes more deeply set than they seemed now.

Behind him stood a brick building with a sharply canted slate roof and tall windows arched at the top. A cluster of small children peered from behind the wall, their eyes big and round with curiosity.

Standing beside Pekkala was a young woman with a softly rounded nose and freckled cheeks. Her long hair was tied in a ribbon, but a breeze had blown a few strands loose. They had drifted in front of her face, almost hiding her eyes, and her hand was slightly blurred as she reached up to brush them aside. Her name was Lilya Simonova. She was a teacher at the Tsarskoye primary school, just outside the grounds of the Tsar's estate.

Each time Pekkala glimpsed that photograph, he felt the same lightness in his chest, as he had done on the first day he caught sight of her at an outdoor party to mark the beginning of the new school year.

He had been passing by on his way from a meeting with the Tsar at the Alexander Palace to his cottage near the Old Pensioners' Stables on the grounds of the estate when the headmistress of the school, Rada Obolenskaya, beckoned to him from across the wall. She was a tall and dignified woman, with grey hair knotted at the back, and a practiced severity in her gaze; a tool of the trade for anyone in her profession.

'Inspector!' she called and, as she approached the wall which stood between them, a cluster of children fell in behind her.

'Some students here would like to meet you.'

Inwardly, Pekkala groaned. He was tired and wanted nothing more than to go home, take off his boots and drink a glass of cold white wine in the shade of the apple tree which grew behind his house. But he knew he had no choice, so he stopped in his tracks and bolted a smile to his face.

It was in this moment that he noticed a woman whom he had never seen before. She was standing just outside a white marquee tent set up in the school playground for the occasion. She wore a pale green dress and her eyes were a luminous and dusty blue.

At first, he thought he must know her from somewhere but he felt quite certain that she was a stranger. Whatever it was, he couldn't explain it; this sudden lurching of his senses towards an inexplicable familiarity. 'Are you really the Inspector?' asked a nervous, little voice. Dazed, Pekkala looked down to see the face of a five-year-old girl peering from behind Madame Obolenskaya's skirt. 'Why, yes,' he replied. 'Yes, I am.'

And now another face appeared, framed by an untidy shock of red hair. 'Have you met the Tsar?'

'Yes,' answered Pekkala. 'In fact, I just saw him today.'

This produced a collective gasp of approval, and now half a

dozen children broke cover from behind Madame Obolenskaya and crowded up to the wall.

'Are you magic, like they say?' asked a boy.

'My mother told me they ride polar bears where you are from.'

'Well, I don't know about that,' muttered Pekkala. Then he noticed the twitch of a smile in Madame Obolenskaya's normally immovable expression. 'Oh, a polar bear, did you say?'

The boy nodded, as curious as he was terrified of what the answer to his question might be.

'Well, of course!' exclaimed Pekkala. 'Do you mean to say you do not ride them here?'

'No,' answered the red-haired girl, 'and the fact is I have never even seen one.'

'I told you,' the boy announced to no one in particular. 'I told you that's what he did.'

Throughout this, Pekkala kept glancing over Madame Obolenskaya's shoulder at the woman in the pale green dress.

This did not escape the attention of the headmistress, and she turned to spot the source of his distraction. 'Ah,' she said, 'you haven't met our new teacher, Lilya Simonova.' 'No,' replied Pekkala, his voice falling to a whisper, as if his throat had filled with dust.

Madame Obolenskaya raised her arm and, with a flip of her wrist, waved towards the new teacher, like somebody hailing a carriage off the street.

Obediently, but not without a faint trace of defiance in her step, Lilya Simonova made her way across the school playground.

What Pekkala said to her in the few minutes of that first conversation was nothing of consequence, and yet the words came so slowly and with such difficulty that it was like talking with a mouthful of cherry stones.

Lilya was polite, but reserved. She spoke very little, which made him speak too much.

At some point, Pekkala heard a click and glanced up to see that Madame Obolenskaya had taken a photograph of the two of them, using a Kodak Brownie camera which she had bought from the DeLisle photographic studio in the arcade at the Gosciny Dvor in St Petersburg. Since it became known that the Tsarina herself possessed one of these cameras, which she used to photograph the daily lives of her family, they had become all the rage in the city.

Madame Obolenskaya had recently set about taking pictures of each class at the school, prints of which would be given out to each student and a copy hung on the wall of her office.

Under normal circumstances, Pekkala would have taken Madame Obolenskaya aside and politely explained to her that the film on which that image had been frozen would have to be destroyed. On the orders of the Tsar, no pictures could be taken of the Emerald Eye. On that occasion, however, he simply asked if he might have a copy of the print.

One year later, having borrowed a rowing boat from the Tsar, Pekkala proposed to Lilya at the pavilion on the little island in the middle of the Lamskie Pond.

A date was set, but they were never married. They never got the chance. Instead, on the eve of the Revolution, Lilya boarded a train heading north towards Finland, on a long and circuitous journey that would eventually deliver her to Paris, where Pekkala promised to meet her as soon as the Tsar allowed him to depart. But Pekkala never did get out. Some months later, he was arrested by Bolshevik militia men while attempting to leave the country. From there, his own journey began, only one that would take him to Siberia.

Along with a scattering of images captured only by the shutter of Pekkala's blinking eyes, this picture was all he had left to prove to himself that his most precious memories had not, in fact, been conjured from a dream.

These thoughts were cancelled by the ringing of the little bell, as yet another stranger tumbled in out of the night.

At that same moment, at the end of a dirt road on the windswept island of Used-om on the Baltic coast, a haggard looking German officer stood looking out at waves which tumbled from the mist and rode hissing on to the pinkish-grey sand.

Clenched between his teeth was a short-stemmed briarwood pipe, in which he was smoking the last of his tobacco.

Another man, wearing the uniform of an air force noncommissioned officer, trudged up the road and came to a stop beside the officer. 'General Hagemann,' he said quietly, as if unwilling to intrude upon his master's thoughts.

The officer removed the pipe from his mouth, clutching the bowl in his leather-gloved hand. 'Tell me some decent news for a change, Sergeant Behr.'

'The fog is due to lift very soon,' Behr said encouragingly, 'and the observation ship reports that visibility in the target area is good.'

A smile glimmered through the fatigue on General Hagemann's face. Although he held a military rank, his heart was not in soldiering. He was a scientist by profession, and his work as head of the propulsion laboratory in the top-secret V-2 rocket facility located in the nearby village Peenemunde had taken over his life, costing him first his marriage, then his health and, he had recently begun to suspect, most of his sanity as well.

Since the first successful launch of a V-2 rocket, back in October of 1942, Hagemann had been working on a radio-controlled guidance system code named Diamantstrahl – the Diamond Stream. If perfected, the system could ensure the accurate delivery of the 1,000 kilograms of explosives contained within each 14-metre-tall rocket. The progress of the war had forced them to go ahead with launches against the cities of London and Antwerp, although, by Hagemann's reckoning, only one in seventeen of these rockets, over a thousand of which had been fired to date, had hit their intended targets. That they had done significant damage to the cities in question was of little consolation to the general because he knew that, even now, as Germany was being crushed between the Anglo-Americans in the West and the Red Army in the East, the delivery of these devastating weapons, with the pinpoint accuracy he felt sure could be achieved, might still tip the balance of the war. And even if it was too late to avoid defeat, the V-2, in its perfected state, might still serve as a bargaining chip in negotiating a separate peace with the western Allies, rather than the unconditional surrender which would otherwise be their only option.

There was no doubt in Hagemann's mind that the future, not only of his country but of all future warfare, depended upon the Diamond Stream project, so named because, in controlled laboratory experiments, the rocket, when functioning perfectly, would emit an exhaust stream of glittering particles which resembled a river of diamonds.

Even as fully armed V-2s were unleashed upon their targets in the west, other rockets, carrying tubes of sand instead of explosives, roared out into the night sky, destined to fall harmlessly into the waters of the Baltic. These were the project's sacrificial lambs. By regulating the mix of liquid oxygen, alcohol and hydrogen peroxide in the fuel system – calculations which sometimes depended on millilitres of adjustment – Hagemann was seeking the perfection of his art.

This evening's offering had been fitted with a mechanism originally intended for steering anti-aircraft missiles. The system, which was much too primitive for use in the V-2, had required so many adjustments before it could be used that Hagemann felt certain this would prove to be another failure.

Sergeant Behr handed over a clipboard. 'Here are this evening's specifics,' he said. Then, he produced a penlight, which he used to illuminate the page, while the general examined the dizzying array of numbers. 'None of these are within the usual parameters.' He clicked his tongue and sighed. After all the years of engineering, he thought to himself, and the thousands upon thousands of experiments, and even with all we have accomplished, there always comes a point when we must stumble out blind into the dark. As he had almost done so many times before, Hagemann reminded himself not to lose faith.

'It's true about the parameters,' Behr replied. 'Some are above the normal range, and some are below. Perhaps they will even each other out.'

Hagemann snuffled out a laugh. He patted Behr on the back. 'If only it were so simple, my friend.'

'Shall I tell them to delay the launch?' asked Behr. 'If you need more time to rearrange the numbers.' 'No.' Hagemann slapped the clipboard gently against Behr's chest. 'Tell them they are clear to go.'

'You are coming back to the ignition area?'

'I'll stay and watch the launch from here,' answered Hagemann.

He was afraid that his subordinates would see the lack of confidence etched upon his face. Some days he could hide it better than others.

'*Zu Befehl!*' Behr clicked his heels. He walked back down the road. Just before the darkness swallowed him up, he stopped and turned, 'Good luck, Herr General.'

'What?' asked Hagemann. 'What did you say?'

'I was wishing you good luck,' said the voice out in the night.

'Yes,' Hagemann replied brusquely. 'That's something we all need.'

He felt a sudden pang of guilt that he had done so little to keep up the morale of his technicians; not even a bottle of brandy to fend off the cold as these men returned to their flimsy, hastily constructed barracks in the village of Karlshagen, on the southern end of the island. Their original accommodations, which boasted not only hot water but a first-class mess hall and even a cinema, had all been destroyed in a massive air raid back in August of 1943. Even though some parts of the sprawling research compound had been rebuilt, the bulk of it remained a heap of ruins, and Soviet advances had recently forced the evacuation of most of the remaining staff to the Harz mountains, far to the south.

At that moment, he heard the familiar hissing roar of the V-2's ignition engine. He could almost feel the rocket rising off the launch pad, as if the great assembly of wiring and steel were a part of his own body. A second later, he caught sight of the poppy-red flame of the V-2's exhaust as the rocket tore away through the night sky.

Almost immediately, the misty air swallowed it up. Hagemann turned and set off towards the launch trailer, a specially built vehicle known as a Meillerwagen.

There was nothing to do now but wait for the report from the observation ship to confirm where the rocket had come down.

He could see the tiny suns of cigarettes as the launch crew moved about, dismantling the V-2's aiming platform so that, by daylight, nothing would remain for Allied reconnaissance planes to photograph. Even the tell-tale disc of charred earth where the ignition flames had scorched the soil would have been carefully swept away by men with wooden rakes, as solemnly as Buddhist monks tending to the sand of a Zen garden.

As Hagemann approached them, he straightened his back and fixed a look of cheerful confidence upon his face. He knew that they would look to him for confirmation that all of their sacrifices had been worthwhile.

Far out in the freezing waters of the Baltic, a wooden-hulled trawler named the *Gullmaren* wallowed in a freshening breeze. Spring had been late in coming and, from time to time, stray clumps of ice bumped up against her hull, triggering loud curses from the helmsman.

Below deck in the ice room, where a boat's cargo of fish was normally stored in large pens, the rest of the three-man crew had gathered around a large radio transmitter.

The radio had been bolted on to a table, to prevent it from sliding with the motion of the waves. In front of this radio sat an Enigma coding machine. It bore a vague resemblance to a typewriter except where the rolling-pin-shaped platen would have been there was instead a set of four metal rotors. Teeth notched into these rotors corresponded to the letters of the alphabet, and they could be placed in any order, allowing the sender and receiver to adjust the configuration of the messages. When typed into the machine, the message would then be scrambled by a series of electrical circuits so that each individual letter was separately encrypted. This system allowed for hundreds of thousands of mutations for every message sent.

Stooped over the radio, with a set of headphones pressed against his ear, was the radio man. Against the damp and cold, he wore a waist-length, black collarless leather jacket of the type normally worn by German U-boat engineers.

Beside him stood Oskar Hildebrand, captain of the *Gullmaren*, his body swaying slightly and unconsciously as the trawler wallowed in the swells.

But Hildebrand was no fisherman, even though he might have looked like one in his dirty white turtleneck sweater and black wool knitted cap.

In fact, Hildebrand held the rank of Kapitan-Leutnant in the German Navy, and for over a year he had served as liaison officer with V-2 Research Facility back on shore.

'Anything?' Hildebrand asked the radio man.

'Nothing yet, Herr Ka-Leu.' But almost as soon as the words had left his mouth, the radio man flinched, as if a slight electric current had passed through his body. At that same instant, miniature lights fitted into the Enigma's keyboard began to flash. 'They have launched,' he said.

From that moment, Hildebrand knew that he had about six minutes before the V-2 reached the target area. His task then would be to note down the point of impact and radio the details back to General Hagemann.

Hildebrand had been in this role of observer for almost a year now, shuttling back and forth across the sea and watching very expensive pieces of machinery smash themselves to pieces as they plunged into the waters of the Baltic. Originally stationed on the coast of France and in command of an S-boat – a fast, low-profiled torpedo cruiser – Hildebrand had, at first, found this new assignment so insultingly beneath him that, even if he could have told people about it, he would have kept silent. It was small consolation that they had allowed him to keep his original radio operator, Obermaat Grimm, and also his helmsman, Steuermann

Barth, who, after years of having almost 3,000 horsepower at his fingertips, thanks to the S-boat's three Daimler-Benz motors, became despondent now that all he had to work with was the trawler's clunky, temperamental diesel.

But in the coming months, as almost everyone they'd ever known in the Navy was removed from their original commission, reassigned as infantry and fed into the vast meat grinder of the Russian front, Hildebrand and his two-man crew had grown to appreciate the obscurity of their position.

Except for the fact that he had been ordered to fly the flag of neutral Sweden while carrying out his work, which meant that he would have undoubtedly been shot if Russian ships prowling these waters had ever stopped and boarded him, Hildebrand's job was relatively safe.

The only thing Hildebrand really worried about was being hit by one of these falling monsters. The fact that these particular rockets did not contain explosive payloads was of little consolation to him, since the amount of metal and machinery contained within them, together with their terminal velocity, was more than enough to turn him, his boat and his crew into particles smaller than rain.

Although Hildebrand was no propulsion engineer, he had pieced together enough to understand that the reason for this incessant bombarding of the Baltic was all part of a search to improve the guidance system by which the V-2s were delivered to their target. From what he had seen with his own eyes, they still had a long way to go.

'I'd better get up top side,' announced Hildebrand. From a cabinet by the ladder, he removed a heavy pair of Zeiss Navy binoculars, with their characteristic yellow-green paint and black rubber bumpers around the lenses. They had been issued to him during his time as an S-boat commander, and if those binoculars could have trapped the memory of things Hildebrand had glimpsed through its lenses, the chalky cliffs of Dover would have glimmered into focus, and the sight of American tankers burning outside Portsmouth harbour, and of La Pallice, his base on the Brittany coast, as he returned from one of his missions, only to find that the port had been destroyed by Allied bombing.

They might have taken his S-boat from him, but Hildebrand was not going to part with those binoculars. Placing the leather cord around his neck, Hildebrand climbed up the ladder, opened the hatch and climbed out on deck.

The first breath of cold air was like pepper in his lungs.

Ice had crusted on the fishing net, which lay twined around a large metal drum balanced horizontally on a stand at the stern of the boat. Even this late in the year, the temperature often dropped below freezing. He went straight to the net and, with his gloved hand, punched at the ice until it began to come away in chunks. Such a build-up on the net was a sure sign, to any passing Russian gunboat, that their trawler was not actually doing any fishing.

The wheelhouse door opened and Barth stuck his head out.

'Is that you, Herr Ka-Leu?' he asked, using the colloquial abbreviation of Hildebrand's rank.

'Just cleaning the net,' replied Hildebrand and, as he spoke, he noticed that their little Swedish flag, tied to a broomstick which jutted at an angle from the bow, had also been encased in ice. Hildebrand made his way over to the pole and shook the flag loose, so that its blue and yellow colours could be seen.

'The Führer thanks you for your fastidiousness,' remarked the helmsman.

'And I have no doubt that he is equally grateful for your sarcasm,'

Hildebrand replied.

Barth glanced up at the sky. 'When's it due?'

'Any minute now.'

The watchman nodded. 'Cold tonight.'

'Keep an eye out for pieces of ice.'

'We've hit a lot of them this trip,' agreed Barth. 'If we stay out here much longer, one of those bastards is going to come right through our hull.' Then he spat on the deck for good luck and shut the door behind him.

Alone now, Hildebrand searched among the stars for the flame of the V-2. Raising the powerful binoculars to his eyes, he stared up at the gibbous moon. The craters of the Ptolemaeus range, like the shell holes of a Great War battlefield, jumped into focus.

'Ka-Leu!' hissed Barth.

Hildebrand lowered the binoculars.

The helmsman was pointing at something off the port bow. Hildebrand could see it now – a chevron of white water caused by the chisel-shaped bow of a small ship ploughing through the water. A moment later, Hildebrand made out the armoured turret-shaped wheelhouse of a Soviet patrol boat, of the type known as a 'Moshka'. They were used primarily as submarine chasers and Hildebrand had seen a number of them during his time out here on the Baltic. He had heard stories of running gun battles between Moshkas and Finnish submarines that had been caught on the surface. Unable to dive without making themselves an easy target for the Moshka's depth charges, the Finns had remained on the surface, exchanging machine gunfire with the Russian sailors until each vessel was so riddled with bullets that both often sank as a result. There were other stories, too, of transport ships crowded with German civilians and wounded soldiers, fleeing the unstoppable Soviet advance. Hoping to reach Denmark, parts of which were still in German hands, these overloaded ships were easy prey for the Moshkas. Thousands of women and children and wounded German soldiers had been lost. Maybe tens of thousands. Their numbers would never be known.

Immediately in front of Hildebrand lay a wooden chest normally used for storing coils of rope. It now contained two Panzerfaust anti-tank weapons, a dozen stick grenades and three Schmeisser sub-machine guns – enough to give the crew of the *Gullmaren* at least a fighting chance if the Russian sailors became too curious. But a fighting chance was all it gave them. The trawler carried no armaments. Its hull was already weak from salt rot and worms which had bored into the keel. Its old diesel engine stood absolutely no chance of outrunning even the slowest of Russian patrol boats. Hildebrand had always counted upon the notion that the greatest defense this trawler could offer them was, in fact, its utter defencelessness. That, and the blue and yellow Swedish flag, which, thanks to his fastidiousness, now fluttered on its broomstick pole.

With the toe of his boot, Hildebrand opened the lid of the wooden trunk and stared at the weaponry laid out in front of him. As mist began to settle on the black barrel of the Schmeisser and on the dull, sand-coloured tubing of the Panzerfaust, Hildebrand tried to calculate exactly how long it would take him to retrieve one of the grenades, unscrew the metal cap at the bottom of the stick, arm the weapon by tugging the porcelain ball attached to a piece of string located inside the hollow wooden shaft, then throw it, not at the Russians but down into the radio room, in order to destroy the Enigma machine before the Russians got their hands on it.

Grimm would be killed in the blast, of course, but the Russians would have shot him anyway when they found out who he was. None of them would survive. Of that, he was quite certain.

As the patrol boat drew near, Hildebrand heard the Russian helmsman back off on the throttle of his engine. Then came a sharp command, a metallic clunk and suddenly the trawler was bathed in the magnesium blast of a search light.

With his eyes forced almost shut by the glare, Hildebrand raised one hand and bellowed, '*Hur mår du?*' – the only words of Swedish that he knew.

While the Moshka's searchlight played along the length of the trawler, Hildebrand caught sight of a heavy machine-gun mounted on a stand at the bow. A Russian sailor stood behind it, leaning into the half-moon-shaped shoulder braces, ready to chop him to pieces with its 37mm ammunition.

In spite of the cold air, Hildebrand was now sweating profusely.

The Moshka was level with them now, still moving but with its engines powered down almost into neutral.

He could see the captain looking from the turret wheelhouse. The man wore a close-fitting fur cap and his meaty hands gripped the metal apron of the turret. He was not smiling.

Neither were the other crewmen, all of whom wore heavy canvas coats with thick fur collars and carried PPSh submachine guns with fifty-round magazines.

'*Hur mår du!*' Hildebrand shouted again, waving stupidly and all the while weaving like a drunkard as compensation for the movement of the deck beneath his feet.

The captain turned to the one of the fur-coated men standing next to him.

The man smiled.

The captain laughed. He raised one hand and swiped it through the air in greeting.

'That's it,' Hildebrand muttered through the clenched teeth of his smile. 'Keep moving, Bolshevik.'

The engine of the Moshka growled and the boat moved on, dematerializing into the salty mist.

Hildebrand tried to swallow, but his throat was so tight that all he could do was hold on to a cable and lean over the side in order to spit. As he moved, the binoculars swung out on their leather strap.

His heart practically stopped. He had forgotten completely about them.

He wondered how the Soviets could possibly have disregarded the sight of a pair of German Navy binoculars hanging around the neck of a Swedish trawler-man. The answer, it seemed clear to him, was that they hadn't. He reached into the wooden trunk and removed a Panzerfaust. Never having fired one before, he wondered how accurate they were.

Hildebrand peered into the black, waiting for the Moshka to reappear out of the gloom and for the night air to be filled with the racing lights of tracer fire as the Russian guns tore his ship apart. But the Moshka never reappeared.

He imagined the Russian captain, weeks or even years from now, waking from a dream in which he suddenly realised his mistake.

Once more Hildebrand broke into a smile, only this one was not conjured out of fear.

Just then, something flickered across the mottled white disc of the moon.

Immediately, he raised the binoculars to his eyes and glimpsed the fiery exhaust of the V-2, trailing a white line of condensation across the firmament. And something else, which he had never seen before. Between the chalky vapour trail and the blowtorch heat of the rocket, Hildebrand perceived a glittering light, as if the universe had inverted and he was not looking up but down into the depths of the sea and the V-2 was no longer a mass of arc-welded technology but a huge and elegant sea creature, followed by a retinue of tiny fish, illuminating its path with their silvery bodies.

'Diamonds,' whispered Hildebrand. And he was so transfixed by the great beauty of this moment that it was only when the V-2 had crossed directly above his head, at a height of about one kilometer, that Hildebrand realised it was not descending, as all of the other rockets had done. 'Are you sure we're in the target area?' he barked at the helmsman.

The wheelhouse door opened and Hildebrand was forced to repeat himself.

'Yes,' answered Barth. 'Why do you ask?' But even before Hildebrand could reply, the helmsman noticed the V-2 as it passed over their heads.

'Shouldn't it be losing altitude by now?' asked Barth. 'It should,' answered Hildebrand, 'as long as we're in the right place.'

'We are, Ka-Leu. I checked.'

'Which direction is it going?' asked Hildebrand.

'North,' replied Barth. 'Due north.'

Hildebrand clambered down the ladder into the hold.

'Is everything all right?' asked Grimm, removing his headphones.

'A chart!' shouted Hildebrand. 'Find me a chart of the area.' Grimm fetched out a map and laid it on the table, sweeping aside a collection of pencils, protractors and decoded Enigma transcripts.

Hildebrand studied the chart, tracing one finger along the north–south line until it came to a stop at the island of Bornholm, 50 kilometers away. 'Son of a bitch!' shouted Hildebrand. 'I think we've just declared war on Sweden.'

'Bornholm is actually Danish,' said Grimm.

'Never mind who it belongs to! Just send a message to the general and ask him what the hell is going on.'

As Pekkala slowly made his way through a bowl of sorrel and mushroom soup which Valentina had brought him, he suddenly felt that he was being watched.

Glancing up, he caught the eye of an ancient, thickly bearded man who was staring at him.

Embarrassed to have been spotted, the old-timer smiled awkwardly and returned to eating his own meal.

This was not the first time that Pekkala had experienced the strange, prickling sensation that the gaze of a stranger was upon him.

Some, like the old man, who had once been a guard at the Winter Palace of the Tsar, recognised his face from long ago. Others had heard only rumours that this quiet midnight visitor was known across the length and breadth of Russia as the Emerald Eye.

Pekkala had been born in Lappeenranta, Finland, at a time when it was still a Russian colony. His mother was a Laplander, from Rovaniemi in the north.

At the age of eighteen, on the wishes of his father, Pekkala travelled to Petrograd in order to enlist in Tsar Nicholas II's elite Chevalier Guard. There, early in his training, he had been singled out by the Tsar for special duty as his own Special Investigator. It was a position which had never existed before and which would one day give Pekkala powers that had been considered unimaginable before the Tsar chose to create them.

In preparation for this, he was given over to the police, then to the State Police – the Gendarmerie – and after that to the Tsar's secret police, who were known as the Okhrana. In those long months, doors were opened to him which few men even knew existed. At the completion of his training, the Tsar gave to Pekkala the only badge of office he would ever wear – a heavy gold disc, as wide across as the length of his little finger. Across the centre was a stripe of white enamel inlay, which began at a point, widened until it took up half the disc and narrowed again to a point on the other side. Embedded in the middle of the white enamel was a large, round emerald. Together, these elements formed the unmistakable shape of an eye. Pekkala never forgot the first time he held the disc in his hand, and the way he had traced his fingertip over the eye, feeling the smooth bump of the jewel, like a blind man reading braille.

It was because of this badge that Pekkala became known as the Emerald Eye. Little else was known about him by the public. In the absence of facts, legends grew up around Pekkala, including rumours that he was not even human, but rather some demon conjured into life through the black arts of an Arctic shaman.

Throughout his years of service, Pekkala answered only to the Tsar. In that time he learned the secrets of an empire, and when that empire fell, and those who shared those secrets had taken them to their graves, Pekkala was surprised to find himself still breathing.

Captured during the Revolution, and after months of interrogation at the Lubyanka and Lefortovo prisons, he was convicted by the Bolsheviks of crimes against the state and sent to labour camp at Borodok, to serve out a sentence of no less than twenty-five years.

Pekkala had been a prisoner for nine of those years when a young, newly commissioned officer in the Bureau of Special Operations came clambering through the forest of Krasnagolyana to deliver the news that Pekkala's sentence had been repealed, but only on condition that he agreed to work for Stalin, just as he had once done for the Tsar.

As a gesture of Stalin's good will, the officer brought with him a satchel containing two trophies which had been taken from Pekkala at the time of his arrest, and which he was now authorised to return.

One was a .455 calibre Webley revolver with solid brass handles, a gift from King George V of England to his cousin the Tsar, and passed on to Pekkala by Nicholas II as a token of his esteem. The second trophy was the emerald eye itself, which Stalin had kept in a purple velvet bag in his desk drawer. The jeweled emblem had been one of his most prized possessions. Often, over the years, when Stalin found himself alone in his red-carpeted office in the Kremlin, he would take out the badge and hold it in the palm of his hand, watching the jungle-green stone drink in the sunlight, as if it were a living thing.

Since that time, maintaining an uneasy truce with his former enemies, Pekkala had continued in his role as Special Investigator, answerable only to the ruler of the Russian people.

'There you are!' exclaimed a Red Army major as he stepped into the fuggy air of Café Tilsit. He was tall and wiry, with rosy cheeks and arching eyebrows which gave him an expression of perpetual astonishment.

On each sleeve of his close-fitting *gymnastiorka* tunic, he wore a red star etched out in gold-coloured thread, to indicate the rank of commissar. Riding breeches, the same dull colour as rotten apples, had been tucked into a set of highly polished knee-length boots. He strode across the room and joined Pekkala at his table.

While they were openly curious about Pekkala, the diners at the café immediately averted their gaze from this officer, having recognised the red stars of the commissar upon his sleeves. Now they busied themselves with scraping dirty fingernails, or reading scraps of newspaper or with a sudden fascination for their soup.

The man who sat before Pekkala now was that same officer who had trudged through the Siberian wilderness to deliver the news that Stalin required his services again.

They had been working side by side for many years now, each having learned to tolerate the eccentricities of the other.

Kirov reached across the table, picked up the half-drunk mug of kvass, took a sip and winced. 'For breakfast?' he asked. Pekkala answered with a question of his own. 'What brings you here at this ungodly hour?'

'I came to deliver a message.'

'Then deliver it, Major Kirov,' said Pekkala.

'We are wanted at the Kremlin.'

'Why?' asked Pekkala.

'Whatever it is, it can't wait,' replied Kirov, rising to his feet.

At the V-2 rocket site, General Hagemann's technicians had just completed the dismantling of the mobile launch platform, which they referred to as a 'table'. The heavy scaffolding, bearing the scorch marks of numerous ignition blasts, had been stacked upon the Meillerwagen, which had been fitted with a double set of rear wheels to take the extra weight of a fully loaded rocket.

The technicians, using their helmets as seats, sat in the road smoking cigarettes which, these days, consisted mostly of corn silk and acorns, while they waited for the order to move out. Assembling and dismantling the V-2 platforms had become second nature to these men. It had to, since their lives depended on the speed with which they worked. During the hours of daylight, once the enemy had spotted the tell-tale fire of a V-2 launch, it was only a matter of time before artillery was brought to bear on the position, or fighter planes equipped with armour-piercing bullets roared in at treetop level. It was the job of these technicians to be long gone by then, and they required little encouragement to carry out their work.

But night-time launches were different, especially this far from the front line. They did not have to fear the prying eyes of artillery spotters, and no fighter-bombers would take to the skies for low-level missions unless they could see where they were going.

For the men of the V-2 programme, darkness had become

the only thing they trusted in the world. That and their ability to vanish before the heat had even left the metal of the launch scaffolds.

General Hagemann waited by the communications truck, in which an Enigma machine, set to the same rotor configuration as the one on the trawler, would receive the message sent by Captain Hildebrand, giving the coordinates of this particular's rocket's crash site.

It was to be the last test launch for at least a week. The reason for this was that the bulk of available V-2 rockets were being pulled back from their launch sites in Holland, where they had been used for bombarding London and the port of Antwerp, and were now to be redirected towards targets in the east. Overseeing the safe transport of the rockets, as well as scouting out new launch sites, was about to become a full-time job for Hagemann.

His troubles did not end there.

Targeting the Russians would only increase the pressure placed upon him by the High Command to solve the guidance problems which had plagued the V-2 programme from the start. Thanks to wildly over-optimistic predictions from Propaganda Minister Goebbels, the German public had been led to believe that miracle weapons were being developed which would turn the tide of the entire war. Even some members of the High Command believed that such things might be possible. But time was running out. Soon not even miracles would save them.

By the small dusty red light of the radio's main console, Hagemann watched the operators scribbling down the trawler's message as it emerged from the Enigma machine. It was a longer message than usual. Normally, Hildebrand just relayed the coordinates of the V-2's splash point. Hagemann immediately began to worry that something had gone wrong.

The radio operator finished transcribing the message, tore off the page on which he had written it down and handed the page to the general.

The first thing Hagemann noticed was that there were no numbers written down, which would have indicated the coordinates where the rocket, or 'needle' as it was always referred to in the messages, had landed. These numbers would then have been tallied with the adjustments made for this particular flight, indicating whether or not they had improved the V-2's accuracy.

Instead, the message read: 'Needle overshot to north-northeast. No splash point indicated. Unusual exhaust pattern observed.'

When Hagemann read those last words, his whole face went numb. 'Reply,' he croaked, barely able to speak.

The radio operator rested his first two fingers on the keyboard of the Enigma machine. 'Ready,' he said quietly.

'Explain unusual exhaust pattern,' Hagemann told the operator.

The operator tapped in the four words. They waited.

'What's taking them so long?' snapped Hagemann.

Before the operator could reply, a new message flickered across the Enigma's light board.

Hurriedly, the operator decoded the message. 'It says "Silver cloud in halo".' The general's heart slammed into his ribcage. 'Silver cloud?'

'That is correct, Herr General. Shall I ask for further clarification?' asked the radio man.

'No,' replied Hagemann, barely able to speak. 'Send a new message, this one to FHQ.'

The operator glanced up. Those three letters stood for Führerhauptquartier and meant that the message would be going directly to Hitler's private switchboard. He hesitated, unsure that he had heard the general correctly.

'Is there a problem?' barked Hagemann.

'No, Herr General!' the radio man waited, fingers poised over the keys.

'The message should read: "Needle overshot Target Area".'

'That's all?'

'No.' But then Hagemann hesitated.

'Herr General?' asked the signalman.

'Diamond Stream observed,' said Hagemann. 'Add that to the message. Send it now.'

Hitler had been waiting for that message for almost two years. Hagemann just hoped to God those boys floating out there on the Baltic were right about what they had seen.

By now, the technicians, sitting in their huddle, had noticed that something unusual was going on. Leaving their helmets, which resembled a crop of large grey mushrooms that had suddenly sprouted from the road, they came over to the radio truck.

Among them was Sergeant Behr. 'What is it, Herr General?' he asked.

Hagemann handed him the message which they had just received. 'Diamond Stream,' whispered Behr.

Soon the words began to echo among the small group of men gathered beside the radio truck.

Hagemann stared at the list of calculations scribbled on his clipboard. He had waited so long for the Diamond Stream to become a reality, rehearsing in his mind the precise array of emotions which hearing those words would evoke. But now that the moment was finally here, and so unexpectedly, the only thing he felt was nauseous.

By now, Behr had also read the trawler's message. 'But why would it have overshot?' he asked.

'I'm not sure yet,' answered Hagemann. 'The Diamond Stream must have had some unintended effect on the propulsion system. I'll have to go over the flight calculations again. It might be a while before I know for certain what took place.'

'Do we have any idea of where it might have come down, Herr General?'

Hagemann shook his head. 'Most likely in the water.'

'And even if the rocket did crash on land,' Behr stated confidently, 'there would be nothing of it.'

Hagemann didn't reply. He knew that whole sections of V-2 fuselage had survived their supersonic impacts, even those which had been fully loaded with explosives. Disoriented, the general began walking down the sandy road towards the ocean, as if he meant to swim out into the freezing waters of the Baltic and retrieve the missing rocket by himself.

'Congratulations!' Behr called after him.

Hagemann raised one hand in acknowledgement as the darkness swallowed him up.

Far to the west, at a British Special Operations listening post known as Station 53A, located in a rural manor house in Buckinghamshire, the messages exchanged between General Hagemann's launch site and the observation ship had been intercepted.

In less than an hour, the message had been decoded by the station's Head of Operations, a former member of the Polish Intelligence Service named Peter Garlinski.

Garlinski, a thin-faced man with round, tortoiseshell glasses and two thin swabs of hair growing on either side of his otherwise bald head, had been en route to England in September of 1939, carrying rotors stolen from a German Enigma machine, when the Germans invaded his country. With no way to return home, Garlinski offered his services to British Intelligence. He had been at 53A ever since, rising to Head of Operations thanks to his ability to stay at his post for thirty-six hours at a stretch, monitoring the airwaves for enemy transmissions, relying on nothing more than strong tea and cigarettes to keep him going.

The capture of a complete Enigma machine from a U-boat that foundered off the English coast had enabled British Intelligence to begin decoding the messages.

For several minutes, Garlinski studied General Hagemann's text, wondering if he might somehow have misread the transmission. He processed it a second time to reassure himself that there had been no mistake. Then he sent the message on to cryptographic analysts at Bletchley Park to await confirmation.

At the same moment as Sergeant Behr was congratulating General Hagemann, two elderly brothers on the Danish island of Bornholm were contemplating murder.

Per and Ole Ottesen were twins who lived together in a lowroofed house, not far from the village of Saksebro. They had spent all their lives on Bornholm, running a small dairy farm which they had inherited from their parents. Neither man had married and now they were both very old.

Due to poor management, the Ottesen farm had shrunk until it was only a shadow of its former self. Their father, Karl Ottesen, had once owned a hundred and fifty head of cattle, exporting not only milk but butter and cheese as well to the nearby Swedish mainland. He had been one of the first people on Bornholm to own a motor car – a 1902 wood-panelled Arrol-Johnston – and even though it could not travel far or well upon the roads of that largely unpaved island, the fact of ownership had been enough to ensure his elevated standing in the community. Lacking such ambition, the Ottesen brothers were content to let the business dwindle until only a few cows remained, whose milk produced barely enough to cover the cost of their feed.

Now they were down to one cow, an irritable Friesian named Lotti. She was blind in one eye and gave no milk and, two days before, as Ole was leading her out of the barn so that Per could clean her stall, she fastened on to the seat of Ole's trousers and tore off a large piece of cloth, exposing the old man's buttocks to the winter cold.

So they decided to shoot her.

Having settled upon this course, it soon became apparent to the twins that neither was prepared to carry out the deed. Lotti had been with them a long time. She was, to all intents and purposes, a member of their family.

The two men sat in spindle-backed chairs beside the fireplace, while they tried to come up with a plan.

'Father would have done it,' said Per.

'He would,' agreed Ole, 'and there would have been no discussion, before or afterwards.'

'You should be the one,' said Per.

'And why is that?' protested his brother.

'I have always been a gentler soul.'

'Gentler!' laughed Ole. 'You son of a bitch.'

'And what does that make you?' replied Per. They lapsed into silence for a while.

'It's got to be done,' muttered Ole.

This time, there was no disagreement from his twin.

Ole leaned back in his chair and rummaged in his waistcoat pocket, emerging seconds later with a two-krone coin between his fingers. 'I'll flip you for it,' he said.

Per squinted at him. 'This is some kind of trick.'

'You can flip the coin,' Ole tossed it into his lap.

'I get to call it as well!'

Ole shrugged. 'You really are a son of a bitch.'

Per settled the coin on his thumbnail, then launched it into the air. Both men watched it tumbling up and then down.

Per caught the coin, slapped it on to the top of his other hand and then fixed his brother with a stare that could have passed for madness.

'Crown or cross?' demanded Ole. The cross referred to a Roman numeral, fixed inside the monogram of the Danish king, Christian X. On the other side of the coin was the king's crown.

Per's hand had begun to tremble.

'Go on!' shouted Ole. 'Choose, damn you!'

'Cross!' he blurted. 'No! Crown! Cross!'

Ole lunged forward. 'You can't have both, you simpleton!'

'Crown,' Per said softly. Then slowly, he lifted his hand. It was the cross.

'Ha!' crowed Ole.

'I meant to say crown,' muttered Per.

'Too late now,' answered his brother as he got up from his chair, reached above the fireplace and took down the only gun they owned, a model 1896 Krag rifle which had belonged to their father, who had served in the Bornholm Militia. 'Make it quick,' commanded Ole, as he handed the rifle to Per.

Per lit a kerosene lantern. Then he put on a thick wool coat with wooden toggle buttons and stepped through the anteroom, where they put their muddy boots in summer time. He closed the door behind him and then opened the second door out into the farmyard.

Sheet ice lay like mirrors in the barnyard and the old man shuffled along carefully, still wearing his slippers.

Arriving at the barn, he opened the heavy door and made his way inside. He was going to close the door again, to keep in what little heat there was, but there seemed to be no point to that and he left it open instead.

Lotti was in a stall among several others, all of them empty except hers. She watched the old man approach, turning her head so she could see with her good eye.

She had won prizes in her day. A medal from the 1935 Agricultural Fair in Sandvig still hung from an old nail above her stall. 'Lotti – Beste Kuh,' it said.

Per stopped in front of the cow. 'Lotti,' he said solemnly, 'I have to kill you now.'

The cow just looked at him and chewed.

After setting down the lantern, Per leaned upon the gun as if it were a cane. Why is this so hard for me, he wondered, but even as the thought passed through his mind, he knew the answer. The death of this animal would mark the end of his life as a farmer. And if he was no longer a farmer, then what was he? What purpose was there left for him in life? And if he served no purpose, then what point was there in going on at all?

At that moment, it would almost have been easier for Per to shoot himself than it would have been to put a bullet through the forehead of that temperamental cow.

Exhausted by such unforgiving thoughts, the old man sat down on a bale of hay. 'To hell with everything,' he sighed.

'I knew you couldn't do it,' said a voice. It was Ole. Hearing no shots fired, he had come to check on his brother and now stood in the doorway, arms folded, with a disapproving frown upon his face.

'I was just . . . collecting myself,' Per replied defensively.

'No, you weren't.'

Per stared at the ground. 'I'm damned if I will shoot this cow.' He held out the gun to his brother. 'You can do it.'

But Ole made no move to take the rifle. The truth was he couldn't do it either. 'God will take her when he's ready,' he announced.

Per rose to his feet, shouldered the gun on its tired leather sling, picked up the lantern and followed his brother out into the barnyard.

At that moment, both men saw what they simultaneously perceived to be a shooting star, so perfectly reflected in the ice which covered the barnyard that there appeared to be not one but two meteors, each one racing towards the other on a collision course.

This was followed by a roar of wind, like one of the katabatic gusts which sometimes blew in off the Baltic, wrenching trees out of the ground and knocking over chimney pots.

The ground shook.

Both men stumbled and fell.

The lantern slipped from Per's grasp and broke upon the ground, sending a splash of blazing kerosene across the ground, which flickered yellow to orange to blue and finally sizzled away into the melting ice.

Then out of the darkness came a thumping, clattering shower of roof tiles, old nails, pitchforks and smouldering bales of hay.

The brothers cowered, speechless, as the trappings of their life crashed down around them.

When this barrage had finally ceased, Per and Ole climbed shakily to their feet and stared at a wall of dust, even blacker than the night, rising from where the barn had been only a moment before. As the dust began to clear, and stars winked out of the gloom, they realised that their barn had been completely destroyed. Somewhere in that tangle of charred beams and splintered planks was Lotti. Or what was left of her. There was nothing to be done about it now.

'God did not waste any time,' remarked Ole.

'He might have been a little less heavy-handed,' said Per, as the two men returned to their house.

A few hours later, just as the first rays of dawn began to glimmer off the rooftops of Berlin, a man named Rochus Misch was woken by the telephone.

Misch opened his eyes. By the pale light which filtered in through his curtains, he noticed that the crack in his ceiling had spread. When it first appeared, back in January, after a British 10-ton bomb known as a Grand Slam had obliterated an apartment block three streets away, Misch had simply painted over the crack. One week later, the crack reappeared after another bomb, this time from an American B-17 flying daylight raids over the city, knocked out power to the entire suburb of Karlshorst. This time, Misch just left the crack alone. It was a rented flat, after all. In the weeks that followed, the crack meandered in a crooked path across the chiffon-yellow paint, travelling like a slowmoving lightning bolt from one end of the ceiling to the other. For Misch, its relentless progress seemed to take on hidden meaning. The closer it came to the opposite end of the ceiling from which it had begun, the more Misch became convinced that when it finally arrived, something momentous would take place.

It was almost there. Holding out his arm and clenching his hand into a fist, Misch measured that the crack had only three knuckle-lengths to go before it reached its destination. What happened then had become the stuff of Misch's nightmares which, like the crack itself across the once-clear field of yellow paint, had worked their way into his waking thoughts until it seemed as if they must consume his mind entirely.

The phone rang again.

Still half asleep, he tossed aside the crumpled sheets and made his way down the hall to where the phone stood on a wooden table, its battered finish partially hidden by a place mat crocheted with the red, white and black design of the National Socialist flag. The phone rested on the white circle in the middle of the flag, concealing all but the outer edges of the swastika, which jutted like the legs of a huge, squashed spider from beneath the heavy casing of the phone.

Misch picked up the receiver. 'Hello?' he said. 'Hello? Who is there?'

There was no answer. In fact, the line was dead.

Mystified, he put the phone down again and glanced at his watch. It was 6 a.m., a full two hours before he had to report for work. That gave him another half-hour of lying in bed. Maybe he could fall asleep. Or maybe he'd just stare at the crack in the ceiling.

Misch had almost reached the bed when the phone jangled yet again.

Muttering a curse, he spun around and stared at it, as if daring it to make another sound.

As the last shadows of sleep drifted from his mind, Misch realised that something was wrong. The phone wasn't actually ringing, at least not in the way it normally did. Instead, after the initial high-pitched rattle of bells, its tone faded out almost apologetically, as if something other than an incoming call was causing the disturbance.

At that moment, Misch felt a faint vibration through the worn-out socks he always wore to bed. It was only because he was standing still that he felt it at all. But the bells inside the telephone responded faintly and at last Misch understood that this vibration was the cause.

But what, in turn, was causing the vibration?

Misch walked over to the window, drew the heavy velvet blackout curtains and rested his hand against the window pane. He felt it, like a weak electric charge, trembling through his skin. It was too early in the morning for an air raid. The RAF night bombers were usually gone by about 2 or 3 a.m. and the Americans rarely arrived before noon. Besides, he had heard no sirens to indicate that he should head down to the shelter in the basement.

And suddenly he remembered a day, back in the autumn of 1939 when, as part of an armoured column making its way across Poland, his column had passed by a huge snub-barrelled cannon being transported on its own railway tracks to the outskirts of Warsaw. In white Sutterlin-script letters as tall as a man he read the cannon's name – Thor. That night, as Misch sat beside a fire made of willow branches, poking the embers with the remains of a Polish cavalry lance from the obliterated Pomorske Cavalry Brigade, he had felt the same trembling of the earth beneath his feet. It was the sound of Thor, launching its 4,700-pound shells at the Polish capital. He had been told that a single shell from that gun could destroy an entire city block.

At last Misch understood what had hounded him from his sleep. Russian long-range artillery had come within range of Berlin. In the days and weeks ahead, what little had remained undamaged by the Anglo-American bombers would be pounded into dust by Stalin's guns.

One hour later, his chin dotted with scabs of bloody tissue paper from a hasty shaving job with a worn-out razor, Misch passed through the security checkpoint at the Old Reichschancellery. He side-stepped the boiler-suited workmen who were making their way across the marble floors, sweeping away fragments of glass from panes broken out of the tall Chancellery windows. The sound of it was almost musical, like that of a wind chime stirring in the breeze.

In January of that year, the German High Command had begun the process of relocating from the Chancellery buildings into the safer, bomb-proof complex below, which was known to all who worked there as the Führerbunker. Hitler himself had relinquished his lavish suite, with its views of the Chancellery Garden, for a cramped and stuffy quarters below ground. Since then, with the exception of short strolls amongst the rubble in the company of his German shepherd, Blondi, Hitler had seldom ventured out into the city. Now he could often be found, at any time of day or night, wandering its narrow corridors on errands known only to himself.

It used to be that Misch would hurry through the halls of this great building on his way to work, barely stopping to notice the beautiful furnishings or the lifesize portraits of statesmen like Bismarck and Friedrich the Great, glowering down from their frames.

But today he did not hurry.

Suddenly, there seemed to be no point.

All a person could do now was to wait for the end of what was to have been the Thousand-Year Reich, whose obliteration after less than a decade of existence would soon play out in the streets of this doomed city.

Misch did not expect to survive the coming battle. These days, in his plodding commute from the flat to his work and home again, the smallest things, even the sound of broken glass as it was swept across a floor, took on a kind of sacredness.

After the checkpoint, Misch descended a staircase broken up into four separate columns, each consisting of eleven steps. As he made his way underground, the air became thicker and more humid. To Misch, it smelled like a men's locker room. In places, the cement ceiling was fuzzed with a curious white crystalline substance where water had leaked through.

Few people outside the Chancellery building even knew of the existence of this underground warren of rooms and narrow passageways, with its battleship-grey walls of re-barred concrete six feet thick and floors lined with burgundy-red carpeting.

In a little alcove 55 feet below ground level, Misch took his seat at a radio transmitter. For the next eight hours, with the exception of one forty-five-minute break, this would be Misch's domain. All radio traffic in and out of this underground complex passed through this single transmitter and it was Misch's task to transfer incoming and outgoing calls to their proper recipients. For the most part, it was mindnumbing work, with long stretches in which the radio fell silent. During these periods, he would sometimes put a call through to his wife, who had gone with their infant son to live with her parents south of the city, where they would be safer from the bombing raids. The strength of the radio antenna also allowed him to listen in to the various German Army broadcast stations, known as Senders, which had once been scattered over the vast areas of conquered territory, from Arctic Norway to the Libyan desert, but were now confined to the few corners of the Reich that the Allies had not yet wrestled from their grasp.

He shared this tedious duty with another radio operator, a squat and fleshy Austrian named Zeltner, whose toes had frozen off when he fell asleep in a bunker outside Borodino in the winter of 1941. The injury removed him from any possibility of service on the front line, and he had helped to run the switchboard at the Chancellery until, like Misch, he had been transferred down into the bunker. Zeltner moved about surprisingly well for a man with no toes and, when in uniform, showed almost no sign of his deformity. This was accomplished by stuffing the ends of his boot with crumpled sheets of newspaper.

Other than this, Misch knew very little about the man with whom he exchanged a few words twice a day, when he began and ended his shift, and whose body heat he each day felt in the padded chair they shared at the switchboard.

'Anything come in?' Misch asked.

'Only this,' replied Zeltner, handing over a message form, which had been filled with only two words. 'It's from a general named Hagemann, somewhere on the Baltic coast.'

Misch squinted at the message form. '"Diamond Stream observed". What the hell is that?'

'The man was probably drunk,' laughed Zeltner. 'I suppose you could do the general a favour and not hand it in.'

Misch tossed it back on to the desk.

Zeltner climbed out of his chair and slapped Misch on the back to say goodbye.

Misch had only been at his station for a few minutes before he heard a familiar shuffling sound coming up the corridor behind him.

He did not turn around. He didn't need to.

Misch heard the sharply exhaled breaths and the switchblade

noise of a man sucking at his teeth.

It had become almost a game for Misch, allowing himself to be sneaked up on in this way.

He felt a hand settle lightly on his shoulder, and then a voice softly calling his name. 'Misch.'

Misch turned, rising from his chair. His heels crashed together as he came face to face with Adolf Hitler.

He wore a pearl-grey, double-breasted jacket, a green shirt and black trousers. Fastened to the jacket was an iron cross from the Great War and a gold-rimmed National Socialist Party member badge with a serial number of 001. In a few days, Hitler would turn fifty-six, but he looked at least a decade older than he was. His pale blue-grey eyes were watery and unfocused and he held his left hand against his side to stop the trembling which had taken over much of his body.

There was a rumour going around that he suffered from Parkinson's disease.

'I will just . . .' Hitler gestured at the headphones lying on the radio desk.

He did not need to say more. This eavesdropping on the outside world had become a regular occurrence.

Misch stepped aside, offering his seat.

'Go up to the mess and have some coffee,' said Hitler. His tone with Misch was gentle, as it often was with those of lower rank who shared this subterranean existence. 'Come back in twenty minutes.' There was no coffee. Not any more. At least not for men of Misch's rank. There was only a substance made from ground chicory root that Misch could not stand. Instead, he used the time to return above ground and smoke a cigarette, since there was no smoking in the bunker.

Just before Misch turned the corner to climb the first flight of steps, he glanced back at the radio station, watching Hitler squint as he fiddled with the frequency dials. Misch had no idea what Hitler listened to while he was gone. Was it music? Was it some message meant for him alone, transmitted from some distant corner of the universe? Misch had resigned himself to never knowing the answer since by the time he returned from his break, the dials had all been returned to their original positions.

With Misch out of the way, Hitler turned the receiver dial until the familiar voice of Sender Station Elbe appeared through the rustle of static. Along with sender stations in Berlin and Belgrade, the Elbe network was the last functioning transmitter in the Reich. Designed to keep soldiers at the various fronts informed about the war, each sender station operated with some degree of autonomy. Of course, they were all controlled by the Ministry of Propaganda, which had instituted strict guidelines as to what music could be played, what news could be broadcast and what kinds of messages could be read out from loved ones at home. But those responsible for each sender station were allowed to choose the scheduling, and could even insert their own news stories, to add local flavour to the regional broadcasts. These included history lessons about famous landmarks, such as a very successful programme about the Acropolis broadcast by Sender Station Athens, shortly before it went off the air back in 1942. There was also a series of lectures on French wine broadcast by Sender Station Paris, although that station, too, had gone off the air months ago.

These stations had proved to be a great success, keeping soldiers in touch with events at home at the same time as the local broadcasts allowed them to glimpse their surroundings through lenses not clouded by war.

No station had proved to be more popular than the Elbe network. Their broadcasts were expertly produced, the signal always strong and easy to locate and, with its lighthearted irreverence, spoke most convincingly to soldiers grown weary of the kind of incessant, humourless and increasingly far-fetched pronouncements about miracle weapons which would alter the course of the conflict.

What only Hitler, and a few others in his administration, knew, however, was that Sender Station Elbe did not originate from the German Ministry of Propaganda.

It was actually run by the British.

This pirate radio station had first come to Hitler's attention back in early 1944, when it came on the air as Sender Station Calais. As it was named after a town on the French coast, those who tuned into its signal could be led to believe that the broadcasts originated from there, when in fact the programmes were being transmitted from England, on the other side of the Channel.

The Calais station had been in operation for some time before anyone in Berlin realised that it even existed. The reason for this was that, at first, no one listening to the programmes thought any of their content worth reporting. It was just the usual array of songs – the 'Erika Marsch', 'Lili Marlene', 'Volks ans Gewehr' – and the predictable anti-American, anti-British, anti-Russian stories.

It was only when a special programme appeared, narrated by a jovial, but disgruntled SS officer known only as Der Chef, that Berlin began to take notice. Der Chef spoke in the blunt, abbreviated language of a front-line soldier. His informal chats, broadcast for five or ten minutes between long stretches of popular music, were filled with sneering remarks about the effete quality of British soldiers, the drunkenness of Russians and the overindulgence of Americans. But he also did not hesitate to share whatever gossip he had picked up about the leadership in Berlin. It was Der Chef who exposed the juicy goings-on between Gerda Daranovski, one of Hitler's private clerks, and Hitler's chauffeur, Erich Kempka. Having left the womanising Kempka, Gerda married Luftwaffe General Christian. Soon afterwards, the jilted Kempka married a known prostitute from Berchtesgaden. Gerda, meanwhile, had begun an affair with SS Lieutenant-Colonel Schulze-Kossens. In other news, Hitler's chief architect, Albert Speer, was having a fling with film-maker Leni Riefenstahl. Three members of Hitler's private staff had been sent to a special venereal disease clinic in Austria. Martin Bormann, chief of Hitler's secretarial staff, kept a mistress at his ski chalet in Obersalzberg, with the complicity of his wife.

There was never anything critical about Hitler himself. That would have been going too far. But these lesser players in the Berlin entourage were fair game.

It was not Der Chef 's rambling gossip that troubled Hitler and his staff. What bothered them was that Der Chef was right. Whoever this man was, he obviously had a source very near to the nerve centre of the German war machine. When the existence of the Calais network was first reported, Minister of Propaganda Joseph Goebbels immediately ordered the signal to be jammed. The signal was so powerful, however, that jamming it also disabled several legitimate sender stations, and Goebbels was forced to rescind the order.

The Ministry of Propaganda then considered broadcasting the truth about the Calais Sender on all the other sender stations, warning soldiers not to listen to Calais and threatening anyone who did with execution. But this idea was also abandoned. To acknowledge the existence of the Calais network would not only call into question the entire German propaganda apparatus, it would also require an explanation as to how the Allies were privy to such sensitive and personal information.

In the end, the Calais Sender was allowed to continue uninterrupted.

Soon after the Normandy invasion, in June of 1944, Sender Calais began rebroadcasting as Sender Caen, and after that as Sender Alsace. This gave the impression that the sender station was setting up shop in the line of the German retreat across Western Europe. In reality, the base of operations never changed and the pirate radio station continued to broadcast from England as it had always done.

Even if Der Chef was correct in his unearthing of such sordid details, the mere mention of them, embarrassing as they might be, had no serious effect upon the German war effort.

But it was not the gossip that caused such great anxiety among those few members of the German High Command who were aware of the station's true source. If Der Chef knew about the sleazy parlour games of Hitler's closest circle, then what else did he know? This was the question which had been nagging Hitler ever since he first tuned in to Der Chef, whose seemingly inexhaustible supply of titbits echoed in Hitler's brain like the relentless ticking of a metronome.

He had ordered his Chief of Security, General Rattenhuber, to conduct a full investigation. But Rattenhuber had found nothing. The best he could do was to tell Hitler that the informant probably worked somewhere in the Chancellery, was probably a low-level employee and had probably been there for a long time.

Probably.

In an attempt to play down Hitler's concerns, as well as his own lack of results, Rattenhuber went on to assure the Führer that once the High Command had relocated down into the bunker complex, where security was considerably tighter than up among the ruins of the Chancellery building, Der Chef 's source of information would undoubtedly dry up.

Every day since, Hitler had listened to the radio station, putting Rattenhuber's pronouncement to the test.

This morning, Der Chef, speaking in his unmistakable Berlin accent, went off on a tirade against the kind of clothing worn by American civilians. Hula shirts. Zoot suits. In spite of himself, Hitler snuffled out a laugh at the description of these preposterous outfits. Other than what he had read in the cowboy novels of Zane Grey, Hitler knew very little about American culture, and what he did know left him unimpressed. Then Der Chef went on to congratulate a number of SS officers who had recently been awarded the Knight's Cross, Germany's highest award for service in the field.

Hitler felt his jaw muscles clench. He had approved that list of Knight's Cross candidates himself not five days before. The award ceremony wasn't even due to take place until next week.

So much for Rattenhuber's fortune-telling, he thought.

He was just about to remove the headphones, after which he would carefully reorient the signal dials to their original position, when suddenly he froze.

That list of officers.

There was something about it.

He struggled to recall. There had been so many lists drawn up recently, so many meetings. It was hard to remember them all.

The candidates had been put forward by his old comrade Sepp Dietrich, now in command of the 6th SS Panzer Army. Initially, Hitler had approved the list as a matter of course but following the failure of the 6th Army to hold back Red Army forces attacking the city of Budapest, Hitler had ordered his approval to be withheld. His secretary, Bormann, had dutifully filed it away among those documents consigned to limbo at the headquarters. Withholding the document was not an outright refusal to issue the medals, only a sign of his disapproval at the performance of Dietrich's soldiers. In practical terms, all it meant was that Dietrich would have to resubmit his request, but Hitler's gesture would not go unnoticed.

What mattered now was not the list itself, but the fact that it had never left the bunker. And yet, here was Der Chef, reading it off word for word.

'The spy is here among us!' Hitler muttered hoarsely.

Misch had, by now, returned from his cigarette break and was busy sucking on a mint in order to hide the odour of smoke on his breath. Hitler could not stand the smell of tobacco.

Hitler turned in his chair and eyed the man. 'He's here!' he whispered.

Misch stared at him blankly. Is he talking about me, wondered the sergeant. Is he seeing ghosts? Has he finally gone out of his mind?

Hitler had hooked his left knee around the leg of the table in order to stop the incessant trembling of his calf muscle. Now he untangled himself from his chair and rose to his feet. Just as he was handing the headphones to Misch, he spotted the message form which Zeltner had filled out the night before. 'What is this?' he asked.

'Something that came last night from a certain General

Hagemann,' Misch explained hastily. 'I was going to give it to you.'

Hitler fished out a pair of reading glasses. Shakily, he perched them on his nose. Then he picked up the form. 'Diamond Stream,' he said. Then he glanced at Misch. 'Are you sure this is correct?'

'The message came through on Zeltner's shift,' Misch explained nervously. 'I doubt there has been a mistake.'

Hitler folded up the message form and tucked it away in his pocket. 'Bring me General Hagemann,' he commanded softly.

10 April 1945

Message from Major Clarke, via SOE relay station 53a, Grenton Underwood, to 'Christophe':
URGENT. SUPERSEDES ALL OTHER WORK ACQUIRE PLANS FOR DIAMOND STREAM DEVICE.

Message from 'Christophe' to Major Clarke:
WHAT IS DIAMOND STREAM?

Major Clarke to 'Christophe':
UNKNOWN AS YET. BELIEVED TO BE OF EXTREME IMPORTANCE. WILL NEED PHOTOGRAPHS. CAN YOU DELIVER?

Message from 'Christophe' to Major Clarke:
CAN ATTEMPT. USUAL CHANNELS FOR DEVELOPING AND TRANSPORT OF FILM NO LONGER FUNCTION DUE TO BOMBING RAIDS. WILL REQUIRE EXTRACTION IF SUCCESSFUL.

Major Clarke to 'Christophe':
ARRANGING FOR EXTRACTION SEND WORD WHEN YOU HAVE RESULTS.

The sun had just risen above the onion-shaped domes of St Basil's Cathedral when Major Kirov and Pekkala arrived at the Kremlin.

Escorting them to their destination was Stalin's personal secretary, a short and irritable man named Poskrebychev. Although he held no rank or badge of office, Poskrebychev was nevertheless one of the most powerful men in the country. Anyone who desired an audience with the Boss had first to go through Stalin's outer office, where Poskrebychev ruled over a dreary cubicle of filing cabinets, a chair, a telephone and an intercom which sat like a big black toad upon Poskrebychev's desk.

After showing visitors into Stalin's room, Poskrebychev always departed, closing the double doors behind him with a dance-like movement that resembled a courtier's bow.

Poskrebychev never attended these meetings but, returning to his desk, he would invariably switch on the intercom and eavesdrop on the conversation. He was able to do this without arousing suspicion because, although a small red light switched to green whenever the intercom was in use, Poskrebychev, after hours of fiddling with the machine, had discovered that, if the intercom button was only half switched, the red light would stay on and he could still hear every word of what was said. This malfunction of technology was the true source of Poskrebychev's power, although it did not come without a price. Often, lying in bed at night in the flat he shared with his mother, Poskrebychev would twitch and shudder as the vastness of the treacheries and horrors which Stalin had conjured into being echoed from the rafters of his skull.

'He has another visitor,' Poskrebychev whispered to Pekkala as they reached the door to Stalin's office. 'Some teacher or other. A strange bird if ever I saw one!'

Pekkala nodded thanks. The doors were opened.

The two men walked into the room and Poskrebychev, with his usual dramatic flourish, closed the door behind them.

Stalin sat behind his desk. As usual, the heavy curtains were drawn. The room smelled of beeswax polish and of the fifty cigarettes that Stalin smoked each day.

Standing at the far end of the room, where he had been admiring the portrait of Lenin on the wall, was a man in a tweed jacket and grey flannel trousers. He turned as Pekkala walked in and bowed his head sharply in greeting. The man had a thick crop of grey hair and a matching grey moustache. His eyes, a cold, cornflower blue, betrayed the falseness of his smile.

He is no Russian, thought Pekkala.

Confirming Pekkala's suspicion, Stalin introduced him as Deacon Swift, a member of the British Trade Commission.

'But of course,' added Stalin, 'we all know that is a lie.'

The smile on Swift's face quickly faded. 'I wouldn't call it that, exactly,' he said.

'Whatever your role with the Trade Commission,' continued Stalin, 'you are also a member of British Intelligence, a post you have held for many years, in Eg ypt, in Rome and now here, in Moscow.' Stalin glanced across at the Englishman. 'Am I leaving anything out?'

'No,' admitted Swift, 'except perhaps the reason for my

visit.' Stalin gestured towards Pekkala. 'By all means attend to yourbusiness.'

Swift drew in a deep breath. 'Inspector Pekkala,' he began, 'I have been sent here by His Majesty's Government on a matter of great importance. You see, we might soon need your help in retrieving one of our agents from Berlin.'

'I imagine you have several agents in Berlin,' said Pekkala. Swift nodded cautiously. 'That is altogether likely, yes.'

'Then what makes this one so special?'

'This is someone we felt might be of particular significance to you,' explained Swift.

'And why is that?'

'The agent, whose code name is Christophe, has been supplying us with snippets of propaganda.'

'Snippets?' asked Pekkala.

'Oh,' Swift let the word drag out, 'nothing of great importance, really. Just the odd detail here and there about goingson among the German High Command, which we then cycle back into our radio broadcasts throughout the liberated territories. Of course, the Germans listen to these broadcasts, too. It lets them know we have our eye on them.'

'So far,' remarked Pekkala, 'I have not heard anything that might be of significance to me.'

'The thing is,' explained Swift, 'this person is known to you.' Pekkala narrowed his eyes in confusion. 'I don't know any

British agents, and no one at all named Christophe.' 'Ah!' Swift raised one finger in the air. 'But you do, Inspector, whether you realise it or not. Christophe is the code name for a woman named Lilya Simonova.'

Pekkala's heart stumbled in his chest. Instinctively, he reached into his pocket, rough fingertips brushing across the crackled surface of the only photo that had ever been taken of the two of them together.

'When was the last time you saw her?' asked Swift.

It had been in Petrograd in the last week of February, 1917. Entire army regiments – the Volhynian, the Semyonovsky, the Preobrazhensky – had mutinied. Many of the officers had already been shot. The clattering of machine-gun fire sounded from the Liteiny Prospekt. Along with the army, striking factory workers and sailors from the fortress island of Kronstadt began systematically looting the shops. They stormed the offices of the Petrograd Police and destroyed the Register of Criminals.

The Tsar had finally been persuaded to send in a troop of Cossacks to fight against the revolutionaries, but the decision came too late. Seeing that the Revolution was gaining momentum, the Cossacks themselves had rebelled against the government. Now they were roaming the streets of the city, beating or killing anyone who showed any signs of resistance.

It was after midnight when the Tsar called him in to his study at the Alexander Palace. He sat at his desk, his jacket draped over the back of his chair. Olive-coloured braces stretched over his shoulders and he had rolled up the sleeves of his rumpled white shirt.

Pekkala bowed his head. 'You sent for me, Majesty.'

'I did,' replied the Tsar. 'Where is your fiancée?'

'Majesty?'

'Your fiancée!' he repeated angrily. 'Where is she?'

'At home,' answered Pekkala. 'Why do you ask?'

'Because you need to get her out of here,' said the Tsar, 'and as soon as possible.'

'Out of Petrograd?'

'Out of Russia!' The Tsar reached behind him and pulled a folded piece of paper from the pocket of his tunic. He slid it across the desk to Pekkala. 'This is her travel permit to Paris. She will have to travel via Finland, Sweden and Norway, but that's the only safe route at the moment. The train leaves in three hours. I have it on good authority that it is the last one on which permits authorised by me will be accepted. After that, my signature will probably be worth nothing.'

'Three hours?' asked Pekkala.

The Tsar fixed him with a stare. 'If you hesitate now, even for a minute, you may well be condemning her to death. The time will come when you can join her, but for now I need you here. Do you understand?'

'Yes, Majesty.'

'Good. Then go. And give her my regards.'

Three hours later, Lilya and Pekkala stood on the crowded railway platform of the Nikolaevsky station in Petrograd.

Many of those fleeing had come with huge steamer trunks, sets of matching luggage, even birds in cages. Hauling this baggage were exhausted porters in their pill-box hats and dark blue uniforms with a single red stripe, like a trickle of blood, down the sides of their trousers. There were too many people. Nobody could move without shoving. One by one, passengers left their baggage and pressed forward to the train, tickets raised above their heads. Their shouts rose above the panting roar of the steam train as it prepared to move out. High above, beneath the glass-paned roof, condensation beaded on the dirty glass and fell back as black rain upon the passengers.

A conductor leaned out of a doorway, whistle clenched between his teeth. He blew three shrill blasts.

'That's a two-minute warning,' said Pekkala. 'The train won't wait.' He reached inside his shirt and pulled a leather cord from around his neck. Looped into the cord was a gold signet ring. 'Look after this for me.'

'But that's your wedding ring!'

'It will be,' he replied, 'when I see you again.'

Sensing that there would not be enough room in the carriages, the crowd began to panic. Passengers ebbed back and forth, as if a wind was blowing them like grain stalks in a field.

'I could wait for the next train,' Lilya pleaded. In her hands, she clutched a single bag made out of brightly patterned carpet material, containing some books, a few pictures and a change of clothes. As of now, they were her only possessions in the world.

'There might not be a next train. Please. You must leave now.'

'But how will you find me?' she asked.

He smiled faintly, reaching out and running his fingers through her hair. 'Don't worry,' he said, 'that's what I'm good at.'

The clamour of those still struggling to get aboard had risen to a constant roar. A pile of luggage lurched and fell. Furcoated passengers went sprawling. Immediately, the crowd closed up around them.

'Now!' said Pekkala. 'Before it's too late.' When, at last, Lilya had climbed aboard the carriage, she turned and waved to him.

Pekkala waved back. And then he lost sight of her as a tide of people poured past him, pursuing the rumour that another train had pulled in at the Finland station on the other side of the river.

Before Pekkala knew what was happening, he had been swept out into the street. From there, he watched the train pull out, wagons rifling past. Then suddenly the tracks were empty and there was only the rhythmic clatter of the wheels, fading away into the distance.

For Pekkala, that day had been like a fork in the road of his life. His heart went one way and his body set off another, lugging its jumbled soul like a suitcase full of rusty nails.

'What is she doing in Berlin?' Pekkala asked, hardly able to speak. 'And why is she working for you?'

'She volunteered,' Swift replied matter-of-factly.

Now Stalin raised his voice. 'If she's working for you, then why do you need us to get her out? Why not just leave her there until Berlin has fallen? I promise it won't be long now.'

'We feel a certain sense of urgency,' Swift replied vaguely, 'and given your army's proximity to the city, such a task might better be accomplished by a man such as Pekkala. It is a small gesture in the grand scheme of things,' Swift said magnanimously. 'We see it as evidence of the many things which bind us in this struggle against a common enemy.'

'When do I leave?' asked Pekkala.

'Soon,' replied Swift. 'Perhaps very soon. Of course we will notify you as far in advance as we can.'

'Then we look forward to hearing from you,' said Stalin. Bowing his head with gratitude, Swift made his way out of the room.

Until that moment, Stalin's face had remained a mask of unreadable emotions. But as soon as the Englishman departed, Stalin slammed his fist down on the desk. 'A gesture of solidarity! Who the hell do they think we are? A pack of errand boys?' Pekkala was still reeling from the news. Stalin's voice reached him as if through the rush and tumble of waves breaking on a nearby shore.

'What are we going to do?' asked Kirov.

'You will do exactly as they say,' replied Stalin. 'You will go to

Berlin and you will bring that woman back.'

In spite of his confusion, Kirov managed to nod in agreement.

'But not', continued Stalin, 'before you discover the real reason they want her.'

'The real reason?' asked Kirov.

'Whatever her value to the Inspector, do you honestly think they would go to all this trouble to retrieve an agent who is merely supplying them with gossip?' Stalin swept one stubby finger back and forth. 'No, Major Kirov, there is more to this than their compassion for a missing operative. She must have got hold of something important, something they want now, or they would simply leave her where she is to wait until the city has fallen. And I want to know what it is.'

'But how are we to manage that?' asked Kirov.

Stalin took out a pen and scribbled an address on a pad of notepaper, then tore away the sheet and handed it to Pekkala.

'Here is the address of someone who might have the answer.'

As soon as he had departed from the Kremlin, Professor Swift made his way to the British Embassy at 46 Ulitsa Vorovskovo. There, in a small, dark room at the end of a long corridor, Swift perched on the end of a stiff-backed wooden chair, nervously smoking a cigarette. The haughty confidence he had put on display before Stalin was now replaced by scowling agitation.

From the shadows came the sound of a deep breath being drawn in. Then a man leaned forward, his face suddenly illuminated by the glow of a glass-hooded lamp which stood upon the desk between them. He had an oval face, yellowish teeth and neatly combed hair shellacked on to his scalp with lavender-smelling pomade. His name was Oswald Hansard and although the brass plaque on his door had him listed as the subdirector of the Royal Agricultural Trade Commission, he was in fact the Moscow station chief of British Intelligence. 'So you think that Pekkala will help us?' he asked.

Swift sipped at his cigarette and then exhaled in two grey jets through his chapped nostrils. 'I think he will follow his conscience, whatever Stalin has to say about it.'

'I'm sure a good number of men and women in this country have followed their conscience, and I dare say it bought them a ticket to Siberia, if they even made it that far.'

'It's different with Pekkala,' remarked Swift. 'Stalin seems to take a perverse pleasure in being stood up to by this Finn. Even though he has the power to make Pekkala disappear from the face of the earth with nothing so much as a phone call to Lubyanka, he won't do it.'

'And why is that, do you suppose?'

'If I had to guess, I'd say it is because he knows Pekkala doesn't care. He's not afraid and there's nothing Stalin can do about it. If you want my opinion, the only thing keeping Pekkala alive is the very fact that he has placed less value on his life than on his work.'

'And that work is what they have in common,' added Hansard.

'The only thing, I'd say, but it's enough.'

'So he will help us?' Hansard asked again.

'I think he might,' answered Swift, 'for the sake of the woman.'

Hansard sat back heavily, vanishing again into the shadows.

'But it's been years since he last set eyes upon her. Surely, he has moved on by now. Any practical person would have done so.'

Swift laughed quietly.

'Did I say something funny?' snapped the station chief.

'Well, yes sir, I think you did. Has there never been someone you loved, from whom you were kept apart by fate and circumstance?'

Hansard paused, sucking at his yellow teeth. 'In practical terms . . .'

'And that's where you really are being funny, sir,' interrupted Professor Swift.

'Well, I'm glad to have kept you so amused,' growled Hansard.

'What I mean, sir, is that practicality has nothing to do with this. Neither has time itself. Once a love like that has been kindled, nothing can extinguish it. It remains suspended, like an insect trapped in amber. Time cannot alter it. Words cannot undo it.'

Hansard sighed and rose up from his chair. He walked out into the middle of the room. Although he had on a grey suit, and a black and white checked tie, he wore no socks or shoes and his pale feet glowed with a sickly pallor. 'Highly impractical,' he muttered.

'As you say, sir,' answered Swift, stubbing out his cigarette in a peach-coloured onyx ashtray on the desk, 'but the world would be a poorer place without people who believed in such things. And besides, in this case, you will admit, it serves our purpose well.'

He gave an exasperated sigh.

The station chief glanced up. 'Something on your mind, Swift?'

'Actually, sir, there is. Pekkala asked me how this woman ended up working for us.'

'What did you tell him?'

'I guessed and said she volunteered. The fact is I have no idea.'

'Nevertheless,' replied Hansard, 'you stumbled into the truth.'

'But what is her story, sir?'

'I suppose it won't hurt to tell you now,' said Hansard. 'She was first approached by the French Security Service, the Deuxième Bureau, when she was living in Paris back in 1938. At the time, she was a teacher at some small private school in Paris. The Deuxième had been keeping their eye on her for some time. They knew she was Russian, of course, and that her parents had been murdered by the Bolsheviks back in the early

1920s. At the time, the Deuxième were concerned that the entire French government had become riddled with Soviet spies.'

'And had it?'

'Oh, yes,' replied Hansard. 'Their fears were entirely justified. That's why they needed someone who could speak Russian, but with enough hatred for Stalin that they could, perhaps, be put to use in ferreting out these infiltrators.'

'And what did she say to that?'

'Apparently, she told them she would rather be a school teacher than some kind of glamorous spy.'

'And yet they persuaded her somehow.'

'Not until the war broke out,' said Hansard. 'As the Germans began their invasion of France, and it became clear that the French army was about to collapse, the Bureau approached her again. This time, it was with an offer to get her out of the country, along with a number of others whom, they believed, might prove useful as agents in carrying on the war effort even after France had fallen. And with France about to fall, the only way they could do that was by delivering those agents to us.'

'How did they come to choose Simonova? After all, she had no training and she had already turned them down once.'

'But that's precisely why they did choose her,' explained Hansard. 'The Bureau suspected that lists of its active agents might already have fallen into the hands of German intelligence, so they chose people who had not become operational, or whose identities might have failed to make their way on to the Bureau's roster.' 'But that can't have been the only reason they chose her.'

'It wasn't,' answered Hansard. 'You see, in addition to French and Russian, she also spoke fluent German. Her father, Gustav Seimann, had been a riding instructor for the Grand Duke of Hesse, a close relative of Tsar Nicholas II's wife, Alexandra. When Alexandra, who was herself a German, married Nicholas, she brought in a number of people from her native country to play various roles in her new life among the Russians. The tutor of her children, for example, was an Englishman named Gibbes. There was also a Frenchman named Doctor Gilliard, whom she put on her household staff. And when it came time to teach her children how to ride, she brought in the Grand Duke's riding instructor. Gustav Seimann settled down in Petersburg and made a new life for himself. He even changed his name to Simonov.'

'That shows a lot of faith,' remarked Swift.

'They *were* faithful,' agreed Hansard. 'Some of these foreigners turned out to be the most loyal members of her retinue. Simonov himself was said to have been killed when he rode out by himself to confront a band of roving Cossacks who had made their way on to the grounds of the Tsarskoye Selo estate. That act of bravery cost him his life, but it shows how he remained loyal right up to the end, and I'm told there are many who didn't.'

'I suppose the Deuxième Bureau were hoping for the same kind of commitment from his daughter.'

'Nothing less would do,' replied Hansard. 'By the time they got to her, the situation in Paris had become critical. The place had been declared an open city, and most of those who could flee did precisely that. Given the situation, this time the woman agreed.'

'How did they get her out?'

'They drove her straight to Le Bourget airfield, just outside of Paris, loaded her aboard one of those lumbering Lysander planes, the kind with the big wheels that can land on just about anything, and two hours later she was in England. They trained her at our Special Operations camp at Arisaig up in Scotland. From there, she went to Beaulieu, Lord Montagu's place over in the New Forest. Less than a month later, they sent her back to France, this time on a fishing boat we modified to transport agents to and from the Continent, operating out of the Helford River estuary. She was put ashore somewhere near Boulogne and made her way to Paris.'

'And nobody became suspicious that she'd been gone all that time?' asked Swift.

'So many people had left the city after the Germans broke through the French lines at Sedan that her absence was not considered unusual. The school had closed, temporarily, and the students had all been sent home. People were scattered all over the country. When things settled down a bit and life in Paris began to return to normal, or as normal as it could ever be under occupation, those who had fled began to return. Simonova simply joined the tide of refugees making their way back into the city. The little school where she worked reopened and, after registering with the German authorities, she simply resumed her work as a teacher.'

'And what then?' demanded Swift. 'How did she help the war effort? Did she start bumping off people in the middle of the night?'

'Hardly,' answered Hansard. 'Remember, she could speak German, and we had known all along that the occupation government would need people who were fluent in that language as well as in French. She volunteered and, sure enough, they put her to work.'

'Doing what?'

'Nothing too onerous. Typing out translations of public notices. Things like that.'

'Doesn't sound like much of a return on our investment.'

'The thing about being a translator is that, sooner or later, an important document is going to end up on your desk. The people who give it to you might not think it contains any vital information, but even the smallest fragment of intelligence can be built up into something useful over time. Before leaving Beaulieu, she had been given a wireless set which she used for transmitting the information back to England.'

'And how did we manage to get her to Berlin?'

'We didn't,' said Hansard. 'The Germans did that by themselves, and we have one man in particular to thank for that. His name is Hermann Fegelein. Before the war, his family managed a riding school down in Bavaria. In the early 1930s, Fegelein joined the Nazi Party and went on to command an SS Cavalry Division on the Eastern Front. In early 1944, he got assigned to Himmler's private staff as a liaison officer. One of the first places Himmler sent him was Paris. When Fegelein got there, he demanded a secretary who was fluent in German and French from the occupation government.'

'And they gave her Simonova?'

'Not right away,' said Hansard. 'He sacked the first two people he was offered, probably because he didn't like the look of them. The thing about Fegelein is that he considers himself a real ladies' man and it wasn't until they sent him Simonova that he was finally satisfied. When Fegelein left Paris a couple of months later, she went with him.'

'As his mistress?'

Hansard shook his head. 'Only as his private secretary, although I dare say he might have other plans for her in the future. In the meantime, Fegelein has become a go-between for Hitler and Himmler; the two most powerful men in the Third Reich. He was, and still is, present at Hitler's daily meetings with his High Command. Whatever's going on, he knows about it.'

'And so does Simonova, by the sound of it.'

'Fegelein is no fool. Even if he did trust Simonova, he would not knowingly have given her access to secrets of national importance. More likely, he just gossiped with her about all the various goings-on in Hitler's entourage. But even gossip has its value and we started broadcasting it back to the Germans, as soon as we had set up the Black Boomerang operation.'

'You mean the radio station? The one that was supposed to be coming out of Calais?'

'Yes,' said Hansard, 'and after that out of Paris and now they're broadcasting as Sender Station Elbe or something. Of course, their location never actually changed. They're in some manor house in Hampshire, I believe, although the operation is so secret that even I'm not sure of the exact location. Thousands of German soldiers and civilians tune into that station every day. It's the most reliable network they've got, and if somebody told them it was run by us, they probably wouldn't believe it. By airing all those bits of gossip from Hitler's inner circle, we not only dishearten the listeners, we intrigue them. Everybody likes gossip, especially the kind we're serving up. But there's an even greater value to this information,' Hansard went on. 'Even if the High Command denies the stories, they know perfectly well it's the truth. And that means they know we have a source' – with his thumb and index finger, Hansard measured out a tiny space in front of him – 'this close to Hitler himself.'

'I understand all this,' said Swift, 'but what I can't quite grasp is why we are going to such lengths to rescue an agent who, for all intents and purposes, is running a Berlin society page! At my meeting with Stalin and Pekkala I said what you told me to say – that we value the lives of all our agents in the field. But you and I both know that we have cut our losses before, and with agents more valuable than this one.'

'And I suspect we would have done the same with Simonova if it wasn't for the fact that HQ back in England seems to think that she can get her hands on something extremely important.'

'And what is that?'

Hansard sighed and shook his head. 'Damned if I know, but it must be bloody important for us to go down on bended knee in front of Stalin and beg for the Russians to help us.' With that, he fished a pocket watch out of his waistcoat pocket.

Swift correctly understood this as a sign that he should take his leave. He stood up and buttoned his jacket. 'I'll let you know if we hear anything from Pekkala.'

Hansard nodded. 'Fingers crossed.'

After sending his message to the Reichschancellery, General Hagemann immediately began organizing a trip to Berlin. Once there, he planned to personally deliver all the details of his latest triumph to Adolf Hitler.

But even before he could locate any transport, a plane arrived at the Peenemunde landing strip, with orders to take him immediately to Hitler's headquarters, where he had been ordered to explain the disappearance of his test rocket.

Hagemann was stunned. It appeared that whatever good news he had hoped to bring about the success of the Diamond Stream device had already been trumped by the missing V-2. God help me, thought Hagemann, if that rocket is anywhere except the bottom of the sea.

Within an hour of receiving the message, the general was on his way to Berlin. There had not even been time to pack an overnight bag. The only thing he had managed to grab from his office, located in a requisitioned farmhouse not far from the ruins of the Peenemunde test facility, was a large leather tube containing schematics of the V-2's guidance system. These diagrams, painstakingly laid out by draughtsmen assigned to the programme, were a vital part of any presentation Hagemann gave to the High Command. To the untrained eye, they represented an indecipherable scaffolding of blue-veined lines, criss-crossed with arterial red pointers, indicating the names and specification numbers of the system's multitude of parts.

This was not the first time Hagemann had faced the wrath of the German High Command and he had come to rely upon the indecipherability of his blueprints to baffle and intimidate his fellow generals. The less they understood, the more they would be forced to rely upon Hagemann's optimistic predictions, and it was these which had kept the V-2 programme alive.

Hitler, on the other hand, seemed to love the labyrinthine complexity of the diagrams. With the schematics laid out in front of him, he would sweep his hands almost lovingly across the skeletal lines of the rocket, demanding explanations for the smallest details, which Hagemann was happy to provide.

The extraordinary cost of the V-2 programme, not to mention the delays caused by Allied bombing and the failure of so many experiments, had earned Hagemann many opponents. As he had been reminded many times by skeptical members of the General Staff, for the cost of every V-2 rocket, the German armaments industry could produce over five hundred Panzerfausts, the single-shot anti-tank weapons so simple and effective that they were now being issued to teams of teenage boys recruited from the Hitler Youth, whose orders were to pedal after Russian tanks on bicycles and engage the 20-ton machines in single combat.

Without Hitler's approval, the whole endeavour would probably have been shelved years ago, but just as easily as he had kept the programme running, he could also destroy it, with nothing more than a stroke of his pen.

Clutching the leather document tube against his chest, it seemed to Hagemann just then that even his magical drawings might not save him now.

Looking down through patchy clouds from an altitude of 10,000 feet, the landscape, just coming into bloom, appeared so peaceful to the general that his mind kept slipping out of gear, convincing him that there was no war, that there had never been a war, and that it was all just a figment of his own imagination.

But as they descended over the outskirts of Berlin, that calm hallucination fell apart. Ragged scars of saturation bombing lay upon the once-orderly suburbs of Heinersdorf and Pankow. The closer they came to the centre, the worse the damage appeared. Whole sections of the city, laid out like a map beneath him, were completely unrecognisable now. The cargo plane touched down at Gatow airfield. As the plane rolled to a stop, Hagemann's gaze was drawn to the carcasses of ruined aircraft which had been bulldozed to the side of the runway.

A car was there to meet him. The last time he had come here, several months before, he had been met by Hitler's adjutant, Major Otto Günsche, as well as the Führer's own chauffeur, Erich Kempka, who had entertained him on the drive to the Chancellery with stories of his days as a motorcycle mechanic before the war.

This time, however, his escorts were two grim-faced members of General Rattenhuber's Security Service, who were in charge of protecting the bunker.

At the sight of them, Hagemann felt his heart clench. He wondered if he was already under arrest.

Neither of the men spoke to him on the drive to the Chancellery building. They sat in the front. He sat in the back.

So this is how a life unravels, thought Hagemann. This brief moment of self-pity evaporated when he saw what was left of the Chancellery. Barely a single window remained intact and the stone work, particularly on the first floor, was so stubbled with shrapnel damage that it gave the impression of being unfinished, as if the masons had abandoned their work before the final touches on the building had ever been completed.

The car came to a halt. The man who had been sitting by the driver climbed out and opened the door for the general.

Hagemann climbed out. 'Where should I go?' he asked. The man gestured up the staircase to the main entrance.

'People are still working in there?' gasped Hagemann. 'But the place is in ruins!'

'Once you are inside, Herr General,' said the man, 'someone will show you the way.'

He took care climbing up the stairs, so as not to trip upon the broken steps. Once inside, he was directed to the entrance of the Führerbunker. Although he had known of the existence of the underground fortress, he had never been down into it. On every other visit, the entranceway had been shut.

He handed his credentials to a guard, who allowed him to pass through the checkpoint after relinquishing his sidearm, a Mauser automatic pistol, which he had never actually fired. He was then escorted down two more sets of stairs, during which time Hagemann noticed the air becoming stale and damp.

Having arrived at the third level below ground, he encountered a new set of guards, who directed him down a narrow corridor to the room where the twice-daily meetings of the High Command had been taking place ever since they migrated underground.

It so happened that Hagemann had arrived just as the midday meeting was about to start.

Entering the conference chamber, Hagemann found himself in a cramped, tomb-like space lit by a single bulb suspended from the ceiling in a metal cage.

At the only table in the room, and sitting on the only chair, was Adolf Hitler. On the other side of the table, herded into a cluster which reminded Hagemann of penguins crowded on to an ice flow, were more high-ranking individuals than he had ever seen collected in one space.

Albert Speer, sweating in a long leather coat, nodded in greeting to Hagemann. Martin Bormann, Hitler's secretary, eyed Hagemann suspiciously, making no attempt to welcome the professor. Beside him stood Joseph Goebbels, in his neatly pressed caramel-brown uniform, as well as Lieutenant General Hermann Fegelein, liaison officer to Heinrich Himmler, Lord of the SS. There were several others whom Hagemann did not know, but he did recognise Christa Schroeder, one of Hitler's private secretaries and the only woman present in the room.

Unprepared as Hagemann had been for this unceremonious descent into the bunker, he now felt equally out of place among this crush of National Socialist celebrities.

But the thing which unnerved Hagemann most of all was the sight of Adolf Hitler himself.

The Führer had aged visibly since their last meeting, even though it had taken place only a few months before. His eyes had taken on a glassy sheen and flaccid skin hung like wet laundry from his cheekbones. His hair, although still neatly combed, looked matted and dull and a salting of dandruff lay across the shoulders of his double-breasted jacket.

One thing that had not changed, however, was the fierceness of his glare, which Hagemann now felt as if a searchlight had been turned upon him.

'Hagemann,' drawled Hitler. 'What have you done with my rocket?'

If there had been any warning, even a couple of seconds, about what the Führer was going to say to him, Hagemann would almost certainly not have said what he said next. Instead, he blurted out the first thing that came into his head. 'I have perfected it,' he answered defiantly.

Hitler paused, slowly drawing in a breath as if he meant to suck in the last remaining particles of oxygen in the room. Then he sat back in his flimsy wooden chair and drummed his fingers on the table. 'This', he asked, 'is what you call the loss of a V-2, whose whereabouts you cannot trace and which, even now, might have fallen into enemy hands?'

'Preposterous!' snapped Goebbels. 'Hagemann, you will be put on trial for this.'

'If you will allow me to clarify the situation,' began the general.

'By all means,' answered Hitler. 'We are all of us here very anxious to see how you interpret perfection.'

'Especially when you don't have the rocket to prove it!' shouted Goebbels.

There was a quiet murmur of laughter in the room.

It was all Hagemann could do not to grab these cackling bullies by their throats and choke the life out of them. Instead of acknowledging this triumph, which signalled the birth of a new age of discovery for the entire human race, very little mattered to the men inside this room except to know exactly how much damage could be done with Hagemann's invention. 'Quiet!' barked Hitler. 'This is no cause for amusement.' Then he turned to Hagemann. 'Well, what have you to say in your defence?'

The general had plenty to say.

Over the next few minutes, he explained how steam, produced by concentrated hydrogen peroxide and catalysed by sodium permanganate, propelled a mixture of ethanol and water along a double-walled combustion chamber contained within the rocket. This double wall simultaneously cooled the combustion chamber and heated the fuel, which was then sprayed through a system of more than twelve hundred tiny nozzles.

'One thousand two hundred and twenty four to be exact,' said Hagemann.

He went on to describe how the fuel combined with oxygen as it entered the combustion chamber, shaping the air with his hands as if to trace the flow of blazing particles.

'When the newly designed guidance system is functioning as it should,' said Hagemann, 'it creates an ideal trajectory for the rocket, which in turn allows for an optimum fuel consumption ratio. This balance of trajectory and fuel consumption, when perfectly aligned, produces an exhaust plume which appears, to observers on the ground, to resemble a halo of diamonds. Hence the name of the device. This phenomenon, known as the Diamond Stream effect, was witnessed by my observers in the Baltic. That is how we know of our success, even without the physical remains of the rocket.' As Hagemann paused to catch his breath, he glanced around the room. His eyes met only the blank stares of the assembled dignitaries.

There were occasions when this labyrinth of chemistry and physics had worked to Hagemann's advantage and listeners, no matter what their rank, would have no choice except to take his word for everything he said.

But this was not one of those occasions. This time Hagemann had lost a rocket approximately 45 feet long and weighing more than 27,000 pounds. Now he very much needed these men to understand exactly what had happened.

'Think of the engine in your car,' he began, and immediately the strained looks of the generals and politicians began to relax. Even the most technologically dense of them could picture what lay under the hood of their automobiles, even if they had no idea about the workings of the internal combustion engine.

As Hagemann continued, he did his best to make his audience feel as if he were speaking to each person individually, but the only one who really mattered in this conversation was Hitler himself. In the trembling hands of this man, who was so obviously being devoured from the inside by the all-consuming fact of his defeat, lay not only the future of the V-2 programme but Hagemann's very existence.

'When your car engine is not tuned correctly,' he explained, 'you end up with a lot of smoke coming out of your exhaust.' There were some nods of agreement.

'This happens,' he continued, 'because your fuel is not being properly burned. When the engine is correctly tuned, you can barely see any exhaust at all.'

'So,' Goebbels said cautiously, 'with this rocket of yours, instead of seeing nothing . . .'

'You see diamonds,' answered Hagemann.

But Speer was not yet satisfied. 'And the guidance is what tunes the engine?' he asked, his eyes narrowed with confusion.

'In a manner of speaking,' agreed Hagemann. 'Think of a clock hanging on a wall. If the clock is not hanging at the correct angle, its timing will be off. You can even hear it when the ticking isn't right.'

'I have a clock like that,' muttered Goebbels. 'No matter what I do, it cannot tell the proper time. And the sound is enough to drive a person crazy, especially at night.'

'Shut up!' barked Hitler. 'This has nothing to do with your clock.' He nodded at Hagemann. 'Go on, General.'

'Think of the ticking of this clock as the result of the spring winding down, just as the exhaust from the V-2's engine is the result of the fuel as it burns. When the clock is running perfectly, the spring will wind down to the end, telling perfect time along the way. But if the clock is out of balance, the clock will usually stop before the spring has properly wound down. Until now, our rockets have been like clocks whose springs are out of balance. The fuel consumption was not optimised and the rockets, whether they were fired against targets or out into the Baltic Sea, did not achieve their true potential. The Diamond Stream device was designed to create a perfect balance in the rocket. Until this most recent test, that balance had not been achieved. But when it did finally work, not only were we able to witness the distinctive exhaust pattern, but the rocket travelled further than any previous test had done before, without any increase in fuel payload. As of last night,' he concluded, 'the Diamond Stream is a reality.'

Over the past few minutes, the focus in Hitler's eyes had changed. He sat forward now and, when he spoke, his speech was no longer barbed with the executioner's sarcasm on which he always relied to chip away at those who had displeased him.

'Why did this rocket work so well', he asked, 'when all of the others had failed?' This was the moment Hagemann had been praying for. From now on, this was a conversation between himself and Hitler. Everyone else in this room had just been relegated to the position of an unnecessary bystander.

'The reason the others have failed', said Hagemann, 'is that all of our previous attempts to install guidance technology in the rockets were thwarted due to vibration from the engines. The result, as you know, has been the high percentage of our rockets not landing where they were supposed to, whether on our test sites or upon the battlefield. Although they created a significant amount of damage to the enemy, they were nevertheless off target when they landed. The control system in this particular rocket was fitted in a newly designed shock-proof housing. This allowed the guidance technology to minimise the fuel consumption, thus allowing it to travel further than had previously been the case. Our original calculations did not take this into account, with the result that we undercompensated the flight curve. Such a thing is easily corrected and, from this point on, the device will be able to perform as we had always intended.'

Hitler fanned his eyes across the others in the room. 'There you are,' he said. 'Easily corrected. Did you hear that, or are there more jokes to be made, Goebbels?'

The room became utterly silent. Goebbels' eyes strained in their sockets as he peered into the corners of this concrete cell, as if searching for some means of escape.

Hitler turned back to Hagemann. 'But where is the rocket now?'

Hagemann opened his mouth to reply. There could be no hiding of the truth. Not now. And he wondered if every measure of confidence he might have gained during these past few minutes would now be squandered by the simple declaration that he did not know.

But before he could speak, Hitler answered his own question. 'It probably fell in the sea.'

'In all likelihood,' Hagemann assured him. Hitler nodded, satisfied.

'There is one more thing,' said Hagemann, almost in a whisper.

Hitler held out one hand magnanimously towards the general. 'Do continue, please.'

Hagemann did as he was told. 'With the accuracy we can now obtain, we are capable of obliterating highly specific targets. By this, I mean we are no longer unleashing the force of the V-2 upon cities, but upon targets of our choosing which lie within those cities. A single house. A single monument. All you have to do is take the tip of your pencil, touch it against a location on the map and give the order. Within the hour, the place which lay beneath that pencil point will cease to exist.'

'What about anti-aircraft fire?' demanded Fegelein. 'Can't they bring it down with that?'

'No,' answered Hagemann. 'By the time the V-2 finishes its journey, it will be travelling at supersonic speed. This means that those who stand in its circle of destruction will receive no warning. Even for those who survive, the sound of the rocket will reach their ears only after the explosion. Once the V-2 has been unleashed, nothing on this earth can stop it.'

'Do you hear?' Hitler shouted. 'This will be our deliverance! Everything we have endured will now be cast into the light of everlasting triumph!'

Now Goebbels spoke. 'As long as the professor is convinced that such results can be achieved with regularity.'

'Not just regularity, Herr Reichsminister,' Hagemann told him. 'With infallibility.'

'Ha!' Hitler crashed his hands together. 'You have your answer, Goebbels!'

'I do indeed,' the Reichsminister said as he fixed Hagemann with a stare, 'provided his deeds match his words.'

'You may leave us now, Professor,' said Hitler. 'We have other matters to discuss.'

Obediently, Hagemann began to gather up his blueprints.

'Leave those,' Hitler waved his hands over the documents. 'I would like to study them.'

'Of course,' replied Hagemann, standing back from the table, 'but I must ask that they be kept in a safe. I cannot overestimate . . .'

'Thank you, Herr General,' interrupted Speer. 'We are well aware of safety protocols. We wrote them, after all.'

There was another grumbling of laughter. This time, even Hitler smiled.

Carrying his empty chart case, Hagemann left the room and made his way along the corridor, heading for the stairs which would bring him back up to the ground floor of the Chancellery building. Even though the meeting had been a success, he still had to stop himself from breaking into a run. All he could think about was breathing some clean air again.

'Professor!' a voice called to him.

Hagemann glanced back to see Fegelein, Himmler's liaison officer, advancing down the corridor towards him, one hand raised as if hailing a taxi, and Hagemann's schematics in the other. 'A final question for you,' he said. 'What are you doing with the charts?' stammered Hagemann. 'Haven't I made it clear enough that the information contained within those diagrams is extremely sensitive!'

Fegelein grinned. 'Which is precisely why Reichsführer Himmler will enjoy looking them over. With Hitler's blessing, I am taking them to Himmler's office now. You should join me! The Reichsführer has some excellent wine at his disposal.'

'I am very busy,' said Hagemann. He had an instinctive mistrust of Fegelein. The soft round chin, full cheeks and shallow brow gave him an innocent and almost child-like face. But this appearance was an illusion.

That Fegelein had managed to advance so far in his career, and yet was so universally disliked, was a testament to the ruthlessness of his ambition. To Fegelein, the price of loyalty could always be negotiated, and friendship had no value at all.

He was not alone in making that equation.

In 1941, Fegelein had been arrested for the looting of money and luxury goods from a train, an offence which could have carried the death penalty – although his real mistake had not been the theft so much as the fact that these items had already been stolen from the safety deposit boxes of Polish banks by men who outranked Fegelein, and were, at the time, on their way back to a warehouse where the loot was scheduled to be divided among the thieves. The charges against him were dropped, on the orders of his master, Heinrich Himmler, which only added to rumours already circulating, that Fegelein led a charmed life. What had been only rumour before was transformed into fact when Himmler appointed him as his personal liaison officer. This, and his marriage to Gretl Braun, sister of Hitler's mistress, Eva, had assured him an almost untouchable position in the Führer's closest circle. The marriage had been conducted hurriedly after Gretl discovered that she was pregnant. The fact that there was some question as to who might be the father of the unborn child, and Hitler's outrage at the circumstances, had prompted Fegelein to come forward and offer his hand. In Hitler's mind, this act of chivalry saved not only Gretl's reputation, but also his own, as the consort of Eva Braun. The marriage had done nothing to temper Fegelein's appetites and while Gretl remained, for the most part, far to the south in her home province of Bavaria, Fegelein had taken up residence with his mistress, Elsa Batz, in an apartment on the ironically named Bleibtreustrasse. Of this arrangement, Hitler was unaware or else he had chosen to look the other way and Fegelein had enough instincts for self-preservation not to ask which one was the truth.

'I have one final question,' repeated Fegelein, as he pursued Hagemann down the narrow corridor. 'It won't take a second, Professor.'

'I was just leaving,' Hagemann muttered.

Fegelein refused to take the hint. 'Then I'll walk up the stairs with you. I could do with a smoke,' he laughed, 'and they don't allow that in the bunker.'

Side by side, the two men plodded up towards the Chancellery.

It was all Hagemann could do not to push Fegelein back down the stairs. He not only mistrusted this slippery emissary of the SS, he despised the whole organisation. Ever since the conception of the V-2, Himmler had repeatedly tried to take over the project. In an obvious attempt at blackmail, the SS had even gone so far as to arrest one of the programme's chief scientists, Werner von Braun, on charges so trumped up that even Hitler, who normally deferred to the man he called 'My Loyal

Heinrich', refused to accept them.

In spite of Himmler's insatiable desire to control the future of the programme, Hagemann had managed to keep the SS at arm's length.

But all that changed in July of 1944, when a bomb planted by the one-armed, one-eyed Colonel Claus von Stauffenberg in a briefing room of the Wolf's Lair command centre failed to kill its intended target, Adolf Hitler.

Even as Stauffenberg and numerous other conspirators were

rounded up and either shot or hanged, the SS, citing concerns for national security, finally received Hitler's blessing to take over the V-2 programme.

Since then, the production and research facilities had been scattered all over Germany, slave labour had been employed to assemble the rockets, and virtually nothing could be accomplished without Himmler's approval.

If it weren't for that fact, Hagemann might well have told Fegelein exactly what he thought of him.

The two men reached the main floor of the Chancellery building, where their side arms were returned to them.

'What did you want to know, Fegelein?' Hagemann asked as he undid his belt and slid the Mauser holster back where it belonged.

Fegelein delayed giving an answer until they had passed beyond the earshot of the guards.

Out on the shrapnel-spattered stone steps of the Chancellery, Fegelein removed a silver cigarette case from his chest pocket, opened it and offered its neatly arrayed contents to Hagemann. Hagemann shook his head. For now, he was more interested in filling his lungs with fresh air than with tobacco fumes.

Fegelein lit his cigarette, inhaled deeply and then whistled out a long grey jet of smoke. 'What I wanted to know, Herr Professor,' he said, 'is how many of these rockets you have left. After all, what use is your guidance system if you have nothing left to guide?'

Even coming from this man, Hagemann could not deny that it was a reasonable question. 'We have, at present, approximately eighty complete rockets. Once the guidance systems have been modified, they will be ready for immediate use.'

'And how long will the modifications take?'

'Only a matter of hours for each rocket.'

'And after the eighty rockets have been fired, what then?' asked Fegelein.

'Our production facility in Nordhausen is still fully functional. At top capacity, we can produce over eight hundred rockets a month,' and then General Hagemann paused, 'provided there is no interference, either from you or from the Allies.'

Fegelein smiled. 'My dear Professor,' he said, 'I am not here to obstruct, but rather to help you in any way I can.'

'Is that so?' asked Hagemann, unable to mask his nervousness.

Fegelein laughed at the general's obvious discomfort. Playfully, he batted Hagemann on the shoulder with the rolled-up blueprints.

'Those are not toys!' snapped Hagemann. Angrily he shoved the leather cylinder into Fegelein's hands. 'If you're going to carry them about, you might as well put them in this.' 'I know what you think of me,' said Fegelein, as he opened the chart case and slid the blueprints inside, 'and aside from the fact that I couldn't care less, surely you can see why I would want to support the development of a weapon that could be our only hope out of this mess.' He waved the smouldering cigarette at the ruins of the buildings all around them. 'I make no secret of the fact that it would benefit me to do so, over and above whatever good it does our country.'

You self-serving bastard, thought Hagemann.

'You may loathe me for my reasoning,' continued Fegelein, 'but it does prove that my offer of assistance is genuine. If I didn't think it would work, I promise you we would not be having this conversation.'

A black Mercedes rolled up to the kerb. Hagemann noticed the SS number plates.

'Ah! Here is my transport.' He turned to Hagemann. 'I must leave you now, Professor, but you should be aware that, once

Himmler has seen these plans for himself, he will want to speak with you immediately. Face to face, you understand.'

Hagemann felt his bowels cramp.

'There is nothing to be nervous about,' Fegelein assured him, 'unless of course he asks you to meet with his friends.'

'What would be wrong with that?' stammered Hagemann.

'The Reichsführer has no friends,' said Fegelein called back over his shoulder, as he made his way down towards the waiting car.

Hagemann was surprised to see a tall woman emerge from behind the wheel. She wore a short greenish-brown wool jacket with flapped pockets at the hip and braided leather buttons, like miniature soccer balls. Her blonde hair was cut to shoulder length, in a style which had grown popular that winter, as if to match the austerity that had worked its way into every facet of civilian life.

So, thought Hagemann, that is the famous chauffeur, known to the world only as 'Fraülein S'. Who she was and where she came from, only Fegelein seemed to know. She was reputed to be the one woman Fegelein, who had a stable of concubines, had failed to bed. Hagemann had heard about this beautiful woman, but this was the first time he had ever set eyes upon her.

As the woman walked around the front of the car, she glanced up at the professor.

Hagemann was struck by the deep blue of her eyes and he realised that that the rumours of her beauty had not been exaggerated.

The woman opened the passenger's side door and Fegelein climbed inside.

Now General Hagemann made his own way down the steps. In days past, he would simply have hailed a cab to take him back to the Gatow airport, but there didn't appear to be any taxis any more. He wondered if the tram system was still functioning, or if that, too, had been put out of commission by the bombing. Hagemann set off in the direction of the airport. It would be a long walk, but the more distance he could put between himself and the confines of the bunker, the happier he knew he would feel.

As Fegelein's Mercedes wove its way past heaps of rubble from the latest air raids, bound for Himmler's headquarters in the village of Hohenlychen, north-west of Berlin, Fegelein scribbled down his report about that day's conference in the bunker.

These days, it was usually bad news, and Fegelein was content to transmit any details from the briefings by secure telegraph from SS Headquarters on Prinz Albrechtstrasse. But good news, such as he'd heard today, required a more personal delivery, especially since he would be arriving with the gift of Hagemann's own blueprints for the Diamond Stream device.

Besides, it gave him the chance to spend more time with Fraülein S.

Her real name was Lilya Simonova, although he rarely used it even when speaking to her directly. Although there were plenty of people around with Russian-sounding names, especially here in the east of the country, Fegelein felt safer not advertising the fact that his own chauffeur was one of them. Besides, it lent her an air of mystery which he was happy to exploit, since it helped to baffle those gossiping fishwives who were always whispering behind his back.

Having served briefly as Fegelein's secretary, Lilya had taken on the role of chauffeur, after his original driver had got drunk and crashed the car into a lamp post on the way to pick him up. This driver's name was Schmoekel and he, like Fegelein, had been a former cavalry man until being invalided home when he had ridden his horse over a mine. The incident had left Schmoekel with a grotesque scar across one side of his face. Unfortunately, it was the side which faced Fegelein when he was sitting on the passenger side of the two-seater car he had been given by the SS motor pool. Fegelein found it unpleasant to have to look at this deformed creature every day and he was more relieved than angry when Schmoekel finally smashed up the car, providing him with an excuse to reassign the mangled cavalryman to a desk job far away.

Replacing Schmoekel with Fraülein S had been a stroke of genius. As she took over the task of shuttling him back and forth from the Chancellery to the apartment of Elsa Batz on Bleibtreustrasse and to Himmler's headquarters at Hohenlychen, north of Berlin, Fegelein had noticed that Fraülein S was a better driver than Schmoekel, as well as a good deal softer on the eyes.

Fegelein was well aware of the rumours, circulated by his jealous rivals in the high command, about his apparent failure to bed this particular woman. One particularly hurtful piece of gossip made out that Fraülein S was 'too beautiful' for him, as if the woman was simply too far out of his league for him to even contemplate what he had so easily achieved with numerous other secretaries before her.

But that, Fegelein protested in his imaginary conversations with these rumour fabricators, was precisely the point. There had been so many others, literally dozens by his count, and every single one of them had since moved on, either because he had fired them or because they had requested transfers which, under the circumstances, he was obliged to grant them.

It had reached the point where he actually required a good secretary, and one who was going to stick around for a while, more than he needed to satisfy his instincts.

Pretty though she was, Fegelein had been forced to forgo any dalliance with Fraülein Simonova in favour of running a competent liaison office. Humiliating as it might have been to hear his manhood criticised, he could reassure himself that these gossip-mongers were simply envious of his marriage, of his standing with the Führer, of the trust Himmler had placed in him and yes, even of the woman who sat beside him now.

'I'm not sure we have enough fuel to reach Hohenlychen,' said Lilya. 'I didn't realise we would be leaving the city.'

'There's a fuel depot in Hennigsdorf,' replied Fegelein. 'We can stop there on the way.'

Lilya glanced at the rolled-up blueprint lying on the dashboard. 'That must be important, for you to be delivering it in person.'

'It's the best pieces of news we've had in months,' replied Fegelein. Then he turned his attention to the pad of paper on his lap, where he had written out the notes for his report to Himmler. 'How does this sound?' he asked. 'The success of the guidance system known as Diamond Stream . . .'

And then he paused. 'Should I call it a system? That doesn't sound quite right to me.'

At first, she didn't reply. The moment she heard the words 'Diamond Stream', the moisture had dried up in her mouth.

'How about "the Diamond Stream technology"?'

'Much better!' Fegelein crossed out the old word and wrote in the new one. 'The success of the guidance technology known as Diamond Stream has revitalised the V-2 programme to the extent that we can now deliver to the German people the reassurance of military superiority, while at the same time making it clear to our enemies that we are far from being defeated on the battlefield.

No,' he muttered. 'Wait.'

'Is it the word "defeated"?' asked Lilya.

'Exactly,' answered Fegelein. 'I can't use that. I can't even mention defeat.'

'How about "Making it clear to our enemies that we are still masters of the battlefield"?'

'Excellent!' He glanced at Fraülein S and smiled. 'Where would I be without you?'

One of the most valuable lessons that Lilya Simonova had learned during the frantic days as British Intelligence rushed her through her training at Beaulieu was that once she had convinced her sources of information that she could be trusted, the sources would repay this trust with loyalty of their own. After this, the sources would remain stubbornly faithful, not only because the bond between them had become a reality, but also because of how much they stood to lose if they were wrong. Not only the life of the agent, but also the lives of the sources depended on the appearance of truth.

To forge that bond with her enemy, knowing all along that it was balanced on a lie, had triggered in her moments of what bordered on compassion even for the monster that was Fegelein.

This was the hardest thing she had ever done. It would have been easier to kill Fegelein than to cultivate his loyalty and trust, even as she was betraying it herself. Before it all began, she would never even have considered herself capable of such a thing. But the war had made her a stranger, even to herself, and now she wondered if it would even be possible to return to a place where she could look in the mirror and recognise the person she had been.

It had taken many months to earn Fegelein's trust. During this time, she had passed every test, both official and unofficial, which

Fegelein could think to throw at her. On the advice of her handlers back in Britain, she had made no attempt to gather information during the time when she was being vetted. No contact had been established with courier agents. No messages had been transmitted. This was because of the danger that false information might be fed to her, and carefully monitored to see if Allied intelligence acted upon it. As Lilya later discovered, Fegelein had employed this tactic several times.

Back in England, Lilya had been told that she should become active as an agent only when she was absolutely certain that her source's confidence had been secured. Her life depended on that decision. That much she had known from the start. What Lilya had not known, at least in the beginning, was that you could never be certain. All you could do was guess, hope that you were right, and begin.

That day came when Fegelein appointed her as his new driver, replacing the grimly scarred man who had held the job up until then. Usually, after his midday meetings with Hitler, it was Fegelein's habit to spend the remainder of his time at the apartment of his mistress, leaving Lilya Simonova outside in the car in which Fegelein would leave behind the briefcase containing any briefing notes to his master, the Lord of the SS.

Fegelein left the briefcase in the car because he thought it would be safer there than in the house of Elsa Batz, whom he cared for, up to a point, but whom he did not trust.

Alone in the car, Simonova would read through the contents of the briefcase and, later, would deliver the information, along with any gossip she had picked up from Fegelein that day, to a courier agent, who then forwarded the details to England.

Lilya knew very little about the courier, other than the fact that he worked at the Hungarian Embassy.

For the transfer, Lilya would deposit information in the hollowed-out leg of a bench in the Hasenheide park, just across the road from the Garde-Pioneer tram station. Occasionally, messages would be left for her there, indicating that she was to make contact with her control officer in England, whom she knew only as 'Major Clarke'. For this purpose, she had been issued a radio, to be used only in such emergencies.

Her last contact with Major Clarke had been only the day before, when he had ordered her to find out all she could about this Diamond Stream device.

And now there it was, barely an arm's length away, resting on the dashboard of the car as they roared across the German countryside, bound for the lair of Heinrich Himmler.

'Wait!' Fegelein said suddenly. 'Pull over! There's something I forgot.'

Lilya jammed on the brakes and the car skidded to a halt, kicking up dust at the side of the road. 'What is it?' she asked.

'It's Elsa's birthday.' Fegelein looked at her helplessly. 'We'll have to turn around.'

'And keep Himmler waiting?'

'Better him than Elsa,' mumbled Fegelein.

As she wheeled the car about, the chart case tumbled into Fegelein's lap.

'I won't be long, but I'll need you to wait in the car. You can look after this while I'm gone,' Fegelein told her, replacing the map case on the dashboard.

'Of course,' she said quietly. 'Where would I be without you, Fraülein S?' repeated Fegelein. As he caught sight of her luminously blue eyes, his gaze softened with affection. Those eyes were like nothing he had ever seen before, and their effect on him had never lessened since the first day he caught sight of her in Paris. She was sitting at a desk in a dreary, smoke-filled room crowded with secretaries typing out documents for translation by the city's German occupation government. Pale, bleached light glimmered down through window panels in the roof, whose glass was stained with smears of dirty green moss. Whenever he thought about that moment, Fegelein would hear again the deafening clatter of typewriters, pecking away like the beaks of tiny birds against his skull, and he remembered the instant when she had glanced up from her work and he first saw her face. He had never recovered from that moment, nor did he ever wish to.

'Where would you be?' she asked. 'In search of the perfect word for your reports to the Reichsführer. That is where you'd be.'

Her words were like a cup of cold water thrown into Fegelein's face. 'Exactly so,' he replied brusquely, turning back to face the road. In that moment he realised that the reason he had not thrown himself at her long ago was because he had fallen in love with this woman, and he could not bring himself to treat her the way he had treated the others, and even his own dismally promiscuous wife.

'Was that General Hagemann I saw with you on the steps of the Chancellery building?' she asked.

'He prefers to be called a professor,' confirmed Fegelein, 'but that was him all right, and since he has just misplaced a very valuable rocket, it may be the last time you see him.' 'He lost a rocket?'

Fegelein explained what he had learned. 'It's probably at the bottom of the Baltic Sea, but I expect the old general would sleep a little better if he knew that for a fact. And I would sleep a little better, too, if you would take my advice and agree to carry a pistol. I'd be happy to provide you with one. These are dangerous times and they are likely to get more so in the days ahead. I gave one to Elsa, you know, and she seems happy with it!'

'Perhaps because she needs it to defend herself against you.' Fegelein laughed. 'Even if that was the case, I'd have nothing to worry about! What Elsa needs more than anything is some lessons in target practice. Believe me, I tried to teach her, but it's pretty much hopeless.'

'Well, I don't want a gun,' said Lilya. 'How many times have I told you that?'

'I have lost count,' admitted Fegelein, 'but that doesn't mean I'll give up trying to make you see some sense.'

The truth was, Lilya did carry a weapon. It was a small folding knife with a stiletto point and a small device, like the head of a nail, fitted into the top of the blade which enabled the user to open the knife single-handedly and with only a flick of the thumb.

It had been a gift from a man she almost married long ago. One late summer day, they had gone on a picnic together to the banks of the Neva River outside St Petersburg and he had used the knife to peel the skin from an apple in a single long ribbon of juicy, green peel. Before them, white, long-legged birds moved with jerky and deliberate steps among the water lilies.

'What birds are those?' she had asked. 'Cranes,' he replied. 'Soon they will begin their long migration south.'

'How far will they go?' she asked.

'To Africa,' he told her.

She had been stunned to think of such a vast journey and tried to imagine them, plodding with their chalk stick legs in the water of an oasis.

Later, when she got home, she had discovered the knife in the wicker basket which they had used to bring the food. When she went to return the knife, the man told her to keep it. 'Remember the birds,' he had said.

It was not until much later that she noticed a maker's mark engraved upon the blade – of two cranes, their long and narrow beaks touching like two hypodermic needles – engraved into the tempered steel.

Of the possessions she had carried with her on that long journey out of Russia, this knife was the only thing she had left. The diamond and sapphire engagement ring, which she had been wearing when she arrived in England, was taken from her for safekeeping by the people who trained her for the tasks which had since taken over her life. She wondered where that ring was now, and also where the man was who had slipped it on her finger, on the island in the Lamskie pond at Tsarskoye Selo, already a lifetime ago.

Then the voice of Hermann Fegelein broke into her memory, like a rock thrown through a window pane. 'I will not always be your commanding officer,' he said. Reaching out, he brushed his hand across her knee.

'I know,' she replied gently, glancing down at his arm.

And if Fegelein could have known what images were going through her head just then, his heart would have clogged up with fear.

Radial artery – centre of the wrist. Quarter-inch cut. Loss of consciousness in thirty seconds. Death in two minutes.

Brachial artery – inside and just above the elbow. Cut half an inch deep. Loss of consciousness in fourteen seconds. Death in one and a half minutes.

Subclavian artery – behind the collarbone. Two-and-a-half inch cut. Loss of consciousness in five seconds. Death in three and a half minutes.

Down in the bunker, the briefing had been concluded.

The generals, having delivered their usual, bleak assessment of the situation above ground, were now sitting down to lunch in the crowded bunker mess hall where, in spite of the spartan surroundings, the quality of food and wine was still among the finest in Berlin.

Hitler did not join them. He remained in the conference room, thinking back to the day, in July of 1943, when Hagemann and a group of his scientists, including Werner von Braun and Dr Steinhoff, had arrived at the East Prussia Army headquarters in Rastenburg, known as the Wolf 's Lair. Hagemann's team had come equipped with rare colour footage of a successful V-2 launch, which had been carried out from Peenemunde in October of the previous year.

In a room specially converted to function as a cinema, Hitler had viewed the film, in the company of Field Marshal Keitel and Generals Jodl and Buhle.

Previously skeptical about the possibility of developing the V-2 as a weapon, watching this film transformed Hitler into a believer.

When the lights came up again, Hitler practically leaped from his chair and shook Hagemann's hand with both of his.

'Why was it', he asked the startled general, 'that I could not believe in the success of your work?'

The other generals in the room, who had previously expressed their own grave misgivings, especially about the proposed price tag of funding the rocket programme, were effectively muzzled by Hitler's exuberance. Any protest from them now would only be seen as obstruction by Hitler, and the price tag of that, for those two men, was more than they were willing to pay.

'If we'd had these rockets back in 1939,' Hitler went on to say, 'we would never have had this war.'

And then, for one of the only times in his life, Hitler apologised. 'Forgive me', he told General Hagemann, 'for ever having doubted you.'

He immediately gave orders to begin mass-production of the V-2, regardless of the cost. As his imagination raced out of control, his demand for nine hundred rockets a month increased over the course of a few minutes to five thousand. Although even the lowest of these figures turned out to be impractical, since the amount of liquid oxygen required to power that many V-2s far exceeded Germany's annual output, his belief in this miracle weapon seemed unshakeable.

Although there had been many times since then when Hitler had secretly harboured doubts about the professor's judgement, now it seemed to him that his faith had been rewarded at last. Even if it had come too late to ensure a total victory over Europe and the Bolsheviks, the V-2's improved performance, if the full measure and precision of its destructive power could be proven on the battlefield, would not go unnoticed by the enemy. And it might just be enough to stop the advance of the armies which, even now, were making their way steadily towards Berlin. But only if he stopped this leak of information that had been trickling out of the bunker.

'Fetch me General Rattenhuber!' he shouted to no one in particular.

Fifteen minutes later, SS General Johann Rattenhuber, chief of the Reich's Security Service, entered the briefing room.

He was a square-faced man with a heavy chin, grey hair combed straight back over his head, and permanently narrowed eyes. From the earliest days of the National Socialist party, Rattenhuber had been responsible for Hitler's personal safety. He and his team were constantly on the move, travelling to whichever of Hitler's thirteen special headquarters was in use at any given time.

Some of these, such as the Cliff Nest, hidden deep within the Eifel Mountains, or the Wolf's Lair at Rastenburg in East Prussia, were complexes of underground tunnels and massive concrete block houses, built to withstand direct hits from the heaviest weapons in the Allied arsenal of weaponry. From these almost impenetrable fortifications, Hitler had conducted his campaigns in the east and west. Other hideouts, such as the Giant in Charlottenburg, the construction of which had required more concrete than the entire allotment supplied for civilian air-raid shelters in the year 1944, had never been put to use.

Rattenhuber was used to departing at short notice. He was seldom given more than a day's warning when Hitler decamped from one headquarters to another and, increasingly over the past few months, he had grown accustomed to being summoned at all hours of the day or night, to answer Hitler's growing suspicions about his safety.

In Rattenhuber's mind, ever since the attempt on Hitler's life back in July of 1944, the Führer had been steadily losing his grip on reality. Having survived the bomb blast that tore through the meeting room in Rastenburg, Hitler had become convinced that providence itself had intervened. Although Rattenhuber did not believe in such lofty concepts, he was quietly forced to admit that it was no thanks to him, or to his hand-selected squad of Bavarian ex-policemen, that Hitler had emerged with nothing more than scratches and his clothing torn to shreds. Those were the physical results, but mentally, as Rattenhuber had seen for himself, Hitler's wounds were much deeper. The sense of betrayal he felt, that his own generals would have conspired to murder him, would dog him for the rest of his days. Behind the anger at this betrayal lay a primal terror which no amount of concrete, or Schmeissertoting guards or reassurance could ever put to rest.

But what consumed him now, was the story of this spy in the Chancellery.

Rattenhuber knew about Der Chef, whose jovial gossip had enlightened him to scandals which even he, in his role as guardian of all the bunker folk, had not known about before he heard it on the radio.

With his mind set on vengeance, Rattenhuber sifted through the list of Chancellery employees. For a while, he had fastened on a bad-tempered old janitor named Ziegler, who had worked at the Chancellery for years. Hauling him off to Gestapo headquarters, located in the crypt of the now-ruined Dreifaltigkeit church on Mauerstrasse, it was Rattenhuber himself who conducted the interrogation. But it quickly became apparent that Ziegler had nothing to hide. He was what he was – just a surly, ill-mannered floor-sweeper with a grudge against all of humanity.

After Ziegler, there were no more leads, and the stone-like face of Rattenhuber, the once-unshakeable Munich detective, was unable to conceal his helplessness.

Standing in the briefing room, Rattenhuber's head almost touched the low concrete ceiling. Directly above him, an electric light dimmed and brightened with the fluctuating power of the generator.

Of all the fortresses which Hitler had put into use, Rattenhuber hated this bunker the most. Worst of all was the quality of the air. There were times when he had virtually staggered up the stairs to the main floor of the Chancellery building. Gasping , he would lean against the wall, two fingers hooked inside his collar to allow himself to breathe.

Hitler sat by himself. Except for a single sheet of paper, the table in front of him was bare.

Rattenhuber came to attention.

Hitler ignored the salute. Without even looking up, he slid the piece of paper across to Rattenhuber.

The general picked it up. It was a list of Knight's Cross recipients. 'Why am I looking at this?' he asked, laying the page back on the table.

Hitler reached across and tapped one finger on the page. 'It never left the bunker.'

'Is that a problem?'

'Indeed it is,' Hitler confirmed, 'because this morning, Der Chef broadcast it to the world.'

There was no need to explain any more. Rattenhuber knew exactly what this meant. The blood drained out of his face. 'I will begin an investigation immediately,' he said.

Slowly Hitler shook his head. 'You had your chance,' he muttered. 'I am giving this job to Inspector Hunyadi.'

'Hunyadi!' exclaimed the general. 'But he's in prison! You put him there yourself. He is due to be executed any day now. For all I know, he might already be dead.'

'Then you had better hope it's not too late,' said Hitler. 'You have already failed me twice, Rattenhuber. First, you let them try to blow me to pieces. Then you stand around uselessly while this spy roams the bunker at will. Now I am ordering you to bring me Hunyadi. Fail me again, Rattenhuber, and you will take that man's place at the gallows.'

Following the directions that Stalin had written down for him, Pekkala made his way to a narrow dreary street in the Lefortovo District of the city. He rattled the gate at 17 Rubzov Lane – a dirty yellow apartment building with mildew growing on the outer wall – until the caretaker, a small hunched man in a blue boiler suit with a brown corduroy patch sewn into the seat, finally emerged from his office to see what the fuss was about.

'He's just moved in,' said the caretaker, when Pekkala had explained who he was looking for.

He unlocked the gate and led Pekkala to a door on the ground floor of the building. 'In there, he should be,' said the man, then shuffled back to the office, in which Pekkala could see a huge grey dog, some kind of wolfhound, lying on a blanket beside a stove.

Pekkala pounded on the door and then stood back. The curtain of the single window facing out into the courtyard fluttered slightly and then the door opened a crack.

'Comrade Garlinski,' said Pekkala.

'Yes?' answered a frightened voice.

'I hear you've just arrived from England.'

'What do you want?'

'Only to talk.' 'Who sent you?'

Pekkala held up his red Special Operations pass book, with its faded gold hammer and sickle on the front.

The door opened a little wider now and the frightened-looking man who had, until the week before, been the head of operations at Unit 53A, the British Special Operations listening post at Grantham Underwood, appeared from the shadows. Even though it was the middle of the afternoon, Garlinski had been asleep. With orders not to leave the flat, he had little else to do except to make his way through the meagre rations that had been left for him in the kitchen. 'Talk about what?' he asked the stranger.

'An agent of yours named Christophe,' answered Pekkala. Garlinski blinked at him in astonishment. 'How the hell do you know about that? I haven't even been debriefed yet.' And now he opened the door wide, allowing Pekkala to enter.

Inside, there was almost no furniture; only a chair pulled up next to the stove. The walls were bare, with fade marks on the cream-coloured paint where pictures had once hung. His bed was a blue and white ticking mattress lying on the floor, with an old overcoat for a blanket.

'Look where they dumped me,' said Garlinski. 'After all I've done, I thought I'd get some kind of hero's welcome. Instead, I get this.' He raised his hands and let them fall again with a slap against his thighs.

With only one chair between them, both men sat down with their back against the wall. Sitting side by side, they stared straight ahead as they conversed.

'What is it you want to know?' asked Garlinski.

'Why were you in such a hurry to leave England?' 'I thought that my cover was blown,' explained Garlinski, 'or that it was about to be, at any rate.'

'What happened?'

'I was on my way home from the relay station,' explained

Garlinski. 'In my briefcase, I had several messages that had come in from SOE agents which I planned to copy and send out to Moscow that evening.'

'Why were you bringing them home with you?'

'Because that's where I kept my transmitter,' said Garlinski.

'Of course, we weren't allowed to leave with these messages, but since I was in charge of the relay station, no one ever checked. Until last week, that is.

'I got stopped at a police checkpoint two blocks from my house. They were looking for black marketers. When they opened my briefcase, they saw the messages and decided to hold on to them until they had been cleared.'

'Couldn't you have told them you were working for SOE?'

'I could have, but it would only have made things worse. SOE would have come down on me like a ton of bricks for removing messages from the station.'

'What did you tell the police?'

'I said I was trying to invent a new code for the army to use. I went on about it long enough that they must have thought I was telling the truth. They still held on to the messages, though, and I knew it was only a matter of time before someone figured out what I was up to. That's why I had to leave.'

'How did you get out of the country so quickly?' asked Pekkala.

'There was a safe house, right outside the underground station at the Angel up in Islington. I went straight there and your people arranged for my disappearance.'

'Did SOE ever suspect you might be working for Russian Intelligence?'

'If they did, I wouldn't be here now, but I don't know how much better off I am, left to rot in a place like this.'

'At least you are alive.'

'If you can call this living,' muttered Garlinski.

'How do you know about Christophe?' asked Pekkala.

'Only that the agent's messages come through our station. My job is simply to take in the raw material, decode it and send it up the chain, and all as quickly as possible. What I can tell you is that the stuff Christophe sent us was usually a mixture of gossip, scandal and shuffles in the High Command. I hear the British use it on the radio stations which they broadcast into enemy territory. It was all pretty straightforward until about ten days ago.'

'What happened then?'

'We intercepted a message from somewhere on the Baltic coast, mentioning something about a "diamond stream".'

'What does it mean?' asked Pekkala.

Garlinski shrugged. 'Whatever it was, it got their attention up at Headquarters. They contacted Christophe, asking for more information, photographs and so on. They're afraid it might be some kind of new weapons system – one of the miracles the German High Command keep promising will turn the tide of the war. But whether Christophe was successful or not, I don't know.'

'The British have come to us, asking if we might be prepared to get Christophe out of Berlin.'

'Berlin?' Garlinski turned to face Pekkala. 'And what fool are you sending on that suicide mission?'

'That fool would be me,' replied Pekkala.

'Well, I'm sorry for you, Inspector, because none of it matters now anyway.'

'Why do you say that?' asked Pekkala, rising to his feet.

'The enemy is done for and they know it. All but a few of them, anyway.'

'It's those few we have to worry about,' Pekkala said as he headed for the door.

'Put in a good word for me, could you?' asked Garlinski. He spread his arms, taking in the hollowness of the dirty room. 'Tell them I deserve more than this.'

'Diamond stream?' Stalin rolled the words across his tongue, as if to speak them might unravel the mystery of their meaning.

'Garlinski said he thought it might have something to do with one of the German secret-weapons programmes,' said Pekkala. 'Is there anyone who might know for certain?'

'We have a number of high-ranking German officers at a prisoner-of-war camp north of the city. It is a special place, where men are slowly squeezed,' Stalin clasped his hand into a fist, 'but gently, so that they barely notice, and before they know it they have told everything. You might find someone there who still has a drop or two of information which we haven't yet wrung from his brain. You'd better send Kirov, though.'

'Why is that?' asked Pekkala.

'Speaking to these men requires some finesse,' explained Stalin, 'and your method of questioning suspects is apt to be a little primitive.'

Pekkala could not argue with that, but he had one more thing to say before he left. 'Garlinski asked me to put in a word for him.'

'A word about what?' Stalin asked.

'About his living conditions here in Moscow. He thinks he deserves something more.'

Stalin nodded. 'Indeed he does, Inspector. Thank you for bringing it to my attention.'

On the island of Bornholm, the Ottesen brothers had done nothing to clean up the mess caused by the explosion the night before, and the yard was still scattered with fragments of splintered wood, old horse tack and a splintery coating of straw.

For now, at least, they contented themselves with simply observing the destruction.

The two men perched side by side upon a bale of charred hay in the middle of their barnyard. Both of them were smoking pipes that had long thin stems and white porcelain bowls with tin lids to dampen the smoke.

Emerging from their house at sunrise that morning, they had discovered, amongst the wreckage, several pieces of what appeared to be metal fins and heavy discs of metal pierced by a multitude of drill holes.

The idea that it might have been an aeroplane was quickly set aside. Where were the wheels, the brothers asked themselves. Where were the propellers? Or the pilot? No. This was no work of human hands.

By pooling their combined intelligence, the Ottesen brothers decided that it must have been a spaceship of some sort. Having arrived at this conclusion, they could advance no further in their thinking, and so they sat down and smoked their pipes and waited for events to unfold. It was not long before three policemen arrived in a truck, ordered the brothers back into their house and then began to rummage through the ruins of the barn.

The Ottesens watched through the gauzy fabric of their day curtains as the policemen removed several chunks of mangled metal from the barn, loaded them aboard the truck and then left without saying goodbye.

Not wanting to disobey orders, the brothers remained in their house for another hour before finally returning to the barnyard.

Soon afterwards, another car showed up and two more policemen climbed out.

'You're too late,' said Per, removing the pipe stem from his mouth. 'The other lot already came and went.'

'What other lot?' demanded the policeman. His name was Jakob Horn and he had served for many years as the only policeman stationed at the southern end of the island. With him was a German named Rudi Lusser who, as part of the small occupation force located on Bornholm, was tasked with accompanying Horn wherever he went, and reporting everything back to Northern District Police Headquarters, located in Hanover. Lusser had been there since 1940, and he had never received much encouragement from Hanover. In fact, he had grown to suspect that his reports weren't even being read. Now that Hanover had fallen to the enemy, Lusser was growing increasingly nervous about his prospects for the future. Lusser and Horn had never got along well. In the early days of their forced partnership, Lusser had been intolerant of Horn and of these islanders, whom he had written off as ludicrously provincial. He had made no attempt to learn Danish and relied instead of Horn's rudimentary grasp of German. Now that the war was as good as lost, Lusser was beginning to regret his previous attitude, and he made every effort to ingratiate himself with Horn and with these men, who might soon be his captors.

Lusser beamed a smile at the brothers, as if he was a long-lost friend.

The Ottesens ignored him. They had always ignored Lusser and now they ignored him even more, if such a thing were possible.

'What other lot?' repeated Horn.

'The other policemen,' explained Ole. 'They must have come down from the north end of the island.'

'Why do you say that?'

'We didn't recognise them.'

Lusser, who could make no sense of what was going on, continued to smile idiotically.

'Did they speak with you?' Horn asked the twins.

'No,' answered Ole. 'They just told us to stay in our house.'

'What did they do then?'

'Took a bunch of stuff from the spaceship,' said Per.

'Spaceship?' asked Horn.

'At first we just thought it was God,' Ole told him.

'But then we found the metal bits,' said Per, 'and that's how we knew it was a spaceship.'

'And what did these men do with the things they found?'

'Put them in their truck and drove away.'

'Where did they go?' asked Horn. 'Which direction?'

Ole aimed his pipe stem down the road towards Arnager, a little fishing village on the southern coast.

Horn shook his head in disbelief. 'Did it not occur to you to wonder why policemen from the north end would be down this way at all, let alone why they would head off to the south when they left here?'

It had not occurred to them.

Horn stared at them for a moment. Then he got back into the car, along with Lusser, and the two policemen raced towards Arnager.

Arriving not long afterwards, they found an empty truck parked at the quayside and three police jackets, stolen from the Klemensker station at the north end of the island, lying heaped on the passenger seat.

When Major Kirov walked into the interrogation room at the Alexeyevska prisoner-of-war camp, which was reserved for high-ranking enemy officers, he found a tall man with pale skin and greying hair, still wearing the tattered uniform of a colonel in the German Army. The colonel sat at a table, hunched in a chair and clasping a green enamel cup filled with hot tea. Except for one other chair, on the opposite side of the table, there was no other furniture in the room.

The soldier's name was Hanno Wolfrum.

He had been in charge of a convoy of trucks fleeing the advance of the Red Army towards the Baltic. Having departed from Königsberg, the column had planned to travel due south to Pultusk, just north of Warsaw and from there to head west towards the German lines. Fearing that his route might be cut off by Russian reconnaissance units, Wolfrum sent his own scouts ahead to ensure that the roads were still passable. As they crossed the Polish border and entered the region of Masuria, Wolfrum's scouts reported that Soviet tanks had been seen on the road to Pultusk. There were no westbound roads between him and the town, and he did not dare retrace his steps towards the north, so Wolfrum had been forced to detour to the east, towards the enemy lines, in the hopes that he could then find another route south. As the column made its way along a winding road which passed beside the Narew river, they came under Soviet mortar fire from the opposite bank. The lead and rear trucks on the convoy were destroyed, stranding the vehicles in between. The drivers and a small number of men who had been serving as armed escorts for the convoy all fled into the surrounding countryside.

Russian soldiers crossed the river, hoping to find food in the trucks. Instead, they discovered engine parts for both V-1 and V-2 rockets. As word of the discovery reached the Russian High Command, specialised troops of the NKVD Internal Security Service were dispatched to the scene. The rocket parts were quickly inventoried and transported to the rear and a hunt began for the men who had been travelling with the convoy.

By then, most of them had already been killed by Polish civilians. Wolfrum himself was found hiding in a barn by Red Army soldiers who had been out foraging. He was brought to the Alexeyevska prison camp, where he underwent weeks of interrogation.

During this time, Wolfrum was neither tortured nor mistreated. His interrogators, who were among the most skilled in the Russian Intelligence Service, were well aware that Wolfrum, in time and if properly treated, would supply them not only with the answers to their questions, but with questions which they had not thought to ask.

At first, Wolfrum claimed to know nothing about the contents of the crates aboard his trucks, but the unexpectedly civilised treatment he received put him off balance. He soon began to give up details about the convoy that showed that he was not only aware of the significance of these engine parts, but that he had been part of the team which designed them. It emerged that Wolfrum had been sent by General Hagemann himself, head of the Peenemunde programme, to the factory in Sovetsk, on the

Lithuanian border, which had manufactured the engine parts and to remove them to safety before the arrival of the Red Army. In addition to this, Wolfrum had been ordered to blow up the factory before he left, a task for which he used so much dynamite that he not only obliterated the factory but shattered half the windows in the town.

Now Kirov studied Wolfrum's appearance. The colonel's tunic, although badly damaged during the days he had spent on the run, was made of high-quality grey gaberdine, with a contrasting dark green collar. All of his insignia had been removed by the camp authorities, leaving shadows on the cloth where his collar tabs and shoulder boards had been, as well as the eagle above his left chest pocket.

Wolfrum himself, although solidly built, looked frightened and as worn-out as his clothes. The skin sagged beneath his eyes and his bloodless lips were chapped. Kirov did not need to be told that it was not the present which terrified this officer, but the future. Wolfrum had already been in captivity for several months and was well aware that he would soon arrive at the limits of his usefulness. Whatever promises had been made by his captors, regarding his treatment in the weeks, or months or even years ahead, had only served to scour every wrinkle of his brain for information they could use. Any day now, the illusion of dignity would be set aside. Whether they put him up against a wall and shot him or else dispatched him to Siberia was all out of his hands now. In the meantime, Wolfrum answered their questions. He didn't care what they were. The oaths of loyalty which he had taken long ago were to a country on the edge of extinction. Besides, there was nothing he knew that was still worth keeping secret. 'You're new,' remarked Wolfrum when he caught sight of the major. 'Are all the others tired out?' Then he sipped at his tea, waiting for the interrogation to begin. They always gave him tea before these sessions and he was almost afraid to tell them how much he had come to value this miniature gesture of kindness.

'I just have one question,' said Kirov, 'and I've been told that you might have the answer.'

Wolfrum sighed. 'I have already explained everything. About everything. But why should that matter?' Placing the mug on the table, he held open his hands, palms rosy from the heat. 'Ask away, Comrade. I have all the time in the world.'

Kirov sat down in a chair on the opposite side of the table.

'What do you know about "Diamond Stream"?' asked Kirov. Wolfrum paused before he spoke. 'Well now,' he said at last, 'perhaps there is something you don't know about me, after all.'

'And what might that be?' asked Kirov.

'That I worked on the Diamond Stream project.'

'What did the project involve?' he asked the colonel. Wolfrum paused. Each time he gave up a new fragment of information, it seemed to him he took another step towards a line beyond which there could be no going back. But he had lately come to realise that the line had been crossed long ago.

'Diamond Stream is the code name for a guidance system for the V-2 rocket. If it had succeeded, we could have dropped one down a chimney on the other side of Europe.'

'If?'

'That's right,' said Wolfrum. 'It was a wonderful idea, but that's all it ever was. I don't know how many test shots we fired in the months before I was captured, but I can tell you that every single one of them failed. The mechanisms we designed were too fragile to withstand the vibrations of the rocket in flight.'

'Do you think it could have worked,' asked Kirov, 'even if only in theory?'

Wolfrum smiled. 'Our theories always worked, Comrade Major. It's why we gave them such beautiful names. But that's all it is, just a theory, and likely all that it will ever be.'

A few days later, a truck pulled up before the gates of the British Propulsion Laboratory, located near King's Dock in Swansea in the south of Wales.

The town had once been a thriving port, but German air raids, which took place mostly at night during the summer of 1940, had reduced much of the docklands to rubble.

The propulsion laboratory, which dealt primarily in steamdriven turbines for powering the engines of battleships, had been one of the few businesses to survive the bombing. This was by virtue of the fact that its large roof, whose dew-soaked slates gleamed in the moonlight, had served as a homing beacon for the attacking squadrons of Heinkels and Dornier bombers. The pilots of these planes had been given strict orders not to damage the roof, and the laboratory had remained intact.

Soldiers of the Army Transport Corps unloaded a crate from the back of the truck. The heavy box was placed upon a handcart and brought inside the red-brick building. The soldiers were joined by two men in civilian clothing, who had accompanied the crate from the moment it had arrived in the English port city of Harwich two days before.

One of these men wore a trilby hat and a brown wool gaberdine coat. He was tall and wiry and sported a pencil-thin moustache. The man made no attempt to conceal the fact that he was carrying a revolver in a shoulder holster.

The other man, who sported a three-piece Harris tweed suit, had a small chin, curly hair gone grey and had not shaved in several days, leaving a stippling of white stubble on his cheeks.

The man with the pencil moustache stood in the middle of the laboratory floor and, in a loud and nasal voice, informed the dozen technicians who were working on the main floor of the laboratory that they had been dismissed for the remainder of the day.

No one argued. No one even asked why. The sight of the gun wedged under the man's armpit were all the credentials he needed.

Only one person was kept behind: a small, bald man with fleshy lips and cheerful eyes. Instead of the faded blue lab coats worn by the other technicians, this man had put on a chef's apron, with a large kangaroo pocket at the front which sagged with pencils, handkerchiefs and scraps of notepaper on which mysterious equations had been written.

'Professor Greenidge?' asked the man with the pencil moustache.
'Yes?'

'My name is Warsop,' said the man. 'I'm with the Home Office.' And, as he spoke, he removed a folded piece of paper from his coat. 'I'd like you to sign this, please.'

'What is it?' asked Professor Greenidge.

It was the man in the tweed suit who answered. 'Official Secrets Act,' he said nonchalantly. 'As soon as you've done that, we can show you what we've got in here.' He gave the crate a jab with his toe. 'I think you'll find it worth your time.' Then he held out his hand to the professor. 'My name is Rufford. I'm a member of Crossbow.'

Greenidge had heard of the Crossbow organisation although,

until now, he had never met anyone who was a part of it. The organisation had been put together to study German rocket technolog y. It was all top-secret stuff, far beyond his own level of clearance.

'What's this got to do with me?' he asked. 'I'm a steam technician. I don't build rockets.'

'We pulled your name out of a hat,' muttered Warsop. 'Now are you going to sign the document or not?'

'I do suggest you sign it, old man,' said Rufford.

'Very well,' said Greenidge, suspecting that he had no choice. With a few swipes of his Parker pen, the professor did as he was told.

'In any of your work,' asked Rufford, 'have you ever come across the mention of a project known as "Diamond Stream"?'

'No,' he replied. 'What would that be?'

'Well,' began Rufford, 'we are hoping it might be the contents of this box.'

As Warsop unlatched the crate, a smell of mud and manure swept out into the room. Warsop reached inside and removed a gnarled piece of machinery, still clogged with dirt and threads of straw. That it had been torn from its mountings by incredible force was clear to see in the bent and shredded steel.

Warsop handed it to Greenidge. 'See what you can make of that,' he said.

Greenidge held the cold metal in his hands for a few seconds, but it was too heavy and he had to put it down upon a work bench. Then he took out one of the many pencils from his apron and began to poke around among a cluster of wires which splayed out of the machine like the roots of a tree wrenched from the ground. After several minutes, he stood back, tapping the pencil thoughtfully upon his thumbnail. 'It appears to be some kind of gyroscopic mechanism, possibly for stabilising an object in flight. It's not one of ours or I would know about it. Where did you get it?'

'From a crash site on an island in the Baltic,' replied Rufford. 'That's about all we can tell you for now.'

'Can you at least inform me of the type of craft it came from?'

'We think it was a test rocket that went off course, probably fired from the German research facility at Peenemunde.'

'So it's either a V-1 or a V-2,' remarked Greenidge.

Warsop glanced at Rufford. 'Might as well tell him,' he said.

'It is the latter,' confirmed Rufford.

'I thought we bombed Peenemunde,' said Professor Greenidge.

'We did,' Warsop answered. 'Just not enough, apparently.'

'Which would imply that the mechanism didn't work.'

'Possibly,' replied Rufford. 'We've managed to salvage a number of rocket parts out of the recent bombings of Antwerp and London . . .'

'London!' exclaimed Greenidge. 'There's been no report of that.'

'Ah,' Rufford scratched at his forehead. 'Well, you see, in order not to generate panic in the city, we have been reporting these rocket strikes as gas-main explosions. Since they come in faster than the speed of sound, the detonation actually precedes the noise of its arrival, which itself is drowned out by the explosion.'

'How long do you think you'll be able to keep that fiction working?' the professor asked incredulously.

'As long as we have to,' said Warsop, 'but that's not why we're here.'

'Yes, quite,' said Rufford, who seemed anxious to defuse whatever animosity was already brewing between the two men.

'We've brought you this piece of equipment, because we've never come across anything like this before. We have reason to believe that the enemy may be close to perfecting a radio-controlled homing system for these weapons.'

'Radio-controlled?' asked Greenidge, and suddenly he understood why they had come to him.

Before the war, he had experimented with radio-guidance technology for weapons, but he had never been able to develop a successful prototype. His government funding had eventually been cut and he came to work at the propulsion lab as a steam-turbine engineer. Now, it seemed, the enemy had fulfilled the dream which had once been his own.

'Any chance you might be able to reconstruct it?' asked Rufford.

Greenidge shook his head. 'Not from what you've given me. This is only part of the mechanism. If you can find me schematics, even partial ones, I should be able to make some headway pretty quickly.'

'We're working on that now,' said Warsop.

'In the meantime,' continued Greenidge, 'I can take apart what we do have here and should be able to tell you what is missing.'

'Then that will have to do,' said Rufford. 'Have you got some place where you can work on it without anyone looking over your shoulder?'

'Yes,' said Greenidge. 'There's space in the storage room at the back.'

'Put a lock on the door,' ordered Warsop.

'There is one.'

'On the inside,' said Warsop, 'so you can keep out any unintended visitors.'

Greenidge nodded. 'I'll see to it right away.' He shook hands with Rufford. Warsop only nodded goodbye.

'I do have one last question,' said Greenidge, as the two men headed for the door.

They turned and looked at him.

'Are you sure there's no one on the other side who knows we've got hold of this?'

Rufford looked nervously at Warsop.

'Why do you want to know that?' demanded Warsop.

'Because if I can build it', answered Greenidge, 'I might also be able to build something which could defeat its purpose. And that's what you really want, isn't it? The simple fact that we might be able to duplicate the technology isn't going to prevent it from being used against us.'

For the first time, Warsop's scowl faltered.

'We're as sure as we can be that the enemy has no idea where these rocket pieces went,' explained Rufford, 'but that's never one hundred per cent. The men who brought us that wreckage took extraordinary risks in doing so, but who knows if someone saw them on their journey, or if the local authorities where the rocket came down have been able to figure out what was taken from the wreck. The way things are in Germany right now, they've got plenty of other things to worry about. Let's hope this stays off their radar.'

'The sooner you get me those schematics . . .'

'People are working on that even as we speak, Professor, but as I'm sure you can imagine, it is easier said than done.'

When the two men had gone, Greenidge turned his attention once more to the piece of wreckage. With one finger, he moved aside the tangled spider's web of multicoloured wires and was startled when something fell out of the mechanism. It tumbled to floor, metal ringing on the concrete. Greenidge bent down and picked it up, relieved to see the solid disc of brass had not been broken by the fall. There appeared to be some writing on it, half hidden by the smear of the same mud that coated the rest of the mechanism. With the side of his thumb, he wiped the dirt away and squinted at the words, struggling to make sense of them. 'Lotti,' he read aloud. 'Beste Kuh.'

Message from Christophe to Major Clarke:
DIAMOND STREAM PLANS ACQUIRED.

Major Clarke to Christophe:
WHAT IS DIAMOND STREAM?

Christophe to Major Clarke:
ROCKET ASSEMBLY. PURPOSE UNCLEAR BUT HIGH VALUE.

Major Clarke to Christophe:
PHOTOS?

Christophe to Major Clarke:
YES. FILM IS SAFE BUT NOT DEVELOPED.

Major Clarke to Christophe:
WE WILL GET YOU OUT. MONITOR SAFE HOUSE. FOLLOW PROTOCOL.

'Inspector?' whispered Major Kirov.

Pekkala was sitting at his desk. With unseeing eyes, he stared at the wall, a look of fixed intensity anchored to his face. His hands lay flat among the dusty white rings of mug stains on the woodwork of the desk, like someone who has just felt the ground shake beneath his feet.

Kirov was careful not to get too close. He had seen this phenomenon before. The Inspector was not asleep. Instead, he had travelled deep inside the catacombs of his mind, leaving behind all but the shell of his body.

When these trances overcame Pekkala, it was important to wake the man gently. Kirov had learned never to jostle him out from this state of waking dreams. The first time he had tried this, the Inspector exploded into movement and Kirov found himself staring down the barrel of Pekkala's Webley revolver. He had drawn the weapon from its holster with a speed Kirov had never seen before in the Inspector, or in anyone else, for that matter. There had been many times since, when, in the carrying-out of their duties, Kirov had watched Pekkala unholster the Webley and, although the Inspector was quick, the pace of his conscious movements was nothing like the speed with which this savagery erupted from his self-hypnotic state.

'Inspector?' Kirov called again. He stood well back from the desk, edged in behind the wheezy iron stove they used to heat their office on Pitnikov Street. 'Inspector, you must wake up. We are wanted at the Kremlin.' The call had come in only a few minutes before, ordering them to appear. Whenever Kirov had to listen to Poskrebychev, and especially over the phone, he always had the impression that he was being barked at by a small and irritating dog. Flinching involuntarily as he listened to Stalin's secretary relay the Kremlin's order, Kirov had glanced at the Inspector, unable to comprehend how the man could sleep through the clattering of the telephone bell, followed by the muffled ranting of Poskrebychev through the receiver.

After a few more attempts at trying to wake the Inspector with only the murmuring of his voice, Kirov removed an onion from a basket where he kept whatever food they had on hand. Removing a knife from his desk drawer, he sliced up the onion and placed it in an iron frying pan, along with a splat of butter, which he stored, wrapped in a handkerchief, on the sill outside the window, where the Russian winter kept it frozen solid.

Resting the pan on the flat surface of the stove, which had almost consumed its daily ration of wood, it was not long before the onions began to sizzle and the room soon filled with their aroma.

Almost imperceptibly, one of Pekkala's hands twitched. Then his fingers began to move, as if, in his unconscious state, the Inspector was playing out a tune upon some ghostly piano.

Sharply, Pekkala breathed in a breath. He blinked rapidly, as the focus returned to his eyes.

'Where were you?' Kirov asked.

Pekkala shook his head, as if he could no longer recall, but the truth was he remembered perfectly. It was simply too complicated to explain.

He had been in St Petersburg, strolling with Lilya along the Morskaya and Nevsky Prospekts. They had stopped to buy chocolate at Conradi's, before going to see a play at the Théâtre Michel. And afterwards, they went for a drink at the Hôtel d'Europe, where the bartender was a man from Kentucky.

These things had never happened. They belonged to a parallel world in which he had never been separated from her, and there had never been a Revolution, and a bank robber named Joseph Dzhugashvili had not murdered his way to the Kremlin, from which he ruled under the name he gave himself – Stalin – Man of Steel.

Only in moments of great stillness, such as that quiet afternoon on Pitnikov Street, could Pekkala glimpse that other life he might have lived.

Sometimes, in that trance of overwhelming memory, he would reach out, as if to pull himself into that second world, only to watch that fragile loophole disappear when sounds or smells or the touch of his well-meaning assistant intruded, and he would find himself once more a prisoner of flesh and bone.

But this time it was different. Although Pekkala had long since resigned himself to the fact that those two paths – the one he had taken and the one he might have done – were never going to converge, still they both had a role to play, in this world if not in the other.

At the outset of her days in exile, Lilya Simonova had clung to every detail of the time she had spent with Pekkala.

But the more time that went by, the more difficult it became. The memories began, very slowly, to fracture. It was as if she had found herself in a room full of broken mirrors and even if she could have glued every shard back into its place, the image could never be properly restored.

Eventually, instead of trying to remember, she did all she could to forget. It was either that, or lose her sanity completely.

But some of them refused to fade away, especially in those moments just before she fell asleep at night, when no amount of concentration could force the memories back into the darkness. The most vivid and tenacious of these were the legends he had told her of the place where he came from.

Pekkala had grown up in the lake region of eastern Finland, not far from the town of Lappeenranta. His father had been born there, and knew the waterways and forest trails as well as if they'd been the creases on his palm. But Pekkala's mother was a Sami, from the northernmost reaches of Lapland. It was from her that Pekkala had learned the stories which he then passed on to Lilya, as they walked the grounds of Tsarskoye Selo in those first weeks of their acquaintance.

He would meet her at the stone wall after she had locked up

the schoolhouse for the day. Then they would walk to the yellow stone house known as the Bath Pavilion, or else they would make their way to the Lyceum garden, where the statue of Pushkin cast his brooding shadow on the ground.

But under the spell of Pekkala's stories, Lilya barely noticed her surroundings.

He told her of the time when, as a child, he had gone to visit his mother's family in the north and, after a three-day journey, arrived to find the men of the village on the point of setting out to hunt a bear. The beast had only recently emerged from hibernation and had already killed three calves from the reindeer herd on which the village relied, not only for food but for clothing.

So sacred was the bear that no one dared to speak its name. Instead, they just called him by a word which meant 'the Walker in the Woods'.

The animal was tracked to its lair and brought down with spears tipped with bone from the reindeer it had killed. Then its corpse was tied to a V-shaped trellis made from birch trees and dragged back to the village. That night, meat from the bear was cooked over a fire made from the same trellis used to haul him in.

The taste of it, Pekkala told her, was rank and sour and, when no one was looking, he spat it back into the fire, where the fat burned with a flame like polished brass.

The next morning, the bear was buried in a hole as deep as the bear had been tall and even though the animal had been cut to pieces for the feast, his bones were now arranged in exactly the way he had carried them in life.

The place where they buried the bear was at the edge of a grove of trees where the People of the Twilight lived. But there were no houses to mark their property or any sign at all that they were there. The name of this tribe was the Sajvva, and they lived in a parallel world, making themselves known only when they had to. They were said to be tall and beautiful, and their skin appeared to radiate a glow like that of polished wood. The Sajvva lived much as Pekkala's people did, catching their own fish from the lakes and tending their own herds of reindeer. These animals they did not share. Only the bear lived in both of their worlds; serving as an emissary between the Twilight World and that of men. They buried his bones with respect, not only for the animal itself but for the Sajvva who considered him a friend.

In time, when he was ready, the Walker would rise up from his grave and piece his body back together, bone by bone, until he was himself again, so he could carry on his ceaseless wandering between the worlds of gods and men.

He had told her that story one evening as they stood at the edge of the Façade Pond, with the Alexander Palace at their backs. The palace had been lit up and the moon had just risen above the trees, casting its mercury light across the still water.

'What strange names they have for things up there,' Lilya had remarked.

'They would have a name for you as well,' Pekkala told her. She turned to him, smiling. 'Oh, really?' she asked. 'And what name would that be?'

'They would call you,' he began, and then he paused.

'Yes?'

'Your name', said Pekkala, 'would be "She Whose Hair Glows Softly in the Moonlight".' Even though the words had just rolled off his tongue, there was something both ancient and haunting about them, as if the name had been waiting for her much longer than she'd waited for the name.

The last thing she heard of Pekkala, after the Revolution drove them apart, was that he had been sent to the labour camp of Borodok, in the valley of Krasnagolyana. As years passed, and only silence reached her from the forests of Siberia, she began to wonder if Pekkala was still alive.

At times like that, she would return to the stories he had told her, until it seemed to her that Pekkala had transformed into the Walker in the Woods, striding through the veil between the worlds of gods and men with no more effort than a sigh.

And then she would not worry any more.

While he waited for Pekkala to arrive, Professor Swift sat in a chair across from Stalin's desk, nervously fingering his gold Dunhill lighter. In the other hand, he held an unlit cigarette, which he was desperate to smoke but did not dare to do in Stalin's presence. Although Swift was well aware of Stalin's tobacco habit, he had been warned by his station commander not to light up before the Boss himself saw fit to fill the room with smoke.

Stalin seemed to know this. Balanced between his yellowed fingertips was one of the many Markov cigarettes he puffed away each morning, often switching to a pipe come afternoon. He tapped the stubby white stick upon the leather blotter of his desk, letting it slide up between his fingers before turning it around and tapping it back down the other way.

'Pekkala appears to be late,' remarked Swift. Stalin responded with a grunt.

Another minute passed.

Swift could feel perspiration sticking the shirt to his back.

'Perhaps I should come back later,' he suggested.

Stalin fixed him with emotionless yellow-green eyes.

'Perhaps not,' Swift corrected himself.

From the outer office an irregular clatter of typewriter keys, which seemed to pause now and then, as if the typist – that little bald man with a shifty expression – were listening for any words that passed between them.

Just when Swift was about to flee from the premises, he heard voices in the outer office. 'Thank God,' he muttered.

The doors to Stalin's study opened.

Poskrebychev swung into the room, his hands touching both door knobs, which caused his arms to spread as if he were some large featherless bird in the moment before it took flight.

Pekkala and Kirov followed on his heels.

Swift was struck by the air of lethal efficiency these two men seemed to exude. He, himself, felt clumsily unprepared. The pretence of his job as sub-director of the Royal Agricultural Trade Commission was, by now, nothing more than an afterthought. The Soviets seemed to have known exactly who he was before he even arrived in the country and the charade that SOE's concern for agent Christophe was purely humanitarian had also crumbled to dust. He felt like a man in a poker game who had bet everything on a bluff, only to realise that he'd been showing his cards all along.

On seeing Pekkala walk into the room, Stalin's whole demeanour seemed to change. He smiled. The stiffness went out of his shoulders. He wedged the cigarette between his lips and lit it with a wooden match which he struck against a heavy brass ashtray already crowded with that morning's crumpled stubs. 'You are going to Berlin!' he announced. 'I hear it's very nice this time of year.'

'And me?' asked Kirov.

'You as well,' confirmed Stalin, 'along with a guide who will lead you to a safe house in the city. There, you will meet agent Christophe and bring her back across the Russian lines to safety.'

'Who runs the safe house?' asked Pekkala.

'We do,' answered Swift. Before continuing, he paused to light a cigarette, flooding his lungs with smoke. 'It belongs to one of our contact agents, who is employed at the Hungarian Embassy.'

'You will be provided with papers', explained Stalin, 'indicating that you are Hungarian businessmen who have been stranded in the city by the bombing and are staying with a member of the embassy until you are able to leave Berlin.'

'Neither of us speaks Hungarian,' said Kirov.

'And nor, in all likelihood, will any policeman who stops and asks for your papers,' answered Swift. 'The contact has been told to expect you. If the police check with him, he will verify your story. There is one other thing.'

'And what is that?' asked Pekkala.

'We have just learned from an informant in the German Security Service that Hitler has assigned a detective, a former member of the Berlin police, to root out a spy whom Hitler is convinced is operating from within his own headquarters. It's possible that they are closing in on Christophe, so the sooner you can get her out of there, the better.'

'A detective?' asked Pekkala. 'But surely they have a Security Service protecting the headquarters?'

'Indeed they do,' confirmed Swift. 'It is headed up by a former Munich policeman named Rattenhuber.'

'Why not use him?' asked Kirov.

'Hitler no longer knows whom to trust,' Swift explained.

'That's why he chose someone from the outside: an old comrade of his from the Great War.'

'Who is this man?' asked Stalin.

'His name is Leopold Hunyadi.'

'Hunyadi!' muttered Pekkala.

'You know him?' asked Swift.

'By reputation, yes. Hunyadi is the best criminal investigator in Germany. When did Hitler assign him to the task?' asked Pekkala.

Swift shook his head. 'We're not sure,' he confessed. 'It must be at least a few days.'

'Then we are already behind schedule,' said Pekkala. Turning to Stalin, he asked, 'How soon can you get us to Berlin?'

'If all goes well,' he replied, 'I'll have you walking the streets of that city by the day after tomorrow.'

The ash on Swift's cigarette was now precariously long and he began looking about for somewhere to tap it out. Stalin made no move to offer up his own ashtray and so, with gritted teeth, Swift tapped out the hot ash into his palm.

'I'll get a message through to agent Christophe,' said Swift.

'She will be waiting for you at the safe house upon your arrival in Berlin.' He made his exit, still carrying the ash on his palm.

The men who remained waited until they heard the clunk of the outer door closing before they resumed their conversation.

'There's something he just told us which doesn't make sense,' remarked Stalin.

'And what is that?' asked Pekkala.

'One of our sources in the Berlin Justice Department informed us that Leopold Hunyadi was condemned to death more than a month ago.'

'What did he do to deserve that?' asked Kirov. 'It's not clear,' answered Stalin. 'All we know is that Hunyadi was sent to the prison camp at Flossenburg to await execution.'

'Maybe they got the name wrong,' suggested Kirov.

Stalin slowly opened his hands and then set them together again, to show that it was anybody's guess.

'If Swift is right, however,' said Pekkala, 'then it will not be long before Hunyadi tracks her down. Lilya's only chance is for us get there first.'

'You depart tonight,' said Stalin. 'The appropriate weapons have been set aside for you at NKVD Headquarters, as well as those false identification papers provided by the British. All you have to do is pick them up and be ready to go by six o'clock this evening.'

As both men turned to leave, Stalin loudly cleared his throat to show he wasn't finished with them yet.

Both men froze in their tracks.

'A word with you in private, Inspector,' said Stalin. 'Major, you can wait in the hall.'

At that same moment, in the Flossenburg Concentration Camp in southern Germany, Leopold Hunyadi was preparing to meet his maker.

He was of medium height, with thinning blonde hair and a round and cheerful face. Hunyadi was in the habit of tilting his head back when he spoke to people, at the same time narrowing his eyes, as if to hide whatever emotions they might disclose. He was not a man who had ever been prone to physical exertion and now, as a result, possessed a belly that sagged over the old army belt he still wore, whose buckle was emblazoned with the words 'In Treue Fest', from his time in the Great War, when he had served as a sergeant in the 16th Bavarian Reserve Regiment.

In 1917, in a battle near the town of Zillebeke in Flanders, he had saved the life of another German soldier who had become entangled in barbed wire while attempting to deliver a message from the trenches to a battery of artillery located just behind the lines. Due to a miscommunication, the battery had opened fire on German trenches, instead of the English lines. In the course of this bombardment, several soldiers were killed and the radio lines had been cut. In desperation, an officer scribbled out a message ordering the artillery to cease fire, handed it to a nearby corporal and told him to deliver it as quickly as humanly possible. The name of this corporal was Adolf Hitler. Shortly after leaving the trenches, he was blown off his feet by an incoming shell and, although unwounded, became stuck in a nest of barbed wire.

At that same moment, Sergeant Hunyadi emerged from the bunker where he had been seeking shelter from the guns. Seeing the corporal tangled like an insect in a spider's web, and hearing the man's cries for help, he used a pair of pliers to cut the soldier loose from the snare of rusty talons.

When the war was over, Hunyadi went on to become one of the most successful detectives in the history of the Berlin police force.

Even though he had refused to join Hitler's newly founded National Socialist Party, an act which would normally have guaranteed the swift termination of his career, Hitler never forgot the debt he owed Hunyadi and refused to have him dismissed.

Although frustrated by Hunyadi's stubbornness, Hitler allowed the detective to continue his work unhindered by any lack of political affiliation.

But Hitler's patience with his old friend came to an end in 1938, when he was informed by his intelligence service that Hunyadi's wife, Franziska, a woman of legendary beauty in Berlin, had been born into a family of Sephardic Jews, who had emigrated from Spain generations before.

Hunyadi was summoned to the Berlin Headquarters of the Security Service. There he was informed that he should immediately begin divorce proceedings against his wife. An excuse would be provided by the courts. The paperwork would be expedited. The whole thing would be finalised within a week, after which his wife would receive permission to leave the country.

When Hunyadi protested, saying that he would rather leave the country with his wife than divorce her and remain in Germany, he was told that this was not an option. His services were required in Berlin. Any failure to carry out Hitler's wishes would result in the arrest of his wife and the certainty of transport to the women's concentration camp at Belsen.

Faced with this ultimatum, Hunyadi had no choice but to agree. The divorce papers were drawn up, Hunyadi signed them, and Franziska departed for Spain, where she was taken in by distant relatives.

With Hitler's blessing, and under his personal protection, Hunyadi continued his work as an investigator, adding to his earlier reputation with a string of successful cases. Hitler himself called upon Hunyadi to undertake a number of investigations, including one in which a British major with a briefcase handcuffed to his wrist had washed up on the coast of Spain. It appeared that the dead man, whose name was William Martin, had been killed in a plane crash off the Spanish coast. Although Martin had managed to make his way into a damaged life raft, he succumbed to injuries and drowned before reaching the shore, where he was found by fishermen as they prepared to set out their nets. Spanish authorities, being sympathetic to the German cause, had allowed German intelligence to open and photograph the contents of the briefcase before turning the body over to the British Embassy. The documents turned out to be a complete work-up of a planned invasion of Sardinia, signed by several members of the Allied High Command. In spite of the fact that Martin had been carrying tickets to a London theatre production, as well as a letter from his fiancée – details which did as much to convince the German High Command as the contents of the briefcase itself – Hunyadi's recommendation was to treat the whole thing as a trick.

Disregarding the detective's warning, Hitler ordered more than 20,000 combat troops to Sardinia, where they prepared for the imminent arrival of the Allies. By the time they figured out that Major Martin and his battle plans had indeed been a decoy all along, the invasion of Normandy had already begun.

Even before Hunyadi had returned from Spain, it came to Hitler's attention through an informant in the Spanish government that the detective had secretly met with Franziska and, in a private ceremony, married her a second time.

Seeing this as a personal betrayal of the trust he had placed in Hunyadi, Hitler ordered the detective to be arrested, stripped of his membership in the Berlin Police Department and sent to Flossenburg. There, he was to await a trial whose outcome was a foregone conclusion.

In November of 1944, Leopold Hunyadi was dragged from his cell, and hauled before a magistrate in an improvised courtroom at the Flossenburg mess hall, where he received the news that he had been sentenced to death by hanging.

From that day to this, Hunyadi had lived in a kind of suspended animation, never knowing which day was to be his last. In the beginning, each time he heard footsteps in the hall outside his cell, his heart would clench like a fist at the thought that they were coming for him now. This happened so many hundreds of times that he grew numb to it, as if a part of him had already departed from his body and was waiting, somewhere beyond the concrete wall, for the rest to follow. Although the tiny window in his cell was too high up for him to have a view, he could sometimes hear the wooden trapdoor of the gallows clunking open in the courtyard just outside his room. Rather than terrifying Hunyadi, the sound gave him comfort, because it meant that the Flossenburg gallows was operating on a drop system, which would kill its victims quickly, rather than a different method, also in use, by which men would be hoisted up a pole and left to dangle while they slowly choked to death.

To pass the time, Hunyadi made contact with the men on either side of him. He could not see or speak to them, so he employed a system known as the Polybius Square, which separated the alphabet into five rows of five letters, each letter in its own box, and with C and K in the same box. By tapping a heating pipe that ran through the rooms, the first set of taps indicating the horizontal position and the second set showing the vertical position within the box, it was possible to spell out letters.

Hunyadi had learned the system early in his career and had often eavesdropped on conversations between prisoners when carrying out investigations, sometimes even using the system to communicate with prisoners he had arrested, who mistook him for another prisoner and often divulged information that they would never have told the police.

Men came and went; all of them high-ranking officers, government officials or political prisoners. From this, Hunyadi came to understand that this particular prison block at Flossenburg had been selected as the final destination for those whose exits from this world had been decreed by the Führer himself.

From newcomers, Hunyadi learned about the advance of the Allied armies, and he guessed that it would not be long before either the Russians or the Americans overran the camp. While his fellow prisoners tapped out their messages of hope that the Allies would save them, Hunyadi realised that the approach of these armies would only hasten their deaths.

The sun had just set that day when the door swung open and a guard named Krol walked in.

Hunyadi had been lying on his bunk. Now he sat up in

confusion. 'What's going on?' he asked.

'Get undressed,' ordered the guard.

Hunyadi, who had been asleep when Krol opened the door, was at first so confused by this command that he just sat on his bunk and did not move.

Angered by Hunyadi's stupor, Krol stepped forward and fetched the detective a mighty slap across the face. 'Strip, damn you!' he bellowed.

Blearily, Hunyadi obeyed.

When at last he stood naked in front of Kroll, the guard turned and marched out of the room. 'Follow me!' he commanded.

As Hunyadi left his cell for the first time in months, another guard fell in behind him and he walked between the two men, the almost noiseless shuffle of his bare feet in stark contrast to the crunch of the guards' hobnailed boots upon the concrete floor.

It was only when they turned a corner and he could see the courtyard dead ahead, that he finally grasped what was happening.

His heart began to thunder, as if it was trying to hammer its way out of his chest.

He could see the gallows now, and on it were three nooses, hanging side by side. Two men, as naked as Hunyadi, stood with the nooses in front of them, hands bound behind their backs. Nobody stood behind the third noose, and Hunyadi understood that it was meant for him.

He did not recognise the men. The paleness of their flesh appeared grotesque.

Why do they need us to be naked? Hunyadi wondered to himself. What final insult is this?

He was halfway across the courtyard now. Little pebbles in the gravel dug into his heels.

He thought of Franziska. He wondered what she was doing now. He had heard stories of people feeling something they described as a kind of snapping shock at the moment when their loved ones passed away, as if some invisible thread were snapping. I wonder if she'll feel it, thought Hunyadi.

And then suddenly Hunyadi realised that the terror which had haunted him for so many days that he could no longer recall what it felt like to live without it was only the fear of dying and not of death itself.

As soon as he understood that, even the fear of dying lost its grip on him and faded away into the still air of the courtyard.

Krol turned and looked back at Hunyadi, to make sure that the man had not begun to falter. And the guard, who had led so many men to their deaths these past few months, was astonished to see Hunyadi smiling.

'Stop!' called a voice.

All three men, the two guards and Hunyadi, came to an abrupt halt. They turned in unison to see a man, wearing the finely tailored uniform of a camp administrator, come tumbling out of the same doorway from which they had only just emerged.

'What is it?' demanded Krol. 'Bring him back,' said the man.

'I will not!' roared Krol. 'I have my orders!'

'Your orders have been overruled,' said the administrator, 'unless you'd care to take it up with General Rattenhuber in Berlin!'

Krol blinked, as if a bright light was suddenly shining into his face. Grabbing Hunyadi by the arm, he marched the naked man back inside, followed by the second guard, who looked as confused as his prisoner.

As the three men stepped into the shadows of the concrete block house, they heard the heavy clunk of gallows trap doors swinging open.

'What is happening?' stammered Hunyadi.

To this, Krol just shook his head in stunned amazement.

'What's happening,' explained the administrator, 'is that your death has been postponed.'

'But why?'

'You have a friend in high places, Hunyadi. Very high places indeed.'

'Hitler?' gasped Hunyadi.

The administrator nodded.

'But he's the one who put me here!' shouted Hunyadi. 'I demand an explanation!' But even as he spoke, Hunyadi became aware of how difficult it was to make demands of any kind when fat, middle-aged and the only naked man in the room.

The administrator, who had retrieved Hunyadi's clothes from his cell, now dumped the reeking garments at his feet. 'Ask him yourself when you see him,' he said.

'Pekkala,' said Stalin, as soon as Major Kirov had left the room, 'there is something we need to discuss.'

'Can this not wait?' asked Pekkala. 'Every minute that I linger here in Moscow brings Hunyadi one step closer to Lilya.'

'It concerns Lilya,' answered Stalin, 'and her family, as well.'

'You mean her husband and their child?'

'Exactly. So you have not forgotten them?'

'Of course not,' replied Pekkala. 'I still remember the photograph you showed me, back when I first agreed to work with you.'

'Yes.' Stalin paused to clear his throat in a long, gravelly eruption from his smoke-clogged lungs. 'Let us talk about that picture.'

When Stalin had sent the young Lieutenant Kirov to retrieve Pekkala from Siberia, it had been with one purpose in mind – to conduct a secret investigation into the death of the Tsar and his family. Although a statement had been issued long ago, confirming the executions in the basement of a house in Ekaterinburg, which had once belonged to a merchant named Ipatiev, Stalin had harboured his own suspicions about the accuracy of the report. He had become fixated on the possibility that one person in particular might have survived – the Tsar's only son, Alexei, whose frailty, caused by haemophilia, had consumed the royal couple even to the end of their days. It was this very frailty, combined with the young man's youth and innocence, which led Stalin to believe the executioners might have taken pity upon the boy, and perhaps even on some of the daughters as well. A steady flow of rumours had circulated, not only in Russia but throughout the world, that various members of the Romanov clan, once thought to have been butchered in captivity, might still be alive, after all. Eventually, inevitably, these suspicions loomed so large in Stalin's mind that he knew he must find out the truth. And even as the thought occurred to him, he realised that there was only one man alive who knew enough about the Romanovs to dig out the truth once and for all. It was the Emerald Eye.

Stalin had kept Pekkala alive for a reason, even if he had not known at the time what that reason might amount to. The execution order had been there on Stalin's desk and he had been about to sign it when he hesitated. Such a thing had never happened before. Even he did not know what had caused his pen to hover over the page. It was part fear, part admiration, part practicality.

Stalin knew where to find Pekkala. What he did not know was whether the Inspector would agree to join forces with a man who had once been his enemy. It would not be enough to simply order him. In order to tip the balance in his favour, Stalin had made Pekkala an offer – complete the investigation, and then Pekkala could go free.

And he had intended to keep his word, at least in the beginning, but by the time Pekkala's investigation was completed, Stalin had changed his mind. Not only would Pekkala's brand of expertise prove useful in running the country, Stalin could not imagine how he'd ever do without it. But he knew that Pekkala could never be forced into such an arrangement. He would have to be persuaded.

In the end, all Stalin needed was a single photograph.

The picture was of Lilya Simonova, sitting at a café in Paris, where she had fled at the outset of the Revolution. Pekkala's plan had been to join her there, but his arrest by Red Guard Militia, at a lonely, snowbound checkpoint on the RussoFinnish border as he tried to leave the country, had put an end to that.

In the photo, Lilya Simonova was smiling. Sitting beside her was a man, slightly built, with dark hair combed straight back. He wore a jacket and tie and the stub of a cigarette was pinched between his thumb and second finger. He held the cigarette in the Russian manner, with the burning end balanced over his palm as if to catch the falling ash. Like Lilya, the man was also smiling. Both of them were watching something just to the left of the camera. On the other side of the table was a pram, its hood pulled up to shelter the infant from the sun.

Procuring such a photograph had not been difficult. Stalin's network of informants had charted the whereabouts of almost every Russian émigré in Paris.

Mother. Father. Child. The picture was perfectly clear. Stalin's purpose in showing the photo to Pekkala had been equally clear – to persuade him to remain in Russia, and carry on the work he had begun when he first attached the gold and emerald badge beneath the collar of his coat. 'You must not blame her,' Stalin had told the Inspector. 'She waited. She waited a very long time. But a person cannot wait forever, can they?' Better, Stalin had explained, that Pekkala should learn the truth now than to arrive in Paris, ready to start a new life, only to find that it was once more out of reach. 'You could still go to her, of course. I have her address if you want it. One look at you and whatever peace of mind she might have won for herself in these past years would be gone forever. And let us say, for the sake of argument, that you might persuade her to leave the man she married. Let us say that she even leaves behind her child . . .'

Pekkala held up a hand for him to stop.

'You see my point,' continued Stalin. 'You and I both know that you are not this kind of man. Nor are you the monster that your enemies once believed you to be. If you were, you would never have been such a formidable opponent for people like myself. Monsters are easy to defeat. With such people, it is only a question of blood and time, since their only weapon is fear. But you, Pekkala, you won the hearts of the people of Russia, along with the respect of your enemies. I do not believe you understand how rare a thing that is. Whatever your opinion of me, those whom you once served are out there still.' Stalin brushed his hand towards the window, and out across the pale blue sky. 'They know how difficult your job can be, and how few of those who walk your path can do what must be done and still hold on to their humanity. They have not forgotten you, Pekkala, and I don't believe you have forgotten them.'

'No,' whispered Pekkala, 'I have not forgotten.'

'What I am trying to tell you', Stalin had explained, 'is that you still have a place here if you want it.' Until that moment, the thought of staying on had not occurred to Pekkala. But now the plans he'd made held no more meaning. Pekkala realised that his last gesture of affection for the woman he'd once thought would be his wife must be to let her believe he was dead.

Now Stalin opened a file and from it he removed a picture, which he slid across the desk towards Pekkala.

It was that same photograph which he had set before Pekkala all those years ago.

A sigh escaped Pekkala's lips. Even though he had recalled every detail of the picture, it still struck him to see it again. It was as if a hole had opened up in time and he found himself again, in this same room, in that moment when the course of his life had been altered by this single frozen image. 'Why show me this again?' he asked.

'The photograph is not complete,' Stalin said quietly, as if hoping that his words might pass unnoticed.

'Not complete? I don't understand,' said Pekkala.

Now Stalin removed a second picture from the file. It was the same size as the first one, and showed almost the same image, but this one appeared to have been taken from several paces further back.

The second photo showed not only Lilya Simonova and the man beside her, as well as the pram that stood between them, but also the tables on either side. From this expanded view, it was evident that the man had been sitting at a separate table and that he was with another woman. The woman was holding a baby in her arms. The baby was laughing and it was this which had drawn the attention of Lilya and the man. The other thing which this photo made obvious was that Lilya Simonova was sitting at the table by herself. A stack of notes, perhaps the uncorrected papers of her students, lay neatly on the table top, and her hand, with a pen tucked in her fingers like a cigarette, lay on the notes, to stop them from blowing away.

As he stared at the picture, Pekkala realised that the first image he had been shown, all those years ago, had, in fact, been cropped to hide the presence of the other woman, the baby and the positioning of the tables.

In the second picture, the narrative had been completely changed.

The first picture was authentic, but the story it told had been a lie.

Pekkala's mind reeled as he tried to grasp the magnitude of the deception.

'I needed you here,' explained Stalin, 'and it would have done no good to force you to remain. The decision had to be yours. That picture came across my desk just as you were completing your first case for me. The subject of the photo, taken by one of our agents in Paris, was actually the man sitting next to your fiancée. His name was Kuznetsk and he was one of the founding members of the French anti-Bolshevik League known as the White Hand. The picture was taken to provide confirmation that the man was, in fact, Kuznetsk, prior to my issuing a liquidation order.'

Pekkala looked down again at the photo. He stared at the woman and the laughing child.

'It was only when the picture was handed to me for approval that I noticed your fiancée, and I realised it could be useful in persuading you to stay and work for us.' 'Why tell me this now?' demanded Pekkala, as he struggled to contain his rage.

'Because you would have learned the truth yourself within hours of reaching Berlin, and I would rather you heard it from me than from her.'

'What difference would that make?' asked Pekkala. 'You're the one who lied to me, not her.'

'And the British are lying to both of us, which is something else we need to talk about if you can hold on to your temper long enough!'

Pekkala stood there in silence, waiting for Stalin to continue.

'In case you haven't realised this already,' Stalin told him, 'the British don't care about Lilya Simonova, at least not enough to come to us and beg for help as they have done.'

'They why would they do such a thing?'

'Because she has something they want.'

Pekkala narrowed his eyes. 'You think this is about the Diamond Stream?'

Stalin nodded.

'But the officer in the prisoner-of-war camp, the one Kirov spoke to. He said they couldn't make it work.'

'And, at the time of his capture, that was probably the truth,' agreed Stalin, 'but much could have happened since then.'

'Assuming you are correct,' said Pekkala, 'and that this device is now operational, that still does not explain why you are in such a hurry to rescue a British agent. Even if they are our allies, you can't honestly believe that they will share the secrets of this weapon.'

'They won't,' confirmed Stalin, 'but Lilya Simonova might.' Pekkala breathed out sharply through his nose. 'And why would she do that?'

'Because of what I am about to offer you,' replied Stalin.

'And what is that?' asked Pekkala.

'A future for the two of you in Moscow.'

'Her home is in Paris, not here.'

'No, Pekkala. That is where you are wrong. Paris was never her home. She did not go there by choice, the way you chose to come

159

to Russia, all those years ago. Bring her back to the place where she is from and I give you my word you can both live out your days in peace, as you were always meant to do.'

'For a price,' muttered Pekkala.

Stalin shrugged and smiled. 'Nothing is free, Inspector. Especially not diamonds.'

'You will have my answer soon enough,' Pekkala told him as he turned to leave.

'That is all I ask,' replied Stalin. 'Now, if you could send in Major Kirov on your way out, I will explain to him what must be done.'

Kirov was waiting in the hallway, having chosen not to linger in the outer office, under the squinting stare of Stalin's secretary Poskrebychev. It was cold in the marble-floored hallway and a pale afternoon light seeped in through the tall windows. The two guards who stood outside Stalin's office had come prepared with winter greatcoats and dense *ushanka* hats which bristled with a brownish-grey synthetic pile known to the soldiers as 'fish fur'. With hands balled into fists inside his pockets and shoulders hunched against the shivers that crabbed across his back, Kirov paced about, wondering what could be taking Pekkala so long.

When Pekkala finally emerged, Kirov sighed with relief. He was anxious to be gone from here, and not just because of the cold. Although he had visited the Kremlin many times, and had always been impressed with its architectural beauty, Kirov never felt comfortable there. Maybe it had to do with the hidden passageways he knew existed behind the wood-panelled walls, along which Stalin was known to tread at all hours of the day or night, carrying his shoes so as not to make a noise. Or perhaps it was the lack of voices. Everyone in this building seemed compelled to speak in hushed tones, as if they knew that whatever they said would be overheard by someone else, invisible and dangerous, judging their every word. Although he had no proof of it, Kirov did not doubt that this was true. And the last thing which made Kirov nervous whenever he stepped into this labyrinth was the fact that he knew he didn't belong here. Although he had reached the rank of major and was, after all, frequently summoned to this building by none other than the Vozhd – the Boss – himself, Kirov had come to realise that he would never belong to Stalin's inner circle. Neither would he ever achieve that indispensability that Pekkala had been given from the start. If it weren't for the Inspector, thought Kirov, Stalin wouldn't even know my name.

'He wants to see you,' said Pekkala.

'What?' asked Kirov. 'Just me?'

'That's what he said.'

'What about?' Have I done something wrong, wondered Kirov.

'He didn't tell me anything,' replied Pekkala.

Unable to hide his nervousness at this unexpected summons, Kirov made his way back through the lair of Poskrebychev and returned to Stalin's study.

Out in the hallway, after only a few paces, Pekkala came to a halt, so overwhelmed by what he had just heard that he could no longer bring himself to place one foot in front of the other.

But it was not rage which sapped him of his strength.

In his years of working with the Kremlin, Pekkala had learned never to apply the rules of other men to Joseph Stalin. With him, different logic prevailed. Only a fool would believe what Stalin said, and most of them had long since paid with their lives for such naivety. With Stalin, what mattered were his actions, not his promises.

The Russians even had a word for this. They called it *maskirovka*. Translated, it meant 'camouflage', but in the minds of men like Stalin it transformed into the art of deception.

In order to survive among men like the leader of Russia, and those who carried out his will because they had been mesmerised by fear, Pekkala had taught himself to see beyond the outrage of dishonesty. Instead, the task became to answer one simple question – What does Stalin want? – knowing that no amount of blood, hypocrisy or lies would sway the Boss from his desires.

As long as Pekkala proved himself useful in fulfilling Stalin's wishes, he was perfectly safe. The trick had become to carry out his master's will, and not lose his soul in the process. Terrible as it was to know that he'd been lied to all these years, Pekkala was not surprised to hear it. He even understood. Stalin had needed him, and so the Boss had done whatever was necessary to continue their fragile alliance.

It served no purpose to be angry with Stalin, now or ever. How could it, when all traces of guilt or remorse had been scalpeled from his character? There were times when Pekkala even pitied the man, existing in the spiritual wasteland of someone whose word counted for nothing.

For Pekkala, what mattered now was not how to grapple with the depth of Stalin's betrayal, but to judge whether the offer he had made would ever be matched by his deeds.

Kirov, meanwhile, stood before the desk of Joseph Stalin.

'Sit down!' the Boss commanded, nodding towards the chair on the opposite side of his desk.

Kirov subsided into the chair like a marionette whose strings had been cut.

'I am placing you in charge,' Stalin announced.

'In charge of what?' Kirov asked breathlessly.

'Of the journey you are taking to Berlin.'

These words so confused Kirov that, at first, he could not bring himself to comprehend their meaning. Blankly, he stared at his master.

'Did you hear what I said?' asked Stalin.

'I heard you, Comrade Stalin,' replied Kirov. 'I just don't understand why you are saying it. I work for the Inspector. It is he who gives the orders. That's the way it's always been.'

'You work for *me*,' Stalin corrected him, 'and it is *I* who give the orders.'

'Of course, but . . .' And suddenly he faltered. Stalin raised his heavy eyebrows. 'Yes?'

'Very well, Comrade Stalin,' answered Kirov, finally coming to his senses.

'Good.' Stalin pressed his palms together. 'Then you may go.'

Kirov knew what he was supposed to do next. He should have

risen to his feet, saluted and left. Instead, halfway out of the room, he all but skidded to a halt and wheeled about.

Stalin was staring at the Major, as if he had just placed a wager with himself on whether Kirov could make his exit smoothly. From the look on Stalin's face, he had just won that little bet.

'Why?' gasped Kirov. 'Why are you doing this to Pekkala?'

'Because I don't trust him,' came the answer.

'Forgive me for saying so, Comrade Stalin, but you have never trusted him.'

'That is true,' agreed Stalin, 'at least with regard to his following my instructions, but he has always managed, one way or another, to carry out the task I set for him. I make no secret, to you or to anyone else, that I find Pekkala to be the most disobedient person I have ever allowed to keep on breathing. We have an unspoken truce, the Inspector and I. We may be very different, he and I, but we do have one important thing in common.'

'And what is that?' asked Kirov.

'The survival of the country,' answered Stalin. 'This has been enough to secure our allegiance to each other. At least, it was until today.'

'What has changed?' asked Kirov.

'This business with Lilya Simonova. For years, she has existed as a kind of dream for Pekkala – a beautiful image of the past, frozen in time since the Revolution began. But now that past has collided with the present, or soon will anyway, if you can get her out of Berlin in one piece.'

'We will do everything we can . . .'

'That is not what concerns me, Major Kirov. If she is there, Pekkala will find her. I have no doubt of that. It's what happens after that which troubles me.'

Now Kirov had begun to understand. 'And you are worried he will not return?'

'What I'm worried about,' answered Stalin, 'is that he will not return with the information these Englishman are so desperate to obtain that they would come to us, cap in hand, to ask for help. I want that information here in front of me.' He jabbed one thick, blunt finger on polished wood. 'And only when I know exactly what it is, will I consider passing it along to those temporary gentlemen from London.'

'I understand,' said Kirov. 'Would you like me to bring in the Inspector so that you can inform him about the change in command?'

'You can take care of that yourself,' muttered Stalin. 'I have another meeting.' And he began to fidget with the papers laid out in front of him.

Kirov didn't tell Pekkala right away. He would rather not have told him at all.

The whole drive back to Pitnikov Street, the two men remained silent.

Pekkala did not press him for information, since it was clear from the look on Kirov's face that a storm was brewing in his head.

The only sound was the soft voice of their driver, Zolkin, as he sang one of his favourite Ukrainian folksongs, called 'The Duckling Swims', about a young man going off to war. His low and mournful voice was interrupted from time to time by a grinding crash of the Emka's mangled gears.

Finally, when they had tramped up to their office on the fifth floor of the building, Kirov revealed what Stalin had told him. As Kirov spoke, he could not bring himself even to look at Pekkala. Instead, he looked out of the window, past the luminous green leaves of basil, sage and rosemary which he grew in earthenware pots upon the windowsill, and rattled off Stalin's instructions.

It seemed to take a long while to explain what was, in fact, a very simple order. By the time Kirov had finished, he felt completely out of breath. And now he waited, looking without really seeing through the dusty windowpanes, for the Inspector to make his pronouncement.

'It's a good idea,' said Pekkala.

Astonished, Kirov whirled about. 'Do you really think so?' he gasped. It was the last thing he had expected to hear.

Pekkala had settled into his chair beside the wheezy iron stove. The stove was not lit and he had put his feet up on the circular cooking plates. From where Kirov stood, he could see the double thick soles of the Inspector's heavy boots, and the iron heel plates, scuffed to a mercury shine. The Inspector seemed perfectly at ease, almost as if the idea had been his all along.

'Congratulations on your first command,' Pekkala added graciously.

'Why, thank you,' stammered Kirov.

'Long overdue, if you ask me,' continued Pekkala.

'Well, now that you mention it,' replied Kirov, his shattered confidence slowly reassembling, 'I have been looking forward to the challenge for some time. I just never thought it would come.'

'Stalin is no fool when it comes to recognising talent.' Overwhelmed, Kirov strode across the room and shook Pekkala's hand.

'Be sure to tell your wife,' said Pekkala. 'I expect she will be pleased.'

'I will!' Kirov replied eagerly.

Elizaveta worked as a filing clerk in the records office on the fourth floor of the Lubyanka building which had, for many years, been the headquarters of Soviet Internal Security.

'As soon as I have picked up our equipment for the journey,' Kirov continued, 'I'll head upstairs and tell her the good news.' 'If that suits you, of course, Comrade Major,' Pekkala answered with a playful gravity.

'I believe it does,' said Kirov, lifting his chin dramatically. Then he set off to Lubyanka.

Arriving at the Lubyanka building, Kirov immediately made his way down to the basement, to consult with Lazarev, the armourer.

Lazarev was a legendary figure at Lubyanka. From his workshop in the basement, he managed the issue and repair of all weapons supplied to Moscow NKVD. He had been there from the beginning, personally appointed by Felix Dzerzhinsky, the first head of the Cheka, who commandeered what had once been the offices of the All-Russian Insurance Company and converted it into the All-Russia Extraordinary Commission to Combat Counter-revolution and Sabotage. From then on, the imposing yellow-stone building served as an administrative complex, prison and place of execution. The Cheka had changed its name several times since then, from OGPU to GPU to NKVD, transforming under various directors into its current incarnation. Throughout these gruelling and sometimes bloody metamorphoses, which emptied, reoccupied and emptied once again the desks of countless servants of the state, Lazarev had remained at his post, until only he remained of those who had set the great machine of Internal State Security in motion. This was not due to luck or skill in navigating the minefield of the purges, but rather to the fact that, no matter who did the killing and who did the dying above ground, a gunsmith was always needed to make sure the weapons kept working.

For a man of such mythic status, Lazarev's appearance came as something of a disappointment. He was short and hunched, with pock-marked cheeks so pale they seemed to confirm the rumours that he never travelled above ground, but migrated like a mole through secret tunnels known only to him beneath the streets of Moscow. He wore a tan shop coat, whose frayed pockets sagged from the weight of bullets, screwdrivers and gun parts. He wore this tattered coat buttoned right up to his throat, giving rise to another rumour; namely that he wore nothing underneath. This story was reinforced by the sight of Lazarev's bare legs beneath the knee-length coat. He had a peculiar habit of never lifting his feet from the floor as he moved about the armoury, choosing instead to slide along like a man condemned to live on ice. He shaved infrequently, and the slivers of beard that jutted from his chin resembled the spines of a cactus. His eyes, watery blue in their shallow sockets, showed his patience with a world that did not understand his passion for the gun and the wheezy, reassuring growl of his voice, once heard, was unforgettable.

As soon as Lazarev caught sight of Kirov's highly polished boots descending the stairs, he reached below the counter, whose top was strewn with gun parts, oil cans, pull-through cloths and brass-bristled brushes, coiled like the tails of newborn puppies, and lifted out a Hungarian-made Femaru Model 37 pistol, still nestled in its brown leather holster. The weapon had been taken from the body of a Hungarian tank officer on the outskirts of Stalingrad in the winter of 1942 and was delivered to Lazarev for just such an occasion as this. In preparation for Kirov's arrival, Lazarev had cleaned the weapon and loaded its 7-round magazine with freshly oiled 7.62 ammunition.

Kirov stared at the weapon, his eye drawn to the curious eyelash-shaped extension on the magazine, designed to rest against the user's little finger when holding the gun.

Lazarev picked up the Femaru and held it out. The metal gleamed blue in the harsh light of the bulb above their heads.

'You will find this less elegant than your issue Tokarev,' he explained, 'but just as lethal under the circumstances you are likely to encounter. More importantly, it is what they'll be expecting if you are ever searched, the point being not to use the gun at all if you can help it.'

Kirov unfastened his officer's belt, the heavy brass buckle emblazoned with a cut-out star, slid off the holster containing his issue Tokarev automatic and placed it on the table. Then, he replaced it with the Hungarian pistol. 'Where do I sign?' he asked.

'No need!' Lazarev waved away the thought with a brush of his hands.

Kirov narrowed his eyes. 'But we always have to sign for weapons, and I know you are a stickler for the rules.'

Lazarev began to look flustered. 'They called me from upstairs,' he explained. 'They said there was no need for you to sign.'

'Who called?' asked Kirov.

Lazarev rolled his shoulders, as if he had a crick in his spine.

'Upstairs,' he repeated quietly.

'Why would there be no signature?' demanded Kirov. Lazarev reached across the counter top and rested his hand on Kirov's shoulder. 'You can sign when you return it,' he said, a pained expression on his face. 'How about that?' Mystified at this breach of protocol, Kirov headed for the door. Then he stopped and turned. 'I almost forgot,' he said.

'What about a weapon for Pekkala?'

Lazarev smiled. 'Do you honestly think you can persuade him

to give up that Webley of his?'

Kirov understood immediately what an impossible task that would be.

On his way to see his wife in the records office at the top of the building, Kirov stopped at the third floor, where he picked up two sets of identity papers. They consisted of a Hungarian passport, a small, sand-coloured booklet printed with the Hungarian crown and shield and the words 'Mag yar Kiralysag' and a German *Reisepass*, containing various travel permits, stamps and handwritten validations. There were also driving licences, food ration books and Hungarian Fascist Party membership cards. Kirov marvelled at the attention to detail that had gone into preparing the books. There must have been half a dozen different inks used in signatures on the pale green pages of the passport, and the books themselves had been worn down in such a way that they even matched the contours of having been carried in a man's chest pocket. If these documents had once belonged to someone else, Kirov could find no trace of alteration in the pictures, which had been heat-sealed into the identity books, cracking the emulsion of the little photograph and overlaying Kirov's face with an image of an eagle from a registration office in the Berlin suburb of Spandau.

'You'd better have this, too,' said the clerk, setting before him a stack of German Reichsmark notes. 'Spend it quickly, if you have the chance,' he advised. 'Pretty soon, it won't be worth the paper it is printed on.' Kirov picked up the brick of cash and turned to leave.

But the clerk called him back. 'You're not done yet!' he said.

'You'll need another set of clothes.'

Led through the office to a room at the back, Kirov found himself in a room full of garments, all of them in various states of disrepair. Here, he was handed an old set of clothes by an even older clerk whom he had never seen before.

The man wore a tape measure around his neck, although he never put it to use. Instead, with a squinting of one watery eye, he judged the length of Kirov's arms and legs and the width of his narrow chest, of which the major was slightly ashamed.

As Kirov held out his arms, the clerk piled on shirts and trousers and a tattered coat for him to try on.

'I do have things at home besides my uniform,' Kirov complained, his nose twitching at the smell of other men's sweat and dogs and unfamiliar cigarettes which had sunk into the cloth.

'But not like these,' explained the clerk. 'You'd be spotted as a Russian the minute you arrived in Berlin.'

'But how?' asked Kirov. 'Clothes are just clothes, after all.'

'No.' The clerk shook his head. 'And I will prove it to you. See here,' he said, holding out the collar of a shirt with a Budapest maker's label. 'The collar of a Hungarian shirt is more pointed than a Russian shirt and the way that the sleeves are attached here is different from what you would find on a German shirt. Even the way the buttons are attached, in two straight lines of thread as opposed to a cross are different from, say, on an English shirt.' With his thumb, he levered up one tiny mother-of-pearl disc, letting it wink in the light to show the manner in which it had been stitched. 'Even if those around you aren't specifically aware of these details, they will nevertheless sense that something is not right. These clothes were carefully gathered from people who had travelled to Hungary before the war.'

'Didn't anybody have anything newer?' asked Kirov. 'Or cleaner, for that matter?'

The clerk laughed. 'That is all part of the disguise! Nobody has new clothes in Berlin any more, or Budapest for that matter, and they haven't for quite some time. Nor do they have the opportunity to clean their clothes as often as they should. Believe me, Major Kirov, you may not like the way you look when I am finished with you, but you will fit right in where you are going.'

'Can you do the same thing for other countries?' he asked.

'Of course!' boomed the old man and he began to sweep his hands around the room. 'Over there is England. There is Spain, France. Turkey. Wherever you go, Major, my job is to make you invisible!'

'Inspector Pekkala is also . . .' began Kirov.

The man held up one hand to silence him. 'Do not speak to me of that barbarian! What he wears does not belong in Russia, or Germany, or anywhere else on this earth! His tailor ought to be shot. And even if he would agree to let me outfit him for this journey, which he wouldn't, it is hopeless anyway. Pekkala will never fit in. Anywhere! It's just who he is. There is no camouflage for such a man.'

At last, Kirov arrived at the records office on the fourth floor, to share the good news of his promotion with his wife.

Elizaveta was in her mid-twenties, head and shoulders shorter than Kirov, with a round and slightly freckled face, a small chin and dark, inquisitive eyes.

Few outsiders were ever permitted past the iron-grilled door which served as the entrance to the records office. But Kirov had that privilege. Thanks to Elizaveta, Kirov had been welcomed into their miniature tribe.

They retired to what had once been a storage room for cleaning supplies used by the maids at the hotel. The space had been converted by the three women who managed the records office, led by the fearsome Sergeant Gatkina, into a refuge where they could smoke and drink their tea in peace.

Elizaveta, wearing a tight-collared *gymnastiorka* tunic, dark skirt and navy-blue beret, sat upon a filing cabinet placed on its side against the wall.

Kirov paced about in front of her, animatedly describing his promotion. He expected that, at any moment, Elizaveta would leap up from her makeshift seat and embrace him.

But this did not happen.

All she said, at first, was, 'Stalin is no fool.'

'How strange,' remarked Kirov. 'That's just what the Inspector told me!'

'Stalin is not raising you up,' she told him, leaning forward and lowering her voice, as people often did when mentioning the name of Stalin. 'In fact, he might as well have sentenced you to death.'

'You're not making any sense!' blurted Kirov. 'I have been promoted!'

'In order to do what?' she demanded. 'Give orders to Pekkala? That's just not possible. As soon as you cross the border into enemy territory, that Finn will do exactly as he's always done.' 'Which is what?'

'Whatever he chooses,' she replied, 'and if that choice is to simply vanish off the face of the earth like some phantom in a fairy tale, who will be held responsible?' She raised her eyebrows, waiting for the answer which both of them already knew.

'He wouldn't do that,' said Kirov. 'He's knows the kind of trouble I'd be in.'

'Of course he does,' answered Elizaveta, 'and that's what Stalin's banking on. You are his insurance policy against Pekkala's 'disappearance, but do not think for a minute that you are actually in charge of this mission.'

'If that's what you think,' Kirov said indignantly, 'then maybe I'll surprise you.'

'That may be so,' she told him, 'but there's something I still don't understand,' she added.

'And what is that?' asked Kirov.

'Even if you do find this woman, does Pekkala really think they stand a chance of getting back together?'

'I'm not sure,' he answered honestly. 'I do know he still loves her.'

'And how do you know that?' she demanded. 'Has he told you so?'

'Not in so many words.'

'Then what makes you think it is true?'

'Pekkala used to send her money every month,' explained Kirov. 'You see, he knew exactly where she lived in Paris, at least until the war broke out. After that, he lost track of her.'

'So they were communicating up to that point?'

'No,' Kirov told her. 'He never told her where the money really came from.' 'Well, where did she think it was coming from?'

'It was transferred from a Moscow bank under the name of Rada Obolenskaya, the headmistress of the school where she had worked before the Revolution. According to Pekkala, Comrade Obolenskaya had always taken good care of Lilya and so she had no reason to doubt that Obolenskaya was actually the source.'

'But why on earth wouldn't he tell her?' Elizaveta exclaimed in exasperation.

'Until today, when Comrade Stalin told him otherwise, Pekkala was under the impression that Lilya had got married, and that she even had a family. He did not want to take the risk of damaging the new life she had made for herself. But he never fell out of love with her and I don't think he ever will, whatever happens when we reach Berlin.'

'If he thinks he can just pick up where he left off,' said Elizaveta, 'then he is just a dreamer.'

'There are worse things to be,' Kirov answered defensively, 'and maybe he just wants to save her life. After all, that's what I'd do for you.'

Only now did she rise to embrace him. 'I want you to make me a promise,' she said.

'What would that be?' asked Kirov.

'If it comes down to you or Pekkala,' she said, her voice muffled against the chest of his neatly pressed tunic, 'promise you'll make the right decision.'

'All right,' Kirov told her softly. 'I will.'

When the money first started arriving in her account, back in the summer of 1933, Lilya Simonova thought that somebody had made a mistake. After receiving her statement in the mail, and seeing that there was considerably more in her account than should have been there, she went to the bank manager to find out what had happened.

'Everything is in order,' he assured her. 'The money has been wired from Moscow.'

'But by whom?'

'Rada Igorevna Obolenskaya,' replied the manager. 'Does that name sound familiar to you?'

'Why yes,' said Lilya, still confused. 'Yes, it does, but . . .'

'I am given to understand,' interrupted the manager, 'that additional amounts will be deposited each month.'

'For how long?'

The manager shrugged. 'No limit has been set.'

'And is there any message from Rada Igorevna?'

'None that I know of.'

'What should I do about this?' Lilya wondered aloud.

'I'll tell you exactly what to do,' said the manager. 'Take the money. Take it and be glad.'

The next month, just as the manager had said, another deposit arrived from Moscow. And it continued to arrive, without fail, for the following eight years.

Lilya Simonova attempted to make contact with her former employer. She had no idea where the headmistress might be living but wrote to the address of the school where they had worked together, hoping that she might still be there or that someone who remembered her might be able to forward it. But she received no reply and, after many attempts, she finally gave up.

In 1937, at a place called the Café Dimitri, where expatriate Russians often gathered to drink tea, Lilya ran into someone she had known in Petrograd before the Revolution. Her name was Olga Komarova and her children had attended the school where Lilya taught. When Lilya mentioned to her the gifts which had been sent by Rada Obolenskaya, a strange look passed over the face of her friend.

'But that's impossible,' said Olga Komarova. 'The school was burned to the ground, right at the beginning of the Revolution. It couldn't have been more than a day after you left.'

'Well,' replied Lilya, 'that explains why no one got the letters I sent. But Rada was a woman of means. I don't think she needed her job to survive financially. Even with the school gone, I'm sure she still had money tucked away.'

Olga Komarova reached across and rested her hand upon Lilya's. 'No,' she said softly, 'you don't understand. The poor woman was in the school when the Red Guards came to burn it down. They told her to leave, but she refused, so they burned the school anyway, with her inside it. Lilya, she's been dead for years.'

'You must be mistaken,' Lilya insisted.

'But I'm not,' said Olga Komarova. 'I saw them drag her body from the ashes. She was still holding that camera of hers. Aside from you and that school, I think it was the only thing she valued in this world.'

The next day, Lilya Simonova went back to the bank manager and told him what she had learned.

'There's a simple explanation,' said the man. 'She must have left it to you in her will. The executors of her estate must have arranged for these payments to be made.'

Lilya took him at his word but, even though it was a tidy explanation, her suspicions were never completely laid to rest. Then, in June of 1941, when the German army launched its campaign against Russia, banking routes between Moscow and Paris, which had been occupied by Germany for the previous year, shut down and the money stopped coming in as abruptly as it had first appeared.

An hour after leaving Lubyanka, Kirov was back at the office on Pitnikov Street.

There, Pekkala informed them that a car was already on its way to transport them to a military airfield on the outskirts of Moscow. As yet, neither of the men knew exactly how they would be arriving in Berlin.

Gloomily, Kirov slouched in the chair by the stove. Little clouds of raw cotton peeked from the chair's tattered upholstery. Kirov's condition did not look much better than that of his chair. He had already traded in his uniform and was now dressed in the Hungarian clothes he had been given. He looked depressingly shabby, unemployed and unemployable.

'You don't look so bad,' said Pekkala, trying to cheer him up.

'That's easy for you to say,' grumbled Kirov. 'You get to wear your own kit.'

'It's because I have a certain universal quality,' Pekkala announced grandly.

'He said you were a barbarian.'

'There are worse things to be called.'

Realising that he was never going to gain the upper hand in this conversation, Kirov turned his attention to the pistol given to him by Lazarev. 'I can't understand it,' he said. 'You have to sign for everything in that place! And you get in all kinds of trouble if you don't return every little scrap of equipment you are issued. Why would they change their minds, all of a sudden?'

'What would be the point of having you sign for a gun you will never return?' asked Pekkala.

'But of course I would return it!' protested Kirov.

'Not if we don't make it back,' replied Pekkala.

Kirov stared at him in amazement. 'Do you mean they don't expect us to survive?'

'It looks that way to me.'

Kirov launched himself to his feet, as if he meant to march back to NKVD headquarters and demand an explanation. Then, realising the futility of such a gesture, he slumped back into his chair.

Just then, they heard the squeak of brakes.

Pekkala walked over to the window and glanced down into the street. 'It's time for us to leave,' he said.

As Kirov and Pekkala set off on their journey to Berlin, Inspector Leopold Hunyadi had only just arrived in the city, still wearing the rags of his prison uniform.

Now he stood face to face with Adolf Hitler.

For this meeting, Hitler had chosen the rubble-strewn Chancellery gardens, where he was in the habit of walking his German shepherd dog, Blondi, at least once every day. He had dismissed his usual escort of armed guards, determined to keep his time with Hunyadi as secret as possible.

'Hunyadi,' muttered Hitler, drawing out the man's name like a growl. 'What have I done to deserve this?'

Hunyadi had no idea what Hitler was talking about, but it occurred to him that if he so much as asked, he might find himself on the next plane back to Flossenburg. So, for now at least, he held his tongue.

Hitler began to walk along the pathway, which had once been lined with flowers but now resembled a gangplank laid across a cratered field of mud. The dog walked on ahead, straining at its leash.

'There is a spy,' continued Hitler.

Hunyadi looked around at the jagged teeth of broken windows. 'Here?' he asked. 'Now?'

Hitler shook his head, then jerked his chin towards the ground.

'Down there, in the bunker.'

'How do you know?'

'Information has leaked out. The Allies are broadcasting it on the radio, as if to taunt me for my ignorance. I cannot allow it to continue. That is why I brought you here.'

'You want me to find the spy?'

'Exactly.'

'But what about your own security service?'

Hitler breathed out sharply. 'If Rattenhuber and his gang of Munich Bulls had done their jobs when they were supposed to, you would not be standing there now.'

'No,' answered Hunyadi. 'I would be dead.'

Hitler glanced at him and shrugged. 'Death awaits us all, Hunyadi.'

Hunyadi cleared his throat. 'If I may ask, why call on me for this? I do not see why you would place your faith in me, especially since you yourself ordered my execution for what you have termed crimes against the state.'

'Ah!' sighed Hitler, resting his hand briefly on Hunyadi's shoulder. 'Yours was a crime inspired by love, misguided of course, but understandable in the circumstances. It is because of this love that I know I can trust you to carry out your task.'

'I don't understand,' said Hunyadi.

'At my request, your wife Franziska has been taken into custody by some friends who have remained loyal to me among the Spanish authorities.'

Hunyadi felt the bile rise in his throat. 'On what charges?' he spluttered.

'I am sure they have come up with something,' remarked Hitler. 'Why don't you just take me back to Flossenburg and hang me?' demanded Hunyadi. 'Why must you put me through this?'

'Because, my old friend, I no longer know whom to trust,' Hitler stamped his heel into the sandy soil, as if to trample out a fire which had broken out beneath his feet, 'down there in the bowels of the Reich. If I give this mission to a member of my own security, who is to say I am not entrusting an investigation to the very people who should be investigated? No, I needed someone from outside. Someone I know will not smile in my face and then stab me in the back, as others have tried to do. Don't you see, Hunyadi? It is your hatred which convinces me that you are the right man for the job, and your love for that woman which has guaranteed your loyalty.' Now he fixed Hunyadi with a stare. 'Do you honestly mean to turn me down?'

'Under the circumstances,' answered the detective, 'I don't see how I can.'

Hitler nodded with satisfaction. 'Then it is settled.' He reached into his tunic and removed a thick envelope. 'Here is everything I know about the case.' He handed the envelope to Hunyadi.

'If what you say is true,' said the detective, 'I may need to question some very high-ranking people.'

'Yes.'

'I doubt they will appreciate the intrusion.'

'Indeed they won't, but you have my word they will endure it. In the envelope I have just given you,' said Hitler, 'you'll find a number that will connect you directly to the main switchboard in the bunker. If anybody tries to obstruct you in your duties, no matter who they are, just have them call and I will personally explain the situation.'

They had reached a place where they could go no further. The path was blocked by a huge piece of smashed masonry and the ground beyond had been cratered by explosions.

From the moment he had set eyes on Hitler that day, Hunyadi's first thought had been to kill the man, with a rock, with his bare hands, with his teeth, and then to simply vanish among the ruins. But what Hitler had said about Franziska paralysed him. He had no doubt that, even with the Allies and the Red Army closing in upon Berlin and the German army little more than a heap of wreckage propped up by pensioners and teenage boys, there were some still prepared to carry out their Führer's wishes. When these men learned of what he'd done, Franziska would be dead within the hour.

He wished he could go back in time, to that moment when he had emerged from his bunker and found the young corporal ensnared by the rusting barbed wire. He wished he could have turned his back and walked back down again into the musty earth, leaving the man to be torn to shreds by their own artillery.

The fact that this had even occurred to him, a man who usually confined himself within a world of fact, not dreams, showed him just how powerless he was.

And Hitler knew it, too. Why else would he have dared to meet Hunyadi alone and without his usual escort of armed guards?

Now, in one last attempt to reason with the man, Hunyadi reached out and took hold of Hitler's arm.

Hitler was startled. Few people ever touched him. Even his mistress seemed to hesitate before allowing her pale flesh to brush against his own, still paler skin.

The dog began to growl, lips curling up around its teeth. Realising his mistake, Hunyadi let his hand slip away. 'Listen to me,' he said. 'We have been bound together all these years by the debt you think you owe me. Allow me to absolve you of that now. Just let us go, me and my wife, and if you cannot do that, then at least let her go free. Don't hold this over me. It may well be that we no longer share that friendship, but at least there was a time when we did not think of each other as enemies. I beg you to remember that.'

Hitler stared at him. A look of intense curiosity spread across his face.

For one brief moment, Hunyadi convinced himself that his wish might be granted, after all.

'The debt I owe you is mine to repay,' said Hitler. 'I will decide when the slate has been wiped clean, and I will decide how it's done.' He glanced up at the sky. 'It will be night soon,' he said. 'Time for me to head back underground. I will leave you here, Hunyadi. You can find your own way home.' With those words, Hitler turned and made his way back towards the Chancellery entrance. The dog followed close upon his heels.

As the sun set over the ruins of the city, the brassy evening light suffused with yellow dust, Hunyadi set off towards his flat on the Kronenstrasse. No one seemed to notice him as he shuffled along in his dirty prison clothes. He looked like just another refugee, of which there were thousands roaming the streets in search of shelter and food.

In spite of the fact that Hunyadi had not been home in weeks, he found the door to his apartment still locked and everything inside untouched since the moment of his arrest. The air was musty and still. In spite of the cold, he opened the windows, then sat down at his desk, turned on the light and read through the report Hitler had given him.

When he had finished, he sat back in the chair, laced his fingers together and set his hands on top of his head. For a long time, he just stared at the open window, watching how the night breeze brushed against the curtains. There must be some way out of this, he thought. Lost in the caverns of his mind, he searched for a solution, but there was none. Hunyadi was utterly trapped. There was nothing to do but proceed with the task he had been given.

He returned the envelope of documents to his chest pocket, rose to his feet, breathed in deeply and strode out of the room.

After a short walk across town, he arrived at the Pankow district police station where, up to the moment of his arrest, he had spent his entire career.

The sergeant on duty was surprised to see him. 'Inspector Hunyadi!' he exclaimed, 'I thought . . .' he hesitated, 'well, I thought they . . .'

'They did,' replied Hunyadi.

The sergeant nodded vigorously. 'And what can I do for you, Inspector?'

'I will be requiring my old office.'

'But I don't think it's available,' spluttered the man. 'It belongs to Inspector Hossbach now.'

'Hossbach!' muttered Hunyadi. An image appeared in his mind of the small, rosy-cheeked man, his face split almost in two by a patently insincere smile. 'And how long did he wait,' Hunyadi asked the sergeant, 'to move into my room after I left?'

The sergeant's tactful silence was an answer in itself. Hunyadi climbed up the first flight of stairs and made his way along a stretch of industrial carpeting worn almost bare by the path of his own feet over the years until he reached his office door.

He did not bother to knock.

Hossbach was sitting with his feet up on the desk, reading

a monthly magazine called *Youth*, which passed itself off as a pictorial journal celebrating what it touted as 'the human body and spirit' but was, in fact, little more than pornography.

As soon as the door opened, Hossbach tossed the magazine over his shoulder and swept his feet off the desk. He snatched up the receiver of his phone, as if to give the impression that he had been engaged in some important conversation. 'God damn it to hell!' he shouted. 'Didn't anyone teach you how to knock?' Then he paused, astonished, the heavy black receiver frozen in his hand. 'You!' he gasped.

'Hossbach.' It looked for a moment as if Hunyadi was going to say more, but he didn't, leaving the man's name to hover in the air like the tone of a lightly struck bell.

'What are you doing here?' asked Hossbach, replacing the receiver in its cradle. 'I thought they shipped you out in chains!'

'I managed to get loose,' remarked Hunyadi.

'So,' Hossbach narrowed his eyes in confusion, 'are you back on the force?'

'Not exactly. I'm doing some work for an old acquaintance.'

'And you need my help?' Hossbach wondered aloud.

'I need you to get out of my office.'

And now the irritating smile began to spread across Hossbach's face. 'Well now, Hunyadi,' he began, 'I'm just not sure that's possible.' Hunyadi removed the envelope from his coat pocket and began to rummage through its contents.

'What are you doing?' asked Hossbach.

'It's in here somewhere,' Hunyadi answered vaguely.

'I'm damned if I'm giving up this office!' shouted Hossbach, the smile still weirdly bolted to his cheeks.

'You may well be, at that,' answered Hunyadi. 'Ah! Here it is.'

He pulled out a business card, bearing the initials AH, intricately twined into a monogram. Below that was a number, written in black fountain pen. Hunyadi placed the card down on the desk and, with one finger, slid it across to the detective. Then he picked up the phone receiver and handed it to Hossbach. 'Make the call,' he said. 'I'll be waiting right outside.'

Having returned to the hallway, Hunyadi closed the office door behind him. He breathed in the familiar smell of the office: a combination of cigarette ash, hair tonic, sweat, the eyewatering reek of mimeograph ink and of over-brewed coffee, although Hunyadi doubted that any real coffee had been drunk here in a long time. The air was filled with the clatter of typewriters and the voices of men who smoked too much, none of which he could distinctly hear, so that they merged into a throaty purr whose familiarity Hunyadi found reassuring.

After a few minutes, the door opened and Hossbach stepped into the hall. He was clutching a small orchid in an earthenware pot. His face was utterly white, as if the blood had drained out of his heart like dirty water from a bath. He said nothing as he walked away to find another office, the orchid stem wobbling over his shoulder, as if waving goodbye to Hunyadi.

On the night of 12 April 1945, Kirov, Pekkala and their guide found themselves strapped into uncomfortable metal seats in the unheated cargo bay of a Junkers transport plane.

Pekkala looked around at the aircraft's curved frame supports, which arched down the bare metal of the interior walls, giving him the impression that he had been swallowed by a whale. Just then, Pekkala could not remember whether the story of Jonah had actually taken place or if it was simply the invention of some long-dead holy man, intended to steer the listener towards some greater truth which now eluded him.

The Junkers had been captured the year before when Russian troops overran an airfield near Orel. Since then, it had been used in several missions that involved dropping supplies or spare parts to Red Army soldiers encircled by the German Army.

On this occasion, however, the cargo was human.

Beside Pekkala sat Kirov. For the fifth time, the major was checking his parachute. Still echoing in Kirov's head were the words of the jump instructor who had met them at the airport and having described how they would be jumping from the aircraft, went on to explain that, if his chute failed, he would reach a terminal velocity of approximately 110 miles per hour, the speed at which he would strike the ground, whether he fell from 500 or 5,000 feet, and that when he did strike the ground, he would break every bone in his body, even the tiny ones in his ears. In spite of the matter-of-fact delivery of this information, the instructor had meant this to be reassuring, since it would all be over in a second and there would be no time for feeling any pain.

Kirov, however, was having trouble seeing it that way. As he peered at the various straps and clips, he realised that he had no idea whether the parachute had been correctly assembled or not, and he was afraid to touch anything in case he accidentally rearranged or broke some important part, which would cause him to be gelatinised on impact.

He cast a scathing glance at Pekkala, who did not seem at all troubled by the fact that they would soon be hurling themselves into space. In fact, to judge from the look on Pekkala's face, he appeared to be looking forward to it.

Muttering curses he knew no one would hear above the rumble of the Junkers' engines, Kirov went back to checking his equipment.

Opposite them was their guide, a grim-faced man with a German accent, who introduced himself as Corporal Luther Strohmeyer.

One year before, Strohmeyer had been an Untersturmführer, or lieutenant, commanding a much reduced company of Panzer Grenadiers from the SS Panzer Division 'Das Reich'. During the same vast clash of armour in which his present mode of transport had been captured, Strohmeyer had been ordered to lead a frontal assault on a town called Fatezh. His orders were to attack without any preliminary bombardment of the town which, since it involved traversing a wide expanse of open ground, was tantamount to suicide. Assuming that there must have been a mistake somewhere up the line, Strohmeyer took matters into his own hands and ordered a mortar barrage on Fatezh. The Soviet defenders, surprised and out-gunned, immediately retreated, enabling Strohmeyer and his men to capture the town without a single casualty.

For this, Strohmeyer had expected an Iron Cross 1st Class at the very least, or perhaps even a Knight's Cross to hang around his throat.

But this was not what happened.

It emerged that Strohmeyer's company had been selected as a diversion for a much larger attack taking place to the north. He and his men were to be sacrificed. None had been expected to survive. As a result of Strohmeyer's successful capture of Fatezh, he was charged with failing to carry out an order in the spirit in which it was given. He still had no idea what that really meant. The result, however, was exile for the duration of the war to a group known as Parachute Battalion 500, formed largely out of troops who, after disgracing themselves in one way or another, had been stripped of their rank and decorations and bundled into a military formation for whom survival was an even more remote prospect than it had been for them when they were regular soldiers.

In May of 1944, the battalion was sent to capture the Communist partisan leader Tito in his remote mountain hideaway near Dvor in western Bosnia. Not only did the battalion fail to capture Tito, but more than eight hundred of the thousand men taking part in the mission were killed or captured, thanks to a tip which the Communists had received before the battalion had even set out on their mission. The man who tipped them off was Luther Strohmeyer, who had passed a message through an informant at the camp where the battalion underwent parachute training. Driven by bitterness at how he had been treated, the fanaticism with which Strohmeyer had entered the war on the side of the Fascists transferred almost seamlessly to the Communist cause.

Only rarely, in the months ahead, would the guilt of what he'd done emerge from the dark corners of his mind to torment Strohmeyer. Then images of the men whose deaths he had assured would flash behind his eyes and he would twitch and jerk his head, as if someone were holding a lit match too close to his face.

As soon as his feet touched the ground in Bosnia, he deserted to Soviet troops stationed in Dvor. From there, he was transferred to Moscow and cautiously welcomed as a hero for his role in saving Tito's life.

Since then, in his work for Soviet Counter-Intelligence, he had taken part in several missions inside Germany, all of them involving parachute drops behind enemy lines. What he had learned from these jumps was not only the technique of hurling himself from a plane travelling 500 feet above the ground but also the fact that, when the time came to jump, he was never afraid. Strohmeyer did not know why he wasn't terrified at moments like this. He knew he ought to be. Before he climbed aboard the plane, and later, after he was safely on the ground, nightmares would crowd his head like flocks of starlings taking to the sky. But as soon as the plane left the ground, all terror ceased and where it went and why, Strohmeyer had no idea, nor did he care to know.

This mission looked to be no different from the rest. A native of Berlin, Strohmeyer had volunteered to escort the Russians into and out of the city, along with the person they had been sent to rescue. He knew nothing of the mission itself, nor did he have an inkling about the identities of the men who sat before him now or the person they had been sent to extract. All he knew was the location of a safe house on Heiligenberg Street in the eastern district of Berlin and the time of the rendezvous, at noon three days from now. Although the men he was escorting were aware of the date, the actual location of the safe house had been shared with him alone by the tweed-jacketed British diplomat named Swift who briefed him on the task which lay ahead. On operations like this, it was standard procedure to compartmentalise information so that no one man knew everything. That way, if anything went wrong and one of them was captured, the entire mission would not be jeopardised.

There was one significant difference in the orders he had been given this time. On his way to the airfield, the NKVD officer who had prepared Strohmeyer for the mission instructed him to shoot both of the men he was guiding into Berlin in the event that, on the homeward journey, either of them showed any reluctance to return to Soviet lines. Exactly what constituted reluctance, Strohmeyer was not told. He had the impression that the Kremlin would rather these men did not survive and yet, clearly, they were needed for the task. One thing the NKVD officer had made clear was that under no circumstances was any harm to come to the person they were rescuing from the city. Strohmeyer knew without having to ask that his own life depended on that.

It was painfully cold in the belly of the plane. In addition to the clothes they would wear on the ground, the only protective garments they had been issued were brown cotton overalls, over which the heavy parachute harnesses had been strapped. Lulled into dream-like stupors by the frigid air, each man disappeared into the catacombs of his own thoughts.

After two hours in the sky, they were startled by a sudden, sharp rattling sound against the hull of the aircraft. This was accompanied, a second later, by a high-pitched whistling of air.

The Junker's engines snarled as the pilot jammed the throttle forward.

Pekkala felt a weight, like chains draped upon his shoulders, as the plane began to climb rapidly.

Kirov glanced at the stranger who was to be their guide, hoping for some kind of explanation.

Strohmeyer pointed at the fuselage just above Kirov's head. Turning, Kirov glimpsed a line of puncture marks, through which the wind was whistling in half a dozen different pitches, as if played by a mad man with a flute.

A moment later, the cockpit door opened and a man in a sheepskin-lined flight suit appeared. 'We've just crossed the Soviet lines,' he shouted at them. 'We took some ground fire from our own side, but it hasn't slowed us down. We're over Germany now. Be ready when the light comes on!'

Kirov stared enviously at the man's flight suit, then looked up at the two jump lights, one red and one green, like knotted fists of glass.

Even as he looked at it, the red 'prepare-to-jump' light burst into colour.

Hurriedly and with his heart-beat pulsing in his throat, Kirov unbuckled himself from the seat.

The other two men did the same. Carrying the heavy rope of their static lines, each man clipped himself to a rail running like a spinal cord down the centre of the roof.

The co-pilot opened the side door and the cargo bay filled with a howling rush of icy air, which drowned out even the perpetual thunder of the engines.

Strohmeyer, who was first in line, walked forward, pulling his static line like a leash, until he stood opposite the opening.

Outside, in the pre-dawn gloom, he saw shreds of cloud sweep past and glimpses of landscape far below.

The red glow vanished and, in the same instant, the cargo bay was flooded by the emerald flash of the jump light.

Without a moment's hesitation, Strohmeyer took two paces forward and flung himself head first through the opening. He extended his arms and legs into a spreadeagle attitude in the peculiar and dangerous fashion taught to German paratroopers. Then the static line, anchored to the middle of his back, came taut. The jolt on his spine almost caused him to faint. As the chute deployed, his legs swung down and he hung like a marionette, drifting now towards the ground.

Passing through a cloud, his clothes became instantly soaked with moisture. By then, the plane was barely audible.

Glancing up, he could just make out the dark silhouettes of the other two parachutes.

Directly below him lay a village. It appeared to be mostly intact although it was still too dark to tell for certain.

The thing he would never forget about these parachute drops was the silence, and how slowly he seemed to fall at first. But the closer he came to the ground, the more the speed seemed to pick up and he realised now that he was heading directly for a grove of trees, in the centre of which he could see the spire of a church.

Remembering the instructions of the jump master who had taught him back in Hungary, Strohmeyer jammed his legs together, hooking his feet, one around the other, so as not to straddle a branch on his way in. At the speed he was travelling, an injury like that would be fatal.

Beyond that, there was little Strohmeyer could do but brace for the impact and hope that his chute did not become entangled in the branches.

He tucked his legs up to his chest as the flimsy top branches clawed past him. He drifted over the largest of the trees and laughed out loud when he realised he had cleared the grove. He was coming down in a ploughed field, the best possible place to land. Strohmeyer barely had time to wonder at his luck when he spotted a thread of black running horizontally across the path of his approach.

The shroud lines of his parachute made a loud zipping noise as they connected with the power line and the silk canopy ruffled as it snagged against a telegraph pole.

As the electric current burst through his back and exploded through the soles of his boots, Strohmeyer had no sensation of actually reaching the earth. The last thought that passed through his mind before his body seemed to fly apart, atomising into the night, was that neither of the men travelling with him had any idea where they were going.

As Pekkala drifted down over the ploughed field, he kicked his legs like a man riding a bicycle until he hit the ground and tumbled forward on to his knees in the soft earth. In a second, he was up, pulling in the lines of his green silk chute. Soon, he had gathered it into a large, messy bundle. Removing his harness, he carried it to a nearby hedge and stuffed it in among the brambles until it was hidden from sight.

After hours of breathing the thin, greasy-smelling air inside the cargo bay of the plane, the damp, leafy scent of the earth filled his lungs like incense in a church.

He looked around. The wind had carried him some distance from the town but he could still see the church steeple, rising up above the trees. He could see neither Kirov nor their guide and, for a moment, he struggled against the fluttering of panic in his chest at the thought that he was lost and entirely alone.

Drawing the Webley from its holster on his chest, he made his way across the field, mud clogging his boots, until he reached a bank of grass. From there, he set off towards the church.

He had not gone far when he spotted the silhouette of a man standing on the churchyard wall, waving to him.

It was Kirov.

Neither man could hide his relief at having found the other in the dark.

It took them a while longer to locate the guide.

As soon as they spotted the man's chute, wafting in the night breeze like some strange, aquatic creature, Kirov set off at a run to help the man, whom they could see lying motionless on the ground.

'Stop!' hissed Pekkala.

Kirov skidded to a halt and turned.

'Don't even get near him,' warned Pekkala. 'He's hit a power line. The current has grounded through his body.'

As Kirov backed away, he watched a sliver of smoke, or maybe it was steam, slither from the dead man's mouth, as if his soul were fleeing from the prison of his corpse.

With no clue as to precisely where they were, and no way to check the body of their guide for maps or any other sign of where they were supposed to go when they arrived in Berlin, the two men headed for the church, weaving between the gravestones until they reached the entrance. But the door was locked and there was no sign of life inside, so they retreated to a clump of trees in the corner of the churchyard to wait out the night. Their clothing had been soaked by the descent through the clouds and they decided to light a small fire, keeping its meagre flames hidden by a circle of stones their muddy fingers gouged out of the ground.

A cold wind raked across the field beyond the churchyard wall, rattling the branches of the trees.

Crouched above the mesh of burning twigs, both men reached their hands into the smoke as if somehow to wash them in the scent of burning alder.

With his head tucked down and chin tucked into the collar of his mud-spattered coat, Pekkala resembled one of the tramps who lived in the Vorobjev woods on the south-west outskirts of Moscow.

'There's no point going on,' said Kirov, struggling to speak as his jaw trembled with the cold.

Pekkala looked up from the fire. 'What?' he asked in disbelief.

'Without our guide,' explained Kirov, 'we'll never find the safe house.'

'We have some clues,' countered Pekkala.

Kirov looked at him in astonishment. 'Such as?' he demanded.

'We know that the contact is Hungarian,' said Pekkala, 'and the date we are supposed to meet at the safe house.'

'It's not enough,' said Kirov. 'Not nearly enough! The rendezvous is three days from now, and even if we can get to Berlin in time, what good is that in a city which is doubtless home to thousands of Hungarians, not to mention the refugees who have been pouring in from the east? You must face the fact, Inspector, that there's no chance of making the rendezvous with Comrade Simonova.'

'There is always a chance,' said Pekkala.

An image appeared in Kirov's mind of the two of them, shuffling from house to house and knocking at every door they came to. It would take them the rest of their lives. Kirov paused before he spoke again. It did not surprise him that Pekkala did not want to turn back, especially with what was now at stake. He knew he would have to choose his words carefully if he was to have any hope of persuading the Inspector to come home.

'Inspector,' he began, as he attempted to reason with Pekkala, 'please consider the possibility that your judgement might be clouded in this instance.'

'It might well be,' replied Pekkala.

Encouraged by the Inspector's admission, Kirov felt it safe to go on.

'When morning comes,' he said firmly, 'we'll return to the Soviet lines.'

'Whatever you think of my judgement,' Pekkala told him, 'I have come too far to turn back now.'

'But it isn't so far!' Kirov tried to reason with him. 'It can't be more than a day or two if we keep up a steady pace. All we have to do is head east. The Red Army is massing on the Seelow Heights. Once we reach the River Oder, we'll be safe.'

'Safe?' echoed Pekkala. 'How safe do you think you will be if we return to the Kremlin empty-handed?'

'But we won't,' insisted Kirov. 'As soon as we reach the Soviet lines, we can make contact with Special Operations in Moscow. They can reschedule the rendezvous at the safe house and find another guide to take us there. We'll make it to Berlin, Inspector. It just might take a little longer than we thought.'

'That is the problem, Major Kirov.' Pekkala picked up a stick and jabbed it at the embers. 'It might only be a matter of hours before Hunyadi tracks her down. So even if we did have the time to spare, Lilya Simonova does not.'

Having tried and failed to reason with Pekkala, Kirov realised that he had only one card left to play. 'Inspector,' he said, 'by the authority of Comrade Stalin, I am giving you an order.' For a moment, there was only the sound of the wind in the branches of the trees.

'And if Stalin was here with us now,' Pekkala gestured at a patch of dirt beside the fire, 'do you think that would change my opinion?'

Kirov stared at the place where Pekkala was pointing, half expecting Stalin to rise like some hideous mushroom from the patchwork collage of dead leaves. 'What would you have us do, Inspector?'

'Give me until the deadline for the rendezvous has passed,' answered Pekkala. 'That's all the time I'll need.'

'How on earth do you expect to find her in three days, with no idea of where she might be hiding?' asked Kirov.

'You let me worry about that,' replied Pekkala.

That same night, Peter Garlinski, former supervisor of British Special Operations Relay Station 53A, was woken by a heavy hand rapping on his Moscow flat door.

Bleary-eyed with sleep, Garlinski went to see what the fuss was about and found himself face to face with a sergeant of NKVD, the Soviet Internal Security Agency. The sergeant was crisply dressed, with dark blue trousers and a *gymnastiorka* tunic. Across his waist, he wore a heavy leather belt with a plain iron buckle and a Tokarev in its polished leather holster.

Garlinski was simultaneously worried by the sight of this man and grateful for the visit. He had not spoken to anyone since the arrival of Inspector Pekkala some days before.

'I have come to get you out of here!' announced the sergeant, a rosy-cheeked man with a double chin and thick, dark eyebrows. His short-fingered hands, the colour of raw pork, were criss-crossed with scars across the knuckles, as if he had once punched his way through a window.

'Out of here?' Garlinski asked suspiciously. 'Where to?'

The sergeant poked his head into the room. 'Some place better than this.'

'Finally!' sighed Garlinski.

'Pack your things,' said the sergeant.

'I have no things.' 'All the better. Follow me!'

They walked towards the gate, the sergeant's iron heel plates sparking off the flint stones of the courtyard. Outside in the street, a car was parked, its engine running.

The sergeant got behind the wheel. Garlinski climbed into the back.

'We have to make a stop at Lubyanka,' said the sergeant, as he put the car in gear and set off down the road. 'You haven't been debriefed yet.'

'I know!' Garlinski replied excitedly. 'I've been waiting for that.'

'It won't take long,' said the sergeant. 'Then we can get you to your new apartment.'

'What about employment?' asked Garlinski. 'I think I could be very useful. I'm trained as a decoder, you know. I was head of a listening post back in England.'

The sergeant glanced at him in the rear-view mirror and smiled broadly. 'Sounds like you'll have your pick of assignments. Not like me. I have no special talents.'

Garlinski found his gaze drawn to the scars on the sergeant's knuckles, but he could make nothing of them and soon turned his attention to the sight of the people walking in the streets, passing through the cones of street-lamp light, still bundled in their winter scarves and furs.

The car pulled in to the Lubyanka courtyard.

Garlinski climbed out and looked around. He had heard that Lubyanka was once a fashionable neo-baroque building and it was still possible to see how grand it must have been before the Revolution. Now the windows were covered by angled metal shields, which prevented anyone from looking out, and strong lights glared down from the rooftops, obscuring his view of the sky.

A shudder passed through Garlinski. Even though he knew that he was being welcomed as a hero for his many years of service to the Soviet cause, the Lubyanka was still a place of nightmares for anyone who knew its history.

'Where do I go?' asked Garlinski.

'I'll walk you in,' said the sergeant.

They entered the building and Garlinski was made to sign a register. The page on which he wrote was partially covered by a heavy metal screen, which hid all but the space in which he wrote his name.

'This way.' The sergeant beckoned for Garlinski to follow him.

The two men made their way downstairs and along a narrow corridor lined with pale green painted doors. Along the way, they passed two guards, with a prisoner shuffling along between them.

The prisoner, a young man with coal-black hair and narrow eyes, immediately turned to face the wall as Garlinski and the sergeant walked by.

There was complete silence in the corridor. Even the floor on which they walked had been covered with thick grey carpeting which dampened the sound of their footsteps.

Garlinski wanted to ask how much further they would have to go but the quiet was so threatening and profound that he did not dare to speak.

At the end of the corridor, they came to another door, which was made of dark, heavy panels and had a slightly arched top.

'It's the old wine cellar,' whispered the sergeant, as he reached into his pocket for the key. 'The men who worked at this place, back when it was still an insurance company, kept a king's ransom in bottles down here for entertaining their wealthy clients. That's all gone now, though, men and bottles both.' He swung open the door and gestured grandly. 'After you, Comrade Garlinski.'

Garlinski stepped inside. The ceiling of the room was arched and the walls were made of brick. The floor had been laid with tiles and there were shallow gutters running along the edges of the floor. He wondered why a wine cellar needed gutters. He looked around for furniture, but there was none. Not even a chair in which to sit.

He turned to ask the sergeant if they were in the right place. The last clear thing Garlinski saw was the fist of the sergeant, knuckles spider-webbed with scars, as it slammed into his face. He sprawled on to the floor, nearly blinded by the pain. Blood from his broken nose poured down the back of his throat and, propping himself up on one elbow, he retched as he struggled to breathe. Dimly, Garlinski watched as the sergeant removed his tunic and belt and hung them on the door handle. Then the man rolled up the sleeves of his thin, brown cotton shirt, the armpits of which were already darkened with sweat.

The sergeant's smile had vanished. His face now appeared almost blank, as if he were only half aware of what he was doing. He reached down, took hold of the front of Garlinski's coat and hauled him to his feet.

'Wait!' called Garlinski, peppering the sergeant's face with blood. 'There must be some mistake. I am a hero of the Soviet Union!'

Without a word of explanation and, using nothing more than his fists, the sergeant beat Peter Garlinski to death, as he had done countless others in the past.

He left the body lying on the floor, removed a handkerchief from his pocket and wiped the blood off his hands. He studied a few new cuts on his knuckles. It was always their teeth that caused those.

Then he put on his tunic and belt and departed from the room, leaving the door open.

A few minutes later, two men dragged away Garlinski's body, while a third mopped down the floor with a bucket of soapy water. Bubbles, poppy red, sluiced along the gutters and were gone.

In the dove-grey light of dawn, with darkness still clinging to the western sky, Pekkala and Kirov set off towards Berlin.

Although it was still cold, the breeze blowing up from the south was not as bitter as it had been the night before. Slowly, as they marched along, the warmth returned to their bones. They thought longingly of food they did not have and of the wheezy stove and battered chairs at their office on Pitnikov Street.

'I knew it wouldn't work,' said Kirov.

'What wouldn't work?' asked Pekkala.

'Me giving you orders.'

'Maybe you should have tried a little harder,' suggested Pekkala.

Kirov turned to him. 'Do you mean it might have worked?' Pekkala thought about this for a moment. 'No,' he said at last, 'but it would have been interesting to watch.'

They soon came across a railway track, which appeared to be heading directly towards the city. They followed it, timing their strides to the laddering of sleepers and smelling the oily creosote with which the wooden beams had been painted.

Through eyes bloodshot with fatigue, Pekkala watched the rails flow out on either side of him, like streams of mercury, converging in the distance. His memory tilted back to when he'd walked along another set of tracks which had been sutured across the earth.

In that moment, the mildness of that spring morning peeled

away, leaving behind a world of bone-white snow and ice-sheathed trees and silence so profound that he could hear the rush of blood through his own veins. The cold slammed into his bones, and his heart seemed to cower behind the frail cage of his ribs.

He was back in Siberia again.

The tracks which he recalled were those of the TransSiberian Railway, which skirted the edge of the valley of Krasnagolyana, home to the labour camp of Borodok.

For much of the year, what few wagon trails criss-crossed that lonely forest lay deep beneath the snowdrifts or else were so clogged with mud that no one, not even the long-legged reindeer, could make their way along them.

During those seasons, the railway became the only means of crossing this vast landscape. It marked the boundary of Pekkala's world. The land he roamed belonged to the Gulag of Borodok, whose trees he marked for cutting with red paint. Beyond the tracks lay the territory of Mamlin Three, another camp, where experiments were carried out on behalf of the Soviet military. At Mamlin, inmates were submerged in icy water until their hearts stopped beating. Then they were resuscitated with injections of adrenalin administered directly into their hearts. The procedure was repeated, with longer and longer intervals between the stopping of the heart and the adrenalin injections until, finally, the patient could not be revived. These experiments were designed to replicate the conditions of pilots brought down in the sea. Other tests, using extremes of high and low pressure, produced a steady flow of cadavers, which were packed into barrels of formaldehyde and sent to medical schools all across Russia.

For Pekkala, to walk across those tracks meant certain death if he was ever caught. But he was drawn to them in spite of the danger.

At night, he stood back among the trees, while the carriages of the Trans-Siberian Express rattled past. He caught glimpses of the passengers, bundled in coats and asleep or staring out into the darkness with no idea that the darkness was staring back at them.

Until that memory finally stuttered to a halt, like a film clattering off its spool, he could not bring himself to step beyond the confines of the rails.

The first rays of sunlight glimmered faintly on the tracks. A moment later, the world around them ignited into a million coppery fragments as tiny stones out in the fields beyond, puddles of dirty water and even the powdery condensation of their breath caught the fireball's reflection.

'What's that?' asked Kirov, pointing up ahead.

Pekkala squinted at some strange, segmented creature, leaning up against one of the telegraph poles which ran beside the tracks. As he looked, it seemed to move, bowing out slightly in the centre and then settling back into its original shape.

'Whatever it is,' he whispered, 'I think it is alive.'

Just then they heard a voice, calling out faintly across the empty fields.

At first, the two men could not even tell its source.

Then it came again, and they realised it was coming from the creature by the telegraph pole.

It was calling for help. Without a moment's consultation, the two men set off running, unsure what they would find but drawn by the exhausted terror in that voice.

Not until they were standing practically in front of it did they fully understand what they were seeing.

A man had been hanged by a rope from one of the crooked spikes used by linemen for climbing to the wires above. But his life had been saved by a boy, who had placed himself beneath the man's feet so that the victim's neck did not bear the full weight of the noose.

It looked as they had been there all night, or even longer. The man's hands had been tied behind his back. He wore heavy wool trousers and thick-soled boots, but only a flannel shirt above the waist. If he'd ever had a coat, it had been taken from him. Even though he was not dead, the noose had tightened on his throat and he was half-choked, breathing in short gasps like a fish pulled up on to a river bank.

The boy was tall and skinny, with a thick crop of ginger-red hair cow-licked vertically at the front. What strength he had was almost gone, and fatigue had made his pale skin almost translucent. His white-knuckled hands gripped the man's trouser legs in an attempt to hold him steady.

While Kirov climbed the pole to cut him down, Pekkala took the boy's place, settling the man's boots upon his own shoulders and feeling the sharp heel irons dig into the flesh above his collarbone.

Carefully, they lowered the man to the ground, cut the rope from around his neck and propped him up against the dirty rails to let him breathe.

The boy sat down on the ground and stared at the men, too tired even to thank them except with the expression in his eyes.

'Who did this?' asked Pekkala. He had learned to speak German while at school in Finland, but his grammar was clumsy and the words crackled strangely in his mouth, as if he were chewing on bones.

'Feldgendarmerie,' replied the boy. Field Police.

Even back in Moscow, Pekkala had heard of these roving bands of soldiers, who rounded up anyone whom they suspected of desertion, or failure to place themselves in harm's way. The execution of these stragglers was summary and swift. Their bodies, sometimes bearing placards on which their supposed crimes were listed, dangled from piano-wire nooses all across the shrinking territory of the Reich.

'My son,' said the hanged man, when he was finally able to talk. He gestured at the boy.

Pekkala wondered what charges had been laid against the man, who was not wearing military uniform, and by what stroke of fortune his son had been around to save him from the improvised gallows of the Feldgendarmerie. 'Where are they now?' he asked. 'These Field Police?'

The man shook his head. He did not know. He brushed his hand towards the north to show in which direction they had gone.

'And to Berlin?' asked Pekkala.

With one trembling hand, the wrist rubbed raw by the wire with which it had been bound, the man reached out and pointed down the tracks. 'But do not go,' he told them. 'In Berlin there is nothing but death and, when the Russians arrive, even death will not be enough to describe it.' 'We must go there,' replied Pekkala. He wished he could explain what must have seemed an act of total madness. Instead, he only muttered, 'I'm afraid we have no choice.'

Neither the man nor his son asked any questions, but both seemed anxious to repay them for their kindness. Motioning for the two men to follow, they pointed across the field towards a grove of sycamore trees, on which the reddening buds glowed like a haze in the morning sunlight. Almost hidden in amongst the branches was a small brick chimney rising from a roof of grey slates patched with luminous green moss.

'That is where we live,' explained the boy.

'We are grateful,' said Pekkala, 'but we must be moving on.'

'If you want to reach your destination,' warned the father, 'then you should wait until the danger has passed. The Field Police barracks is on the outskirts of the city and they usually head back well before sunset. By mid-afternoon, it should be safe to travel. Then you can enter Berlin after dark.'

Pekkala hesitated, knowing he should take the man's advice but so anxious to press on towards Berlin that his instincts faltered as they balanced the need against the risk.

'We have food,' said the boy. Knowing that only one of the men could understand what he was saying, he motioned with his hand to his mouth.

Kirov had been trying without success to follow the conversation between Pekkala and the half-hanged man. But he understood the gesture perfectly. He touched Pekkala on the arm and raised his eyebrows in a question, knowing that he could not speak without giving away the fact that he was Russian.

Feeling the touch against his arm, Pekkala glanced at the major. The reminder that he was responsible, not only for what might happen to himself but to them both, returned him abruptly to his senses. Pekkala gestured towards the house in the distance. 'Thank you,' he said quietly.

Without another word, the four of them set off across the field.

At the edge of the woods, the ground sloped away sharply, revealing a small farmstead tucked away in a hollow.

A dog was sprawled dead outside the farmhouse door. It had been shot several times and its blood had leaked out into the mud on which it lay.

Ringing the small farmyard were racks of small cages, the doors of which were open.

'*Fasane*,' said the father, gesturing at the cages. Pheasants. The father fluttered his fingers, to show they had all flown away. 'I let them go,' he explained. His voice was still hoarse and the chafing of the noose had rubbed a bloody groove beneath his chin.

'But why?' asked Pekkala.

The father shrugged, as if he wasn't even sure himself. 'So that they would have a chance,' he said. And then he went on to describe how the band of military police had spotted the birds as they took to the air and had come to investigate. The first thing they did was shoot the farmer's dog after it growled at them. Then, finding that the farmer had released the birds, which might otherwise have fed the hungry soldiers, they accused him of treason and immediately condemned him to death. At gunpoint they had marched him out across the field until they came to the telegraph poles. When they brought out the rope, he asked them why they had not hanged him from a tree by his own house. They told him it was so that people passing on the tracks could see his body, and think twice before they, too, betrayed their country. They tied a noose and hauled him up to hang him slowly, rather than breaking his neck with a drop.

Unknown to the military police, the boy had followed them. As soon as the soldiers had departed, the boy rushed in and set his shoulders underneath the father's feet. And they stood there through the night, waiting for someone to help.

The boy fetched a shovel from the back of the house in order to bury the dog. Kirov went with him, to share in the burden of digging, while the father brought Pekkala into the barn. There, he opened up a horse stall, in which something had been hidden underneath an old grey tarpaulin. The man pulled back the oil-

215

stained canvas, revealing two bicycles.

Their chains were rusted, the brake pads crumbling and the leather seats sagged like the backs of broken mules. But the tyres still held air and, as the father pointed out, this way was better than walking.

When the dog had been buried, they sat down to a meal of smoked pheasant served on slices of gritty bread which had sawdust mixed into the flour. Meagre as it was, this seemed to be the only food they had left.

By two o'clock that afternoon, the father announced that it was safe for them to travel.

They walked out to the narrow road that ran beside the farm.

'Stick to the back roads,' advised the father. 'Just keep heading west and you'll be there in less than a day.'

'Good luck to you both,' said Pekkala, and he shook hands with the man and his son.

'*Udachi*,' replied the father, wishing them good luck in Russian.

Kirov gasped to hear the sound of his own language.

But Pekkala only smiled.

The man had known all along where they came from.

Wobbling unsteadily upon the bicycles, Kirov and Pekkala set off towards Berlin.

At that precise moment, Inspector Hunyadi was sitting alone in a conference room in the Reichschancellery building, waiting to begin the first of several interviews of members of the German High Command about the leak of information from the bunker.

In choosing a location for these interviews, Hunyadi had been given little choice, since this was one of the few places left in the Chancellery with its roof remaining intact.

This had, until not too long ago, been the location of Hitler's meetings with his High Command; one at midday and the other at midnight. It was a grand, high-ceilinged room, with white pillars in each corner and paintings of different German landscapes – the Drachenfels Castle overlooking the Rhine, a street scene in Munich, a farmer ploughing his field at sunrise on the flat, almost featureless plains along the Baltic coast. In between these paintings, windows taller than a man looked out on to the Chancellery garden. In the centre of the room stood a long, oak table, on which the maps of battlefields would be unfurled and gestured at by field marshals waving ceremonial batons. Along the back wall, comfortable chairs with padded red leather seats had welcomed those whose presence was not immediately required.

At least, that's how it used to look.

One night in late October of 1944, a 250-pound bomb dropped by an American B-17 landed in the Chancellery garden, barely fifty feet from the outside entrance to the briefing room. The explosion blew out the windows, spraying the back walls with glass, shrapnel and mud. The upholstered chairs were hurled into the air, along with the briefing-room table, in spite of the fact that it normally took ten men to lift it. In a matter of seconds, every piece of furniture in the room was wrenched into pieces, some of which became embedded in the ceiling.

At first, Hitler had insisted that the briefings continue in their usual location. The windows' holes were sealed up with plywood. The wreckage of the table was removed and those in attendance did their best not to stare at the gashes in the walls, from which shards of window glass still protruded like the teeth of sharks.

Maps were spread out upon the floor and men crouched down to trace their fingers along routes of advance and retreat.

Forty-eight hours after the explosion, just as the midnight meeting was about to commence, a twisted dagger of metal from the bomb's tail fin fell from its resting place in the ceiling and stuck into the floor, right in the middle of a map of the Schnee Eifel mountains.

That was too much, even for Hitler, and before he left the city for another of his fortresses, he ordered a new location to be found. By the time he returned, in January of the following year, the only place left was the bunker.

Since the power was out and the windows were blocked up with plywood, Hunyadi had resorted to a paraffin lamp to light the room. The yellow flame, tipped with greasy black smoke, writhed behind the dirty glass shroud. Most of the furniture had been removed. But the conference table was still here, along with a couple of chairs. It was enough to serve Hunyadi's purposes, but little more. In addition, the paintings had all been removed. Now

Hunyadi surveyed the dreary expanses of yellowy-brown paint on the empty walls, studded with the hooks from which the portraits had once been suspended.

Hunyadi had considered summoning everyone on his list to the police station, where he could have questioned them in one of the holding cells, but he wanted to play down the appearance of a formal interrogation. In addition, German military law usually required that any interrogation of a military official be carried out by someone of equal rank. Not only did Hunyadi lack the pay scale of the officers who would soon be marching through that door, but he wasn't even a soldier.

No matter what location he chose, the reception was likely to be chilly, especially since most, if not all of them, would already know why they were being summoned. Even to be questioned meant that their loyalty had fallen under suspicion.

As the minutes passed, Hunyadi felt the quiet of the room settling like dust upon his shoulders. Even though his rational mind assured him that he was not back in a cell, he still felt trapped in this windowless space and it was all he could do not to bolt into the street. He thought about all the people he had sent to prison over the years. Rarely had he ever felt pity for the people he'd helped to convict, but now he grasped the full measure of their suffering. It was strange that this had come to him only after his release from Flossenburg. In the weeks he had spent in that cell so much of his mind had shut down that every emotion, no matter how extreme, had been dulled to the point where he felt almost nothing at all. Maybe that was the true punishment of prison – not the loss of time but rather the inability to feel its passing.

A few minutes later, the door burst open and there stood Field Marshal Keitel, with cheeks almost as red as the crimson facing on his greatcoat. Without waited to be welcomed, he stamped into the room, removed his hat and tossed it on to the table. Then, resting his gloved knuckles on the polished surface, he leaned across until the two men's faces almost touched.

'You miserable little man!' he spat. 'Did you ever stop to think that I have a war to run?'

Keitel, in his early sixties, had greying hair, a high forehead and fleshy ears. When he closed his mouth, his teeth clacked together like a mousetrap, causing the flesh around his jowly chin to quiver momentarily.

'I just have a few questions,' said Hunyadi, removing a notebook from his chest pocket, along with the stub of a pencil.

'Please sit,' he told the field marshal, gesturing at a chair on the other side of the table.

'I won't be here long enough!' roared Keitel. 'Just hurry up and ask me whatever it is you need to ask, so you can report back to the Führer that I am not the source of any information leak.'

'So you are aware of the leak?'

'Of course! For months, there have been rumours.'

'What kind of rumours?'

Keitel breathed in sharply through his nose. 'Things finding their way on to the Allied radio network.'

'What things?'

Keitel shrugged angrily. 'Useless gossip, mostly. The sordid details of people's lives.'

'The Führer seems to think it is more serious than that.' Slowly, Keitel leaned away from Hunyadi. He pulled himself up to his full height, fingers twitching inside grey-green leather gloves. 'He has no proof of that, at least none that I have seen or heard about. If you ask me, he's chasing a ghost, and we have other, more important things to occupy our minds. It is simply a distraction, which is exactly what the Allies had in mind.'

'So you will admit the leak exists?' The field marshal shrugged. 'Possibly.'

'And where, if you had to guess, would you say the leak is coming from?'

'If you ask me, they are the kind of details one hears talked about among the secretaries, of which there are several working in the bunker.'

'So you think it is one of them?'

'I'm not accusing anyone,' snapped Keitel. 'It's just a hunch, but one that carries weight if you can see this from the Allies' point of view.'

'And how is that?'

'Whoever they are using for this, if there is anyone at all, is someone they consider expendable.'

'How so?' asked Hunyadi.

'How long did the Allies think they could go on telling bunker secrets before Hitler sent a man like you to find the source? Now have you asked enough questions or are you going to keep me here all day?'

'No, Field Marshal,' said Hunyadi, closing his notebook. 'You are free to go.'

The next man through the door was Hitler's adjutant, SS Major Otto Guensche. He had come straight from his duties at the bunker and wore a brown, double-breasted knee-length leather coat over his dress uniform. He was very tall, with sad and patient eyes; a man who looked like he was used to keeping his mouth shut.

Hunyadi realised at once that he would get little out of

Guensche. After a few, perfunctory questions about life in the bunker, all of which Guensche answered in a slow and quiet voice, as if he was certain that others were listening, Hunyadi sent him away.

There followed a line of secretaries – Johanna Wolf, Christa Schroeder, Gerda Christian and Traudl Junge. If anything, these women were tougher than the field marshal. They gave almost nothing away, but from the upward darting of their gazes and the twitching of the muscles in their jaws, it was clear to Hunyadi, from his years of questioning suspects in the ding y, glaringly lit interrogation cells of the Spandau prison, that these women had plenty they could tell. The question was whether they had, and Hunyadi did not think so. Their loyalty ran so deep that it was oblivious to the kinds of political manoeuvrings that other, more highly placed members of the Führer's entourage might have found tempting.

After the secretaries, Hunyadi interviewed Hitler's chauffeur Erich Kempka, a rough, sarcastic man, who was himself a victim of the rumour leak. The story of his infidelities had been described more than once by 'Der Chef'.

Then came Heinz Linge, one of Hitler's valets, so nervous that he might have uttered some inconsequential detail in his sleep and thereby brought about the downfall of the Reich; his right eye began to twitch uncontrollably and Hunyadi dismissed him earlier than he had planned to out of fear that the man might be about to suffer a heart attack. After Linge's departure, Hunyadi glanced at his watch and realised that the day was almost over.

His final visitor was Hermann Fegelein, Himmler's emissary to the Führer's court and, judging from the reputation that preceded him, someone universally disliked.

Unlike all the others, Fegelein appeared completely at ease, and it was this which made Hunyadi suspicious.

'Why am I here?' demanded Fegelein.

'The Führer believes that there is a leak of classified information from his Berlin Headquarters. Some of it is finding its way to the Allies, who are broadcasting it from their radio stations.'

'You mean "Der Chef"?'

'You have heard of him?'

'Everybody has, but if that's why you've brought me in I can tell you right now you are wasting your time.'

'You may be right,' answered Hunyadi, 'but I must speak with everyone who has access to classified information in the bunker. And that would include you, Gruppenführer, since you attend the Führer's briefings every day.'

'That's my job,' he replied.

'Nevertheless,' said Hunyadi, 'we must satisfy the Führer's curiosity.'

Fegelein slumped down into the chair on the other side of the table. He breathed in deeply and then sighed. 'So ask away.'

'I only have one question,' said Hunyadi. Fegelein blinked in confusion. 'That's all?'

'If there was a leak,' asked Hunyadi, 'then where, in your opinion, would it come from?'

Fegelein thought for a moment before he replied. 'Somewhere down the line,' he said. 'Down the line?'

'Someone who has learned to slip between the cracks,' explained Fegelein. 'A person you see all the time but never notice. But you are wasting your time looking at me, and others like me. My kind of people do not risk our lives on spreading gossip. We have far too much to lose for that.'

'Thank you,' said Hunyadi. 'You may go.'

Fegelein stood up and turned to leave. But then he turned back. 'Why only one question?'

Hunyadi smiled, almost sympathetically. 'If you were indeed the source of the leak, would you have admitted that to me?'

Fegelein snorted. 'Of course not!'

'Precisely,' said Fegelein.

'So why bring us in here at all?'

'Firstly, because that is what Hitler wants. And secondly, so that there can be no doubt, in the mind of whomever is divulging this information, that they are being hunted now.'

Fegelein nodded, impressed. 'A tactic which might lose you some friends before this investigation is over.'

'There are no friends,' said Hunyadi, 'only the enemies I have already and those who do not know enough to hate me yet. In my line of work, that is an occupational hazard.'

'If only there were someone you could turn to for help.' Hunyadi stared at him. 'Meaning what?'

'Such a person might be very valuable.' Fegelein held out his arms and let them fall back to his sides. 'Don't you think?'

'If you are implying that I can request assistance from the SS, I am already aware of that.'

'The SS is a large organisation which does not take kindly to strangers snooping about in their business,' Fegelein told him flatly. 'What you need is someone who can get the job done while still maintaining absolute discretion.'

Hunyadi narrowed his eyes with suspicion. 'And this person might be you? Is that what you're suggesting?'

'It might be.'

Now I know why they hate you so much, thought Hunyadi.

'And why', he asked, 'would someone like you make me an offer like that?'

'Because I know who you work for, and I have lately found myself on the wrong end of his sympathies. Any gesture I can make to remedy that situation is worth doing. So you see, if I help you, then I am also helping him. All I ask in return is that, when the time comes, you remember who your friends are.'

'I'll keep it in mind,' Hunyadi answered cautiously.

Fegelein handed him a business card. On one side, in embossed letters, were his initials, HF, and on the other side was a Berlin telephone number. 'This is how to reach me, day or night,' said Fegelein.

After the man had departed, Hunyadi turned his thoughts to the things he had learned that day. The most useful information had come, not from what his visitors had said, but from what they did not say. Tomorrow, he would go to the bunker, and report his findings in person to Hitler. The news was unlikely to go down well, and Hunyadi wondered if the messenger would be the first to fall.

That evening, after a meal of quail braised in a mushroom and cognac sauce, delivered from the kitchens of Harting's restaurant on Mühlenstrasse to the apartment of his mistress, Fegelein sat in a high-backed chair made of crushed yellow velvet, smoking a cigar. Lazily, he held the phone receiver to his ear while his master, Heinrich Himmler, grilled him about the meeting with Hunyadi.

'What did he want?' demanded Himmler. 'What is he looking into?'

'A leak,' replied Fegelein. 'A flow of information from the bunker which has been finding its way into the hands of the Allies. Apparently, you can hear it almost every day on that pirate radio station of theirs.'

'Is there any truth to it?'

'No idea,' sighed Fegelein, 'but even if there is, it's nothing serious.'

'Nothing serious!' scoffed Himmler. 'How the hell can you say that?'

'Because the information is useless,' explained Fegelein.

'It's just gossip. There's nothing to indicate that military secrets are being passed on to the enemy, at least from the bunker.'

'Then why did he have to bring in a detective?' 'Not just any detective,' said Fegelein. 'It's Leopold Hunyadi.'

'Hunyadi!' exclaimed Himmler. 'The last I heard, he was going to be shot, or hanged or something.'

'He appears to have dodged both the bullet and the noose,' replied Fegelein. 'I must say I am not at all surprised. I have looked at Hunyadi's police record. It is very impressive. He has received all four grades of the Police Meritorious Service medal.'

'Four?' asked Himmler. 'I thought that there were only three – gold, silver and bronze.'

'They gave Hunyadi one with diamonds, created just for him. Hitler personally stuck the badge on him, back in 1939. Do you know he also speaks four languages, including Russian, Spanish and Hungarian?'

'Yes, yes, Fegelein,' Himmler replied angrily. 'Anyone would think you were starting up a fan club for Hunyadi! And none of this explains why Hitler did not give the case to our own man, Rattenhuber. He's in charge of security in the bunker and he's the one who should be investigating this.'

'And he would be,' answered Fegelein, 'if Hitler trusted anyone at all down there in that concrete labyrinth.'

'Do you mean he suspects us? The SS?'

'I mean he suspects everyone, Herr Reichsführer.'

There was a long pause, during which time Fegelein studied the whitening ash of his cigar as it slowly extinguished itself. Knowing Himmler's distaste for tobacco, he did not dare to take a puff even when talking to the man on the phone, for fear that Himmler might hear the popping of his lips as he drew smoke. 'We need to keep our eye on this,' Himmler said at last. 'If it does turn out that one of our own people is involved, it will destroy whatever faith Hitler has left in us.'

'I have taken steps to see that does not happen.'

'What steps, Fegelein? What have you been up to?'

'Just extending the hand of friendship to a colleague,' replied Fegelein. 'I told Hunyadi to come to me if he ever needed help.'

'And why would he go to you instead of anybody else?'

'Because I let him know that I can be discreet, and I predict that he will soon accept my offer.'

'As soon as he does that,' said Himmler, laughing softly, 'he will belong to us. But what makes you so sure he will call upon you?'

'Everyone needs someone like me at one time or another,' answered Fegelein, 'and I sense that Hunyadi's time is coming.'

'Let us hope so,' said Himmler. As usual, he hung up without saying goodbye.

For a moment, Fegelein listened to the rustles of static on the disconnected line. Then he put the phone down and set about puffing his cigar back to life.

As Kirov and Pekkala made their way along a muddy road, still 30 kilometres from Berlin, they did not see the roadblock until it was too late.

The windswept farmland had given way to shallow, rolling hills. Through this, the road twisted and turned, the way forward obscured by thick forests of poplars and sycamores, whose patchwork bark seemed to conjure up the shapes of faces, staring wall-eyed at the travellers as they passed by.

They were coasting down a hill, bicycle chains clattering over the spokes, banking to the right and then sharply to the left. It was all they could do just to stay in their seats. Just before the bottom of the hill, the road straightened out, and it was here that a squad of German Field Police had chosen to set up a barrier made from downed trees blocking first the left-hand side of the road and then the right, so that anyone hoping to pass would have to zigzag through the obstacles.

There was nothing that Pekkala or Kirov could do. They had no time to draw their guns or to retrace their steps. They barely had time to stop before they reached where the policemen were standing.

Two men, each wearing long rubberised canvas trench coats and carrying sub-machine guns, stood in front of the first blockade of trees. Hanging from forged metal links around their necks were the half-moon shields of the German Field

Police, each one emblazoned with a large eagle and the word

'Feldgendarmerie', which had been daubed with a yellowishgreen paint that glowed in the dark.

The police grinned, pleased with the success of their trap, as Kirov and Pekkala skidded to a halt in front of them.

At first, it seemed as if these two 'Chained Dogs' were the only ones manning the roadblock, but then the woods appeared to come to life, and half a dozen more police emerged from bunkers on either side of the road.

'Papers!' barked one of the policemen, holding out his hand. Fumbling in their pockets, Pekkala and Kirov each produced their documents. As they undid the buttons of their coats, the policeman caught sight of Pekkala's Webley, tucked away inside his shoulder holster. Immediately, the man swung his sub- machine gun up towards his chest. 'Slowly now,' he said.

Pekkala removed the revolver. Grasping it by the brass butt plates so that the barrel pointed at the ground, he handed it over. As he did so, he noticed for the first time how young these soldiers were.

They could not have been more than sixteen years old, gaunt and acne-spattered faces peering from beneath the iron hoods of their helmets. With underfed and spindly bodies tented beneath their raincoats, they looked like scarecrows come to life.

And yet Pekkala knew what casual brutality could come from those whose youth had shielded them from any frame of reference but the one they had been taught since birth. They were the children of the later war and when they crossed paths with the Red Army, these boys would be the last to surrender, if they were even given such a chance. Now the two men were searched, and

Kirov's gun was also confiscated.

'Herr Hauptmann!' shouted the boy who had demanded their papers.

Another man emerged from the bunker on the left. He wore the rank insignia of a captain, and his silver-braided epaulettes were trimmed with the dull orange piping of the German Field Police. The captain was considerably older than the others, his unshaved chin flecked with a grey haze of stubble. He might have been their father, or even their grandfather. The man carried a short-stemmed pipe, which he paused to light as he made his way on to the road. Unlike his men, this officer did not wear a long coat. Nor did he carry the half-moon badge of his profession. Instead, he was bundled in a field grey tunic, so worn that it seemed to be moulded to his body. Across his back and down his forearms, the woollen fabric had faded almost white. Pinned to his left chest pocket was an Iron Cross 1st Class and tucked into a buttonhole were two medal ribbons, one for an Iron Cross 2nd Class and another to commemorate his service on the Russian front.

'You were right, Herr Hauptmann!' exclaimed the boy. 'You said we might catch a few more of them if we stayed out after dark, and look what we have here!' He shoved the two men forward.

'Thank you, Andreas,' said the captain, sounding more like a schoolmaster than a commanding officer.

The boy handed him the papers belonging to Pekkala and Kirov, saluted and stood back.

Puffing thoughtfully at his pipe, the captain flipped through the Hungarian identity books, unfolding the insert at the back which identified both Kirov and Pekkala as tradesmen for a company called Matra, located in the Hungarian city of Eger, which had a contract to make footwear for the German military.

Ever since they had first come in sight of the roadblock, neither Kirov nor Pekkala had spoken a word. Pekkala could feel his heart beating against a leather strap of his empty holster which he had strapped across his chest. He had designed the contraption himself, so that the gun could be carried at an angle that was easiest to reach, which put the Webley just beneath his solar plexus on the left side of his ribcage.

Both men realised that they were completely at the mercy of their captors. There was nowhere to run, no chance of fighting their way out and, unless this captain intervened, these boys would soon have them swinging from ropes.

'They are Hungarians,' said the officer, more to himself than to the others.

'Shall we hang them?' asked Andreas, unable to conceal the excitement in his voice.

Wearily, the officer glanced up at him. 'These papers are in order and, in case you had forgotten, Hungary is one of the few allies we have left. Besides, according to these documents, these men work for a company that might well have made your boots.'

'Then we should hang them just for that,' piped up the other boy. He pointed at the muddy clumps of leather on his feet.

'I've only had these things three weeks and they're already falling apart.'

The officer just shook his head. 'Indeed they are, Berthold, but perhaps they were not built to last.' Berthold blinked at the officer in confusion, unable to grasp the meaning of his words.

'And what about these guns, Herr Hauptmann?' Andreas held them up for the officer to see.

'Why shouldn't they have guns?' asked the captain. 'Everyone else does.'

'Well, what are they doing out here?' demanded Berthold. 'It looks pretty suspicious if you ask me.'

'But nobody is asking you,' replied the captain. 'Put them in the truck tonight. Then, in the morning, you take them in to Major Rademacher. He can decide what to do.'

Growling under their breath, Berthold and Andreas turned and shoved their captives past the second barricade.

They left their bicycles propped against the felled trees of the roadblock and followed the policeman down the road.

'And make sure they stay put!' the officer called out before he climbed back into his bunker.

The truck which the captain had mentioned was hidden in the woods only a short walk down the road. It had been painted with a curious camouflage pattern, made from leafy branches which had been laid upon the metal bonnet and cowlings and then painted over with a lighter shade of green than the original colouring, leaving the silhouette of the branches behind when the second coat had dried.

Andreas climbed into the back, which was covered with a canvas roof. 'In!' he barked at the two men, motioning for them to climb aboard.

Sitting across from each on the hard wooden benches, Kirov and Pekkala were handcuffed to a metal rail which ran behind each bench.

Andreas patted Kirov gently on the face before climbing out of the truck. 'Good night, gentlemen!' he said, as he shuffled away through the leaves.

The sun was just rising over the shattered rooftops of Berlin when Leopold descended to Hitler's private quarters on the fourth and deepest level of the bunker.

There, Hitler welcomed him into a small, cramped sitting room, whose space was largely taken up by a cream-white couch, a small coffee table and two chairs. Hitler was already dressed. He gave the impression of being a man who seldom slept at all, and Hunyadi suspected that this was not far from the truth.

Here, in the stark electric light, Hitler's skin looked even paler and more bloodless than it had done in the Chancellery garden. He stooped as he moved about, as if, somehow, he felt the weight of the tons of earth between them and the ground above. He was dressed, as he had been before, in a pale green-grey double-breasted jacket, a white shirt and black trousers, neatly pressed.

'So, Hunyadi!' he growled, 'have you caught our little songbird yet?'

Hunyadi was startled by the power in his voice. From his outward appearance, Hitler appeared as someone who could barely speak at all. 'Not yet,' he replied, 'but I have learned a few things since we last spoke.'

Hitler held his arm out towards the couch and gestured at Hunyadi to sit. Hitler lowered himself down in one of the chairs, settled his elbows on to the wooden arms, and leaned forward expectantly.

Before Hunyadi could speak, a door on the far side of the sitting room opened and Hitler's mistress, Eva Braun, appeared, wearing a blue dress flecked with tiny white polka dots and low-heeled black shoes. She had a round, guileless-looking face, with a softly shaped chin and narrow, arching eyebrows. These were darker than her brownish-blonde hair, which had been combed back to reveal her forehead.

To Hunyadi, who immediately rose to his feet, she looked like she was getting ready to go to a party.

Behind her, through the open door, Hunyadi could see an unmade bed. But it was a small bed, and he struggled to imagine how two people could have fitted in it comfortably. The furnishings in the room – everything from the lampshade to the pictures on the walls – showed nothing that would indicate the presence of a man. Hunyadi wondered if they slept in separate rooms, even though both of them were crammed together in this dungeon. It may have been a well-decorated dungeon, but it was a dungeon, nevertheless.

Hitler's relationship with Eva Braun was not widely known outside the bunker. She rarely appeared with him in public and it was only when her car was stopped for driving erratically across the Oberbauer Bridge, early in 1944, that Hunyadi had learned of her existence. The police officer who pulled her over, an old friend of Hunyadi's named Rothbart, had been on the point of arresting the woman for being drunk behind the wheel, along with her loud and even more inebriated companions who occupied the back seat, when two carloads of SS security appeared to escort the woman away. Rothbart's name, home address and service number were taken down by an irate SS officer, whose sleeve bore the black and silver cuff title of the Führer's Headquarters. Then, after warning Rothbart to keep his mouth shut, the officer helped the woman out of the driver's seat, opened the rear door of the sedan and waited until she climbed in beside her friends before getting in himself behind the wheel.

The last thing Rothbart heard as the car sped away into the dark was laughter and the popping of a champagne cork from the back seat of the car.

'That was Hitler's girl!' Rothbart had confided to Hunyadi. It was the first time he had ever heard the name of Eva Braun.

'And who is this?' she asked, barely glancing at Hunyadi as she walked into the sitting room. Instead, she busied herself with attaching a small golden ring into her earlobe.

'My name . . .' began Hunyadi.

'Is not important,' Hitler said abruptly. 'It's a friend of mine from the old days. That's all. He's working on something for me.'

'I see,' said Eva Braun and, in an instant, it was as if Hunyadi had ceased to exist. 'I am going up to the canteen to get some breakfast,' she told Hitler. 'Is there anything you want?'

'A glass of milk,' he replied, 'but do not hurry back on my account.'

Then the two men were alone again.

With clawing fingers, Hitler beckoned at Hunyadi. 'Tell me!' he whispered urgently. 'Tell me everything you know.'

'Based on what you've told me,' said Hunyadi, 'I believe you are correct. There is a leak.'

'Yes? And?' Hitler's eyes bored into the detective. 'Everyone I spoke to is aware of it,' continued Hunyadi.

'However, I do not believe that the person responsible for the leak is operating from inside the bunker.'

Hitler sat back suddenly, as if he had been pushed by a ghost.

'But how could it be otherwise? The information is coming from here and nowhere else!'

'I agree,' said Hunyadi, 'but I believe that this is happening indirectly. Somebody who works here, among you, is speaking to someone on the outside. A wife. A husband. A lover, perhaps, but in any case it's someone they trust implicitly.'

'What brings you to this conclusion?' asked Hitler.

'The one thing shared by everyone I spoke to yesterday was their fear. Fear of you. Fear of the Russians. Fear of the judgement they may have to face some day. None of them, not even the lowest in rank, would risk their lives to smuggle out the gossip you are hearing from Der Chef.'

'And yet that is exactly what they're doing!'

'Without realising it, yes,' agreed Hunyadi. 'I am willing to bet that your informant does not even know that he or she is delivering secrets to the enemy and, given how long this information has been leaking out, we can be sure of two things.'

'What two things?' demanded Hitler.

'The first', replied Hunyadi, 'is that the relationship required to enable such a transfer of information is a long-standing one. The second is that consistency of the information, and the kind of information you have been able to pinpoint as having come directly from your headquarters, implies that it is being passed on in the course of normal conversations. It is just chatter, which people feast upon no matter where or who they are. It is part of human nature. There is nothing threatening, perse, in the information itself, at least as far as we know. This is why the informant believes there is no danger in discussing it.'

'Then we arrest them all!' cried Hitler, leaping to his feet.

'Interrogate everyone! Smash their fingers with a hammer one by one until we get the answers we are looking for!'

Hunyadi waited patiently for Hitler to finish his tirade.

A faint flush of colour brushed across his cheeks, but now it drained away again, leaving his face even more bloodless than before. He slumped back into his chair. 'I see that you do not share my enthusiasm, Hunyadi,' he muttered.

'You cannot arrest everyone,' stated the detective. 'We do not have the time to pursue so many suspects.'

'And why not?'

Because, Hunyadi thought but did not say, by the time I have questioned them all, both you and this city will belong to Joseph Stalin. 'The first thing we have to do is stop the leak,' he said, 'before it grows too big to control. After that, you can start thinking about punishment.'

Hitler nodded slowly. 'Very well,' he said, 'but how do we accomplish that?'

'With respect,' said Hunyadi, 'I suggest that we don't even try.'

'What?'

'Do nothing,' replied the detective.

'Nothing!' Hitler's breath erupted into a long gravelly laugh that finished in a spasm of coughing. 'But why?'

'Because you must understand this leak for what it is,' said Hunyadi. 'As far as we know, it exists as nothing more than a distraction, to make you second-guess the loyalties of those around you. In this, it has already achieved its objective.' 'I am perfectly aware of that,' said Hitler. 'What worries me is not what I'm aware of, but that which I strongly suspect.'

Hunyadi sighed and nodded. 'There is a path we can pursue.'

'Go on.'

'The information seeping from this bunker is smuggled out of Germany the same way it's smuggled back in.'

Hitler narrowed his eyes. 'You mean by radio?'

'Precisely, and since there has been no interruption to the flow of information, we can assume that messages are still being transmitted from an illegal wireless set. And if we can locate it . . .'

'And how big are these wireless sets?'

Hunyadi shrugged. 'The smallest of them can be hidden in a briefcase.'

Hitler shook his head. 'And how do you plan on finding such a tiny object?'

'I have an idea,' answered Hunyadi, 'but it will require you making an announcement at your next briefing.'

'What sort of announcement?'

'One that is incorrect,' Hunyadi told him, 'and yet which would prove irresistible to whomever is causing the leak.'

'You mean some shred of bunker gossip?' asked Hitler intently. 'A sordid affair? A child born out of wedlock?'

'No,' said Hunyadi, 'because even if those details might get passed along to the Allies, they are not truly matters which concern us.'

'I see,' Hitler murmured, touching his fingernails against his lips. 'So it must be something bigger. Something of real significance.'

'A military secret,' suggested Hunyadi, 'and yet one which the Allies would be unable to confirm, at least not for a few days.'

'A few days?' echoed Hitler. 'Is that all?'

'If I am correct that the radio operator is still transmitting messages, we should not have long to wait.'

Hitler breathed in deeply, then let his breath trail out. 'Yes,' he whispered, as Hunyadi's plan took shape inside his brain. 'I think I know exactly what to say.'

'And from this,' continued Hunyadi, 'we will be able to locate not only the radio operator, but also to confirm whether information of strategic value, rather than just parlour chat, is being funnelled to Der Chef.'

'We'll do it!' Hitler clapped his hands together, the sound like a gunshot in the confined space of the room. But then he paused, and his hands drifted down once more on to the wooden armrests of the chair. 'But that still does not explain how you plan to catch this radio operator?'

'Yes,' agreed Hunyadi, 'which brings me to my final request.'

'Name it and it will be granted if such a thing is possible.'

'I might need to disrupt the power grid.'

'Which power grid?' demanded Hitler. 'The one to the Chancellery? To the bunker itself?'

'No.' Hunyadi paused. 'I mean the whole city.'

Hitler stared at him blankly for a moment. 'You're going to shut off the power to Berlin?'

'Possibly.'

Hitler puffed his cheeks and looked around the room. By the time his gaze returned to Hunyadi, Adolf Hitler was smiling. 'By God, Hunyadi, you can plunge us into darkness for a decade if you think it just might work!'

'Gentlemen!' said Hitler, rising from behind the table in his briefing room.

Across from him, members of the High Command waited expectantly for his announcement. They stood shoulder to shoulder, crammed into the little space like commuters on the metro.

'Gentlemen,' said Hitler, 'I am pleased to report that the Diamond Stream device is now fully operational, and is currently being installed in all V-2 rockets.'

'How long will it take before launches commence?' asked Fegelein, who stood at the front of the jostling crowd.

'It is imminent,' replied Hitler. 'Tell that to Himmler when you see him.'

'At once!' barked Fegelein, cracking his heels together.

That night, lying on the bed in the apartment of his mistress Elsa Batz, Fegelein drank cognac from a bottle, stark naked except for his socks. He had decided to wait until morning before driving to Himmler's headquarters with news of the Diamond Stream device. Bad news Fegelein usually dispensed by telephone, but good news, such as this, he preferred to deliver in person. Himmler normally went to bed early and any benefit Fegelein might have derived from heading out immediately to Hohenlychen would be cancelled out by having woken up his master.

'The idea of it!' huffed Fegelein. He paused to take another swig of cognac.

'Of what?' asked Elsa. She was sitting at a table by the window, wearing a white dressing gown, and casually filing her nails. Elsa was a round-faced woman with platinum-blonde hair and rosy cheeks, who had formerly been employed as an exotic dancer at the 'Salon Kitty' on Giesebrechtstrasse. Available solely to high-ranking members of the military, Salon Kitty was one of the only nightclubs allowed to operate in Berlin, for the reason that it was secretly run by the SS. What went on there was filmed by members of Rattenhuber's Security Service, to be used later as blackmail or as an excuse for arrest. From the first moment Fegelein saw Elsa Batz, one night back in the summer of 1944, he had known that their lives would somehow become entwined. From her languid movements, up there on the stage, and the sleepy sensuality in her eyes, Fegelein perceived a strange familiarity about her from which he could not walk away. This fact brought him no joy. He knew, from all the other mistresses he had kept over the years, exactly how complicated and expensive this was going to be. With equal certainty, he knew that the physical attraction he felt for Elsa Batz had nothing to do with whether or not he would actually like her. In fact, in a very short time, he might well grow to despise her. But that had nothing to with how badly he needed to possess her.

Fegelein was well aware that Salon Kitty was nothing more than a honey trap. He even knew where the cameras were located and the names of men who had, when confronted with the evidence of blackmail, chosen to end their own lives rather than end up like dogs on Rattenhuber's leash.

That was why, in a very short space of time, he persuaded Elsa to quit her job and then set her up in this luxurious apartment on Bleibtreustrasse.

It was here that he spent several nights a week, at times when his wife, Gretl, would assume that he was up at Himmler's headquarters at Hohenlychen, north of the city. The fact that Fegelein kept a mistress, in spite of the occupational hazard associated with marrying Eva Braun's sister, did not come as a surprise to anyone who knew him. Fegelein felt fairly certain that even his wife was aware of the apartment on Bleibtreustrasse, although she never mentioned it. His wife, it seemed, neither knew, nor cared to know the details. In marrying a man like Fegelein, contending with a mistress was inevitable.

Much to Fegelein's surprise, he and Elsa Batz did not grow to hate each other. It was true that they had very little in common, but what they had turned out to be enough. Unlike all the other women he had kept, Elsa Batz remained content to be Fegelein's mistress. She never set her sights on being anything more than she had ever been to him, and this alone ensured the survival of their relationship.

'The idea', continued Fegelein, 'that, after everything I've done for Hitler, he would so much as entertain the notion that I might be guilty of treason is just absurd.'

The rustle of the filing ceased. 'But you say there is, in fact, a leak of information.'

'Probably,' replied Fegelein. He was staring at the ceiling as he spoke. 'But it's just small stuff. With a million Russian soldiers waiting on the Seelow Heights, ready to pour into Berlin any day now, we all have more important things to care about.' He took another drink. The cognac burned in his throat. 'It's trust I'm talking about. Hitler should trust me in the same way Himmler does, and in the same way that I trust Fraülein S!'

At the mention of that name, Elsa Batz felt something twisting in her guts. Fegelein often mentioned his secretary, and always in the most glowing of terms. It had lately occurred to Elsa that she might not be Fegelein's only mistress. She had satisfied herself with being who she was because she knew that, sooner or later, Fegelein would abandon his post as Himmler's liaison. When the battle for this city commenced, Fegelein himself would not be part of it for any longer than he had to. When the time came to run, it was she, and not Fegelein's dreary wife, who would accompany him to safety. He was her ticket out of here. All she had to do was make sure nothing came along to change his mind.

'She trusts me, too,' muttered Fegelein, more to himself than to Elsa. 'Trusts me with her life, and so she should.'

'I trust you,' Elsa said softly.

Fegelein glanced across the room at her. 'What?'

'I trust you with my life,' she told him.

He blinked at her uncomprehendingly. 'What are you talking about, woman?'

Fegelein often scolded her like this, but there was something in the coldness of Fegelein's voice this evening which caused a feeling of dread to wash over Elsa Batz. In that moment, she suddenly realised that she was about to be replaced by this mysterious Fraülein S. It seemed obvious, now that the idea had presented itself. She had been ignoring all the signs. Until this moment, her safety had relied upon doing nothing. But now, to do nothing would not just be the end of her cosy apartment on the Bleibtreustrasse. It would be suicide.

'Who is this man who's asking all the questions?' she asked, changing the subject.

'Some Berlin cop named Leopold Hunyadi,' answered Fegelein.

'A policeman?' she asked. 'Just an ordinary policeman?'

'Not quite,' said Fegelein. 'First of all, he's the best detective in Berlin. And secondly, he's an old friend of Hitler's. They go way back, apparently, but how they know each other I have no idea. I hear he's not even a member of the National Socialist Party, so what their friendship's based on I have no idea.' Then he laughed. 'Probably not what ours is based on, anyway!' He patted the empty space beside him on the bed. She got up and walked out of the room.

'Elsa!' Fegelein called after her. 'Elsa! Come on! I was kidding!'

But there was no reply.

With the cognac swirling in his brain, Fegelein settled his head back into the pillow. The last thought through his head before he slipped beneath the red tide of unconsciousness was of Fraülein S, and the sacred bond of loyalty they shared.

The sun was setting as Hunyadi emerged from an underground station just outside the Berlin Zoo. Air raids had wrecked part of the station's structure above ground, but the metro had continued to function. Not far from the Zoo station stood a huge concrete tower, built to support one of several anti-aircraft batteries engaged in the defence of Berlin.

Hunyadi made his way to the tower and, escorted by a Luftwaffe officer in command of the anti-aircraft defenses, travelled in a rattly lift to the top of the tower. Here, on a wide circular platform, an 88mm flak gun pointed at the sky, its barrel ringed with more than a dozen bands of white paint, each one of which marked the downing of an Allied plane.

In a recessed alcove on this platform, Hunyadi found what he was looking for – a field radio station powerful enough to communicate with other flak towers all over the city.

Hunyadi's inquiries as to where it might be possible to monitor not just military radio traffic, but all radio traffic coming in or out of the city had led him to this place.

He handed a radio operator a scrap of paper on which a series of numbers had been written. They represented all the frequencies known to have been used by Allied agents in transmitting messages to their bases in England and Russia.

After leaving instructions with the radio operator to inform him of any traffic on those frequencies, Hunyadi went down to the second level of the flak tower, entering into a bare concrete room filled with unpainted wooden crates of 88mm cannon shells. By shifting some of the crates around, although it took all his strength just to drag them, he fashioned for himself a place to sit. From one pocket, he pulled a piece of cheese wrapped in a handkerchief and from another pocket came a hunk of dark brown Roggenbrot. With no idea how long he'd have to wait, Hunyadi settled down to eat his dinner.

He was fast asleep, four hours later, when the wail of air-raid sirens jolted him awake. His first reaction, like that of every other inhabitant of this city, was to scurry to the nearest underground shelter.

He rushed towards the door, barely able to stay on his feet since the hard wood of the ammunition crate had given him a case of pins and needles. Arriving in the doorway, Hunyadi was almost knocked down by a dozen men trampling up the stairs to take their positions at the flak gun. He stepped aside to let them go by and was just about to make his way downstairs when the last man to pass called him back. 'Stay here,' he warned. 'By the time you make it down into the street, the bombs will already be falling. Besides, you're safer up here than down below.'

There was no time for Hunyadi to question the wisdom of this, because, at that moment, the room was filled with a deafening crash which dropped the detective to his knees.

'Have we been hit?' he asked.

'No!' The man laughed, holding out his hand to help Hunyadi to his feet. 'That's us firing at them! And you'd better get used to it, old man, because we're just getting started.' Dazed as he was by the blast, the only words which really struck him were 'old man'.

I'm only forty-five, he thought, but perhaps, these days, that does make me old, after all.

And then the lights went out.

He staggered back to his throne of crates, just as another shattering boom filled his ears. Vaguely, above the high-pitched ringing in his ears, Hunyadi heard a metallic clang as an empty shell casing was ejected from the breech of the 88 on to the concrete platform above him.

Hunyadi put his hands over his ears, careful to keep his mouth open to equalise the change in pressure caused by the explosions above him, and hunched over with his face almost touching his knees.

How long he stayed that way he could not tell. The firing of the gun became a nearly constant roar, the echo of one blast overlaying the next until he could scarcely tell one from the other. Sometimes, he heard the drone of planes above him and the muffled thump of bombs exploding, as well as the sharp commands of gun aimers and loaders, but it all reached him in a chorus so jumbled that the sounds seemed to come from a dream.

He had no idea if the radio man, up on the firing platform, was still monitoring the frequencies. More likely, thought Hunyadi, he is too busy doing his usual job. Hunyadi took some comfort in the fact that anyone with access to a secret transmitter would probably have sought shelter along with the rest of the city's population, rather than stay at their post and risk being blown to pieces by the very people they were trying to help.

From time to time, Hunyadi was aware of men moving about in the darkness around him as they hauled fresh boxes of cannon shells up to the firing deck. Occasionally, someone would shine a red-filtered torch as they searched among the crates.

During a lull in the firing, Hunyadi rose up from his throne of ammunition boxes and climbed the concrete staircase to the gun platform. The air was filled with gun smoke, which seeped into his lungs and filled his mouth with a metallic taste, as if from resting a coin upon the tongue. Moving past the silhouettes of men, Hunyadi made his way through the carpet of spent shells to the chest-high wall of the platform. From here, he watched searchlights rake across the night sky, like swords wielded by some clumsy giant. In some places, dust from the bombing plumed so thickly that the searchlights seemed to break against the clouds, fragmenting their beams and angling them back to the earth. Distantly, he heard the shriek of falling bombs and then he saw the flash of their explosions, which vanished into tidal waves of smoke.

'When you stopped firing the gun,' Hunyadi said to a man who came to stand beside him, 'I thought it was over.'

'We are just cooling the barrel,' replied the man. His features were so hidden in the darkness that it seemed to Hunyadi, still disoriented by the concussive force of the explosions, that the night itself had taken shape and was conversing with him now.

'It's beautiful, don't you think?' asked the man.

'Beautiful?' asked Hunyadi.

'A terrible beauty, I grant you,' said the darkness, 'but a beauty nonetheless.' He raised an arm and pointed at the sky.

'See there!'

Hunyadi looked upwards, just in time to see a searchlight fasten on a plane. It looked no bigger than an insect, and it was hard for him to imagine something which seemed so small being capable of so much damage. Although he had lived through numerous air raids, he had always been below ground when they took place. All he had ever known of these attacks was the panic of rushing to the shelters and the distant, rumbling earthquake of the bombs as they exploded. And he was well acquainted with the aftermath, as he made his way through shattered streets, dodging fire trucks and ambulances driven by civilians wearing yellow armbands and strange, wide-brimmed helmets which made them appear like Roman gladiators. But he had never actually seen a raid in progress, as he was doing now, and he could not deny that the man had been telling the truth. There was a mesmerising beauty to this vast apocalypse.

Now two other searchlights zeroed in upon the bomber, so that it seemed to balance, helpless and impaled upon the icy spear points.

Hunyadi heard a sharp command from somewhere behind him and he turned just as the cannon fired. The roar and the sudden change in pressure shoved him off his feet. He stumbled back and fell against the wall. His head was filled with a shrill ringing sound, as if a tuning fork had been struck inside his brain. Even over this, he heard the sound of laughter and a hand reached from the dark to help him up again.

The last thing he saw before he clambered back down into the magazine was the bomber, bracketed by tiny sparks as the anti-aircraft shells exploded around its wingtips. There was a momentary smear of orange fire as shrapnel tore the bomber to pieces. Then the night became empty again, and the searchlights resumed their awkward sweeping of the sky.

The sun had not yet risen above the trees when Kirov and Pekkala, still handcuffed to the bench of the truck, were awakened by the sound of someone shuffling towards them through the leaves.

The boy named Andreas climbed in and sat beside Pekkala, a sub-machine gun laid across his lap.

His friend, Berthold, clambered into the cab, started the engine and soon they were driving down the road, heading west towards Berlin.

Andreas studied the two men, who avoided his gaze.

'Do you speak German?' asked the boy.

Pekkala had been staring at the floor, but now he raised his head. 'A little,' he replied.

Kirov kept silent.

'We have to do what the captain says or we will get in trouble,' explained Andreas, 'but do you know what Major Rademacher will say when we arrive with you?'

Pekkala shook his head.

Now Andreas leaned forward. He had no gloves and wore a dirty pair of grey wool socks with the ends cut off, allowing his fingers to poke through. His pale skin and dirt-rimmed fingernails stood out against the black sides of the sub-machine gun.

'Major Rademacher will say we should not bother him with questions. He will say that we have wasted valuable fuel on this foolish errand.'

'So you will get in trouble, either way,' said Pekkala. Andreas nodded. 'Exactly.'

'And what will he say then, this Major Rademacher?'

'Maybe he will tell us to shoot you.' Andreas shrugged.

'Maybe he will shoot you himself. It all depends.'

'Depends on what?'

'On whether he is drunk or sober. On whether his wife yelled at him. On whether he enjoyed his breakfast. You see,' explained Andreas, 'there is no rule but what he says, and what he says will be a mystery, even to himself, until he says it.'

It was mid-morning when Fegelein's car pulled up outside the brick building in which Himmler had established his headquarters at Hohenlychen, located in the countryside not far from the village of Hassleben. The Hohenlychen compound was, in fact, a rest home managed by Himmler's medical adviser, Dr. Karl Gebhardt. Himmler had moved there shortly after Hitler's descent into the Reichschancellery bunker complex.

The building which Himmler had taken over had a sharply angled roof, scaled like the skin of a snake with red terracotta shingles. From a height of a tall man up to the gutters on the top floor of the three-story building, the bricks had been painted bone-white. Below that, they had been left plain. The windows on the ground floor were curiously arched, in order to allow in more light than the windows on the floors above. But Himmler kept the windows shuttered. The ground floor had once been a day room for recuperating patients, but now served as a place for Himmler to conduct his meetings with a daily stream of visitors.

Himmler himself rarely appeared before 10 a.m. His early mornings were taken up with bathing and a daily massage from his steward, Felix Kersten.

Knowing his master's schedule, Fegelein had scheduled his visit to coincide with the moment when Himmler would emerge from his private quarters; a time when his mood was likely to be at its best.

'Shall I wait here?' asked Lilya, sitting behind the wheel. She was dazed and tired. Fegelein had left her sitting in the car for the entire night, while he bedded down with Elsa Batz. She had not kept the engine running, for fear of draining the fuel tank, and it had been a cold night. Even the blankets, which she kept in the trunk for such occasions, had not been enough to keep her warm. At 6 a.m., just when she had managed to doze off, Fegelein had rapped his gold wedding ring upon the driver's side window, jarring her awake, before jumping into the passenger seat and ordering her to drive to Hohenlychen.

Fegelein cast a glance at his driver. She looked exhausted.

He knew it was his fault. With anyone else, he would not have paused even to consider this, but Fraülein S was different.

'No,' he said. 'No need to wait outside. Come in and get warm by the fire.'

Normally, she would have driven the car to a stable which had been converted into a garage for Himmler's various automobiles. There, she would have waited for Fegelein to send for her.

It was useless to protest.

Following in Fegelein's footsteps, Lilya entered the building. It was the first time Lilya had been inside Himmler's headquarters.

She found herself in an immaculately tidy room, with Persian carpets on the floors, a leather couch and two upholstered chairs beside a hearth in which a small coal fire had been lit, to fend off the chill of the morning. There were several paintings on the walls, all of them of landscapes depicting gardens congested with wildflowers, tumbledown farmhouses and quiet streams, surrounded by drooping branches of great willow trees. She was struck by the sense of confinement in these pictures, a feeling which was amplified by the shutters on the windows, excluding all natural light. Electric lamps with heavy, green glass shades cast their glow across the polished wooden side tables on which they had been placed.

One other thing she noticed was the absence of the smell of cigarettes. It was such a constant everywhere else that, like the ticking of a clock, the very lack of it caught her attention. Only then did she recall that Himmler could not stand the smell of tobacco and that he had attempted, unsuccessfully, to cut it from the rations of his soldiers in the field.

I have entered the lair of the beast, thought Lilya. And yet she was not afraid. Having come this far, and in the company of Himmler's trusted adjutant, she realised that she had moved beyond the greatest danger.

At that moment, the inner door opened and Heinrich Himmler stepped out of the shadows. He was of medium height, slightly built, with close-cropped hair, a small chin and shallow, grey-blue eyes, almost hidden behind a set of round silver-rimmed glasses. He wore a clean white shirt, slate-grey riding breeches, and close-fitting black riding boots.

'Ah!' he said, gasping as he caught sight of Lilya Simonova. 'I see we have a guest.' In spite of his jovial tone, there was menace in his voice at this unexpected intrusion.

Fegelein, attuned to every inflection of his master's voice, quickly introduced them. 'The celebrated Fraülein S,' remarked Himmler. 'Fegelein has sung your praises many times.'

Fegelein's face reddened. 'She was cold,' he struggled to explain. 'I brought her in so she could warm up by the fire.'

'I will not detain you any further,' said Lilya, turning to leave.

'Nonsense!' exclaimed Himmler. 'Sit! Sit!' he gestured to a chair. 'I will have coffee brought to you.' The rigidity had vanished from his tone, now that his authority had been established. It was he, and not Fegelein, who allowed strangers to stand in his presence.

The two men retired to the inner room, where Himmler kept his office.

As the door opened and shut, Lilya caught a glimpse of wood-panelled walls, dark green curtains covering the windows and a large desk heaped with paperwork laid out in ordered piles, like some architect's half-finished vision of a city not yet built.

As Lilya stared at the sputtering flames, she struggled to hear what the two men were saying.

'Another mistress, Fegelein?' laughed Himmler.

'No, Herr Reichsführer!' he protested. 'It is nothing of the sort.'

'Do not play coy with me. I know about that little pied-àterre you keep on Bleibtreustrasse.'

'One lady friend is enough.'

'Apart from one's wife, you mean?'

'I swear there is nothing between us. She is my driver, nothing more!'

'If you say so, Fegelein. But now, having seen her for myself, I must admit I might forgive you the transgression.'

'I bring good news,' said Fegelein, anxious to change the subject. 'The Diamond Stream device is fully operational.'

'Are you certain?'

'Hitler himself made the announcement. Diamond Stream is to be installed in all remaining V-2s.'

Himmler grunted with approval. 'You realise, Fegelein, that this could change everything?'

'Yes! That's why I came here in person, Herr Reichsführer, just as soon as I possibly could.'

'We must find a way', said Himmler, 'to ensure that, from now on, Hagemann answers to us. To us and to nobody else.'

'But how?' asked Fegelein.

'We'll try a little flattery and, if that doesn't work, I'm sure we can come up with some way to blackmail him into seeing things our way. He must have some weakness. Have you seen him at the Salon Kitty?'

Fegelein shook his head. 'I don't think he goes in much for cabarets.'

'Gambling?'

This time Fegelein only shrugged.

'Well, find something!' ordered Himmler. 'And if nothing turns up, invent it. A well-placed lie can break him just as easily as the truth and as soon as we have shown him we can do it, he will come around.'

Fegelein said nothing, but he knew exactly what was going on.

At this stage, even rockets equipped with the Diamond Stream device would not be enough to ensure a German victory, as Hitler perhaps believed. But they, and control over the men who had built them, might well be enough to alter the peace that came afterwards.

Even Himmler understood that the war was lost and that nothing could be done until Hitler was out of the picture. But that day was fast approaching and Himmler had convinced himself that he had to be ready to take his place as leader of the country, or whatever remained of it.

Himmler had even gone so far as to send out feelers to the Swedish diplomat Count Bernadotte, hoping to make contact with the Allies.

'They respect me,' he had confided to Fegelein. 'They view me now, as they have always done, as a worthy adversary.'

In this, Fegelein knew, Himmler was as delusional as Hitler. But he was right about one thing – the Allies would indeed respect the weaponry he still commanded.

Fegelein knew perfectly well that he was about to become irrelevant. From now on, he would have to fend for himself, or else be banished to the same corridor of hell where a place had been made ready for his master. But Fegelein wasn't worried. He had already begun to prepare for his departure from this doomed city and for the new life he would begin far away, with Fraülein Simonova at his side.

Hunyadi opened his eyes.

He had fallen asleep, still seated on his throne of ammunition crates, with his elbow on his knee and his chin resting in the cup of his palm.

Someone had hold of his shoulder and was shaking him gently awake.

Blearily, Hunyadi focused on a man wearing the blue woollen tunic of a Luftwaffe flak gunner.

'They've picked up a signal,' said the man. 'Our radio man says you're to come up at once, before we lose it.'

With his feet effervescing from pins and needles, Hunyadi hobbled after the man, following him up to the firing deck.

It was dawn. Mist blanketed the city, punctured here and there by monstrous cobras of smoke where buildings had caught fire.

Men, stripped to the waist, were washing the soot from their faces in a bucket of water. One man was busy painting another white ring around the barrel of the gun.

The radio operator beckoned him over. 'We have a signal on one of the frequencies you gave us.' He took off his headphones and handed them to Hunyadi.

Hunyadi pressed one of the cups to his ear and heard a series of faint beeps, divided into sets of five. 'Definitely some kind of code,' remarked the operator. Hunyadi nodded in agreement.

'The signal is strong,' the radio man continued, 'but I have no way to pinpoint its location.'

'You let me worry about that,' replied Hunyadi. 'Just tell me if the signal cuts out.' On the flak tower's telephone network, he put in a call to the Plotzensee power station, which managed the western districts of the city. Earlier in the day, Hunyadi had contacted each of the four major power stations in the city, with orders to wait for his call, at which point they would cut electricity to the entire district under their control. 'Now,' he commanded.

'Are you sure you want to do this?' said a voice at the other end.

'Now!' shouted Hunyadi. Through a pair of binoculars, he watched a carriage of the city's S-Bahn electric-railway system grumble to a halt at the edge of the western district. People came out of their houses and looked around.

'Anything?' he called to the radio man.

'Still transmitting,' came the reply.

Over the next minute, Hunyadi put in three more calls to other power stations scattered across the city. The Humboldt station, in the north of Berlin, had been hit by incendiary bombs during the raid and was already suffering a black-out. The rest, in turn, cut their power for five seconds before switching it back on again.

Such losses of electricity were not uncommon in a city constantly struggling to repair bomb damage. Some power cuts lasted for days.

It was only when the Rummelsburg station, which governed the eastern district of the city, cut its electricity that the radio man called out that the transmission had ceased abruptly.

Five seconds later, Rummelsburg switched the power on again.

'Nothing,' said the radio operator.

'Wait,' ordered Hunyadi. Seconds passed.

Then, suddenly, the radio man called out, 'He's back! He's back!'

Hunyadi walked to the eastward-facing corner of the platform and looked out towards the Friedrichshain Park, the sprawling cemetery and the Baltenplatz circle in the distance, as if to glimpse the signals, rising like soap bubbles into the morning sky.

'Congratulations, Inspector!' called the radio man. 'Whoever you are looking for, he is as good as in the bag.'

But Hunyadi's face betrayed no sign of satisfaction. As far as he was concerned, his work was only just beginning.

After travelling along the pot-holed forest trail for half an hour, the Field Police truck carrying Kirov and Pekkala emerged from the woods and pulled out on to the highway leading into Berlin. The road was wide and empty and scattered with burnt-out vehicles, which slowed their progress considerably. In the distance, they could make out several towns, their black church spires propping up the egg-shell-white sky.

By mid-morning, they finally reached the outskirts of Berlin. Here, they saw the first signs of the Allied bombing campaign, which had reduced much of the city to ruins. They could smell it, too – a damp sourness of recently extinguished fires, mixed with the eye-stinging reek of melted rubber.

Pekkala watched crews of women and old men pulling yellowy-grey bricks out of the wreckage of destroyed houses, loading them into wheelbarrows and carting them away. The dust of these pulverised structures so coated the clothing and the faces of these clean-up crews that they seemed to be made of the same dirt as the bricks. It gave the impression of some vast, wounded creature, slowly piecing itself back together. As Pekkala looked out at the ruins, which stretched as far as he could see in all directions, such a task seemed all but impossible. The Red Army, with its terrible desire for vengeance, had not even set foot inside the city yet. And if the defenders of Berlin were anything like the boy who sat before them now, there would be nothing left at all by the time the fighting was over.

The truck turned sharply off the road, and pulled into a courtyard where several other vehicles stood parked against a high wall, on which pieces of broken glass had been embedded in a layer of cement.

'Welcome to the Friedrichsfelde Reform School,' said Andreas, 'which is now the headquarters of Major Rademacher.'

They piled out into the courtyard.

Berthold and Andreas marched the two men into the building.

Major Rademacher was eating his lunch, which consisted of a pickled egg and a raw onion, sliced and mashed together upon a slice of pumpernickel bread. He washed this down with some powdered milk, which he swilled from an oval-mouthed canteen cup.

It irritated the major to eat meals so hopelessly cobbled together by his adjutant, Lieutenant Krebs, who doubled as his cook, his house cleaner and his valet. He could not blame Krebs for his choice of food. To have found an onion was a triumph, and an egg, even if it was pickled, was nothing short of miraculous.

But he was still in a bad mood about it and, when the two half-trained Field Police privates arrived with their latest set of prisoners, they were doomed to feel his wrath.

Rademacher shoved his plate of food aside, snatched the Hungarian identity books from Berthold's outstretched hand. He glanced at them and then tossed them back on to the desk, where Andreas had carefully laid out the guns belonging to Pekkala and Kirov, like duelling pistols ready for selection. 'What are you doing to me?' he groaned. 'I send you out to catch deserters and this is what you bring me? Two Hungarian shoe salesmen?'

'The captain . . .' Andreas began.

'Oh, shut up!' ordered Rademacher. 'You always blame everything on him.'

'But it's his fault,' protested Berthold. 'He told us to bring them to you.'

'What you have done', explained Rademacher as if addressing children even younger than they were, 'is provide these . . . these . . . what the hell is a rude name for Hungarians?'

'I don't think there is one,' said Andreas.

'It's bad enough just being Hungarian,' added Berthold.

'Well, all you have managed to do', continued Rademacher, 'is provide them with a taxi service into the city, using up valuable fuel in the process.' As he paused for breath, Rademacher's gaze snagged upon the pistols. He snatched up the Webley and brandished it towards Kirov and Pekkala. 'What the hell were you planning to shoot with this, anyway? Elephants?' Disgustedly, he tossed it back on to the desk.

'What should we do with them?' asked Berthold.

'How should I know?' demanded Rademacher. 'They're not my problem.'

'We could hang them,' suggested Andreas.

'No, you idiots!' boomed Rademacher. 'Just get them out of here and then get out, yourselves.' With the movements of a magician, he waved his hands over the guns on his desk, as if to make them disappear before their eyes. 'And take these with you!'

Kirov and Pekkala retrieved their papers, holstered their guns and then the four men shuffled quickly out into the hallway. Rademacher pulled his plate back in front of him. For a moment, he stared at the pulp of egg and onion smeared upon the dirty-looking bread. Then, with a growl, he shoved it away once again.

'I told you,' Andreas said to Pekkala as they made their way back to the courtyard. 'There's no law but what he says there is, and what he says is different every time.'

'You were right about the fuel, anyway,' said Pekkala.

The two boys climbed back into the truck. Driving out of the courtyard, they slowed down as they passed Kirov and Pekkala.

Andreas leaned from the open window of the cab. 'Next time,' he said, and then he smiled and clamped his fingers to his neck.

Pekkala and Kirov emerged from the courtyard on to Rummelsburger Street and began walking west, towards the centre of the city.

'Well, Inspector,' said Kirov. 'You have one day before the scheduled rendezvous. Surely you can see we have no chance of finding her at all, let alone within twenty-four hours.'

'I am inspired by your faith in me,' remarked Pekkala.

'I'm here, aren't I?' replied Kirov. 'Now would you mind sharing with me exactly what the hell you plan to do?'

'If we can't find her,' explained Pekkala, 'we find the man who will.'

It took a moment for this to sink into Kirov's brain. 'Hunyadi?'

'Exactly.'

'And how do you propose to do that?'

'I have a pretty good idea,' replied Pekkala.

Hunyadi was in his office, staring at a map of Berlin. With a magnifying glass, he studied the layout of the streets in the eastern quadrant of the city, as if to find in it some hint as to the whereabouts of the radio transmitter.

A gentle knocking on the door made him look up. Through the blurred glass pane, Hunyadi could see that his visitor was a woman, even though he could not make out the features of her face.

'Come in,' he said.

The door opened, and an expensively dressed lady stepped into the room. She wore a knee-length navy-blue skirt, with a matching jacket piped in white, with large white buttons. Her hair was startlingly blonde. Freckles dappled her round face, making her look younger than she was. It was her eyes that gave her away. They looked strangely lifeless, as if they had witnessed more misery than one person should see in a lifetime.

Slowly, Hunyadi climbed to his feet. 'I think you might have the wrong room,' he said.

'Inspector Hunyadi?'

'It seems you're in the right place, after all.' He gestured at a chair on the other side of his desk. 'Please,' he said, gently.

The woman looked at the chair, but she did not sit down.

'My name is Elsa Batz,' she said, unbuckling her handbag to

remove her government-issued identification book.

As she did so, Hunyadi caught a glance of a small pistol in her bag, jumbled in amongst a hairbrush, a tube of lipstick and several crumpled scraps of paper, which appeared to be restaurant receipts.

Elsa Batz handed him the identification.

Hunyadi opened the flimsy booklet and inspected the even flimsier pages inside. He noted that she lived on Bleibtreustrasse, not far from the notorious Salon Kitty nightclub.

'How may I help you?' he asked, returning the booklet to her outstretched hand.

'I hear you have been looking for a spy,' said Elsa Batz. Hunyadi felt his stomach muscles clench. 'Fraülein Batz,' he said, 'what gave you that idea?'

'There is a chauffeur,' replied Elsa Batz, letting her tongue rest upon the last word as if unable to conceal her disgust for the profession. 'She works for Gruppenführer Hermann Fegelein.'

'And her name?'

'Lilya,' she replied. 'Lilya Simonova.' And then she added contemptuously, 'She used to be his secretary.'

'Simonova,' repeated Hunyadi. He began to take notes on a piece of paper.

'He calls her "Fraülein S".'

'And you suspect her of treason?'

'I do.'

'On what grounds?'

'I just do.'

Hunyadi paused and glanced up from his writing. 'That isn't much to go on, Fraülein Batz.' 'Sometimes a hunch is enough,' she replied.

'Are you, perhaps, an acquaintance of the Gruppenführer?' She nodded. 'Which is why I know that my hunch is correct.'

We all do what we have to in order to survive, Hunyadi thought to himself, and I think I know exactly what you do.

'Herr Fegelein has perhaps expressed his doubts to you about this Fraülein S?' he asked.

'No!' spat the woman. 'He thinks she's wonderful. He even fired his driver so that she can drive him around the city instead.'

'I see. And this is what makes you suspicious?'

'Yes!' she called out in exasperation. 'She could be running a whole circus of spies and he wouldn't even notice.'

'A circus?'

'Well, whatever you would call them, then.'

'But you have no actual proof,' remarked Hunyadi. 'Only . . .' he paused, 'intuitions.'

'That's right,' she answered defiantly, 'and they have served me very well so far.'

'I promise to look into it,' said Hunyadi, rising to his feet to show that this little interview was at an end. But he wasn't quite finished with her yet. 'One more thing, Fraülein Batz,' he said.

She raised her sculpted eyebrows. 'Yes?'

'If I could just take a look at the gun you are carrying in your handbag.'

Her cheeks turned red and she immediately became flustered, but she did as she was told, retrieving the gun from her bag and placing it upon the desk in front of him.

It was a Walther Model 5, a small 6.35 mm automatic of a type often carried by high-ranking officers for personal protection, rather than for use in combat. A tiny eagle, with a three-digit number beneath, had been stamped into the metal slide and also into the base of the magazine.'

'This is a military-issue gun,' remarked Hunyadi.

'I suppose it must be,' she replied.

'And where did you get it?'

'From Hermann,' she told him, and then, as if that were not formal enough, she added, 'from Gruppenführer Fegelein. He also gave me a permit.' Rummaging in her purse, she produced a small card, which she now handed to Hunyadi.

The permit was genuine, but it had been issued by Fegelein himself, which he lacked the authority to do, no matter how high his rank.

Hunyadi glanced at Elsa Batz.

She sensed his hesitation. 'Keep it if you need to,' she told him. 'I never use it anyway, and I'm tired of carrying it around.' Fegelein had given her the gun soon after they began seeing each other. On what she recalled as their first official outing, he drove her to the ruins of a house on the outskirts of the city. The building had been destroyed earlier in the war by a stray bomb. Fegelein walked her into what had once been a neatly tended garden but was now completely overgrown. From the skeletal frame of an old greenhouse, he removed three earthenware flower pots, placed them on the garden wall, then stood back ten paces and motioned for Elsa to join him.

'A present for you,' said Fegelein, holding out the gun on the flat of his palm.

'What do I need that for?' she asked, refusing to take the weapon from his hand. 'I won't always be around to protect you,' Fegelein told her, 'and there's no point having one of these unless you know how to use it.'

He showed her where the safety catch was, and how to aim, and how to level out her breathing just before she pulled the trigger.

Her first shot ricocheted off the wall, leaving a pink gash on the red brick. The second and third shots also missed.

'Well, it's a good thing I don't have you for a bodyguard,' laughed Fegelein.

He had a particularly annoying laugh.

Elsa was already feeling annoyed that Fegelein had brought her here, instead of to some charming restaurant, but to hear the stuttering hiss of Fegelein's laughter so enraged her that she strode forward to the wall, set the barrel of the gun against each flower pot and blew them all to pieces one by one.

This only made him laugh more. 'That's one way of doing it!' he shouted.

She wheeled about. 'I don't want it! Can't you see?'

The smile had frozen on his face, and all amusement vanished from his eyes.

It was only in this moment that Elsa realised she was pointing the gun right at him. She lowered it at once, immediately terrified of what he might do to her now.

But Fegelein only sighed and told her to put it away.

Since then, she had kept the gun in her purse, letting it rattle around amongst the spare change and cosmetics.

'Keep it,' she repeated to Hunyadi.

'No,' replied the inspector, returning the weapon and her permit. 'I've seen all I need to see.' He knew that, technically, he should have confiscated the gun, but right now there were more important things to do.

After Elsa Batz had departed, leaving behind the faint odour of perfume, Hunyadi picked up the phone and called General Rattenhuber at the bunker.

Rattenhuber did not sound pleased to hear from him. 'What do you want?' he demanded. 'Make it quick! I'm very busy.'

'Is Fegelein on the premises?'

'Probably,' snapped Rattenhuber. 'The midday briefing is about to start and Fegelein is scheduled to be there. Why? I thought you'd already spoken to him.'

'I did,' confirmed Hunyadi, 'and now I need to speak to his secretary.'

'What? You mean the pretty one who chauffeurs him about?'

'That's her.'

'Do you want me to put her under arrest?' asked the general.

'No!' Hunyadi answered quickly. 'Just tell her to report to Pankow district police headquarters before the end of the day.'

'Fegelein's not going to like this,' muttered Rattenhuber. 'He's very protective of her.'

'Is that going to be a problem for you?' asked Hunyadi.

'Not at all, Inspector,' replied Rattenhuber. 'I'd be happy to make that man squirm.'

'What do you want?' demanded the officer on duty at the Ostkreuz district police station. The tiled walls gave off a strange glow as they reflected the dusty light bulbs hanging from the ceiling.

'I am here to see Inspector Hunyadi,' replied Pekkala.

'Hunyadi?' barked the man. 'Well, you've come to the wrong place! Who said you could find him here?'

'I must be mistaken,' said Pekkala.

'Damned right you are mistaken! He works over at the Pankow station. Every policeman in Berlin knows that.'

'And where might I find the Pankow station?'

'Where else? On Flora Street!'

'I apologise,' Pekkala told him. 'I am not familiar with the city.'

The apology seemed to soften the policeman's tone, although only slightly. 'Walk out the door,' he told Pekkala, 'turn left and head up to the Ostkreuz tram stop. If it's still running after last night's air raid, take the tram to Pankow-Schönstrasse and the station is right around the corner from there.'

Pekkala bowed his head in thanks, turned and walked out of the door.

Kirov was waiting outside. He fell in step with Pekkala as they headed up the street. 'Well?' he hissed. 'He works out of a police barracks in the north of the city,' answered Pekkala. 'That's where we're going now.'

'And when we do find him?' asked Kirov. 'What then? Do you honestly think he'll lift a finger to help us?'

'He will if he thinks it's worth his while.'

'And how do we convince him of that?'

'Take a look around you, Kirov, and tell me what you see.' Without breaking his stride, Kirov glanced up and down the street. 'What am I looking for?'

'Just tell me what you see,' insisted Pekkala.

'A city which was once perhaps quite beautiful.'

'And now?'

'It's a junk yard.'

'And things will get worse, much worse, before this war is over.'

'I won't argue with that.'

'And neither would Hunyadi, I expect,' said Pekkala. 'Any fool can see which way this war is going. There may be some who still believe a miracle can save them, but I doubt an old policeman like Hunyadi would be one of them.'

'So we are all agreed that Germany will lose the war,' muttered Kirov. 'Is that enough to make him change his mind?'

'It might be,' answered Pekkala, 'if we offer to take him with us back to Moscow.'

Kirov stopped in his tracks. 'And why would he want to do that?'

'Because there is neither a present nor a future here. In Berlin, there is only the past.'

'And if his loyalty prevents him?'

'Then we will have no choice but to convince him otherwise.'

'You must not worry!' exclaimed Hermann Fegelein, sitting beside Lilya as she pulled up in front of the police station.

'I'm not worried,' she answered quietly, staring straight ahead through the rain-spattered windscreen.

But Fegelein knew it was a lie, and it made Fegelein angry that a dishevelled Berlin cop would rob this woman of her peace. With his rank, and the backing of Himmler, Fegelein had no doubts that he himself was untouchable. But this poor woman was only a secretary, with no real way to defend herself against such serious allegations, especially if, as seemed to be the case, this inspector had found no one else on whom to put the blame. As far as Fegelein was concerned, the fact that Hunyadi was hauling in Fraülein S was the most obvious sign that he had reached a point of desperation.

Fegelein almost felt sorry for Hunyadi, ordered to pursue a mirage which existed only because Hitler said it did. Even if the Allies had managed to get their hands on a few juicy pieces of gossip, none of that would win or lose the war. And all the while the real danger – a million Russian soldiers massing on the banks of the River Oder, 80 kilometres to the east – continued unhindered by the Führer's dilapidated war machine.

'This man is just doing his job,' said Fegelein, trying to console her. 'He interrogated me, for God's sake, and I'm still here, aren't

I?' Fegelein laughed and rested a hand upon her shoulder. 'I know how these people work. Just reply to his questions. Don't tell him anything he doesn't ask to know. Keep your answers short and simple. You'll be out of there again in no time!'

Lilya got out of the car, shut the door and walked up the concrete steps to the entrance of the police station.

The sergeant at the desk insisted on escorting her to Hunyadi's office. Along the way, the sergeant mentioned that he would be off duty soon and asked if she might like to have a drink.

She glanced at him and gave a noncommittal smile. 'I'm not sure that will be possible,' she told the man.

Encouraged by the fact that he had not been rejected outright, the sergeant knocked upon Hunyadi's door, opened it without waiting for an answer from inside, and held out his hand for Lilya to enter the room. 'I know where we can get champagne!' he whispered.

These words did not escape Hunyadi. 'Close the door on your way out,' he ordered.

When Lilya and Hunyadi were alone, he gestured for her to sit down. 'Please,' he said.

She did as she was told.

For a moment, Hunyadi said nothing, but only studied his visitor. Fegelein might be a snake, thought the inspector, but he has good taste in women. 'How long have you worked for the Gruppenführer?' he asked.

'Almost two years.'

'And where were you hired?' 'In Paris,' she answered. 'I was working for the occupation government, translating documents.'

'From German into French?'

'And the other way around. Yes.'

'And he hired you on the spot?'

'More or less.'

Hunyadi felt the woman's stare burning against his face. He noticed that her right fist was tightly clenched, like someone who meant to lash out if provoked. 'And has the Gruppenführer been a suitable employer?' he asked, saying the words with unusual emphasis, so that she might grasp their proper meaning.

'I am his driver. Nothing more,' she replied. 'For anything else, there are others.'

'Elsa Batz, for example.'

'Yes, as a matter of fact.'

Hunyadi sat back in his chair and knitted his fingers together. 'Do you know why I have called you in?'

She nodded. 'Information has been passed to the Allies. They say there is a leak from Berlin Headquarters.'

'Who is they?'

Lilya breathed out sharply. 'The source of the leak may still be a secret, Inspector, but the fact that you are trying to find its source is not. Anyone who sets foot in the bunker knows exactly why you're here.'

'And have you set foot in the bunker?'

'No,' she replied. 'Never.'

'But you must have heard things. Gossip and so on.'

'I hear only what Gruppenführer Fegelein wants me to hear, and he has the full trust of Heinrich Himmler, as well as the highest security clearance. Forgive me, Inspector, but you might as well accuse the Führer himself.'

'And if you were me, Fraülein S, whom would you accuse?' She considered for a moment before replying. 'Someone like me,' she replied. 'Someone who is an outsider. Someone who wouldn't be missed.'

Hearing these words, a dazed look swept across Hunyadi's face. In that moment, he was not thinking of the beautiful woman who sat before him, or of the reason she sat before him now. Hunyadi was thinking of his wife. He stood, resting his fingertips upon the desk, as if uncertain of his balance. 'Thank you,' he said hoarsely. 'You can go.'

As Lilya Simonova left the building, taking the back stairs so as to avoid the duty sergeant. At the end of the staircase, the door opened out into a narrow alley, separating the police headquarters from a now-abandoned block of flats on the other side.

It was raining harder now. The air smelled of damp ashes. For a minute, she rested with her back against the wall, feeling her heart rate slowly return to normal. Slowly, she unclenched her fist, revealing a small vial encased in a thin coating of brown rubber. The inner glass container was filled with potassium cyanide. She had been given the vial before she left England, what seemed like a lifetime ago, and had carried it with her ever since. Lilya had not known, when she walked into the police station, if she would ever walk out of there again. One question too many from the Inspector, and all she had to do was slip the vial into her mouth, bite down, and the shimmering liquid would snuff out her life before she could draw another breath. But Hunyadi had been kind to her. Too kind, perhaps. She was not out of danger yet. The time might come when she would have to put the vial to use. She slipped it into a tiny opening in the collar of her leather jacket. Then she walked out to the street, where Fegelein was waiting in the car.

'You see?' he asked with a smile, when she had taken her place again behind the wheel. 'There was never anything to worry about, was there?'

'No,' she replied softly, as she put the car in gear. 'It was just as you said it would be.'

'What the hell is this about?' demanded General Hagemann. He sat in the back of an SS staff car as it hurtled towards Himmler's headquarters.

Three hours earlier, he had been in the middle of a dense pine forest, 20 kilometres east of Berlin, scouting new areas for deploying his mobile V-2 launch trucks. Then the staff car had appeared, slipping along a road which was little more than a horse track, its glossy black finish overpainted with sprays of khaki-coloured mud splashed up from the hundreds of puddles it had driven through to get this far.

Two men had climbed out, wearing the black uniforms of the Allgemeine-SS. Both men were clearly irritated to have left the relative comfort of their barracks. Brusquely, they ordered General Hagemann into the car.

Hagemann gave one helpless glance at the men who had been assisting him.

The look on the face of Sergeant Behr, who had stood by him since the earliest days of the V-2 project, confirmed the general's own worst fears – that he was unlikely to survive whatever journey awaited him in the back of that SS staff car.

It would have been useless to protest. Hagemann simply ordered Sergeant Behr to take command of the mission, climbed into the back of the car and lit his pipe. As the smoke swirled around him, the general attempted to compose himself so that, at least, he might meet his end with some degree of dignity.

Hagemann realised, as the car slewed around and began making its way back in the direction from which it had come, that he might never know what he had done to deserve this punishment. There would be no trial. These days, there was no time for such elaborate productions. In all probability, the general guessed, he would simply be driven to some part of this bleak forest even more remote than the one where he had been when the men arrived to collect him. He would be walked into the woods, and forced to kneel in the dead leaves. He could almost feel the dampness in the ground against his skin as it soaked through the fabric of his trousers. And then he would be shot.

Hagemann found himself almost impatient for them to get on with their task.

But the car continued on its way.

By the time they emerged from the forest and turned on to the main east–west highway, known as Reichsstrasse I, Hagemann was beginning to wonder if he had perhaps misjudged the situation. A flicker of hope appeared in his mind. He leaned forward and cleared his throat. 'Where did you say you were taking me?' he asked the men.

'We didn't,' replied the guard in the passenger seat.

The general's optimism crumbled. He slumped back in his seat and folded his arms across his chest. As he did so, he felt the shape of his gun in its holster on his waist. It occurred to him that, provided he moved quickly, he might be able to draw the gun and shoot himself before the men in the front seat could stop him. That would, at least, deprive them of the twisted pleasure they were sure to take in carrying out their duties, and would bring an end to his suffering.

But he quickly set aside the idea. The truth was, he didn't have the courage to shoot himself and he knew that he would probably only make a mess of it if he tried.

They did not travel into Berlin, but instead took a ring road, skirting around to the north.

By now, more than an hour had passed since Hagemann had climbed into the car and he had become completely confused.

Finally, Hagemann could stand it no longer. 'What the hell is going on?' he demanded.

'Himmler wants to see you,' said the driver.

'You didn't hear it from us,' added the man in the passenger seat, 'but I think he is giving you a medal.'

Hearing this, Hagemann's whole body went numb. 'A medal?' he whispered. 'From Himmler?'

He had never actually met the Reichsführer before. In that, Hagemann considered himself lucky. Few people, no matter how highly they were ranked, emerged from meetings with the Lord of the SS without having been blackmailed, intimidated or otherwise brought to their knees. For a while, Hagemann had convinced himself that he might be able to avoid meeting Himmler altogether, and he would gladly have done without the medal in order to continue that streak of good fortune. But there was no way out of it now.

For the rest of the journey, Hagemann sat there in silence, slowly reassembling his self-control.

Arriving at the compound at Hohenlychen, the car pulled over in front of the red-brick building which served as Himmler's residence. 'In there,' said the driver. 'No need to knock. You are expected.'

Hagemann got out of the car and made his way into the building. Passing through the front door, he found himself in an elegantly furnished space, which had the appearance of an upscale doctor's waiting room.

There was a door on the other side of the room but it was shut and Hagemann, being uncertain as to whether he should knock, decided to wait here instead.

He was just lowering himself down into one of the leather chairs when the door opened and Himmler appeared from the darkness on the other side. 'Hagemann!' he exclaimed with a smile. 'I have looked forward to this meeting for a long time.' He strode into the room and shook the general's hand, as if they had always been friends.

Dazed, the general managed to nod in greeting.

'Sit!' commanded Himmler.

Hagemann felt his legs practically give out from under him and he subsided into one of the chairs.

'I hear congratulations are in order,' said Himmler, sitting down opposite him.

'They are?' asked Hagemann.

'Come now,' Himmler laughed. 'There's no need for false modesty here.' He leaned forward and wagged a finger at the general. 'I have learned that the Diamond Stream device is now fully operational. Even now, I expect, our rockets are raining down upon the enemy with pinpoint accuracy!'

Hagemann's mouth dropped open with surprise. 'But that's not true!' he gasped. 'More tests are required. We haven't yet . . .' Himmler held up one hand, commanding the general to silence. 'I understand,' he said. 'The need for secrecy is paramount, and I'm certain you are acting on the highest authority.'

'There is no secret!' blurted Hagemann. 'It's not ready yet! It worked once. That's all. Before we can even install the devices, they must be properly calibrated. I'm still trying to get my hands on more components.'

Himmler was staring at him. 'Are you serious?' he asked.

'In your presence, Herr Reichsführer, I would not dare to be anything else.'

Himmler nodded slowly. He looked like someone waking from a trance. 'You will keep me informed,' he said.

It appeared that the meeting was over, almost as soon as it had begun.

Once more, Hagemann shook hands with the Lord of the SS, but at the moment when he tried to release his grip, Himmler refused to let go.

'It is important that you understand the gravity of the situation,' said Himmler quietly. 'I am, as you know, in overall command of Army Group Vistula; the only force that stands between the Red Army and Berlin.'

'Yes,' answered Hagemann, gently trying to remove himself from Himmler's grasp. He began to overheat. Droplets of sweat prickled his forehead.

'If you were to look at our strength on paper,' continued Himmler, 'you would see a formidable presence. Tanks. Guns. Tens of thousands of combat-ready troops.'

'Yes.' Hagemann gave up his attempt to untangle himself from Himmler's soft, persistent grip. He surrendered his arm, as if it no longer belonged to him and, with his free hand, wiped away the sweat which had leaked into his eyes and blurred his vision, distorting Himmler's face into an Impressionistic smudge.

Now Himmler stepped even closer, his emotionless grey eyes

fixed upon Hagemann's face. 'But if you were to see what is actually there on the ground,' he said, 'you would realise how little of Army Group Vistula actually exists. It is a legion of shadows, and shadows will not stop the enemy. But your rockets can, at least long enough to allow us to forge a truce with the western Allies. The Americans, the British, the French – they all realise that we are not the true enemy. The enemy lies to the east, General, the Bolshevik hordes who will, without your help, seek to wipe us from the face of the earth. Now,' he smiled faintly, 'have I made myself clear?'

Hagemann, tasting the salt of perspiration in the corners of his mouth, could only nod.

At last, Himmler released him. 'Go now,' he said.

Hagemann staggered out to the waiting staff car. Within a few minutes, they were on their way south towards Berlin and the dreary forest track where the general had left his crew. He imagined them there still, sitting on their helmets in the rain and waiting for him to return.

'No medal?' asked the driver.

'No medal,' said Hagemann. He was staring at his hand, as if to reacquaint himself with it. The marks of Himmler's fingers still showed upon the chapped skin of the general's knuckles.

'I heard there was a medal,' the driver said to the man in the passenger seat.

'That's what I heard, too,' replied his friend.

The driver glanced in the rear-view mirror, his eyes making contact with Hagemann's. 'Maybe next time,' he said.

Back at his headquarters, Himmler had not yet left the room where his meeting with the general had taken place. Instead, he paced angrily back and forth upon the Persian carpet, breathing in short whistling breaths through his nose. From his pocket, Himmler removed a small, leather-bound case containing an Iron Cross, 1st Class, which he had intended to present to General Hagemann. But the general's denial had spoiled everything.

Now he wondered if Fegelein, who had brought him news of the Diamond Stream's operational capability directly from Hitler's bunker, might somehow have misunderstood. Or perhaps he was being misled. Furious at the thought that someone, maybe even Hitler himself, might have lied to him, Himmler returned to his office and called the bunker.

'Get me Fegelein!' he ordered.

There was a long wait. At last, he heard Fegelein's voice.

'Herr Reichsführer!' Fegelein shouted down the line. 'I have just come out of the midday meeting. I will have the usual report drawn up within the hour. Was there . . .'

Himmler didn't let him finish. 'Did you, or did you not, hear Hitler say that the Diamond Stream was working?'

'Yes! I did. Absolutely.' There was a long pause.

'Is that everything, Herr Reichsführer?' asked Fegelein.

Without replying to the question, Himmler crashed the phone down into the receiver. Then walked to the front door, opened it and pitched the medal case out into the courtyard. The case popped open and the Iron Cross, its silver edges gleaming, skittered away into the mud.

That afternoon, in the eastern district of the Berlin, not far from the Karlshorst Raceway, Inspector Hunyadi wandered slowly down the street, wearing paint-spattered blue overalls, frayed at the heels, and with a hat pulled over his eyes. He carried a metal toolkit in one hand. To people passing by, he looked like some weary electrician or plumber, walking to a job because he no longer possessed a car, or else the fuel to run it. There were many such men in Berlin, too old to be conscripted by the regular army and too young to be entirely overlooked, whose trades were valuable enough to keep them out of uniform. Most of them would have been retired by now, but there was no one else to do the work. And soon, even their trades would be abolished. In the hundreds, they were being summoned by the authorities, given armbands printed with the word 'Volksturm' and, after half an hour's training in the use of a hand-held anti-tank weapon known as a 'Panzerfaust', they were cobbled together into suicidally primitive squads whose purpose was the defence of Berlin. In the meantime, there was nothing to do but to wander the streets, drunk if at all possible, visiting old friends and taking their last tours of the city.

But if those people passing by had looked more closely, they might have noticed the way he kept raising his hand to the right side of his head, and the thin strand of wire running out of his sleeve to the small earpiece he attempted to conceal in his palm.

And they might also have noticed a delivery van, bearing the logo of a non-existent floor-tile company named Ender & Söhne, following slowly in Hunyadi's path along the street. Although the van was painted to look as though its sides were made of stamped metal, the panels were, in fact, constructed out of wood. This was in order not to cause any malfunction of the radio-detection equipment contained inside it, along with two technicians, who hunched over a direction-finding apparatus known as a Nahfeldpeiler.

Ever since the radio men on top of the Zoo tower anti-aircraft station had located an Allied transmission signal in the eastern portion of the city, Hunyadi had been making his way along every street in the district, slowly closing in upon the operator.

Hunyadi had established that these transmissions were being made at regular times, either around midday or in the early evenings. He had a hunch that the operator, whoever he or she was, had been leaving their job during their lunch break in order to send messages, or else was waiting until rush hour, when the noise of buses and trams out in the street would be at their loudest, obscuring any sounds made by the transmitter.

Now it was lunch time, and the detection equipment had picked up a signal, somewhere in the area of Lehndorffstrasse. Hunyadi edged his way down dirty alleyways between the houses, searching for the fuse boxes which, for fire-safety reasons, were located outside and usually close to the ground. Among the rubbish bins, the shards of broken beer bottles and hissing, homeless cats, Hunyadi crouched down, opened the rusty metal fuse boxes and unscrewed the stubby porcelain fuses one by one.

Back in the delivery van, the technicians listened, headphones pressed against their ears, for the moment when power to the agent's radio transmitter was suddenly cut off by the removal of the fuse. When and if that happened, they would send a signal through to Hunyadi, who carried a portable radio strapped against his chest.

Hunyadi's bones were aching. The radio set was small but heavy and carrying the added weight upon his chest had begun to hurt his back. Besides that, many of the fuses were corroded and twisting them out of their sockets had blistered his fingertips so badly that he now wore leather gloves to protect them.

Now and then he would stop, hands pressed against the small of his back and quietly groaning with pain, and he would glance up at the windows, wondering if this plan of his would ever yield results.

After checking every house on Lehndorff, Hunyadi turned the corner and began to make his way down Heiligenbergerstrasse. It was a narrow, gloomy street filled with blocks of flats, some of which showed damage from bombs that had fallen on the nearby Karlshorst Station.

At the first house, he managed to locate the fuse box behind a crate of old milk bottles. The bottles had long since been emptied of milk but were now partially filled with dirty looking rain water, capped with a greenish scum of algae. Holding his breath, Hunyadi lifted the crate, careful not to rattle the bottles, and placed it down beside him.

He kept drifting off in his thoughts. Sometimes he thought of his wife. He hoped they were treating her well. In other moments, he thought of his days at Flossenburg. It was strange, the way he recalled it. There was no terror in his memory, although he had often been terrified. Instead, there was a curious finality about his imprisonment, as if everything that happened before his release belonged to one life, and everything since was part of another. And, in this second life of his, each tiny detail, even those things which were unpleasant, appeared miraculous to him. How can a person know the value of his life, he thought, until he stands upon the brink of its extinction?

Hunyadi's daydreams exploded as a high-pitched whine drilled into his skull from the radio speaker plugged into his ear.

He froze, his fingers locked upon the circular glass fuse which he had been unscrewing at that moment. The technicians in the truck were signalling to let him know that the transmission they had been monitoring had just been interrupted. Hurriedly, he screwed the fuse back in. The signal from the radio truck abruptly ceased.

Hunyadi stared at the number written in black paint above the fuse. It was flat number three. The house only had three storys, with one main fuse per story. Now he knew where the agent was hiding.

Peering upwards, his gaze following the metal ladder of the fire escape, he saw the flutter of a curtain in one of the windows at the top of the building.

His heart began thundering.

He heard the slam of doors as one of the two technicians left the van and ran into the alleyway. From the man's silhouette, Hunyadi could see that he had already drawn his gun.

'Watch the fire escape,' whispered Hunyadi. The man nodded.

Hunyadi pushed past him, coming around the building to the front entrance, where he found the door to the foyer unlocked.

He made his way in and began to climb the stairs. The steps were bare and rickety and there was no way to move quietly. Speed was more important now.

At the front of each landing, a window looked out on to the street and wintery grey light shone in over the worn floorboards.

By the time he reached the third floor, Hunyadi was breathing heavily.

There was only one door. Hunyadi didn't bother to knock. Instead, he raised one booted foot and kicked the door completely off its hinges.

Although this was the first enemy agent that Hunyadi had run to ground – such tasks were normally reserved for the Secret State Police, the Gestapo – there was a cruel sameness to the manner in which this arrest took place.

Hunyadi had lost count of the number of times he had burst in upon criminals, having tracked them to their lairs in every squalid corner of the city.

Realising at once that there was no escape, these criminals reacted in a variety of ways. Some fought back, with knives or guns or whatever object they could lay their hands on. Hunyadi had once been attacked with a rolling pin and, on another occasion, had a bird cage thrown at his head, with a squawking parrot still inside. He had shot men dead, and women too, but only when it would have cost him his own life not to do so. More often, they gave up without a fight. What Hunyadi saw when he charged into the single-room flat was a short, slightly built man with a dark moustache and a thick head of hair. He wore a grubby white undershirt and a pair of pinstripe woollen trousers, with braces pulled up over his narrow shoulders.

The man was hunched over a small fireplace, attempting to set fire to a sheaf of documents. He appeared to have been taken completely by surprise, at least until the power had gone out. There was even a cup of hot tea steaming on the mantelpiece.

He was using wooden matches to set the fire, but without much success. Several of the matches had already been burned, their blackened remnants lying on the hearth beside his bare feet. There had been no time for him to pack his radio and it lay on a desk by the window, its power cord snaking up to a light socket which dangled from the middle of the ceiling. The suitcase in which he stored the radio was still lying open on his bed. Beside it, Hunyadi saw a small-calibre pistol.

The man glanced up at Hunyadi. Then he looked towards his pistol, as if to gauge whether he might reach it before the stranger killed him with the gun in his own hand. Realising it was hopeless, he fumbled with another match, still hoping to set fire to the documents.

Hunyadi strode across to the room, tilting the gun in his hand and cuffed the man across the temple with the butt.

The man collapsed, an unlit match still pinched between his fingers.

Hunyadi looked down upon the agent. In his experience, it did no good, at times like this, to scream and make a show of force. 'Get up,' he said quietly. 'You need to come with me.'

The man stared at the inspector, his dark eyes gleaming with fear. The gun had cut a gash across his forehead, and blood was running down across his face.

Still holding his pistol, but no longer aiming it at the man, Hunyadi held out his free hand, in order to help the agent to his feet.

Hunyadi knew that this was a dangerous moment. If he was not careful, he could easily be pulled off balance, but it was important to offer this gesture – to force the criminal to understand that the chase was over, that he was caught, and that to offer resistance could only end in death.

The agent took hold of Hunyadi's outstretched hand. Hunyadi helped the man to his feet. Then he handed the agent a set of handcuffs which were attached, not by a chain but by a single, heavy swivel bolt. 'Put them on,' he said.

With blood trails lightning-branched across the side of his face, the agent did as he was told. From the way he handled the cuffs, it seemed to Hunyadi that this might not be the first time he had been arrested.

When the agent's hands were firmly locked in front of him, Hunyadi placed his hand upon the man's shoulder and marched him out through the door.

The agent did not resist. There was, Hunyadi observed, a quiet dignity in this man's acceptance of defeat. I ought to have let him drink his tea, thought the policeman. Or fetch his coat. And maybe a pair of shoes. So docile was the prisoner as he descended the stairs, that Hunyadi felt it safe to release his grip upon the prisoner.

'You should have used a car battery,' remarked Hunyadi.

The agent turned and looked at him, a baffled expression upon his face. 'To power the radio,' continued Hunyadi. 'That way, I wouldn't have caught you when I pulled the fuses.'

A look of tired resignation filtered into the man's eyes. He turned away and continued down the stairs.

By now, they had reached the second floor. Rain streaked the windows on the landing.

At that moment, the agent appeared to stumble.

Hunyadi, who was right behind him on the stairs, reached out to steady him.

The prisoner tipped forward, as if he were about to fall.

'Careful!' called Hunyadi, suddenly realising that if the man did not regain his balance, he would crash into the window panes.

In that same moment, Hunyadi understood what was happening.

But it was too late.

The agent dived head first through the window. The crash was almost deafening.

Hunyadi saw the man, his eyes closed, the terrible whiteness of torn flesh mixing with the jagged hail of glass shards. He saw the agent's bare feet, the soles dirty from walking on the old floorboards. And then there was nothing but the gaping hole where the window had been.

He heard the sound of the body hitting the street. Hunyadi rushed to the window opening.

The man lay twisted on the ground.

He had gone head first into the pavement. His skull was shattered, and the torn scalp with its long, dark hair lay draped over the dead man's face.

The technician who had been guarding the fire escape came running from the alleyway. He skidded around the corner, and barely missed colliding with the body. For a moment, he just stared at the corpse. Then he slowly raised his head and looked up at the window.

Through the daggers of the broken window panes, Hunyadi felt the cold rain touch his cheeks. 'Now there will be hell to pay,' he thought.

Later that day, Hunyadi sat at his desk, staring at a pile of unopened mail, all of which had arrived at his flat while he'd been away at Flossenburg. Bills. Subscriptions. Reminders about doctor and dentist appointments. He had brought them with him to the office on the first day, intending to sort through it all. But there had been no time. Even now, he made no move to open the dozens of envelopes.

All Hunyadi could think about now was who he could turn to for help.

Immediately following the death of the radio operator, who had quickly been identified as a low-level employee at the now defunct Hungarian Embassy, a search of the room had revealed a handful of coded messages. These messages had been transcribed on rice paper, which could have been eaten by the radio man if he had been able to get to them in time.

As he held the messages in his hand, a taste of marzipan had flooded into Hunyadi's brain. He had been reminded of the almond pastries he had enjoyed as a boy, which had been baked on sheets of rice paper. He remembered peeling off the delicate strips of paper and eating them first.

He could make no sense at all of the code, and he knew better even than to try. Officially, the only people in Berlin who might assist him in such matters were the SS Intelligence Service, but

Hunyadi had serious misgivings about bringing them into the picture.

The reason for Hunyadi's reluctance to hand over the codes to the SS was that he now felt convinced that someone in their ranks was behind it. These coded messages, if they could only be deciphered, might provide all the evidence he needed, but only if the SS was prepared to confirm their own involvement in the breach. And that, Hunyadi wagered to himself, was very unlikely to happen.

As the minutes passed, Hunyadi reluctantly arrived at the conclusion that he would have to call upon Fegelein. However much Hunyadi disliked the man, Fegelein was the only person within reach who might have access to someone with code breaking skills. Although Fegelein was a high-ranking member of the SS, Hunyadi's recent conversation with Rattenhuber, Head of Security in the bunker, and everything else he had heard about the man, pointed to the fact that Fegelein had fallen out with his masters. Fegelein's assistance in finding the source of the leak might just be enough to tip the balance back into his favour. From that point of view, Fegelein needed Hunyadi even more than Hunyadi needed him.

Hunyadi reached into the pocket of his waistcoat and removed the calling card on which Fegelein had written his phone number.

With his hand hovering over the telephone, Hunyadi paused, knowing that this call, whatever its results, would set into motion events he would no longer be able to control.

He picked up the receiver.

The station operator clicked on to the line.

'Call this number,' said Hunyadi. When the telephone rang, Fegelein was standing on the little balcony of Elsa Batz's apartment on Bleibtreustrasse. He was smoking a cigarette and gazing down at the street below, where the caretaker of his building, an old man named Herr Kappler, was sweeping the pavement with a twig broom that looked as if it should be ridden by a witch. The soothing rhythm of the twigs against the concrete was shattered by the ringing of the telephone.

'It's for you,' Elsa called from the living room.

'Who is it?' he asked without turning around.

'Inspector Hunyadi,' she replied.

Fegelein flicked his half-finished cigarette down into the street, narrowly missing Herr Kappler, and walked back inside the apartment.

He took the receiver from her hand. 'Hunyadi?'

'Yes. I'm calling to see if that offer of help is still on the table.'

'Of course,' answered Fegelein. Then, seeing that Elsa was lingering in the room and doing her best to eavesdrop on the conversation, he frowned and shooed her away.

She turned up her nose and wandered off into the kitchen.

'What kind of help do you need?' asked Fegelein.

'I would rather talk about it in person, if you don't mind.'

'When? Now?' 'Yes. As soon as possible.'

Fegelein glanced at his watch. 'Do you know Harting's restaurant?'

'Yes. On Mühlerstrasse. It's practically across the road from me.'

'Can you meet me there in half an hour?'

'I can,' confirmed Hunyadi.

'I'm on my way,' said Fegelein. 'If you get there before me, just tell the manager you are my guest.'

The door to Harting's restaurant swung open, and Leopold Hunyadi stepped in out of the rain.

The head waiter approached him, a menu clutched against his chest. 'Do you have a reservation, sir?'

'I am a guest of Gruppenführer Fegelein,' answered Hunyadi.

The man cocked an eyebrow. 'One moment, please,' he said. Then he spun on his heel and vanished back into the kitchen.

While he waited, Hunyadi looked around at the dark wood tables, slotted into booths separated by screens of frosted glass into which elaborate floral designs had been carved. Except for the fact that the windows facing the street had been spiderwebbed with tape to prevent them shattering from the concussion of falling bombs, the restaurant showed no sign of having prepared itself for the Armageddon that was coming. He wondered what would be left of the place by the time the Red Army had finished with Berlin.

Now Herr Waldenbuch, the manager, appeared, sweeping wide the leather-padded double doors which led into the kitchen. He was a man of medium height, with a bristly moustache, small, darting eyes and a round belly precariously contained within a linen waistcoat. Before he spoke, he paused to wipe the perspiration from his face with a dark blue handkerchief. Then he stuffed the handkerchief into his waistcoat pocket and offered his sweat-moistened hand for the detective to shake. 'A friend of Hermann Fegelein, you say?'

'A guest,' Hunyadi corrected him.

'Follow me, if you please,' Waldenbuch said quietly and escorted the detective through the kitchen where, Hunyadi could not help but notice, he was studiously ignored by the staff, and brought him to one of several locked doors at the back of the restaurant. From a bundle of little brass keys, Waldenbuch selected the one he needed, opened the room and gestured for Hunyadi to enter.

'I have not seen you here before,' remarked Herr Waldenbuch.

You might have done, thought Hunyadi, if one meal here didn't cost a man like me his salary for the week. But he kept that to himself and only nodded.

'The Gruppenführer is often late,' confided Herr Waldenbuch.

'In that case,' replied the detective, 'and since he will be picking up the tab, you might as well bring me some lunch.'

'What would you like?' asked the manager.

Hunyadi shrugged. 'After where I've been, Herr Waldenbuch, anything at all would suit me fine.'

Waldenbuch bowed his head sharply and left.

Alone now in this airless little room, it occurred to Hunyadi that this could all be a part of a trap. Fegelein's attempt to re-ingratiate himself with Hitler's entourage might have nothing to do with helping this investigation and everything to do with getting him arrested on charges of conspiracy. If that is the case, thought Hunyadi, I'll be on my way back to Flossenburg before this meal is even on the table.

To take his mind off these grim thoughts, Hunyadi studied the pictures hanging on the walls. They showed the restaurant in earlier days – men in high-collared shirts and women with complicated hats staring with bleached-looking faces through the persimmon-coloured light of old sepia prints.

He wondered if these pictures would survive the coming fight. Lately, Hunyadi had become morbidly obsessed with trying to guess whether the objects that passed through his life were doomed to perish in the flames which would engulf this city, or whether they would be carted back to Russia as souvenirs, or if perhaps they would remain here, untouched, to decorate the walls of whatever city rose up from the ashes of this war.

At that moment, Fegelein arrived. He wore a brown leather greatcoat over his uniform, the hide darkened across his shoulders by the rain that was falling outside. 'Welcome to my private dining room,' said Fegelein as he shrugged off the coat and draped it over an unused chair.

'Yours?' asked Hunyadi.

'There are three things a gentleman needs in life,' said Fegelein. 'A good barber, a good tailor and a table at his favourite restaurant. I went one further, and made sure it came with a room.' He settled himself into a chair opposite Hunyadi. 'Now then, Inspector, what is it I can do for you?'

Both men fell silent as Herr Waldenbuch entered with bowls of carrot and fennel soup, the deep orange colour seeming to radiate its own light in the confines of that windowless room. He placed them down before the men, bowed his head, and left. Hunyadi wondered where on earth such food could still be found in this beleaguered city.

As soon as they were alone again, Hunyadi reached into his pocket, withdrew a crumpled sheet of paper on which the agent's coded message had been written and slid it across the table to Fegelein. 'I was hoping you might be able to make sense of this.'

Fegelein picked up the document and stared at it. 'This is some kind of military code.'

'That much I've already guessed,' said Hunyadi.

'And did you also guess that it isn't one of ours?'

'More or less.'

Fegelein laughed quietly. 'And you think I know how to read it?'

'Probably not,' answered Hunyadi, 'but I imagine you know someone who does.'

'It has to do with your investigation?'

'It does.'

'Where did it come from?'

Hunyadi paused to clear his throat. 'For now, Herr Gruppenführer, the help I'm asking for will have to be a one-way street.'

Neatly, Fegelein folded the page and tucked it away in his pocket. 'I'll see what I can do.'

From the distance came a wail of air-raid sirens, the sound muffled by the thick walls of the restaurant. Instinctively, both men stood up to leave, each one calculating the distance to the nearest of the city's many bomb shelters, the locations of which had long ago been branded on their minds.

As they made their way out, they found that the main dining room was already empty. Food lay uneaten on plates. Mozart played softly on the gramophone.

The men stepped out into the street. It was almost dark now and the sirens were much louder here, the rising, falling moan shuddering into their bones. People hurried past them, clutching cardboard suitcases already packed for the hours they knew they would spend below ground.

Now they could hear the heavy drone of bombers in the distance, and the dull thump of anti-aircraft fire from the outskirts of the city.

'It must be done quickly,' urged Hunyadi. 'I don't think there's much time. And the discretion you promised . . .'

Fegelein patted the pocket where he had stashed the message. 'It goes without saying, Inspector.'

Arriving at the Pankow district police station, Pekkala went in to find Hunyadi, while Kirov remained out of sight in an alleyway across the road.

The rising, falling wail of the air-raid sirens filled the streets. The duty officer at the front desk sent Pekkala up to the receptionist on the next floor, where Hunyadi's office was located.

'You'd best be quick,' said the duty officer. 'You've only got about ten minutes before the bombs start falling.'

The receptionist was an elderly woman named Frau Greipel. She had worked on that floor of the police department for many years and considered it her personal domain. The men who worked here, aware of just how miserable she could make their lives if she wanted, knew better than to question her authority.

As a rule, Frau Greipel did not take kindly to strangers, and most of them were sent packing down the stairs much faster than they had come up, especially if air-raid sirens had already begun to sound.

But she did not chase away Pekkala. There was something in the bearing of the man which was both familiar and strangely comforting to her, as if he knew his way around the place, even though she was certain he had never been there before. Frau Greipel escorted Pekkala to Hunyadi's office, knocked on the door, opened it and found the room empty. 'He must have gone to the shelter already,' she said. 'Would you like to leave a message?'

'Yes,' replied Pekkala. 'Please tell him I have come about the Diamond Stream.'

Back at her desk, Frau Greipel made him repeat the words as she wrote them down. 'Are you sure he will know what that means?'

'I believe so,' said Pekkala.

'And your name?'

'Pekkala.'

She made him spell it out.

'And what kind of name is that?' she asked. 'Where does it come from?'

Receiving no answer to her question, Frau Greipel looked up and realised that the man had already gone.

As she had done many times before, Frau Greipel locked her desk drawer, put the key in her pocket and after making sure that she was the last one on the floor, she turned out the lights and made her way downstairs, heading for the shelter across the road.

In the gloom of the darkened police station, Pekkala appeared from a storage closet and made his way to the office of Inspector Hunyadi. Once inside, he turned on the desk lamp and began searching for anything which might reveal the man's home address. It did not take more than a moment to locate the pile of unopened mail, addressed to Hunyadi's flat in Pradelstrasse.

Tucking one of the envelopes into his coat pocket, Pekkala left the room. Out in the street, Kirov was waiting. 'Did you find him?'

'Not yet, but I know where he is.'

'Where to?' asked Kirov.

Before Pekkala could answer, the deep thud of anti-aircraft guns sounded from the west. Layered beneath that sound was the rumble of aircraft engines – hundreds of them by the sound of it.

'For now, we follow them,' answered Pekkala, nodding towards the stream of people heading down into a concrete staircase, above which, in large white letters, they could read the word 'Luftschutzraum'.

After leaving Harting's restaurant, Hunyadi made his way down the stairs of the public air-raid shelter on the corner of Köpenicker and Manteufelstrasse.

He had been here many times before, since the shelter was the closest to his office. Each shelter had its own character. Some always seemed to be filled with crying babies. Others featured music played on violins and accordions. A few served food. This shelter was a relatively quiet place, perhaps due to the fact that it absorbed the entire population of the police station every time there was a raid. Hunyadi had come to recognise many of the regular inhabitants, some of whom he never saw except down in the shelter. Berlin had become a place where each person had two neighborhoods; one above ground and one below.

Now, as Hunyadi plodded down the steps among dozens of others seeking refuge from the approaching raid, he noticed two men in front of him, neither of whom he had ever seen before. One was tall and broad-shouldered and wore a heavy, hip-length coat. The other was thin, with narrow shoulders and rosy cheeks. Neither man spoke to the other, although it seemed clear to Hunyadi from that they were travelling together. The other thing he noticed, from the particular rumple of their coats beneath the arms, was that both men appeared to be armed. Men that age who weren't in military uniform, and carrying guns to boot, could only mean one thing, thought Hunyadi. Secret State Police. Gestapo. He wondered whether they had come to make an arrest or had been on their way somewhere else and got caught in this part of town when the sirens went off. Whatever the answer, Hunyadi knew better than to ask.

Fegelein did not go to a shelter.

As the first bombs began to fall out on the western edges of the city, he made his way to the Salon Kitty club. The place had only just opened its doors for the evening when the sirens sent both dancing girls and their clientele of high-ranking officers scuttling for the shelter, except for Fegelein and one solitary figure sitting at the bar and drinking a glass of beer.

The stranger's name was Thomas Hauer and he was a former agent of the German Spy Agency known as the Abwehr. His former boss, Admiral Canaris, who had once controlled this powerful branch of German Military Intelligence, was at that moment a prisoner in the same cell at Flossenburg prison that Hunyadi himself had occupied only a few days before.

The path which had led Canaris to Flossenburg was not nearly as direct as Hunyadi's.

The German Intelligence apparatus had once comprised two branches, one being the Abwehr, managed by Admiral Canaris, the other a rival service known as the Sicherheitsdienst, run by Heinrich Himmler's SS.

As these competing services vied with each other for control, Himmler personally set out to destroy the Abwehr. By 1944, Himmler had finally succeeded.

On a freezing February afternoon, both Field Marshal Keitel

and General Jodl arrived at Abwehr Headquarters in Security Zone II of the Zossen military complex outside Berlin. The two high-ranking officers made their way to a camouflaged bunker set among a stand of tall pine trees. There, they informed Canaris of Hitler's decision to merge the Abwehr and the Sicherheitsdienst. In the meantime, Canaris was to 'hold himself in readiness' at the remote castle known as Burg Lauenstein in a mountainous region of southern Germany known as the Frankenwald.

In spite of the veiled language, Canaris had no illusions about the fact that he was, in reality, being placed under house arrest. The charges against Canaris stemmed from his suspected contacts with British agents, as well as providing information to Vatican officials, but the real reason for his removal had more to do with the scheming of Heinrich Himmler.

Within hours, Canaris had vacated his office and departed south, in a Mercedes staff car driven by his faithful chauffeur, Ludecke.

In the coming weeks, Canaris was left to stroll about the grounds of the castle in the company of his two dachshunds. He received almost no information about what was going on in the outside world and was simply left to contemplate his doom.

In late June of that year, to Canaris's surprise, he was abruptly released and allowed to return to his home at 14 Betazeile in Berlin, where he soon realised just how busy his adversaries had been during his stay at Burg Lauenstein. By the time Canaris emerged from his gentle incarceration, the network he had so painstakingly assembled had been effectively dismantled. All Abwehr departments had been absorbed by their counterparts in the SS and Abwehr field agents were recalled, reassigned or dismissed according to their relevance in Himmler's future undertakings.

The final blow for Canaris came several months later, when a safe was discovered at the Zossen complex which contained irrefutable evidence that Canaris had been aware of a plot to assassinate Hitler in July of 1944. The attempt had ended in failure and resulted in the executions of numerous high-ranking German officers.

Convicted of treason, Canaris had been sent to prison to await his execution. Unlike Hunyadi, he would never leave Flossenburg alive.

Back while Canaris was still wandering the ground of Lauenberg Castle, Himmler had given Fegelein the task of reassigning all remaining Abwehr agents to posts in the newly formed Reich Intelligence Service.

During the course of this task, while rummaging through the admiral's private papers in the hopes of finding something he might be able to use as blackmail against some high-ranking official, Fegelein discovered a list containing the names of a dozen agents whom Canaris had never registered with the Abwehr. These young men and women, who had been trained by Canaris himself, were kept in reserve for missions which, for one reason or another, it was better to keep off the books.

Rather than simply hand the list over to Himmler, Fegelein sought out these agents on his own, sensing an opportunity more lucrative than the half-hearted thanks of his employer. Of the dozen agents, some were known to be dead, others had never returned from missions and were presumed lost and two committed suicide when they learned that Fegelein was on their trail. Only one man, Thomas Hauer, had proved practical enough to stay alive. And Fegelein assured him he could stay that way, and even prosper by it, provided he could prove his worth. In the short time they had known each other, Hauer had done this many times over.

Now the former agent glanced across as Fegelein entered the room. 'Nice of them to give us the place to ourselves,' he said.

'Anyone would think you planned the air raid.'

'I didn't have to,' answered Fegelein, as he walked behind the bar, searched through the bottles until he found the one he wanted. 'The Royal Air Force have been hitting us almost every night for a month and they are admirably punctual.' With that, he poured himself a glass of Pernod. 'I acquired a taste for this in Paris,' he said, holding up the honey-coloured drink as if to gauge its clarity. Then he added a splash of water from a pitcher on the counter and the Pernod turned a cloudy yellow colour.

'It smells like liquorice,' remarked Hauer.

'A distant relative of absinthe,' said Fegelein. 'They say that it opens the mind.' He took a drink.

'Is that what it's doing to you?'

'Unfortunately, not enough to help me translate this.' Fegelein tossed the page of code on to the counter.

Ignoring the shudder of bombs, which had now begun exploding in the centre of Berlin, Hauer took the page and spread it out before him, pinning it to the table at each corner with his thumbs and index fingers. 'Why come to me with this?' he asked, studying the page as he spoke. 'Why not bring it to the Reich Intelligence Service?'

'Because I have a nasty suspicion that they might already know what it says.'

'Then this is an internal investigation.' 'That's a good way to describe it.'

'Well,' said Hauer, 'at first glance I would say this is a Goliath cipher.'

'Goliath?'

Hauer sat back on his stool, releasing the pressure of his fingertips from the page. As he did so, the paper seemed to flinch as if it was in pain. 'How much do you know about cryptography?'

'Enough to know when I need help from you.'

'The Goliath cipher is one of several codes used by the Allies,' explained Hauer. 'It was developed by the British in the first years of the war. Nowadays it is considered somewhat antiquated, although it's still reliable and often used by agents who have been in the field a long time. Each message possesses its own branch code, without which it is virtually impossible to unravel the message.'

'Well, where do they keep the branch code?' asked Fegelein.

'On a piece of silk,' replied Hauer. 'It's about the size of a handkerchief and can be folded or crumpled into something the size of your little finger. Printed on the silk are dozens of little squares, each one containing the numbers for a separate branch code. As each one is used, the radio operator simply cuts it out of the handkerchief and destroys it with a match. Or else the whole patch of silk can simply be dissolved in a combination of vinegar and hot water.'

'So,' Fegelein muttered with a sigh, 'without the silk, there is nothing to be done.'

A bomb exploded two blocks away. The lights flickered.

'Not necessarily,' answered Hauer.

'What do you mean?' 'Over the course of the war, the Abwehr amassed quite a collection of these silk sheets, either captured from agents who didn't have time to destroy them before they were arrested or else from supply canisters dropped by the Allies over our territory, which we got to before the agents did. What we discovered was that some of these branch codes repeat and, by experimenting with various algorithms, we have been able to apply a variety of branch codes to messages we've intercepted. It doesn't always work, but we have met with some success.'

'And do you have those algorithms? Are you able to decipher this?'

'The answer to both questions is maybe.'

'You do have them, don't you?'

'Let's put it this way, Herr Gruppenführer. Admiral Canaris was not so naive as to think that even though his headquarters might be safe from enemy air raids, it was proof against the scheming of the SS.'

'You mean that there are still Abwehr files out there some place?'

'Yes,' confirmed Hauer, 'although you'll never find them, and if you want my help with this you won't even bother looking.'

'Fine!' Fegelein exclaimed irritably. 'I don't have time for that now, anyway.' He reached across and tapped his finger against the page. 'Decoding this is all that matters, and it's got to be done now. Tonight.'

Hauer took one of the cardboard beer mats scattered across the counter, flipped it over and copied out the message with the stub of a pencil that he fished out of his pocket.

'Why are you doing that?' asked Fegelein.

'It's a standard precaution,' replied Hauer. 'If something happens to me, then you won't lose the message, just the messenger.'

'Abwehr logic,' muttered Fegelein.

Hauer paused. 'If you don't like it, then you can find somebody else.'

'No,' said Fegelein, 'you can do this however you want. Just get it done.'

'I didn't say for certain I could do it.'

'I have great confidence that you will,' said Fegelein, 'because you know that I will pay you generously, and not in German currency which is about to become worthless.'

Now that Hauer had copied out the message, Fegelein took the original, folded it up and tucked into his chest pocket.

'I know you'll pay me,' Hauer replied calmly, 'right up until the day that you don't need me any more. And then I will be dead.'

Fegelein raised his Pernod and clinked Hauer's glass. 'We're both going to hell, my old friend,' he said. 'It's only a question of when.'

When the raid was over, Hunyadi returned to the station and was pleased to find it still intact, although the concussion had blown in several windows. Men were sweeping up the jagged shards and Hunyadi sidestepped their brooms as he walked past.

Just outside his office, Frau Greipel was sitting at her desk, exactly as she had been before he left to meet Fegelein. Hunyadi wondered if she had even left the building during the raid.

'You had a visitor,' she said to the detective.

'I think we all had visitors,' replied Hunyadi, 'although whether it was the Royal Air Force or the Americans I didn't stop to find out.'

'No, Inspector,' said Frau Greipel. 'I mean someone was here to see you, a man in an old-fashioned coat, just before the sirens went.'

'What did he want?'

'I wrote it down,' she muttered, looking at the note pad on her desk. 'He said it had something to do with a stream of diamonds, or a diamond stream. I'm not sure which, or even what he meant.'

For a moment, Hunyadi stopped breathing. 'Who was he?'

'I don't know,' she replied. 'I'd never seen him before. He had a foreign accent. I didn't recognise it.' 'Did he identify himself?' asked Hunyadi, his voice growing increasingly urgent.

'Yes,' she told him. 'He said his name was Pekkala.'

Hunyadi's eyes narrowed as he searched his mind for anyone he might have known by that name. There was only one man he had ever heard of named Pekkala, but Hunyadi seemed to recall that he had died years ago, swallowed up in the bloodbath of the Revolution. 'What was he like?' asked Hunyadi.

Frau Greipel described him as well as she could. She wanted to tell Hunyadi about the strange feeling she had experienced when the man had been standing in front of her, right where Hunyadi stood now. But she could not find the words to express herself, and anyway, it all seemed vague to her now, as if it had been part of a dream. Frau Greipel had worked with Inspector Hunyadi for many years and she knew he was not the kind of man who dealt in vagaries and dreams. What pleased Hunyadi were specifics, and of those she had nothing to offer, beyond the few details of Pekkala's physical presence.

'Did he say where I could contact him?'

To this, Frau Greipel only shook her head.

'And when he left,' asked Hunyadi, 'did you see where he went? Please, Frau Greipel, this could be extremely important.'

'The sirens were going. Everyone was heading to the shelters. I should think he went there, too.'

Hunyadi tried not to vent his frustration. Instead, he took a deep breath and rubbed his hands against his face, feeling the stubble on his cheeks. 'Frau Greipel,' he said, 'I think we have both done enough for today.'

'Yes, Inspector Hunyadi,' she replied. 'I do believe you're right.'

After an early dinner, Fegelein and Elsa Batz had just dozed off when the telephone rang beside their bed.

Elsa sat up, immediately awake. Nobody ever calls with good news after suppertime, she thought. She looked across at Fegelein, who lay sleeping beside her, a pillow over his face as if he were trying to smother himself.

The phone rang again.

'Hey,' said Elsa, nudging Fegelein with her foot. He grunted and rolled over on to his side.

'It's probably for you,' she told him, raising her voice. Fegelein turned on to his back again, tossing the pillow aside. 'Then pick it up!' he told her sharply. 'The phone's on your side of the bed.'

Cursing under her breath, she picked up the receiver and handed it to him. 'I suppose you don't want me around for this call, either,' she snapped.

'How the hell should I know?' he replied. 'I don't even know who is calling.'

Elsa pushed aside the black cord that attached the receiver to the telephone and slipped out of the bed. Then she retreated to the kitchen, shutting the door behind her.

It was Hauer on the phone. 'I've had some success,' he told Fegelein. 'Some?' barked Fegelein, still half asleep. 'What do you mean "some"?'

'Using one of the branch codes from the Abwehr files, I was able to obtain a partial translation of the document, which amounted to about a fifth of the words. The branch code was not exactly the same, but it appears to overlap in some places.'

'What did it say?' demanded Fegelein.

'I managed to translate the words "arrival", "location", "Christophe" and "diamond" in that order.'

'Diamond?'

'Correct,' replied Hauer. 'Does that mean anything to you?'

'Yes. Maybe. Never mind. But what the hell is Christophe?'

'You're paying me to decode the message,' answered Hauer, 'not to interpret what it means.'

'Are you sure that's what it said?'

'If the coding sequence hadn't worked,' explained Hauer, 'it wouldn't have said anything at all.'

'Fine.' Fegelein slammed down the phone.

The kitchen door opened and Elsa stuck her head out. 'Do you want tea?'

'No!' he shouted, and followed that up with a string of obscenities.

'You're insane,' Elsa told him. Then she slammed the door shut.

Fegelein sat on the bed, trying to encompass what he had just been told. The words which Hauer had untangled from the coded message appeared to confirm that the leak from the bunker was real, and not, as he had suspected, simply the result of Hitler's increasingly paranoid frame of mind. But the more Fegelein thought about it, the less sure he became that this was the same leak.

The information that Hitler had pointed to as having been smuggled from the bunker was all just gossip. There was nothing of any military value. All that the Allies could do with these scraps of chat was to serve them back to the place where they had come from, with no more purpose than simply to embarrass those who heard it. If the Allies could only know how well this little game had played out, Fegelein told himself, they would be more than satisfied.

But the message hidden in this Goliath cipher was different. The Diamond Stream programme was a high-value military secret.

In that moment, Fegelein reached a conclusion which was so simple and, now that he had thought of it, so obvious, that he immediately accepted it as the truth. This secret, thought Fegelein, had nothing to do with the rumours mongered by Der Chef on Allied radio. In his search for the leak, Hunyadi had stumbled upon a completely separate operation.

There were only three people, aside from himself, who had studied the blueprints of the Diamond Stream device that Hagemann had brought to the bunker.

One was Hitler, the other was his own boss, Heinrich Himmler, and the last person was the man who drew them in the first place – General Hagemann.

He could safely rule out anyone else. An assortment of highranking officials had seen Professor Hagemann lay out those plans on Hitler's briefing table, but none of them would have been able to decipher what they meant well enough to relay the information to the Allies. And none of them had even touched the plans, let alone had time to draw or photograph them.

Fegelein could rule out Hitler and Himmler right away. That left only Hagemann.

It seemed so perfectly clear to Fegelein that he wondered why he had not suspected it from the start, even without the decoded message.

Believing that the war was lost, Professor Hagemann was attempting to ingratiate himself with the enemy, in order to secure better treatment when the last shots had been fired, but also to be able to continue his work. Hagemann was a scientist, after all. Those people had no moral direction. To them, their work was everything. They didn't care who they were working for, as long as they were left alone to pursue their calculations.

Fegelein decided that he must speak to Hitler directly. He would tell the Führer everything he knew, before Inspector Hunyadi figured it out for himself. Breaking the news, and maybe even preventing Hagemann from carrying out this act of treachery, would raise Fegelein to the stature he had always craved among the rulers of this country. All previous sins would be forgiven.

Fegelein picked up the phone, ready to call the bunker switchboard. But then he paused, as the idea, which had seemed so brilliant only a moment before, now began to unravel.

How would he explain the manner by which he had decoded the message? No one would believe him if he said that he'd done it himself. Then it would only be a matter of time before it emerged that he had failed to turn over the list of reserve Abwehr agents to the proper authorities. It wouldn't take the SS long to track down Hauer, and Fegelein had no doubt that the bastard would tell them whatever they wanted to hear if it meant saving his own skin.

Even if the SS did arrest General Hagemann, they would hang Fegelein from the same noose.

Fegelein returned the phone receiver to its cradle. Only one course of action remained and that was to tell Hunyadi nothing. At best, that would buy him some time before Hunyadi found the source of the leak on his own and Hitler's vengeance took its course. Fegelein had seen with his own eyes what became of the conspirators in the attempt to assassinate Hitler in July of the previous year. Films had been made of men slowly hanging to death from meat hooks. For a while, it had seemed as if the butchery would never end. Fegelein knew that, eventually, he would be implicated, whether he was guilty or not. His offer to help the inspector would be more than enough to seal his fate.

For Fegelein, the time had come to put in motion a plan on which he had been working for months. In the apartment of his mistress, he had hidden two forged Swiss passports – one made out to himself and the other in the name of Lilya Simonova – along with travel permits to Geneva and enough cash and jewellery to make a new start with Lilya.

The idea of escaping with his wife had never entered Fegelein's mind. And as for Elsa, he felt sure that she would understand. She had accepted her role as his mistress for precisely what it was and no more – a business transaction. Fegelein did not love Elsa and, as far as he knew, she had never expected him to.

But Fegelein had fallen deeply and permanently in love with Lilya Simonova. He had never told her this, not in so many words, because he was afraid that she would misunderstand his true feelings, and would think that he was simply trying to add her to what was, under the circumstances, an embarrassingly long list of conquests.

In addition to not confessing his love, Fegelein had also neglected to tell Lilya that he planned to run away with her to Switzerland. Fegelein had kept quiet about this because he knew that if he did not pick precisely the right moment, she would refuse on principle to come along. But now circumstances had changed and Lilya would be forced to realise that if he was arrested on charges of treason, then she would almost certainly be next.

From this point on, every minute counted.

Fegelein stood up and buttoned his tunic. 'I'm going out!' he shouted at the kitchen door, behind which Elsa Batz had taken refuge.

There was no reply.

Two minutes later, Fegelein was striding down the middle of the empty street, which was still littered with chunks of plaster and broken masonry from the most recent air raid, on his way to make his feelings known to Lilya Simonova.

When the droning all-clear sirens reached them in the bowels of the shelter, Kirov and Pekkala had shuffled up the stairs along with all the others, emerging into a night in which the air was filled with dust and a smell like burned electrical wiring from the super-ionised air caused by the detonation of high explosives.

No street lamps had been lit and people made their way about with torches, hands shielding the beams so that their fingers glowed like embers.

Bomb damage to roads along the way, some of which had been cordoned off by civilian air-raid volunteers, forced them to detour several times before they arrived at their destination.

Hunyadi's three-story building had sustained some damage, caused by what appeared to be one huge bomb, which had landed in the next street over, leaving a crater some 20 feet deep in the road. The houses on either side had tumbled back into themselves, exposing rooms where beds perched precariously at the edge of splintered floorboard cliffs and clocks still hung upon the walls.

Hunyadi's apartment building appeared structurally sound, although some of the upper windows were broken, and the main doors had been wrenched off their hinges.

Pekkala looked at the little array of mail boxes located just outside the door until he found Hunyadi's name and flat number. As he and Kirov made their way inside, they received suspicious glances from some of the inhabitants, but nobody spoke to them. Like Hunyadi at the entrance to the air-raid shelter, the tenants had quickly reached the conclusion that two men in plain clothes wandering the halls of their building could only be members of the secret police.

Hunyadi's room was at the end of the corridor on the second floor.

Pekkala knocked quietly on the door, but there was no answer.

After waiting until the hallway was empty, Kirov forced the lock and the two men drew their guns as they entered the flat.

The room was clean but the furnishings had all seen better days. In the tiny kitchen, a pot of cold ersatz coffee, black as tar and smelling of chicory root, lay on the single gas ring on the stove. One cream-coloured enamel cup and a matching bowl, its blue rim chipped around the edges, lay in a wooden drying rack beside the sink. With the exception of a few pictures he saw hanging on the wall, which showed Hunyadi at various police gatherings, each one with a date ranging from the 1920s to the late 1930s, Pekkala realised that the flat was almost as spartanly furnished as his own place back in Moscow.

Kirov was thinking the same thing. 'At least it looks like he sleeps in the bed,' he remarked, 'instead of lying on the floor.'

Pekkala glanced at the bed. Made for one person, it was barely wider than an army cot and, like an army cot, it had been properly made, the corners tucked in hospital-style and the undersheet folded over the top of the blanket at precisely the width of a hand. Then Pekkala noticed a small framed black-and-white photograph on the bedside table. It was the only picture in the room where Hunyadi did not appear in uniform. Standing beside him was a woman with a narrow face and long dark hair. Hunyadi had his hand around her waist. They were standing on a balcony overlooking the ocean. The shape of an archway in the corner of the photo looked Mediterranean – Greek, Italian, he couldn't quite be sure. In the background, Pekkala could just make out a sailing boat at anchor on the dull grey carpet of the water, and he wished he could have seen how blue it really was.

The picture caught him by surprise. It seemed so out-of-step with everything else in the room. Hunyadi lived by himself. That much was perfectly clear. So was this woman just a current girlfriend? Given that the photograph appeared to have been taken some time ago – the whole of the Mediterranean coastline had been a war zone for the past five years – and since there was no other trace of her in the flat, this seemed unlikely. Was it a relative? Pekkala discounted that, too, based on the lack of physical resemblance and the way couple were standing, hip to hip, his arm around her waist. A former wife? That seemed the least likely of all, not only because of the existence of the photo but also where he had placed it. Or was she dead? The tumblers in Pekkala's mind clicked into place. That had to be the answer.

Pekkala felt a sudden and involuntary compassion for Hunyadi. He tried to shake it from his thoughts, but the idea would not budge. Before he even walked into this room, Pekkala had already taken stock of the similarities between his own life and Hunyadi's. Both were involved in the same kind of work. Both were in the service of men who would answer for their deeds for all eternity. Both men walked the razor-thin line between trying to do good in a land which was governed by evil, and in becoming that evil themselves.

Seeing the trappings of Hunyadi's life had only added to Pekkala's empathy. For those who did not know better, a life pared down to such a threadbare minimum might have seemed like a negation of its own existence. But that was only an illusion. The contents of this room belonged to a man who knew that, between one day and the next, he might lose everything. And the only way to carry on was not to care too much. During his years in Siberia, Pekkala had learned that the more tightly you cling to everything you value in the world, the less precious it actually becomes. Somewhere along the way, thought Pekkala, Hunyadi had formed the same equation in his mind.

But this photo had struck Pekkala most powerfully of all. If he failed to locate Lilya and to bring her safely from the cauldron of Berlin, she stood almost no chance of survival. And then that crumpled photo he had kept for all these years would transform into a symbol of remembrance, and not one of hope, as it was now.

Pekkala began to steel himself for what he might soon have to do.

If Hunyadi refused to help, they would have no choice except to abandon the search and get out of Berlin as fast as possible. They would also have to kill Hunyadi. Simply tying him up and leaving him here in his flat, to be discovered in a matter of hours by the inquisitive tenants of this building, would not buy enough time to escape. And it was not simply a matter of getting out of Berlin. They had to retrace their steps all the way to the Russian lines, through a countryside crawling with execution squads.

Just then, they heard the rattle of a key in the door.

When Fegelein arrived at the boarding house on Eckertstrasse, where Lilya Simonova rented a room, he found the night watchman asleep, head resting on his folded arms.

It was a dingy place, its walls badly in need of repainting, and the floorboards scuffed to splinters.

Without waking the old man at the front desk, Fegelein made his way up to the third floor. Although he had never actually set foot inside the building before, he knew exactly where she lived. He even knew which room was hers by looking from the street. Many times, he had driven past this boarding house, sometimes with Elsa in the car, and glanced up at Lilya's window, hoping to catch a glimpse of her.

In sharp contrast to the luxurious surroundings of Elsa's apartment on Bleibtreustrasse, he found the hallway cluttered with pieces of broken furniture and there were brown stains on the ceiling where water had seeped through from leaking pipes. It smelled of sour milk and cigarettes.

Fegelein felt a sudden stab of guilt that Lilya had been forced to live this way. Of course, she would not have been able to afford anything better on her salary, but he could easily have requisitioned her a better place. To do so, however, would have sent her the wrong message. He did not want to simply buy her off. Nor did he want her for his mistress. He already had one of those and one was quite enough. What he had wanted for a long time now, as much as could ever be possible, was to know her on equal terms.

And now he would, if only he could persuade her to come with him.

With one knuckle jutting from his fist, Fegelein rapped softly on the door. He waited, and then he knocked again.

A light came on, splashing its glow like a liquid underneath the door and out on to the landing, just touching the tips of his boots.

'Who is it?' Lilya asked, her voice gritty with sleep.

'It's Hermann,' he said quietly. It was the first time he had ever used his Christian name with her.

A deadbolt lock clunked back and Lilya opened the door. She wore a blue wool dressing gown, held against her body by her folded arms. Blonde hair straggled down in front of her face. Her bare feet were cold upon the floor and she stood with the toes of one foot balanced upon the arch of the other, like a long-legged water bird.

To Fegelein, she had never looked more beautiful.

'What is it?' she asked.

'May I come in?' he asked, suddenly nervous in a way he'd never felt in front of her.

'What's going on?' she persisted.

'I'll tell you everything,' said Fegelein, 'but I don't want to do it out here.'

She stood back to let him pass. 'I'm sorry about the mess,' she said.

But there was no mess, at least as far as he could tell. A few books lay scattered on a coffee table and two mismatched chairs flanked a little fireplace which did not look as if it had been used in quite some time.

Lilya gestured at one of the chairs and sat down in the other. Fegelein took his seat. 'I am sorry to come to you in the middle of the night,' he said, 'but there is something I have to tell you. Something which cannot wait.'

Still hugging her arms against her chest, Lilya waited for him to explain.

'The war is almost over,' said Fegelein, 'and you and I both know how it will end.'

'Why are you telling me this?' she asked.

'Because the time has come when we must begin fending for ourselves. We must look to the future. Whatever loyalties we've had until now belong to the past. Do you understand what I am saying, Lilya?'

'I think so,' she replied cautiously.

Fegelein rubbed his hand across his forehead. This was already more difficult than he had been expecting. 'We need to leave,' he said.

'We?'

Now he looked her in the eye. 'Yes. We.'

'But what about . . .?'

He held his hand up sharply, commanding her to silence, as if he could not bear to hear her speak the names of those other women. 'I have made my choice,' he said, 'and it is you.'

'But leave for where?' she asked.

'Switzerland,' he told her, 'at least to begin with. After that, maybe South America. But none of this can happen if we just sit back and wait for events to unfold. Any delay, and it might be too late. Then all the plans I've made . . .' Now it was she who cut him off. 'What plans?' she asked.

'Passports. Transit papers. Money. You must not worry. I have thought of everything.' Tentatively, Fegelein reached out to take her hands in his.

But her arms remained folded.

'I have great affection for you, Lilya,' Fegelein began, but he could scarcely draw the breath into his lungs to go on speaking.

'Surely you must know that by now,' he gasped. 'I am trying to save you.'

'And why do I need saving?' she demanded.

'If you stay here in this city,' he replied, 'you'll almost certainly be killed, by the Russians when they get here and if not by them, then by our own secret police.'

'The secret police?' she asked. 'What would they want with me?

'It won't be long before they are looking for anyone who has had dealings with me.'

'But why?'

'Because of the things that I have done,' he said flatly, 'and what they are it's better you don't know for now. I'll be happy to discuss all this with you as soon as we are safely in Geneva, but right now you need to realise that I'm the only chance you've got.'

'When are you planning to go?' she asked.

At least, thought Fegelein, she isn't trying to talk me out of leaving. He grasped at this as a sign that she might actually go with him. 'First thing in the morning,' he told her. 'We will travel by car to the Charlottenburg Station. Then we board a train, whatever one is there, just as long as it's leaving Berlin. One way or another, we will make our way to Switzerland. I have money. More than enough. And I have documents which will guarantee we are not stopped.'

She opened her mouth to speak.

But Fegelein couldn't wait. 'For the love of God, say yes!' he blurted out.

'I'll need to pack a few things,' Lilya told him.

'Of course!' exclaimed Fegelein, overwhelmed that she had finally agreed. 'One suitcase, though. That's all. You understand?'

She nodded.

They walked to the door.

'I'll be back for you at 9 a.m.,' said Fegelein. 'You must be ready.'

Her lips twitched, in what Fegelein took for a smile.

He leaned across, gently taking hold of her shoulders, and kissed her on the cheek. 'I'll see you very soon,' he said.

As soon as Fegelein was gone, Lilya unfolded her arms, which were now so cramped that at first she could barely move them. Tucked up the sleeve of her dressing gown was the stiletto knife she always carried with her and which she had almost used on Fegelein in the moment she saw him at the door.

Now Lilya put on her clothes and hurriedly began to pack a suitcase. She threw in an assortment of undergarments, a pair of shoes, a hairbrush, and a clunky dynamo torch made by a company called Electro-Automate, which she had brought with her from Paris. The dynamo operated by repeatedly squeezing a lever attached to the side of the torch, removing the need for expensive and increasingly hard-to-find batteries. The wheezy grinding of these dynamos was a common sound as people made their way about in the dark. Almost everyone carried torches of one kind or another, since no street lights were illuminated in the city at night in case they could be seen by bombers overhead.

Of all the things she crammed into the case, only the torch was important, but this had nothing to do with the light it cast upon the cracked paving stones of Berlin.

The torch housed a roll of film, containing images of the

Diamond Stream schematics. Lilya had photographed the blueprints on the same day Fegelein had borrowed them from General Hagemann, having left them in the car while he paid a visit to his mistress.

To hold the film, the dynamo contained within the torch had been replaced by technicians at Beaulieu House, where Lilya had undergone her training in England. The new dynamo was only half the size of the original, allowing the film to be stored in the remaining space.

She had carried the Electro-Automate with her when she returned to France, back in the summer of 1940. Although her bags had been searched many times since then, in France as well as in Germany, the fact that the torch still worked had always been enough to satisfy the inspectors.

By the time Lilya had finished, a little over six hours remained before Fegelein was due to return. By then, she knew that she would have to be long gone from here. Although Lilya was not scheduled to arrive until noon at the safe house where she would rendezvous with Allied agents sent to evacuate her from Berlin, she had no choice but to make her way there now and hope that her contacts would be there.

Slowly, Hunyadi opened his eyes.

A deep, numbing pain pulsed rhythmically against his right temple.

Struggling to focus, he realised he was in his flat and that a handkerchief had been stuffed in his mouth.

Hunyadi went to remove it, but his hands had been tied with the laces of his own shoes to the arms of the chair in which he sat. His trouser belt had also been used to bind his legs together at the ankles.

The last thing he recalled was opening the door to his apartment.

Everything between that moment and this was a blank.

And now a man appeared in front of him. His hair was greying at the temples and old scars creased his weathered skin. From Frau Greipel's description, Hunyadi realised that this must be the man who had come looking for him at the station.

Although he was helpless, Hunyadi was not terrified. If this stranger had intended to kill him, he would certainly have done so by now.

'Are you going to be quiet?' asked the man. Hunyadi nodded slowly.

The handkerchief was removed from his mouth.

'You are Pekkala,' said Hunyadi. 'That's right,' replied the man. Hunyadi listened to the stranger's voice, trying to place his accent. Although he spoke German well, this man was not a native speaker. His first guess was Russian, but the accent was layered with something else, clipped and sharp, which he could not immediately place. 'Frau Greipel said you wanted to talk to me.'

'Yes.'

'Then you must understand that there are easier ways than this.'

'Under the circumstances,' replied Pekkala, 'I am inclined to disagree.'

Who are you? thought Hunyadi. Why would you take the risk of coming here? But he kept his questions to himself.

'You are searching for someone,' said Pekkala.

'Yes,' confirmed Hunyadi. 'That's how I make my living, more or less.'

'And have you found who you are looking for?'

'Not yet,' admitted Hunyadi.

'But close, perhaps.'

'If you will walk with me back to the Pankow station, I would be happy to share with you the results of my investigation.'

'I told you this wasn't going to work,' said a voice standing directly behind him.

Hunyadi was startled, not only to discover that there was another person in the room but to hear the man speaking in Russian. Until this moment, Hunyadi had remained relatively calm, but now his pulse began thumping in his neck.

The Russian stepped around from behind Hunyadi. He was holding a Hungarian-made pistol and staring intently at Hunyadi. 'You understood me, didn't you?'

'Yes,' answered Hunyadi. There was no point in denying it. Kirov bent down, so that the two men were looking each other directly in the eye. 'Listen,' he said, quietly. 'This person you are looking for, we are looking for them, too, and we think you might know where they are.'

'What gives you that idea?' replied Hunyadi, speaking in the stranger's tongue, although it had been many years since he'd been able to practise his Russian.

Now it was Pekkala who spoke. 'Because you are Leopold Hunyadi, and you would not have been chosen for this work if you weren't the best man for the job.'

'I am sorry to disappoint you,' said Hunyadi, 'but I have not found them yet. And even if I had, what on earth makes you think that I would help you?'

'Because it might save your life,' answered Kirov, 'and not helping us certainly won't.'

Hunyadi coughed out a laugh. 'I don't think you understand the situation,' he told the two men. 'Hitler himself assigned me to this case. If I don't solve it, he'll do worse than anything you boys can throw at me. So go ahead and shoot, you Bolshevik gangster.'

Kirov glanced at Pekkala. 'We're just wasting our time here, Inspector.' He set the gun against the base of Hunyadi's skull.

'Inspector?' said Hunyadi.

'That's right,' said Pekkala, raising his hand to show Kirov he should wait before pulling the trigger. 'I am Inspector Pekkala, of the Bureau of Special Operations in Moscow. The man with the gun against your head is Major Kirov.' 'By any chance are you related to the man they called the Emerald Eye?' asked Hunyadi.

'Related?' Now it was Kirov's turn to laugh. 'He *is* the Emerald Eye!'

Hunyadi blinked in confusion. 'But I heard that he was dead.'

'I heard those same rumours,' said Pekkala, 'and there were

times when they almost came true.' Now he turned up the collar of his coat, revealing the badge the Tsar had given him long ago.

Astonished, Hunyadi stared at the emerald. As it caught the light, the jewel appeared to flicker, as if to mirror the blinking of his eyes.

'We did not come here to end your life,' Pekkala told him.

'We came here to save someone else's. If what you know and what we know could be combined, such a thing might still be possible. And in exchange, I offer you a guarantee of help in escaping the battleground this city is about to become.'

'This city is my home,' replied Hunyadi, 'and there's no point asking me to leave it, even if that means my dying here.'

'I understand that you might not value your existence enough to tell us anything at all,' continued Pekkala, 'and as for why you would assist in saving someone who has conspired against your master, I cannot even conjure up a reason.' Now Pekkala pointed at the picture of Hunyadi and the woman.

'But what about her life?' he asked. 'Have you considered what might happen to her when the Red Army arrives?'

'Of course I have considered it!' shouted Hunyadi. 'You think I'm doing this for Hitler? He sentenced me to death at Flossenburg for marrying the woman in that picture.' 'Then why are you still alive?' asked Kirov.

'So that I can find the source of the leak of information from headquarters,' answered Hunyadi. 'There is no other reason.'

'Where is your wife now?' asked Pekkala.

'In Spain,' replied Hunyadi, 'where I was foolish enough to think she would be safe. But even as we speak, she is being held as ransom, to make sure I do as Hitler has commanded.'

'And when you appear before him empty-handed, what then?'

demanded Pekkala.

'I may yet succeed.'

'You might,' agreed Pekkala, 'but is that still a chance you are prepared to take?'

'I have no choice.'

'You do now,' Pekkala told him. 'We, too, have people in Spain and I can see to it that both of you are saved.'

'Even if that's true,' said Hunyadi, 'why should I trust you any more than I trust him?'

'Because I am also being held to ransom,' replied Pekkala. 'I did not come to Berlin out of loyalty to any cause, any more than you are here because of one.' Reaching into his coat pocket, he removed the crumpled photo of himself with Lilya and held it out for Hunyadi to see. 'The woman in that picture is the one I'm trying to save, and she means every bit as much to me as your wife does to you.'

'Now will you help us or not?' demanded Kirov.

For a while, Hunyadi said nothing. He just stared at the floor, breathing slowly in and out. Finally, he spoke. 'Untie me,' he said quietly.

'Do as he says,' ordered Pekkala.

'Inspector,' Kirov muttered nervously. 'Now.'

Kirov sighed. Then he holstered the pistol and loosed Hunyadi from his bindings.

Slowly, Hunyadi rose to his feet. 'Two days ago,' he told them, 'I located a transmitter at the house of a Hungarian diplomat. I think it has something to do with the leak of information from the bunker.'

'A Hungarian, you say?' asked Kirov.

'That's right,' said Hunyadi. 'He was just about to transmit a message when I burst into the room.'

'And you recovered this message?'

'I did, but it was encrypted.'

'Where is it now?'

'I gave it to someone who offered to help me decode it without letting the authorities know. You see, this leak could be coming from anywhere, and I don't know who to trust.'

'But you trust this person?'

'Not at all,' replied Hunyadi, 'but I had no one else to turn to.'

'And has it been done?'

'Not yet. Not as far as I know. The man said he would contact me as soon as he had anything, but I haven't heard from him.'

'And the Hungarian?' asked Pekkala. 'Where is he?'

'In the morgue at the Köpenick police barracks,' answered Hunyadi. 'He killed himself before I had a chance to question him.'

'And who is at the Hungarian's place now?'

'Nobody. It's empty.'

'Can you take us there?'

Hunyadi looked around the room. He seemed to be making an inventory in his head of all of his meagre possessions. Then he stepped over to the bedside table and picked up the cheap wooden frame which held the photograph of his wife. Grasping the flap which helped it stand upon the table, he tore away the cardboard backing of the frame. Then he removed the photo and tucked it into the inside pocket of his coat. At last, he turned to Kirov and Pekkala. 'Follow me,' he said.

When Fegelein returned to the apartment on Bleibtreustrasse, he found Elsa fast asleep and sprawled across the mattress, still wearing her transparent nightgown.

Rather than make room for himself on the bed, which would almost certainly have woken her again, Fegelein sat down to rest in the yellow chair by the phone stand.

He told himself he would not sleep, but he dozed off anyway, his chin sunk down on to his chest.

Four hours later, he woke to the sound of the caretaker, sweeping the pavement with his witch's broom.

At first, Fegelein was startled to find himself in the chair and it took him a moment to recall why he was there. He glanced at his watch, gasping when he saw the time. It was 9.30. He should have been at Lilya's half an hour ago.

Elsa was still asleep, which did not surprise Fegelein. She regularly stayed in bed until noon.

As quietly as he could, Fegelein got out of the chair and made his way to a bookshelf built into the wall on the other side of the room. Behind the collected works of Goethe, which he had never actually read, was a panel that operated on a spring-loaded latch, opening when it was pushed. With gritted teeth, he set his hand upon the panel and applied pressure until the panel clicked open. He looked back to see if Elsa had been woken by the noise.

She had not moved. Her breathing was slow and deep. Behind the panel was a small briefcase, containing the jewelery and travel documents he and Lilya would need for their escape. The briefcase had been a present from his wife, who had ordered it to be embossed with his full initials and last name – H. G. O. H. Fegelein, and suggested that he use it for his daily meetings with the High Command. However, on the first day he brought it in, Hitler had remarked that the golden initials looked 'flashy'. This meant, of course, that Fegelein could never use the briefcase for its intended purpose, but he had discovered that it was just the right size for stashing the jewellery and passports. After removing the briefcase from its hiding place, Fegelein was about to press the panel back in place when he paused. The first click had not woken Elsa, but the second one probably would. So he only pushed the panel part way closed and then carefully replaced the books. Standing back, he surveyed his work to see if it would pass inspection. It was barely noticeable, and Fegelein doubted whether Elsa even looked at the bookcase.

There was no time to pack a bag. He simply lifted his leather greatcoat from the hook in the entrance way, opened the door as quietly as he could and stepped out into the hall.

Before he closed the door behind him, Fegelein glanced back at Elsa. He had known long ago that this day would come. In fact, he had rehearsed it so many times in his head that he had managed to convince himself he would feel nothing when the moment finally arrived. But now that he was actually leaving, without a word of goodbye, he still felt sick about it.

He closed the door and made his way down the stairs, keeping to the outer edge of the steps so as not to make them creak. By the time he reached the street, Fegelein was no longer preoccupied with leaving Elsa behind. Instead, his thoughts turned to the future and the wonderful life he would have in the arms of Lilya Simonova.

Just as Lilya Simonova was reaching for the handle, the door seemed to open by itself.

The safe house on Heiligenbergerstrasse had not been difficult to find and she encountered no one as she climbed the stairs. Pausing to examine a newly replaced window on the second floor, she looked out into the street to make sure she hadn't been followed.

Although Lilya had never actually met the agent with whom she was to rendezvous that day, she did know him by sight, since they had crossed each other's path more than once in the Hasenheide park where messages were left in the hollowed-out leg of a bench. The first time had been just as she was leaving the park, having timed her exit perfectly to coincide with the arrival of a tram at the Garde-Pioneer station, on which she would begin her journey home.

The thickly moustached man was short and frail, with rumpled clothes that looked as if they needed cleaning. He looked lonely, sad and preoccupied. The man had caught her attention because of the way he glanced at her as she walked by. It was not the casual wolf-like stare she often received from men when she was out walking on her own. This glance was furtive and suspicious, like that of someone who knew more than he could say. Afraid that he might have been sent to follow her, Lilya Simonova boarded the tram and then immediately exited through the door on the other side. She doubled back on her tracks, following the man across the park.

He sat down on the bench, fetched a newspaper from his coat pocket and began to read. It was only after several minutes that he reached down, retrieved the message Lilya had placed there and made his way out of the park.

This time, she did not follow him.

Whenever they crossed paths again, although she felt his stare upon her like the heat from a lamp held too close, Lilya never looked him in the eye.

Now she wondered what she would say to him.

But the man who stood before her in the doorway was not the same person she had encountered in the Hasenheide park.

It took her a moment to realise she knew who he was.

Her heart slammed into her chest so hard it was as if she had been thrown against a wall.

But his presence here was so unexpected, so impossible it seemed, that she forced herself to think she was mistaken.

He spoke her name, so quietly she barely heard him.

In the instant that she heard Pekkala's voice, Lilya found herself back on the crowded railway platform of the Nikolaevsky station in Petrograd, just about to board the train, the last time she had held him in her arms.

Then all the years between that day and this receded into darkness, like a butterfly folding its wings.

Pekkala reached out to take her hand. 'Come inside,' he said, 'and I will tell you everything.'

He led her into the flat, and gently closed the door. Two other men were waiting, one of whom she recognised as the policeman who had questioned her two days before. This man looked as astonished to see her standing there, as she was surprised to see him.

With shock still crackling like sparks along the branches of her nerves, she sat down on the bed.

Pekkala knelt before her and explained the situation they were in. But he paused before he had finished, unsure whether she had heard a single word he'd said. 'Lilya?' he asked.

'Don't ever leave me again,' she told him.

He breathed in sharply, as if dust had been thrown in his face. 'I swear that all the days which we have left I'll spend with you,' he said, 'but what we must do now is leave this place. All hell is about to break loose.'

Hunyadi had been sitting in a chair by the empty fireplace, just staring at Lilya Simonova. 'But you were never in the bunker!' he blurted out suddenly, as if a conversation had been playing in his head this whole time and had just now transformed into words.

Lilya glanced at Hunyadi, then turned again to face Pekkala, a questioning look on her face.

'It's all right,' Pekkala told her. 'It doesn't matter now. You can tell him, if there's anything to tell.'

'Everything I learned, I learned from Fegelein,' she said.

'He was the leak, and he had no idea,' muttered Hunyadi.

'The poor fool has been hunting himself!'

Kirov rested a hand upon Hunyadi's shoulder. 'It's time to go,' he said.

Hunyadi rose stiffly to his feet. 'I thank you, gentlemen,' he told them, 'but after what I have just heard, I believe I've found a way to solve this case without ever mentioning the name of Lilya Simonova. Hitler will be satisfied, and he will never even know that you were here.'

'The choice is yours,' said Pekkala, 'but what about your wife in Spain? What will become of her?'

'She'll be released,' answered Hunyadi. 'And as for me, although I've always wanted to see Moscow, I believe I'll take my chances in Berlin.'

'Fegelein?' Hitler's voice sounded hoarse and faint. His laboured breathing slid in and out of the static on the telephone line. 'Fegelein is the leak?'

'That's right,' answered Hunyadi. By agreement with Pekkala, he had waited several hours before telephoning the bunker. By the time Hunyadi placed the call, the others would already have escaped the city.

'And can you prove this?' demanded Hitler.

'You should be able to correlate every piece of information broadcast on the Allied radio network with times when Fegelein was present in the bunker.'

'I may require more proof that that, Hunyadi. He is Himmler's liaison, after all.'

'If you detain Fegelein and no more leaks emerge, then you'll know that you have the right person.'

There was a long silence. 'Very well,' Hitler said at last. 'I'll send Rattenhuber to pick him up.'

'I suspect that he will be at the house of his mistress, Elsa Batz.'

'His mistress?' Hitler's voice rose suddenly in anger. 'That man has a mistress?'

'Yes, I thought you knew.'

'Of course I didn't know!' shouted Hitler. 'The bastard is married to Gretl Braun! Between you and me, Hunyadi, there's a good chance he might soon be my brother-in-law!' By now his voice had risen to a roar. 'How the hell am I going to explain that to Eva? What's this woman's name again?'

'Elsa Batz,' repeated Hunyadi. 'She lives at number seventeen Bleibtreustrasse.'

'I'll send Rattenhuber over right away. And thank you, Hunyadi, for everything you've done.'

'My wife,' said Hunyadi.

'She will be released within the hour, and you are free to join her, my old friend.'

When Fegelein arrived at Lilya's flat, he found the door unlocked and the room empty.

She must have panicked, thought Fegelein. I'm almost an hour late, after all. But where could she have gone?

The only place that made any sense to him at that moment was Elsa's. Lilya must have been on her way there at the same time as I was coming here. With no other way of accounting for her absence, Fegelein hurried back to the apartment on Bleibtreustrasse. Inside the building, he stashed the briefcase in the little closet under the main stairs, where the caretaker, Herr Kappler, stored the witch's broom which he used for sweeping the pavement.

Fegelein entered the apartment just as Elsa was getting out of bed. As always, the first thing she did was to go to her handbag on the side table and retrieve her lipstick. Then, looking in the little mirror which hung by the door, she daubed her lips a poppy red.

Fegelein never understood why she did this. The lipstick was made by the French company Guerlain and was from the last remaining stock in Berlin, making it ridiculously expensive. Most of it ended up on the rim of her coffee cup, requiring her to apply it again as soon as she had finished eating. But there was no time to think of that now. 'Where did you go?' she asked, still looking at her own reflection in the mirror.

Normally, Fegelein could have spat out a lie as quickly as

speaking the truth, but he was so distressed at not finding Lilya that his mind had just gone blank. 'I was taking a walk,' he muttered.

She laughed quietly. 'That's a first.'

He didn't care whether she believed him or not. 'Has anyone been here since I left?' he demanded.

She turned. 'Why would anyone come here at this hour of the morning?'

Fegelein just shook his head. 'It doesn't matter,' he said, heading for the kitchen. He hadn't had any breakfast and his stomach was painfully empty.

'What's wrong with you today?' she asked.

'Nothing,' he snapped. 'Leave me alone.'

Just then, there was a knocking on the door.

Fegelein's stomach flipped over. Lilya is here, he thought. But now he had no idea how to explain what she would be doing at the apartment. Although Lilya often stopped here to pick him up in the car, she always called up from Herr Kappler's phone at the front desk. He was afraid of the scene Elsa would make in front of Lilya, when she realised he was leaving her behind.

I'll say there is an important meeting at the Reichschancellery bunker, Fegelein thought to himself. I'll say the phone downstairs is out of order. That's why she had to climb the stairs. If Lilya will just play along with me for a couple of minutes, we can leave this place without Elsa causing a commotion. Of course, she will figure it out soon enough, but by then Lilya and I will already be gone.

The knocking came again.

'I'll get it!' said Fegelein, striding across the room towards the door.

But Elsa was standing right there and before Fegelein could do anything about it, she had already opened the door.

Fegelein stopped in his tracks. It was not Lilya.

Instead, Herr Kappler had come to the door, stooped and smiling and holding out Fegelein's briefcase. The gilded letters of Fegelein's name glinted in the morning light. 'Found this under the stairs,' he announced. 'Thought Herr Fegelein might want it back.' Kappler handed the briefcase to Elsa, bowed his head in a quick bobbing motion and headed back downstairs.

When they were alone again, Elsa turned to Fegelein. 'What is this?' she asked, holding out the briefcase. 'What have you got in here?'

'Nothing!' Fegelein blurted out.

'It doesn't feel like nothing.' She placed it on the table by the door and flipped the latch.

'Don't open it!' he commanded.

But it was too late. She flipped up the lid of the briefcase and stared at the tangle of gold chains, diamond rings and jewel studded brooches. She reached into the hoard and picked out the two Swiss passports, which were held together by a rubber band.

'Please,' said Fegelein.

But she didn't seem to hear him.

She slipped off the rubber band and opened each passport in turn. Then she dropped them back into the briefcase. 'You were going away with her,' she whispered.

'Yes,' admitted Fegelein. There was no point in lying any more.

'And you were leaving me here.' It wasn't a question. She already knew the answer.

'Elsa,' he began, but then his voice died away.

As Fegelein stumbled about in his mind, trying to think of what to say next, Elsa Batz reached into her open bag and withdrew the

Walther automatic which Fegelein had given her. She raised the gun and aimed across the room. That day of their first outing flooded back into her brain. The flower pots set up along the wall. The first shot gashing off the wall and the others which peeled away into space. She heard again the clench-jawed hissing of his laughter.

The first shot caught Fegelein in the throat. He dropped to his knees just as the second shot hit him in the chest. By the time the third shot tore off his right ear, Fegelein was already dead.

He tipped face down upon the floor.

She thought how strange the gun smoke smelled as it mixed with the scent of her perfume.

Two minutes later, General Rattenhuber walked into the room, followed by a guard from the Chancellery, who was carrying a sub-machine gun.

Elsa barely glanced up as they entered. She had sat down in the yellow chair and was still holding the Walther automatic.

Rattenhuber recognised the woman from her days as a dancer at the Salon Kitty club. 'You are Fegelein's mistress,' he said.

She nodded wearily. 'And do you plan on using that again?' asked Rattenhuber, nodding at the pistol in her hand.

Elsa shook her head.

'Then kindly drop it to the floor,' said the general. She let the gun slip from her grasp.

Rattenhuber walked over to Fegelein, stuck the toe of his boot under the dead man's chest and rolled him over. 'I see you left nothing to chance,' he remarked to Elsa Batz.

At that moment, Rattenhuber's guard called out to him.

'You need to see this,' he said, pointing at the open briefcase on the table by the door.

Rattenhuber made his way over to the table, lifted up a handful of the jewellery and let it sift back through his fingers again. Then he examined the Swiss passports. At the sight of Fegelein's name, he let out a small choking noise. 'And who is this?' he demanded, holding up the other passport.

'His secretary,' answered Elsa. 'Lilya Simonova.'

'And where is she now?'

'God knows,' said Elsa Batz.

Rattenhuber turned to the guard. 'Search the body,' he commanded.

The guard placed his sub-machine gun on the bed, knelt down and began going through Fegelein's pockets. He soon discovered a crumpled sheet of paper, bearing a cryptic series of numbers set into sequences of five.

'Let me see that,' said Rattenhuber.

The guard held up the paper and the general snatched it from his hand. 'Son of a bitch,' he muttered.

'What is it?' asked the guard.

'A code used by the Allies, called Goliath.' 'What will happen to me now?' asked Elsa Batz. She spoke in a half-drugged voice, the way people talk in their sleep.

'Now you will come with us,' replied the general.

'If you're going to shoot me,' said Elsa, 'I'd rather you just did it here.'

'Shoot you?' snorted Rattenhuber. 'The way I see it, Fraülein Batz, you just prevented a traitor from fleeing the course of justice. I think it is more likely that Hitler himself will pin a medal on your chest.'

Heinrich Himmler sat in his office at Hohenlychen, a telephone receiver pressed against his ear. 'Are you certain, Rattenhuber?' he asked. 'Are you absolutely sure that it was Fegelein who leaked the information from the bunker?'

'I don't see how it could be otherwise,' replied Rattenhuber.

'We found a message in his pocket which was written in a code used by the Allies.'

'And have you managed to translate it?'

'Some of it,' confirmed Rattenhuber.

'What did it say?' demanded Himmler.

'It mentioned the Diamond Stream project.' There was long silence at the other end.

'Herr Reichsführer?' asked Rattenhuber, wondering if the line had been cut.

'Yes,' Himmler said at last. 'This coded message, do you know if it has been sent? Or was it intercepted in time?'

'That is impossible to say,' answered Rattenhuber, 'but I must ask you whether Fegelein was ever in possession of the Diamond Stream schematics.'

'Yes,' sighed Himmler.

'And how did this come about?'

'I asked him to borrow the plans from Professor Hagemann so that I could look at them myself.' 'Then we must assume the worst,' said Rattenhuber.

'And Hitler knows about all this?'

'He does.'

'My God,' whispered Himmler.

'A word of advice, Herr Reichsführer.'

'Yes? Yes? What is it?' Himmler demanded anxiously.

'You must distance yourself immediately from Fegelein, as well as anything to do with the Diamond Stream project. Remove any trace of your involvement. Do you understand what I am saying?'

'I do,' replied Himmler, 'and will see to it at once, Rattenhuber.'

Professor Hagemann was sitting in the basement of a ruined house, in a forest west of Berlin. His faithful sergeant, Behr, had just delivered to him a mess tin full of greasy-looking stew. Outside, technicians were assembling a mobile launch pad for one of the few remaining V-2s in the German rocket arsenal.

The planned construction of the hundreds of V-2s demanded by Hitler at the last meeting had never materialised. The factory that manufactured engine parts, located in the mountains of Austria, had just been overrun by the American Army. Newly made dies for the Diamond Stream guidance components, which were to have been installed in the new missiles, had never been put into use. In addition to this, a train carrying the last reserves of rocket fuel, bound for a different assembly area near the old Peenemunde research facility, had been destroyed by British Mosquito fighter bombers before it ever reached its destination.

Only six V-2 launch teams remained in operation, of which General Hagemann's was one. They were scattered at various sites within a 10-kilometre radius. Within twenty-four hours, the last of the operational rockets would have been fired, at which point Hagemann had instructed the launch team commanders to return to Berlin. There, these highly trained technicians would be armed with whatever antiquated weapons were available and incorporated into makeshift squads tasked with defending the city against the vast firepower of the Red Army.

By Hagemann's own estimation, their chances of survival were zero.

In the meantime, Hagemann and his crew continued to carry out their duties, but in the trance-like state of those who could no longer find a reason to go on, but went on anyway.

Now the professor pulled a battered aluminum spoon from his boot and stirred it in the contents of the mess kit. He ladled up some of the oily mixture, which bristled with fish bones, as well as some pine needles that had fallen into the cooking pot. He was just about to take a mouthful when Behr appeared at the top of the basement stairs.

'There's a call for you on the field radio,' he said. 'It's from Hohenlychen.'

'Himmler?'

Behr nodded grimly.

Hagemann dropped the spoon back into his soup. 'What the hell does he want now?'

'He didn't say,' replied Behr. 'He just told me it was urgent.' With a sigh, Hagemann put his mess kit down upon the floor, trudged up the stairs and out to the radio truck, one of which accompanied each V-2 launch team.

'Hagemann!' Himmler's voice burst through the sandpapering noise of radio static. 'I have been looking forward to speaking with you!'

'How may I be of service, Herr Reichsführer?' he asked.

'I want you to come up to my headquarters.'

'When?'

'At once! We have much to discuss.' 'We do?' asked Hagemann.

'Yes,' said Himmler. 'I want you to meet some friends of mine, so that we can talk about your future.'

In that moment, Hagemann tumbled back in time to the day he had arrived in Berlin, summoned by Hitler to explain the disappearance of the V-2 test rocket. And afterwards, when Fegelein had followed him out of the bunker, what was it exactly that he said? That in dealing with Himmler, there was nothing for Hagemann to be nervous about, unless Himmler asked him to meet with his friends. When Hagemann had asked what would be wrong with that, Fegelein had said – because the Reichsführer has no friends.

At the time, Hagemann had not grasped the meaning of Fegelein's remark. But now he understood. If Hagemann went to this meeting, it would be the last thing he ever did. Those so-called friends would put a bullet in his head.

'I would be happy to meet with you!' lied Hagemann. 'I will leave at once for Hohenlychen. There's no need to send a car.'

'My friends and I will be expecting you,' replied Himmler and then, as usual, he rung off without saying goodbye.

Hagemann turned to his men. 'All further launches have been cancelled,' he said.

'What?' Behr asked in disbelief. 'But what should we do with the rockets?'

'Destroy them,' said Hagemann.

'And what then?'

'Then you will need to trust me, Sergeant Behr,' said Hagemann, 'if you want to get out of this alive.'

A Sherman tank attached to the armoured section of the U.S. 44th Infantry Division made its way slowly along a muddy road north of Reutte in the Austrian Alps.

The tank was called the Glory B, a name coined by its commander, twenty-two-year-old Lieutenant Silas Hood from Jamestown, Rhode Island.

Hood had been ordered to patrol the roads north of Reutte. For this, he had requested infantry support but none was available so the tank set out by itself along the forest roads.

German resistance had all but disintegrated in this area, but men continued to be killed by mines, some of which had been planted in the ground months ago.

Standing in the turret, Hood watched the road ahead of him through a pair of binoculars, searching for any tell-tale changes in the earth that might signal the presence of a mine. There were several different kinds of mine used by the Germans. The first was an anti-personnel device known as a Schumine. When stepped on, a small canister the size of a coffee can would spring into the air and explode, spraying the area with ball-bearings. The second kind was a glass mine, which had no metal parts that could be picked up by a metal detector. They would tear out of the ground in a shower of jagged shards, causing terrible injuries to anyone standing nearby, but of no real concern to the crew inside a tank.

The third sort was known as a Teller mine. It was a large, round disc, about as thick as a man's outstretched hand, containing a shaped charge of 1 kilogram of ammonite explosives, which could blow the track off a Sherman tank, shattering the wheel bogies and leaving the vehicle helpless. With bad luck, the charge could penetrate the underside, in which case the crew would be cut to pieces by ricocheting chunks of metal.

'Slowly,' Hood called down to the driver. He focused his binoculars on the road fifty feet ahead of the tank. 'Slowly,' he called down again. A fine rain had begun to fall and Hood pulled out a handkerchief to wipe the moisture off the binocular lenses.

Then the tank came to a sudden halt.

'Not that slow!' barked Hood.

'Lieutenant,' called a voice from down below. It was the driver, Elmer Hoyt. 'There's a guy standing in the road.'

Hood raised his binoculars again and a German officer suddenly leaped into view. He was a tall, dignified looking older man, wearing a long greenish-grey coat with red facing on the lapels. The braid on his peaked cap was gold. In one hand, he clutched a white pillowcase. In his other hand he held a leather tube about the length and thickness of his arm. The man looked tired, as if he had been waiting a long time for someone to come along. But he did not look afraid.

'Son of a bitch,' said Hood. 'I think that is a general.'

'What the hell is he doing?' asked Hoyt.

'He's trying to surrender, I guess.' Hood waved at the man to come forward.

The general set off unhurriedly towards the tank, his arms held out to the sides and the white pillow case hanging limply in the damp air. A few paces short of the iron monster, he stopped. 'My name is General Hagemann,' he said, 'and I wish to surrender with my men.'

Inside the tank, Hoyt laughed. 'Looks like his men made up their own minds what to do.'

'What's that you're carrying?' asked Hood, nodding towards the leather tube. 'Is that some kind of weapon?'

'Documents,' answered Hagemann, 'which I believe will be of interest to your superiors.'

'And what about these men of yours?'

'With your permission,' said Hagemann. Then he turned and nodded towards the forest. 'Come out!'

The woods began to stir, as if the trees were tearing themselves free of their roots. A moment later, the first of Hagemann's technicians appeared out of the shadows, hands raised. Then came another and another and soon there were almost fifty men, standing with their hands raised on the road.

Hood watched this in amazement. It was not lost on him how differently his day might have turned out if these soldiers had chosen to fight. 'Turn us around,' he called to Hoyt.

As slowly as before, the Glory B returned to Reutte, with General Hagemann and his exhausted comrades shuffling behind.

Kirov woke that morning to the rumble of thunder.

At least, that's what he thought it was.

Since leaving Berlin two days before, they had kept to the back roads, avoiding the highway and veering to the north, where the landscape was forested and offered them greater protection.

Throughout that time, the air had been filled with the distant booming of artillery. But this was different. As sleep peeled away from his bones, Kirov realised that it was not thunder, after all, but rather the noise of machines. Tanks. Hundreds of them, by the sound of it. He could feel the vibration of their engines through the ground on which he lay.

Kirov raised himself up on one elbow and looked around the clearing. The small fire they had lit the night before had burned down to a nest of powdery grey ash.

Pekkala and Lilya were gone. Except for Lilya's suitcase, which remained where she had left it, and marks on the ground where they had each settled down by the fire, there was no sign of them at all.

Kirov didn't think much of it, assuming they had simply woken before him and now, perhaps, were gathering sticks to rekindle the campfire, over which they might cook breakfast from their meagre stores of food. As Kirov rubbed the sleep out of his eyes, he recalled a moment from the night before, when he had been woken by the crackle of a burning twig.

By the coppery light of the flames, he saw that his companions had not yet gone to bed. They sat cross-legged on the ground, their faces almost touching as they spoke in voices too faint for Kirov to hear.

Pekkala must have sensed that he was being watched. Suddenly, he turned and stared at Kirov, so quickly that there was no time to look away.

Ashamed to have been eavesdropping, Kirov opened his mouth, ready to apologise.

But Pekkala smiled at him, to show that there was nothing to forgive.

For a second longer the two men watched each other, coils of smoke rising lazily between them.

Then Kirov closed his eyes and slept again.

Now he climbed to his feet and hauled on the crumpled coat which had served him as a groundsheet in the night. The rumble of the tanks became a constant in his ears. They appeared to be coming from the east and heading for Berlin, but they could just as easily have been retreating German forces as advance units of the Red Army, so he decided to stay where he was, hidden from the road, until he knew one way or the other.

Hoping to track down Pekkala, Kirov ventured away from the stone ring of the campfire and began to wander through the woods. Morning sunlight, flickering down through the first leaves of the spring, dappled the earth on which he trod. As he clambered across the trackless ground, Kirov thought back to the day in Siberia he had parked his car at the end of a dirt logging road and went to find the legendary Inspector in order to tell him he was needed once again. It seemed so distant now, like memories stolen from a man who had lived long before him.

Eventually, Kirov arrived back the campfire, hoping they might have returned. But except for the suitcase, there was still no sign of the Inspector, or of Lilya.

A great uneasiness began to spread across his mind.

The sound of the tanks was louder now. Kirov could make out the rumble of individual engines and the monstrous squeaking clatter of tracks.

Perhaps they are out on the road, thought Kirov, and he looked down at the suitcase, thinking he should pick it up and join them. He took hold of the case, lifted it up and was startled by the fact that it felt empty except for a single object rattling about inside. Kirov dropped to one knee and opened the case. It contained only a clunky dynamo torch, engraved with the words 'Electro-Automate'.

Now his gaze was drawn to the fire, where something lay among the ashes. Reaching into the grey dust, he picked it out and saw that it was the remains of Lilya's hairbrush. The varnish on the brush had all been burned away and only neat lines of holes remained of where the bristles had been anchored. But that wasn't the only thing. Now that he looked, he could see the frail teeth of a zip, twisted by the flames, and glass buttons melted into shapes like tiny ears. He realised that it all belonged to clothes that she had been carrying with her in the suitcase.

'Why would she do such a thing?' Kirov wondered aloud, still staring at the campfire, as if the carbonised remains of all these things might somehow call out to him in reply. Tucking the torch into his pocket, Kirov made his way out to the road, hoping to find their tracks in the dirt before the fastapproaching tanks obliterated every trace of movement in their path. But there was nothing to tell him which way they might have gone.

Struggling to gather his thoughts, Kirov pressed his hands against his face. As he did so, his fingers brushed against some unexpected object, pinned beneath the collar of his coat. Fumbling, he undid the clasp and removed what had been fastened there.

It was the emerald eye.

'Mother of God,' whispered Kirov, as he finally grasped what his fears had been whispering to him.

Overwhelmed, he did not even dive for cover when the first tank rumbled into view.

It was a Soviet T-34. Red Army soldiers clung to the distinctive sloping armour, their faces, guns and uniforms all swathed in a coating of dirt. The men stared at Kirov as the tanks rolled by. One of them split his earth-caked face, revealing a set of broken teeth.

More tanks followed, raising the dust until Kirov could barely see the iron monsters, even though he could almost reach out and touch them.

When the column had finally passed, he walked out into the middle of the road.

'Pekkala!' Kirov called into the forest.

Then he waited, counting the seconds, but no sound returned to him except the rustle of wind through the leaves.

Finally, he turned towards the east and started walking.

One week later, Kirov stood before his master at the Kremlin.

On Stalin's desk lay the dynamo torch that Lilya had left in the suitcase. The day before, as soon as he arrived in the city, Kirov had handed it over to the Lubyanka armoury, along with the Hungarian pistol he'd been issued.

'What is that doing here?' asked Kirov.

'We found a roll of film inside.'

Kirov thought of the number of times he had almost thrown it away on his journey back to Moscow. Although it barely worked, he had kept it because it was better than nothing, and because regulations required him not to abandon any useful equipment acquired while in enemy territory.

Now Stalin shoved across the desk a stack of newly printed photographs. 'Go on,' he said. 'Look.'

Kirov leafed through the images before him, but all he could make out was a tangle of lines, forming shapes which made no sense, and German words, all of which appeared to be abbreviated, whose meanings were all lost to him.

'What you see there,' Stalin explained, 'are details of a missile guidance system which might have won Germany the war if they had managed to build it in time. If only it could have been ours.'

'But surely now it is,' said Kirov.

'Yes and no,' replied Stalin.

'What do you mean, Comrade Stalin? Are the details incomplete?'

'Oh, no, Major Kirov. It's all there. Unfortunately, we have just learned that a certain General Hagemann was recently captured by American forces in Austria and he was carrying an identical set of plans, which he promptly handed over to his captors. Since our marriage of convenience with the Allies will soon be coming to an end, the fact that we both now possess the same technology more or less cancels things out. Nevertheless, you are to be congratulated for returning with such valuable information,' and then he added, 'even if it was by accident.'

Kirov felt his heart sink.

'Along the way, however, you appear to have lost something of great value to me.'

There was no need for Stalin to elaborate.

Kirov wanted to explain how Pekkala and Lilya had simply disappeared while he was sleeping, and even though that might have been the truth, it would never have passed for an excuse.

'I could try to find him,' he suggested faintly. 'If you give me some time, Comrade Stalin . . .'

Stalin laughed. 'Do you know how many lifetimes that would take? If we ever see Pekkala again, it will be at the time and place of his own choosing and not ours.'

Kirov bowed his head, knowing that Stalin was right. He guessed how things would play out now. The drive to Lubyanka in the back of a windowless lorry. The walk to the cellar down the winding stone staircase towards the dome-shaped cells, which he would never reach, because the guard escorting him would put a bullet in the back of his head just as he reached the bottom of the stairs. Kirov bowed his head and waited for sentence to be passed.

Just then, he heard a rustling sound.

Glancing up, Kirov saw that Stalin was holding out to him a single sheet of paper. It was old, discoloured and dog-eared at the corners, as if it had passed through many hands before arriving on the master's desk.

In the upper left-hand corner, neatly printed in blue ink, was the hammer and sickle seal of the Soviet Union, surrounded by two sheaves of wheat, like hands at prayer. The document, dating back to June of 1929, had been issued by the Central Committee of Prison Labour for the Region of Eastern Siberia. It stated that Prisoner 4745, a tree-marker in the valley of Krasnagolyana, was assumed to have perished of natural causes in the winter of 1928. His body had not been recovered. It was signed by someone named Klenovkin, commandant of the camp at Borodok.

'Do you know the identity of prisoner 4745?' asked Stalin. Kirov shook his head.

'It was Pekkala.'

'But I don't understand,' said Kirov. 'This says he died seventeen years ago!'

'That document was prepared as part of my agreement with the Inspector, back when he first agreed to work with me. The deal I made was not simply to release him, once he had solved his first case, but to wipe him from the memory of this country, as if he had never been here. So you see, Major Kirov, I can hardly punish you for failing to return to Moscow with a man you never met.' Kirov opened his mouth but no sound came out.

'Consider yourself lucky,' said Stalin, 'and I suggest that, first thing in the morning, you return to work before this streak of good fortune runs out.'

Dazed, Kirov turned to go.

But Stalin wasn't finished yet. 'Will you ever forgive him for leaving?' he asked.

'There is nothing to forgive,' replied Kirov.

When Stalin was alone again, he got up from his desk and walked over to the window. Standing to one side, so that he could not be seen by anyone looking from below, he gazed out over the rooftops of the city. The sun had set, and dusty purple twilight fanned across the sky. For a long time, he stood there, as if waiting for something to appear. Then he reached out with both arms and drew the blood-red curtains shut.

Emerging from the Kremlin, Kirov set out through the darkening streets, bound for the tiny flat where he knew his wife would be waiting. As Kirov strode along, he reached into his pocket and closed his hand around the oval disc of gold, feeling the emerald press against the centre of his palm. Kirov did not know how long he'd have to wait before its true owner returned, but he swore a quiet oath to keep it safe, until that day finally came.

At that same moment, far to the north in the wilderness of Finland, the Walker in the Woods lay down to sleep. Beside him lay his wife, her hair glowing softly in the moonlight.

RED ICON

1944: THE GERMAN ARMY CRUMBLES BEFORE THE UNSTOPPABLE SOVIET FORCES.

In the midst of fighting, two Russian soldiers find
a priceless icon in the crypt of a German church.

STALIN CALLS UPON HIS MOST TRUSTED INVESTIGATOR, INSPECTOR PEKKALA.

To unravel the secret of the icon's past, Pekkala traces its last known
whereabouts to a band of self-mutilating radicals, who were hunted to
extinction years ago by the Bolshevik Secret Police. Or so it was believed.

With the reappearance of the icon, they have returned to claim the treasure
they say belongs to them alone, bringing with them a new and terrible
weapon to unleash upon the Russian people.

ONE MAN HOLDS THE KEY TO ARMAGEDDON. ONLY PEKKALA CAN STOP HIM.

"The novel's canvas, a cyclorama of vivid scenes are shot through with
tension and drama. The author's descriptions — sharp, palpable and
distinctive — are to savor."

-THE WASHINGTON POST

"The author's portrait of Stalinist Russia is vivid, his characters are
compelling, and his stories downright captivating."

- BOOKLIST